P9-BYH-280

Praise for
THE PURIFICATION CEREMONY

"WONDERFUL...
Dickey's *Deliverance* blended with a healthy
dose of Carlos Castaneda...An utterly satisfying
novel that transcends conventions."
Maine Sunday Telegram

"SPELLBINDING...
Sullivan writes with a sense
of poetry and place."
Orlando Sentinel

"OUTSTANDING...
a real, old-fashioned thriller...It has taken days
to shake the suffocating feeling of being tracked
down while I'm walking in the woods."
Los Angeles Times

"HIGH-QUALITY WRITING...
A graphic, nail-biting chase
built around an unnerving mystery...
Mark Sullivan's *The Purification Ceremony*
succeeds on several levels."
Arizona Daily Star

BODY LANGUAGE

"James Hall is a writer I have learned from over the years. His people and places have more brush strokes than a Van Gogh. He delivers taut and muscular stories about a place where evil always lurks beneath the surface. They are gripping stories and BODY LANGUAGE is no different."

—Michael Connelly, author of *Void Moon*

"BODY LANGUAGE seduces you, then it grabs you, and it never lets you go. This is a first-rate thriller by a masterful writer."
—James Patterson

"Alexandra Rafferty is a fabulous addition to the ranks of law enforcement. She is smart, competent, the consummate professional, and her job as a Miami P.D. photographic specialist places her at the heart of the crime scene, with a cold eye for detail and a passionate commitment to justice."
—Sue Grafton

"BODY LANGUAGE is a sizzling tale of sex, blood, and obsession."
—Stephen Coonts

"This Florida-based thriller gives mystery readers a new heroine—a methodical, nurturing and tenacious Alexandra Rafferty. She is one character with whom you will be pleased to become acquainted." —*The Oakland Press*

ROUGH DRAFT

JAMES W. HALL

St. Martin's Paperbacks

ROUGH DRAFT

Copyright © 2000 by James W. Hall.

Library of Congress Catalog Card Number: 99-055532

ISBN: 0-312-97492-2

Printed in the United States of America

St. Martin's Press hardcover edition / January 2000
St. Martin's Paperbacks edition / January 2001

10 9 8 7 6 5 4 3 2 1

In memory of my father, J. Noble Hall Jr.,
my best reader, my biggest fan.
You were something else, Daddy-O.

ACKNOWLEDGMENTS

My deepest thanks to a host of helpers on this one: Carol Cope, Steve Murray, Joe Wallace, Toby Berk, and Steven Seehafer, who all provided invaluable information and assistance. And to Evelyn and Richard and Les, for reading and rereading and being there when it counted. And thanks to Rita Thievon Mullin, whose fine book *Who's For Dinner?* (Crown) formed the basis for much of Hal Bonner's musings.

"Pray look better, sir . . . those things yonder are no giants, but windmills."

—MIGUEL DE CERVANTES

ROUGH
DRAFT

PROLOGUE

"He changed his story," Hannah Keller said, looking back toward the TV cameras. "Now Mr. Marquez is claiming he was not insane at the time he threw his daughter out the third-story window."

There was the usual clamor of questions. Hannah waited till they'd died out and responded to the one she was prepared to answer.

"Mr. Marquez has now told our investigators that his daughter was crying constantly for three days and three nights and he believed she was possessed by the devil and that's why he tossed her out of his apartment window."

"The devil?" The *Herald* reporter in the front row smiled thinly. "So is Mr. Marquez claiming he murdered his daughter as a form of exorcism?"

It got a snicker from a few of the other reporters, but the remark wouldn't make the evening news. Too cynical even for Miami. Anyway, this wasn't going to be a lead story. Child killing wasn't the grabber it once was, too common, an urban cliché. In the *Herald* the Marquez girl would get less than a paragraph. It probably wouldn't even make TV.

Hannah Keller glanced at her watch, straightened her papers on the podium. She was tall and wide-shouldered, blond, green-eyed, with strong cheekbones. She was under no illusions about why the brass had offered her a two-step pay increase to leave homicide and stand before the cameras every day. They wanted an appealing face to divert the TV viewing public from the latest criminal outrage. Though she'd loved homicide, the raise was too large to ignore. So late last year, the bright boys upstairs got their prominent cheekbones, and Hannah started taking home five hundred more a month.

Tom Berry, the *Herald* guy, had his hand up again. Hannah scanned the group of reporters, pretended she didn't see him.

"So if there's nothing else," she said.

Berry stood up. He raked his hand through his shaggy hair.

"Got anything new on J. J. Fielding?"

Hannah closed her eyes, summoning her patience.

"Okay, okay," Berry said. "So you're pissed off at me. Hey, I'm sorry, Hannah, I was just doing my job."

Hannah looked out toward the video cameras at the rear of the room. She never knew which snippet they were going to use. This sentence, that one. Whatever suited their purpose. She had to assume that anything she said might wind up on the evening news, the official word of the Miami Police Department. Holding her tongue had become her major professional skill.

"Mr. Fielding is now a fugitive from justice. As you know, last Friday U.S. federal marshals attempted to serve Fielding with an indictment on fourteen counts of money laundering, but because someone in the U.S. Attorney's office chose to leak the news to our friend here, Mr. Berry, and Mr. Berry and his editors decided to run the story without consulting the U.S. Attorney's office, Mr. J. J. Fielding managed to drop out of sight before the marshals could serve their warrants."

"And that's all?" Berry was still on his feet. "Nothing new?"

"Well, there is one thing," Hannah said.

Some of the reporters were flipping their notebooks closed, checking their beepers.

"Before Mr. Fielding disappeared, he managed to divert a sizable sum from a couple of accounts of Nation's Trust."

"How sizable?" Berry said.

The TV guys were shutting down their cameras, a couple

of on-screen reporters were on their cell phones already, checking their next assignment. Nobody cared about money laundering, some banker who'd been playing footsie with the cocaine cartel. A decade or two earlier it was hot stuff, but it wasn't fashionable anymore, didn't have the lapel-grabbing power these guys needed.

Hannah shuffled her papers.

"How sizable, Hannah?"

She kept her voice deadpan, a little understatement for this heard-it-all group.

"I believe the amount is somewhere in the neighborhood of four hundred and sixty-three million dollars, which would make J. J. Fielding's embezzlement the largest in U.S. history."

Berry stared up at her, his mouth sagging.

Hannah said, "As a result of their investigation, the U.S. Attorney's office has frozen several accounts that Fielding was managing, small offshore companies apparently fronts for the drug cartel."

"Frozen for how long?" a TV woman asked from the rear of the room. Everyone perked up now.

"Indefinitely," Hannah said.

"Neat trick," said Berry. "Your dad seizes their assets, so now the only way the cartel can get their money back is to go after Fielding. Track him down, do the government's job for them."

Hannah looked at him for a long moment. Then lifted her eyes and gazed out at the others.

"So, if there's nothing else," she said, "I'll see you all again tomorrow."

Hannah was walking back to her office when Tom Berry trotted up beside her.

"Hey, that was cute, Hannah. Like an afterthought, dropping that bombshell."

"Glad you liked it."

Tom was shorter than Hannah by almost half a foot and had to trot to stay up with her stride.

"So, I was wondering, Hannah, maybe you'd be willing to put a word in for me, help me get a chance to speak to your father?"

She halted abruptly and swung around.

"Jesus, I don't believe you. You actually think I'm going to arrange an interview with my dad? Man, you don't get it, do you?"

"I know, I know. You're pissed off at me, your dad is pissed off. Hey, everybody I know is pissed off at me. I'm used to it. All I want to do is ask Assistant U.S. Attorney Keller a few questions, try to get the complete story on this. It's going to be national now, Hannah. The largest embezzlement in U.S. history. Man, we're talking major news event here."

"What you mean is, you think this could be your ticket to the big time. The *Post*, the *Times*."

"Well, yeah, sure, it's got big-time potential. But the point is, your father, he's going to be the key guy on this. And he won't return my calls."

"You're amazing, Tom. Dad spent an entire year digging up the evidence he needed to put Fielding away, and you, in one stupid, greedy, me-first story, shoot the whole thing down. And now you expect him to talk to you, give you an inside track?"

"If you asked him, he would. Come on, Hannah. I know you're mad at me at the moment, but, hey, we're on the same side. I want to see Fielding captured, your dad wants to see him captured. If I can do this story right, it might help."

"Bullshit, Tom. Bullshit. I'm not doing it. You want to talk to my dad, you'll have to find some other way."

She headed on down the corridor. Tom called out, a last pleading. But she kept on going.

Back at her office, Gisela Ortega was sitting in her chair, grinning at her as she entered the room.

"What?"

"What do you mean, what?" Gisela said.

"That grin. What happened, somebody ask you to get married?"

Gisela was wearing a pale yellow dress with small roses printed on it. One of the quietest outfits she owned. She had short black hair and bright green eyes. She'd been working as Public Information Officer for six years, an old-timer by Miami PD standards. Showed Hannah the ropes two years ago when she transferred in from homicide.

"Nobody asked for my hand," Gisela said. "I'm grinning about you, not me."

"Oh, you heard about my little show downstairs?"

She shook her head. Grinning wider.

"Okay, so what is it, Gisela? Tell me. Don't do this. I hate guessing games."

"You got a phone call."

"Yeah?"

"Some guy, he was very nice. He sounded young. Very hip."

"He saw me on TV and wanted a date."

She shook her head. Really pleased with herself.

"He said he had good news for you, and I told him you were busy and I was your best friend so it was okay to tell me. I am your best friend, aren't I, Hannah?"

"You won't be much longer if you keep doing this."

"The guy's name was Max Chonin. Does that ring a bell?"

Hannah looked at the far wall. A photo of her mom and dad on a cruise they'd taken last summer. Both of them wrapped in sheets for some goofy shipboard toga party.

Hannah shook her head.

"Never heard of him."

"Literary agent. New York City."

Hannah smiled.

"Oh, that guy," she said, feeling her pulse jump. "What? He wants to represent my book?"

"No," Gisela said. "Guess again."

"Gisela, stop it. Just tell me."

"He sold your book."

"What?"

"He sold your book, *First Light*."

"He couldn't have. I just sent it to the guy two weeks ago. He was going to look at it, tell me what he thought."

"He got it, gave it to some hotshot publisher he knows, and the guy wants to buy it. That is, of course, if you're interested."

"Really!"

Gisela kept on grinning. "Really," she said. "Really, really, really."

"My God. I don't believe it."

"And that's not even the best part," Gisela said.

Hannah stepped over to the visitor's chair and sat down. Her knees were mush. She'd sold her goddamn book. Her novel about a female police officer who does secret after-hours crime fighting. A year of writing it in the early morning before Randall got up and went to school and she headed off to work. Using her police stories, the droll talk, some of the macabre events that were the daily reality around this city.

"Okay," Hannah said. "I'm ready, I'm sitting down. What's the best part?"

"Well, he didn't tell me the exact figure, but he said he didn't think you were going to need to keep taking shit from reporters anymore unless you really wanted to."

Hannah was stopped at a light on Bayshore. Dialing her mother for the fourth time and for the fourth time getting no answer. She'd already called her father's office and was told he hadn't come to work that morning.

It was noon and the traffic was light through Coconut Grove.

She went back to her driving, heading up the steep hill into the heart of the Grove, then down the long shady avenue past the big stone churches and private schools and Mediterranean villas.

Ed Keller had probably decided to take the day off, still reeling from Berry's article and disgusted by the information leak in his office that had cost him a year's work. He and Randall would no doubt be snook-fishing on the bay. For the last month since school let out, her six-year-old son had been spending his days with his grandparents while Hannah was at work. "Club Granddad" is what Ed Keller called it. He was happy as hell to take charge of the boy, spoil him any way he and Martha could dream up. They'd been covering Hannah's day-care needs since her marriage broke up six years ago. Her Prince Charming turned out to be a child molester. First year of marriage, the son of a bitch was caught in the backseat of a car raping a fifteen-year-old high school girl. So much for Hannah's good judgment in men.

She pulled into the driveway of her parents' Gables-by-the-Sea ranch style and parked. Her father's Buick was still at the curb. Her mother's fifteen-year-old Mercedes was in the garage, the door up.

Hannah was shivering. Her hands were cold even though it had to be near ninety degrees. She couldn't remember the last time she'd been so excited. Maybe when Randall was born, holding him that first time. But that was the only time even close.

She hadn't called the agent back yet to get the details. She wanted to save that, do it in front of her parents. They'd be whooping with excitement. That's who they were. They rooted for her at every step. Her biggest fans. And both of them were book lovers. Big-time readers. It's where she'd caught the fever, a kid growing up in this very house. Bedtime stories were her earliest memories, *Jack and the Beanstalk*, her father playing the parts, doing voices. Her mother's quiet melodious voice reading *Black Beauty*. When she told them the news, Ed would drive off to the liquor store, buy the most expensive bottle of champagne they had, and the family would sit around on the deck all afternoon howling over Hannah's triumph. Middle of the day, it didn't matter. That's who they were, parents of a daughter who could do no wrong. And boy did they love to celebrate.

The kitchen door was open. Hannah stepped inside and saw immediately that something was wrong. A burner on the gas stove was fluttering its blue flame. A pan of grits had tumbled onto the floor and spilled across the tile. They looked as hard and cold as white rubber.

Hannah came around the breakfast counter and called out for her mother.

Then she stumbled hard against the refrigerator, nearly went down. Dressed in white linen, Martha Keller was sprawled in front of the stove. There were three bullet wounds in her upper torso. Chest, lungs, stomach. The bloodstain against the white dress had taken the shape of a large, disfigured butterfly.

Hannah stood for a moment, staring at her mother's body just as she had stared at hundreds of other corpses in the last five years. Countless gunshot victims who had come to rest in the same eerie, inert pose as Martha Keller.

Hannah dropped her purse and stepped close to her mother's body and kneeled down to feel for a pulse. But there was none. The flesh was cool and her mother's eyes were open, her face holding a look that was neither frightened nor angry nor in any distress at all. She looked composed. A quiet calm, as if she were simply daydreaming there on the Mexican tiles.

Hannah rose and turned to the kitchen window. She could see her father's fishing skiff still tied to the dock in the wide canal.

She whirled around and called out her son's name. And called it out again.

She snatched up her purse and drew out her Glock nine.

She was a police officer now. Not the daughter of the deceased.

She edged to the swinging door that opened onto the living room. She pointed the pistol upward and slung aside the door and stepped across the threshold.

Twenty feet away she saw her father's legs, his body hidden by the green corduroy couch. He was wearing his blue seersucker trousers, part of an ensemble he'd worn hundreds of times before. White shirt and his blue tie with sailboats printed on it, blue-striped seersucker suit coat. His plantation owner's look.

Hannah inched across the room, panning the pistol back and forth as she moved past the two couches and overstuffed chairs. Her heart was numb, her breath tight in her lungs. Some essential muscle in her soul had short-circuited. She was only dimly aware, seeing the room as if through some weirdly distorted lens. An undersea vision, cloudy and wavering.

"Randall!" she called, and swung around to aim her pistol at the empty bedroom doorway. "Randall!"

She stepped forward, around the end of the couch.

And the pistol nearly fell from her hands. She gasped, staggered forward.

Her father was lolling on the Oriental rug, one arm trapped behind his back at an obscene angle, the other arm extended across the rug. In his hand he gripped the chrome Smith & Wesson .357 revolver, the one pistol in his collection he kept loaded. His white shirt was punctured in three places and the blood had pooled around his left armpit.

His face was hidden by a glossy photograph.

She inched forward, aiming her pistol at the doorway to the den. She crouched down, blinded by tears.

"Randall!" she screamed "Randall!"

The killer had used a blue pushpin from the bulletin board in her father's study to fix the photograph to his face. He'd gouged the thumbtack into the flesh of Ed Keller's forehead to hold in place the eight-by-ten glossy of J. J. Fielding, banker, money launderer, fugitive.

"Randall!"

She pushed herself back upright and edged across the room toward the bedroom. She hopped through the door, swinging the pistol from side to side. The bed was made, the room tidy. Light streamed in through the French doors that opened onto the patio.

"It's me, Randall. It's Mommy."

At the foot of the bed, the green and gold throw rug was

askew as if Ed Keller had come running from the bathroom at the sound of the shots, kicked it awry. Hours ago. Breakfast time.

She moved to the bathroom, stepped inside, slung the shower curtain aside, and pointed the Glock at the bare porcelain.

She turned and went back into the bedroom and halted.

It wasn't a noise that stopped her or a scent or anything out of place. It was some disturbance in the air, some barometric flutter her sensors had detected.

"Randall?" she said quietly. "Is that you, Randall?"

She drew aside the folding louvered door and stepped into her parents' closet. There at the back under a pile of Hannah's own laundry, clothes she'd brought over to her mother's because her own washer had broken down, there beneath her jeans and blouses and underwear, in the heavy-scented mass of work clothes and after-work clothes, she saw Randall's bare foot.

"Randall?" she whispered.

The pistol dropped from her hand.

"Randall?"

She fell onto the pile of laundry, throwing aside the cotton jerseys and denim. And Randall looked up at her with the dull, unfocused flatness of the blind. His unruly blond hair was damp with sweat. His white skin flushed, the freckles on his cheek seemed to be glowing.

"I was fishing," he said, his voice empty.

"Randall, are you all right?" She inspected his limbs, his torso. Then drew him to her, hugged his small, perfect body against hers.

"I was on the seawall," he said, his mouth near her ear. "I was fishing."

"Don't," she whispered. "We can talk later."

"I saw them go in the kitchen door. Three men."

She relaxed her hold on him. He lifted his head, stared up at his grandparents' clothes hanging above him.

"Two short men and one tall," he said.

He drew out of the embrace and spoke as if in a trance. A few words, a pause, his eyes detached.

"They had on white pants. White shirts. And white hats. Like painters. Like house painters. I thought they were doing work for Granddad. Then I came inside and I found them lying on the floor. There was blood all over. They're dead, aren't they, Mommy? Granddaddy and Nana are dead."

She nodded.

"But you're all right, Randall. You're going to be just fine."

"I was fishing," he said. "There were three of them. They looked like house painters."

"It's okay, it's okay, Randall."

His body was rigid. Face slack, eyes filmed over, Randall stared off at some invisible spot in the air, his lips pursed as if he were blowing bubbles of silence.

And those were the last words he spoke. For days he did not utter a sound. Those days stretched into silent, agonizing weeks. Hannah rarely left his side. For long hours, he curled up in her lap and the two of them rocked. His eyes were disengaged. He sat in the living room and gazed out the window. He lay in bed beside her and peered up at the ceiling. He sat motionless in the bow of his skiff while Hannah steered them up and down his favorite mangrove canals and pointed out the great blue herons, the ospreys. Sometimes he turned his head in the direction she pointed, but his eyes were empty.

He ate little, slept not at all. His blood pressure fluctuated wildly. The first psychiatrist Hannah took him to prescribed a mild antianxiety drug, but it had no effect. The next two psychiatrists told her that she should simply stay on her present course, give Randall as much love and reassurance as she could. Keep talking to him in normal tones, touch him gently and often. Be there for him when he was ready to speak. This was a trance that only he could break and only when he was ready.

After three weeks of Randall's silence, Hannah had almost given up, resigned to life with a mute son, a boy stunted forever. Destroyed because his mother hadn't been there to protect him.

Then one morning at breakfast as she set a plate of blueberry pancakes before him, he looked up and said, "Hi."

She held back the tears. Pretended it was a perfectly ordinary moment.

"Hi," she said. But Randall would say no more for the next hour.

Midmorning they were sitting on the dock, watching the mangrove snappers cruise beneath their dangling legs. Hannah's pulse was wild. Randall looked over at her and said, "I'm sorry, Mom."

"Sorry?" she said. "You haven't done anything, Randall. Nothing at all."

She hugged him against her chest and wept.

A month and a half after the murders, the FBI's forensics people were still nowhere. Dozens of hair or fiber samples at the scene, but nothing useful. No usable fingerprints, no DNA samples. Particles of sand in the carpet, dirt, pebbles, sandspurs, smudges of dog shit, leaves, twigs. Everything and nothing.

According to the ballistics reports and the trajectory studies done later by the FBI, a single pistol was used, a thirty-two caliber, and all three shots were fired by a person taller than six feet. Beyond that, there was no physical trace of the shooter and his accomplices, nothing but the molecules of their breath still circulating in the room and that photograph tacked to her father's forehead.

Frank Sheffield, the FBI's lead investigator on the case, dismissed the photo as a red herring. Too obvious, too convenient to be believed. According to Frank, the three men had walked into the study, grabbed the first item they saw that might incriminate some other party, and left it on the scene. Such arrogance didn't fit their profile of J. J. Fielding, leaving behind a calling card. Anyway, the guy was a banker, a high-powered number-cruncher. Not a killer.

Oh, sure, they were still seeking him on the money-laundering charge, but he wasn't the FBI's prime suspect for the murders, not even close. There were dozens of others on the list ahead of him, bad people, serious felons, all of whom had been Ed Keller's target at one time or another. All considered far more likely than Fielding to order a hit or do the deed themselves.

With Randall back in school and Hannah on leave, she spent her days scouring old newspaper files, questioning Fielding's associates at Nation's Trust, searching for any scrap of evidence that might point to the man's whereabouts. At one point she showed up on the porch of Maude Fielding, the banker's abandoned wife. After a moment's hesitation, Mrs. Fielding invited her in, made her tea, listened to her story. Said nothing till Hannah asked the one question she'd come for, "Was your husband capable of murder?"

Maude Fielding smiled quietly.

"My dear," she said, "who among us isn't capable of it?"

For weeks Hannah took notes, developed theories, relentlessly badgered Frank Sheffield. A nice guy, mellow, looked more like an aging tennis bum than an FBI agent. Lived in a dinky motel on the beach at Key Biscayne, ran around shirtless when he wasn't at work. Hannah knocked on his motel room door at six in the morning, ten at night, bombarded him with seven, eight phone calls a day. "Did you consider this?" "Have you looked into that?" "The shooter was taller than six feet. Fielding was six foot one."

"A lot of people are over six feet, Hannah. And who were the other two guys with him, his chauffeur and butler?"

Frank Sheffield was always patient and respectful, looking her straight in the eye, though he must have considered her a flaming crackpot.

Because of course she was. During her years with homicide she'd often been on the receiving end of the same kind of lunacy. A victim's family member calling every day, convinced that unless they did so the investigation would be shelved. Pestering, pestering.

But she couldn't help herself. So inflamed with rage, she couldn't stop. Picking up the phone, dialing it again, "Frank Sheffield, please." The secretaries started recognizing her voice. Frank was in a conference. Frank was in the field.

Weeks like that. Every waking moment on the phone or at the library. Until one evening as she was setting the phone back on the hook after sharing another brilliant idea with Frank Sheffield, she turned to find Randall staring at her from the doorway of her study. His mouth twisted, eyes red.

"What is it?" she asked him. "What's wrong, Randall?"

He took a breath, a tear gleaming on his cheek.

"Please stop," he said. "I can't take it anymore. I want it to be over."

So she stopped. No more calls. No faxes. Nothing.

J. J. Fielding was never seen or heard from again. No one at the FBI ever informed her directly, but she knew how it worked. Without a prime suspect or fresh leads, the probe of her parents' murder gradually faded from their high-priority roster. Until finally the case slipped quietly to the Bureau's back shelves.

ONE

There were no windows in room 2307 of the FBI office building at 26 Federal Plaza in Lower Manhattan. An interior room, plain white walls, naked except for an FBI seal and a TV screen flush-mounted beside it. Gray carpet, and a long cherry table with fifteen green leather chairs. Five of them occupied today. A couple of minutes earlier the small talk had died away, now everyone was quiet, eyes down, sipping their coffee, waiting for Special Agent Helen Shane to arrive.

One look around the conference table and Frank Sheffield knew a serious mistake had been made. He didn't belong here. Not with these people. Unless maybe he'd been ordered to New York on a Saturday morning to face a reprimand for his total and unwavering lack of distinction. Twenty-one years with the Bureau without a single commendation. A record so undistinguished it had given Frank Sheffield a kind of reverse fame.

He worked out of the Miami field office, one of the busiest in the country, over seven thousand cases last year, six hundred-fifty agents and support personnel responsible for FBI activity from Vero Beach all the way to Antarctica. Frank hadn't heard of any major crime outbreaks in Antarctica, then again, you could never be sure when the penguin population might start acting up.

It wasn't that Frank was a screw-off. He did his job as well as the next guy. But he wasn't at the head of the line volunteering for extra duty, and he sure as hell didn't have that spit-shined gung-ho bearing that bumped you steadily up the ladder. He served warrants, sat in surveillance vans, carried crates of subpoenaed documents from banks and boiler room operations. He sat in meetings half of every day, adding to his collection of doodles. Mostly he kept his head down, went home at five, took his kayak out on the bay, paddled ten miles around Key Biscayne, good weather or foul, and by the time he got back to his little stretch of beach, all the day's aggravations were magically erased.

Any way you looked at it, Sheffield didn't belong in this room with this bunch of fired-up overachievers who spent all their waking hours keeping America safe and their careers revving in high gear.

Across the table was Deputy Assistant Director Charlie Pettigrew who ten years ago was Special Agent in Charge of the Miami field office, Frank's boss. Somehow Charlie had parlayed one minor talent into major career advancement. Not exactly a yes-man, still Charlie was a guy who could sing harmony to any tune. Great at meetings, aligning himself with the right position. These days Pettigrew was fourth down the chain of command from Director Robert Kelly. Charlie was looking slim and spiffy, sharply creased white shirt, jeans. But Frank detected a little upper-echelon worry in his old buddy's eyes. Bigger concerns, more shades of gray than the old days in Miami, gunning for dopers, tearing holes in the cocaine pipeline.

On the other side of the table, slouching in his seat, was a kid named Andy Barth, twenty-something, with the long stringy blond hair and wolfish face of an undercover dope cop. Frank had seen the kid's picture a lot lately in internal press releases. The Bureau's computer guru, headed the cyber-crime division, fastest growing section in the FBI. Andy wore ratty blue jeans and a fresh white T-shirt. He was helping himself to the basket of Danish in the middle of the table. Taking one, offering them around, taking another. A boy with serious cravings.

At the head of the table was Abraham Ackerman, senior United States senator from New York, and Chair of the

Armed Services Committee. For a man in his early fifties he obviously kept himself gym-pumped. His dark wavy hair was swept back on the sides, and he was wearing a blue baseball hat with the FBI logo embroidered in gold on the front. Probably a gift from Director Kelly. Ackerman wore a yellow golf shirt, faded jeans, and running shoes. Very casual on this Saturday morning, just one of the guys. Former college quarterback, Penn State, missed the national championship by a field goal. Two feet wide right. Frank remembered it because he'd won two hundred bucks on the game. With a mediocre team around him, Ackerman had thrown for over three hundred yards, run for a hundred more, almost won the championship single-handedly. A man who could carry ten guys on his back, haul them to the mountaintop. He'd done it then, been doing it ever since. Maybe not an astronaut, never walked on the moon, but the next best thing.

As Chair of the Armed Services Committee, the guy was used to five-star generals kowtowing to him, sitting there in a row, chests dripping with medals and ribbons while the senior senator from New York chewed them out or blasted holes in their latest budget requests.

That morning there was a hum rising from Ackerman's flesh like the tick of radioactivity. Not exactly the look of a grieving father. Frank had seen the story on the evening news a few weeks back, Ackerman, wiping tears from his eyes, had taken questions from reporters. Joanie, his only daughter, a teenager, had been killed in a skiing accident in Aspen. Took a wrong trail in the tricky light of dusk, and smashed into a tree. Tragic mess.

But this morning the man looked like he was totally back to business. The way he lifted his eyes and measured each person in the room, his gaze swinging sharply to the doorway as Helen Shane made her entrance.

"Good news," she said, shutting the door behind her, moving breezily to a chair two down from Sheffield, giving him a quick once-over as she eased into the seat. She set a file folder on the table in front of her, brushed a strand of hair from her face. "I just got off the phone with Director Kelly. And I'm happy to report that we're fully green-lighted. It's a go."

"All right!" said Andy Barth. And took a celebratory bite from a cherry Danish.

Helen was wearing black linen slacks and a clingy white blouse. She had straight shoulder-length red hair and her tense green eyes looked out from under long bangs. The rest of her face was an odd mix of slightly oversized features that somehow looked good in photographs but seemed a little out of whack in real life. He'd heard she was a fashion model in high school, on the covers of *Seventeen*, and even *Glamour.* Graduated Columbia, then joined the G-men. God knew why. Maybe Frank would ask her about it later, take her out to lunch, maybe some of her ambition would rub off. This was, after all, the lady they said was destined to be the first female director of the FBI.

Thirty-two, worked out of the D.C. field office, and even Frank Sheffield, who didn't ordinarily pay attention to such matters, was fully aware of her recent successes. The latest one had gone down last August when Helen spearheaded the biohazard unit that thwarted a major smallpox virus attack. It was Helen's team that took down the high-tech plague lab operating inside a condo only a canister toss from the White House.

Ackerman was staring at Helen Shane. His eyes jacked up to full voltage.

Somewhere down the hall a phone rang, and that seemed to wake him from his fierce appraisal. He leaned to the side and scooped up a slim leather briefcase and slapped it down on the conference table. He unzipped it slowly and withdrew a handful of eight-by-ten glossies. Ackerman stared down at the top photograph for a moment, his face going slack, the color draining.

He pushed the stack to his right, directly in front of Charlie Pettigrew.

Charlie tried to nudge the stack on to Andy Barth, but the senator shot out his hand and took hold of Charlie's wrist.

"Look at them," he said.

"I've already seen them, sir."

"Look at them again. I want you to keep these images in your mind. I want you to remember them every second of every day from now until you catch this fucking animal. Look at them, Mr. Pettigrew."

Charlie stared at the photographs. He went through the stack slowly. There were five. He lingered on the last one, then slid them to Andy Barth.

Barth had a piece of Danish in his mouth when he peered at the top photograph. He flinched, didn't swallow and didn't chew as he suffered through the rest.

"I'm sure you've all witnessed autopsies as a part of your training," the senator said. "And you have strong stomachs for this sort of thing. But you should remember as you look at these photographs that this girl, my daughter, was alive only seconds before this was done to her. This carnage. She was laughing. She was red-cheeked and brimming with life."

Impassive, Helen Shane took her look and passed the photos on to Frank.

The girl was sixteen. Though if Frank hadn't known her age already, he wouldn't have been able to tell from the photos. She had dark curly hair and plump cheeks with a short upturned nose. But her face was spattered with gore and whatever her final expression might have been was now concealed by the mask of blood.

Her head was tilted back into a depression of snow. Around the rest of her body the snow was shadowed with blood. In the second and third photographs, the injuries were visible. The fourth and last were close-ups of the gaping wounds in her chest.

"This wasn't any skiing accident," said Sheffield.

"That's right, Frank," said Pettigrew. "That was only the cover story."

"Tell him," Ackerman said. "Tell him what this animal did."

The light was buzzing in the senator's eyes.

Helen Shane leaned forward in her chair, rested her fore-arms on the edge of the table.

"He was hiding in the trees on the edge of the ski slope. As Joanie passed by, he stepped out, clotheslined her, dragged her ten yards into the underbrush."

"My forensics are a little weak," Frank said. "What're these wounds?"

"After he strangled her," said Helen with the lilt of a schoolroom recitation, "Joanie was alive but unconscious. That's when he tore open her parka and made a crude incision directly below the xiphoid, a triangular cartilaginous mass at the base of the sternum. Once he'd broken through the skin, he apparently widened the laceration with his fingers, and when the breach was large enough, he inserted his hand into Joanie's chest cavity, took her heart in his fist, and crushed it."

Sheffield felt a light-headed swirl begin to form behind his eyes. The silence thickened, a breathless interlude.

"This is why we're here," the senator said, staring at Sheffield. "Because some man in his jungle mansion was unhappy with Joanie's father. Unhappy that I ordered a na-palm strike on his coca fields. Unhappy that I approved a half-dozen separate guerrilla operations that caused him great financial losses. This unhappy man in his jungle mansion hired a monster that you people refer to as Hal to retaliate for his losses.

"Until my daughter was slaughtered, I was not aware that such a monster existed. Nor did I know that your Bureau has been pursuing this beast for the last ten years without success. But now that I do know, now that I've seen what complete incompetence has been operating here, an incompetence which has led to this, this atrocity, I have made it my mission to change that. And I will not rest until this mission is complete."

Out in the hallway, a man laughed, and a woman's high cackle answered back. The intrusion seemed to push Acker-man deeper into his rage.

He raised his huge fist and hammered it against the table,

then pushed his chair back a few inches from the table as if he meant to hurl himself at the whole incompetent group of them.

Helen lifted her eyes and gave the senator a serene half smile as if the two of them shared some secret.

"His name is Hal Bonner," Helen announced. Then she was quiet for a moment, letting the silence dance around her.

Frank watched as she sat, eyes lowered, running a slender finger around the rim of her mug. Then touching the edge of a black TV channel changer.

Eyes still down, Helen said, "Bonner is twenty-nine years old, a white male. He's approximately six feet tall. Born in Indiana, raised in foster care, no juvenile record. He was fifteen years old when he first came to the attention of the police in Indianapolis. Fourteen years ago, during a two-week period in the middle of July, Hal Bonner wiped out his former foster parents. Four women and three men ranging in age from thirty-six to sixty-seven. By the time the connection to Bonner was made, he'd vanished."

Helen looked up, glanced around the table. Letting a few more seconds tick off her theatrical clock. Frank was watching her. Everyone else was too.

"He started out with simple strangulation," she said. "The first four were killed that way. But by the time he got to number five, Hal was tearing them open, crushing their hearts. Like he did to Joanie. That's been his MO ever since. Only for the last ten years he's been getting paid."

"Not your average hitman," Andy said.

The senator cut his eyes to Andy, scowled, and looked back at Helen.

"And that's all, Mr. Sheffield. Ten years, that's all your people have."

"Now he's a hired gun for the Cali cartel," Andy said. "They use Hal for special occasions, when they want to inspire the serious heebie-jeebies. Make an example of someone."

Andy looked around at the silent group, took another bite from the remaining Danish.

"Senator Ackerman is correct," Helen said. "Hal's extremely slippery. Apparently he's spotted every sting we've thrown at him. For ten years we've had him as a level-one priority and we've consistently bombed. Even using our best undercover people, Oscar winners, Hal saw through them every time. Got a whiff of something wrong, stepped back into the shadows, and was gone. But we think we have a winner this time. Something Hal won't be able to resist."

"All right," Ackerman said, rapping his knuckles impatiently against the table. "Show him the photograph."

Helen reached below the table and came up with a file folder. She laid it on the table next to her coffee.

"Fourteen years ago when Hal murdered his foster parents, he also was quite thorough about destroying any sign of his presence in those homes. Photo albums, schoolwork, drawings, everything. Very meticulous for a young man of only fifteen. As if he already had a life plan and knew exactly what he needed to do, obliterate any trace of his past life. But we did manage to locate one photo from a school in Evansville. A junior high school he attended for a few months."

She took a thumbnail photograph from the folder and slid it across the table to Frank. He picked it up, studied it for several moments.

The boy was wearing a madras shirt buttoned to the top, and he stared grimly into the lens. A crudely handsome young man with heavy eyebrows and coarse, dark hair which was chopped and mangled as though he had been barbered by someone with failing eyesight and a palsied hand. His eyes were gray and widely spaced and protruded slightly. Already at thirteen or fourteen his cheeks were shadowed by a thick beard. As though he were cursed by a heavy flow of testosterone, launched into manhood years before he was ready.

"We've aged him," Helen Shane said. "Brought him up to date. Agent Barth directed the work, using the TS-38 software system he designed."

Andy showed them a gloating smile.

Helen picked up the TV remote and aimed it at the set and it crackled to life. Slowly she clicked through four different renderings, leaving each one on the screen for half a minute. Hal Bonner as a twenty-nine-year-old, side view and front. Hal with long hair. Hal with a trimmed beard. Hal with a shaggy beard and short hair. Hal Bonner clean-shaven and bald. She left the last one on the screen.

It was excellent work, but like every computer enhancement he'd seen, something was lost from the original photograph. Some spark in the eyes. While everyone stared at the television screen and murmured, Frank took another look at the small class photo.

He'd never believed in reading things into people's eyes. All that windows-of-the-soul bullshit. But Hal Bonner's eyes were tempting. In the class photo there was a brooding defiance in them that Sheffield had seen once or twice in the eyes of torture victims. Soldiers who'd suffered excruciating ordeals in POW camps, and because they'd managed to survive the worst their captors could inflict, they no longer knew real fear or cared quite as much as they once had about the suffering of others.

In Hal Bonner's eyes there was also a glint of bitter humor. This was one smug little alien bastard. On the television screen, however, his eyes were flat and empty. Drained of any hint of humanity by the digital rendering.

For several moments after Helen snapped the television off, Senator Ackerman continued to stare at the blank screen.

Sheffield took a breath, the photos of Joanie Ackerman and Hal Bonner still burning in his head. He didn't have a weak stomach, but just now the floor felt soft beneath him, the room expanding and contracting with each breath.

Charlie Pettigrew pushed his chair back and stood up, trying in some measure to assume control of the proceedings. Though even a casual observer could tell poor Charlie was a distant third in this group's pecking order.

"So, I suppose you're curious to know, Frank, where you fit into all this."

"It crossed my mind."

"Well, actually there are several reasons," the senator said.

Frank waited. This wasn't the time for witty comebacks.

"You worked a murder case five years ago," Charlie Pettigrew said. "Ed Keller, Assistant U.S. Attorney."

"Yeah, Ed Keller and his wife, Martha. Sure I remember it. Never solved."

"And a certain persistent relative."

"You mean Hannah, their daughter."

"That's right."

Helen Shane was studying Frank, her eyes scouring his features. It was the same way Frank's ex-wife had looked at him most of the time. Collecting faults, adding them to the heap.

"You think Hal Bonner was involved in the Keller murders?"

"No, Frank," said Helen. "We're interested in the daughter. Hannah. Whatever you can tell us about her. We understand she made quite a fuss about the way you were handling the case. There are a dozen letters from her in our files, protesting the direction you took on the investigation."

"She had her own theory, yeah. There were a lot of midnight phone calls. She showed up on my front porch a few times."

"Is the woman unbalanced?" Ackerman asked.

"She'd just lost her parents, Senator. She was deeply distraught."

Ackerman nodded. It seemed to be an emotion he vaguely understood.

The senator fixed Sheffield with an earnest, vote-getter look.

"I knew your father, Frank. Not well, but I knew him. I was greatly saddened by his passing. I had the utmost respect for the man."

Frank nodded.

A lot of people had known Harry Sheffield. Liked him, respected him. He was that kind of man. Friends in high and low places and everywhere in between. The folks who showed up at his funeral could've been herded directly onto the next Noah's Ark, diverse enough to be the complete breeding stock for a new world. Before Harry died there'd been talk of politics. Democratic nominee for Florida governor. Maybe something national. It all seemed possible for Harry Sheffield, retiring chief of police for Dade County, the most colorful, media-friendly, and well-loved cop the city had ever known. Sixty-one, still a young man. But even with all that charisma circulating in his veins he wasn't immortal. The night of his retirement party, Harry Sheffield had returned home from the festivities at about 1 A.M. He took out the garbage, set it on the street, went back in and got a cold beer from the refrigerator, sat down in his favorite easy chair, turned on the television, and somewhere deep inside his chest, the tectonic plates shifted and Harry Sheffield had a seven-point-five heart attack. An old story. Nothing unique about it. Two hours after retiring from the job he loved, Harry lay dead in his recliner, a can of Schlitz malt liquor going flat on the table beside him.

That was over ten years ago, and still to this day people like Ackerman were bringing it up, passing on their condolences.

"So," Sheffield said, "is anybody going to tell me why I'm here?"

"You'll be our Miami tour guide," Helen Shane said, "and our specialist on Hannah Keller." Helen Shane showed him a smile. Lots of teeth, not much sincerity.

"Specialist? I barely know the lady."

"For someone who barely knows her, you certainly filled your reports with detailed observations about her." Helen's smile became demure.

Frank had never come close to slapping a woman before, but he was picturing it now. A good rap on the cheek, just hard enough to wake Helen from her terminal smugness.

"And what does Hannah Keller have to do with this guy Bonner?"

"Let's just say they share a common obsession," Helen said.

"And what's that?"

"J. J. Fielding."

"Largest embezzlement in U.S. history, that J. J. Fielding?"

"That's right, Frank. The man Hannah Keller believes murdered her parents. The same man Hal Bonner has been searching for without success for these last five years."

Frank looked around at the four of them. No one making eye contact.

"Are you going to explain the operation to me or are we going to do this dance all morning?"

Helen looked across the table at Pettigrew, a quick, wordless exchange.

She turned to Frank, gave him a vacant smile.

"For the purposes of this meeting, Frank, all you need to know is the overall shape of the plan. Actually it's very simple. We'll dangle Fielding in front of Hannah, then we dangle her in front of Hal Bonner. We convince Hal that the only way he's going to locate J. J. Fielding is to follow Hannah. We send Hannah to half a dozen locations around the Miami area that we've preselected, our hot zones. We'll be rigorously monitoring all traffic in and out of those locations until Hal makes his appearance. He thinks Hannah's going to lead him to Fielding, when he sticks his nose out of the shadows, we take him down."

"What? You have Fielding in custody?"

"Not exactly," Pettigrew said.

Helen relaxed in her chair. She reached out and touched a finger to her coffee mug, basking a little more.

"I don't get it," Sheffield said. "Why bother with Hannah at all? Why not just dangle Fielding directly in front of Hal?"

"Too obvious. He'd know it was a trap. Like I said, the man's extremely cautious."

"Has Hannah agreed to all this?"

"Let's put it this way, Frank. Ms. Keller will be a nonvoting participant in the operation."

"You're doing this without her knowledge?"

"I can assure you, Frank, that Ms. Keller will be more than happy to play the role we've assigned her."

Helen lifted her eyes and gave Frank the full wattage of her scorn.

"And how the hell do you know it'll be Hal," Frank said, "not one of the other ten thousand goons they have working for them?"

"Hal's their major search-and-destroy guy," Charlie said. "He's been working this from day one when Fielding disappeared. He has a way of getting people to talk. He'll be the one they use."

Sheffield shook his head. Enough cocksure arrogance floating around that room to power Manhattan through a July heat wave.

"And how're the Cali people going to know J. J. Fielding's surfaced?"

"They'll know."

"How?"

"We have a mole, Frank. He works in the cartel's computer division. It's his job to alert the Cali people that Fielding has popped up."

Helen sat forward in her chair, craned around for a face-off with Frank.

"Let me remind you, Agent Sheffield, you're here merely as a consultant. Whether or not you understand and approve of all the nuances of our strategy is quite irrelevant. The only other thing you need to know is that the operation has a running time of exactly seventy-two hours. No more, no less."

"Seventy-two hours? What, the Bureau's run short of funds again?"

Helen Shane sliced him with a glare.

"We're limited by certain technical restraints that will become clear to you later. So, that's all we have. Seventy-two hours to catch Hal Bonner. But let's get this clear, Agent Sheffield, we're not asking for your approval on any of this."

Frank looked across at the FBI seal. Mouth shut.

"Frankly," the senator said, "I like the seventy-two-hour time frame. When Bonner realizes he has only three days to get to Fielding, the time pressure will be just the thing to make him blunder. He thinks this is his last chance to locate Fielding, he starts to hurry, makes a mistake. That's when we take him."

Ackerman raised his big right hand and slapped the table hard, crushing the very thought of Hal Bonner.

The room was silent for a moment, everyone watching Ackerman's palm grinding against the glossy wood.

Helen Shane cleared her throat, gave the senator a small smile, and said, "There'll be more detailed briefings this afternoon after lunch, then we'll get everything in place on Sunday, and we'll commence the operation at one minute after midnight Monday morning. So do you think you can take seventy-two hours out of your schedule next week, Frank? Put aside your other assignments and give us three days of your valuable time?"

Frank stared across the far wall. The flush-mounted television was dark now. This was the last group of people on earth he wanted to spend time with. He'd rather lock himself in a room with a dozen copperheads.

"Did you see the pictures of Joanie, Frank?" the senator said.

"I saw them, sir."

"Maybe you need to take another look. Refresh your memory. See what's at stake here."

Frank looked down the long table at Abraham Ackerman. The senator had been intimidating generals so long he'd probably started to believe his power was boundless. But losing his daughter like that must have been a brutal reminder of the limits of his authority.

Sheffield picked up the snapshot of Hal Bonner and took another look.

Helen leaned close, lowering her voice.

"He's got that kamikaze thing going, doesn't he? A guy who doesn't mind dying, but by god he's going to take as many others down with him as he can."

Frank looked at her. Pretty woman with a cold, slippery smile.

"So are you on board, Frank?" Ackerman said.

Sheffield turned back to the senator.

"I'm not my father," Frank said. "Not even close."

"We're aware of your record," the senator said. "But I wanted you to have this opportunity. A larger venue, a chance to excel."

Helen chuckled.

Maybe what the woman needed was something a little stronger than a slap. Like a short jab to the solar plexus.

"Sure," Frank said. "I guess I could shift some things around on my calendar."

The senator nodded curtly. A man used to getting his way.

He stood up, stepped over to Charlie Pettigrew, and the two men huddled in the corner of the room.

Sheffield kept his seat, staring at the blank TV screen. He was trying to figure out why the mention of Hannah Keller's name had put an extra bump in his pulse.

"Welcome aboard, Frank," Helen said. "This should be fun."

He turned slowly and squinted at her.

"Fun?"

"Sure," she said. "And maybe you'll even learn something."

"Yeah? And what the hell am I going to learn from you, Shane?"

"Maybe how to act like a grown-up."

"Trust me," Frank said. "It'll take more than seventy-two hours to accomplish that."

TWO

Monday morning, 11 A.M., Hal was in Milwaukee.

Every city was the same. Buildings and streets and sidewalks and cars, horns honking, airplanes flying overhead, places to shop, places to work. The cities had different names but that was the only difference Hal Bonner could see.

Hal was in a hotel, it could be any hotel. Standing at the front desk. There was a black woman in a white blouse and burgundy skirt behind the desk typing on her computer. She looked up at him and asked if she could be of any help.

"I locked myself out of my room."

"What room is it, sir?"

"Fifteen twenty-six."

She tapped on her computer.

"I'm sorry, but I'm going to need to see some ID, sir."

"My wallet's locked in my room. I went to get some ice and the door shut and locked me out." He held up the ice bucket he'd taken from a maid's cart.

The young woman considered her options. She looked down the counter at the tall man who was the manager. He was on the phone with someone.

"And could I have your name, sir?"

"Randy Gianetti."

The young woman looked at her computer screen. She made a face to herself, coming to a decision. Then she opened a drawer and took out a credit card room key and ran it through the magnetizing unit and handed it to him.

"Thank you very much," said Hal.

"You're welcome. Sorry for the inconvenience, Mr. Gianetti."

He stood there for a moment. Maybe he was supposed to say something else. He wasn't sure. No one had ever said that to him before. Sorry for the inconvenience. That was a new one.

"You're welcome," he said to her.

He could tell from her look that this wasn't the right response.

He nodded and smiled. That usually worked when he'd made a mistake. Or sometimes he shrugged.

At that moment the desk clerk's phone rang and she answered it. Hal stood there a few seconds longer, then turned and went back to the elevator.

Hal looked at himself in the mirrored walls of the elevator. He was wearing jeans and a white button-down shirt. His hair was cut very short. He wasn't good-looking or bad-looking. He resembled a lot of people.

He got off on the fifteenth floor. He took two steps to his right and looked over the railing. He could see fifteen stories down into the lobby where there were trees and a fountain and people milling around. He could see the counter where he'd just been. The black woman on the phone. She had forgotten about him by now. Later she would remember him when the police came, but by then it would be too late. She would describe Hal and the police would make sketches. He'd seen some of the sketches. His employer had sent them to him so he could see what the authorities had. The sketches always looked like someone else. Someone meaner than Hal, someone dumber.

Hal found room 1526. NONSMOKING it said on a silver plaque. There was a peephole above the plaque.

Hal stuck the credit card key in the slot and pulled it out and the small green light came on and he pushed the door open.

Randy Gianetti was sitting on the side of the bed smoking

a cigarette and lacing up his right shoe. He had black hair, curly.

"What the hell?" he said.

"This is a nonsmoking room," Hal said. "There is a plaque on the door."

"Who the hell are you, coming in here like that?"

"My name is Hal."

"What're you going to do, bust me for smoking in my room? Jesus."

"Are you Randy Gianetti of Detroit, Michigan?"

"That's right."

"Randy Gianetti, I was sent here by people you have cheated."

Randy took the cigarette from his mouth.

"Hey, get in line, fella," he said. Trying to joke with Hal, giving him a stupid grin. Like he was going to try to be his buddy, kid his way out of this.

"You may remember Jose Cardona. He lives in South America. He shipped you some merchandise, but the money you were supposed to pay him never arrived in his bank account."

"It didn't?"

The man started to stand up, but Hal stepped forward and shoved him back onto the bed. He was a big man, taller and heavier than Hal, but not nearly as muscular. There was a silver pistol lying on the bedside table. But the man was used to kidding his way out of trouble. He was sneaky, not strong. Not a dangerous man. Hal could tell all that in an instant. It was in the man's eyes. It was in his sweat, his odor, the shape of his mouth, the way his eyes moved. It was in his clothes. The shiny blue shirt he wore, the heavy gold bracelet. Everything about the man was weak.

"I've got the money," Randy said. "Actually, you want to know the truth, I got it with me in that suitcase over there. The full amount. Really. Take a look. It's in hundred-dollar bills. I been scraping it together. I know it's a little late, but it's there, all of it, every single last dollar."

"I don't want money."

"You just said . . ."

"I'm not a bill collector," Hal said.

He had used this line before and had seen the thing happen in their eyes. The same thing that was happening in Randy's eyes, all his false courage fizzling. A weak man terrified. Desperate. Going to lunge for his gun. Try anything he could to squirm out of danger.

Hal was calm. This moment was exactly like the moment before it and the moment that would come after it. Every moment was equal. He was always alert, always relaxed. He was a bird pecking for worms in the damp grass, ready to eat or burst into flight. He was a snake sunning himself on a rock. Tranquil and alert, relaxed and vigilant.

The phone in his pocket chirped.

"That mine or yours?" Randy said. Trying another smile.

Hal took out the phone and said yes.

The voice in his ear was a woman's. She worked in an office in Panama or perhaps Costa Rica. Every week or two it changed. He'd been in some of those offices. One desk, two phones, a fax. A woman answering the phone who didn't know anyone's name or even who she worked for. A woman who was good at dictation, taking it all down word for word, passing messages on. Remembering none of it.

"Yes, it's Hal," he said. "I'm in the middle of something."

It was amazing, talking to this faraway woman. Hal's voice was penetrating the walls of this room. Zooming out into the sky and bouncing from one satellite to the next, zing, zing, across the black vacuum of space. Hal Bonner was in two places at once, three, four places, multiple Hals zinging around the solar system.

The woman spoke to him for several moments, explaining his next assignment, then said, "Do you understand?"

Hal watched Randy Gianetti of Detroit. Randy was still trying to decide if he should lunge for his gun. It was the most important decision he would ever make and he had not prepared himself for it. He had lost his instincts for survival.

His reactions were slow and uncertain. He had talked his way out of danger too many times. Now that was his only skill.

"Do you understand?" the woman said. "You will be able to find *Deathwatch.com* on the Internet?"

"Don't worry," he said. "I'll figure it out."

"So finish up whatever you're doing, Joe says, get right on this. It's urgent. And something else."

"Yes?"

"He said if you don't get it right this time, if you don't find Fielding, Joe is going to have to make a personnel change."

"A personnel change," Hal said.

"You understand what that means?"

"I understand," Hal said. "Good-bye."

The woman said good-bye and hung up.

Hal put the phone back in his pocket. The phone was smaller than a wallet. He would keep this phone for a few more days, then he would pitch it in a garbage can and buy another one. It was harder that way for people to listen in, track him down. Hal was not stupid.

"There are only two ways to kill a person," Hal said. "Did you know that, Randy?"

"Only two ways," the man said. He was having trouble with his voice. It was dry and scratchy.

"Yes," Hal said. "Either you attack the heart or you attack the brain."

"Yeah? Okay."

"Myself, I prefer the heart."

Randy glanced back at the gun on the bedside table.

"You're that guy," Randy said. "The one they send, you don't use anything, just your hands. That's who you are, isn't it?"

"That's who I am."

Randy looked at the blank wall. His face was soft now. Eyes watering.

"Jesus Christ," he said. "Jesus, Mother, and Mary. I thought you were like an urban myth."

"What's that?"

"You know, like a lie. A fiction."

"No," Hal said. "I'm real."

Randy turned his head and looked at Hal.

"Is it quick, the way you do it?"

"Not particularly, no."

"Is there a lot of pain?"

"From what I can tell, yes, I think there is."

"Shit," Randy said. "Shit, shit, shit."

Randy sniffed and wiped his nose.

"You could take the money," he said. "It's all yours. No one would ever know."

"I'm going to take it anyway," Hal said.

"Shit," he said. "Jesus God." His eyes were watering more.

"Would you like to use your gun, Randy, or do you want me to do it my way?"

The man lifted his cigarette and took a drag on it and blew out the smoke.

"You'd let me do it?" Randy said. "Really?"

"I don't care. If you'd rather not be the one for whatever reason, religion or something, I don't mind. But you have to decide right now. I've got other business to take care of."

The man looked at him. He was cowering. It was what animals did when they were cornered. They signaled the attacker that they offered no resistance. They were not a threat. It sometimes worked in the wild. Sometimes they escaped by cowering. But in a hotel room in Milwaukee it was useless.

Hal stared at the man and said nothing. Randy sighed.

"All right," Randy said.

"Which is it?"

"I guess I'd rather do it myself. If it's all the same to you."

Hal stepped over to the bedside table and picked up the pistol.

"It's better in the shower," Hal said. "Less noise, less mess."

The man followed Hal into the bedroom. He hesitated a moment outside the shower, grimacing at Hal like he'd changed his mind. Hal just looked back at him, hard, unblinking. Then Randy began to strip off his clothes and when he was down to his underpants, he said, "Can I leave these on?"

"Sure," Hal said. "Whatever you want."

Randy got in the shower in his underpants and turned on the water. The hot water and the cold, getting it the right temperature. Then he stepped under the full force of the spray. Hal handed him the pistol. The man looked at the gun in his hand and he looked at Hal.

"I could shoot you," he said.

Hal nodded.

"You could try."

The man put his face into the stream of water, then he looked back at Hal. He was holding the pistol by his side.

"I fucked up," the man said. "I thought I was so smart."

"Sorry to inconvenience you," Hal said.

Randy looked at him. Puzzled. He swallowed.

He raised the pistol and pressed the muzzle against his temple.

He cocked the hammer back. Then he took the barrel away from his temple and slid it into his mouth.

His hand quivered, but he could not bring himself to fire.

He withdrew the barrel and looked at Hal.

"I'm not sure how to do it, which way is best."

"A big gun like that," Hal said. "One way is probably as good as the other."

"All right," Randy said. "All right then."

He jammed the barrel against his temple. He closed his eyes hard and fired.

Hal stepped back to avoid the spray. He watched Randy Gianetti's body slump to the floor of the shower.

Hal stayed there a few seconds more, watching the blood swirl down the silver drain. Randy Gianetti was twitching. But he didn't twitch for long.

                              *   *   *

The taxi driver took Hal to an electronics store. Best one in Milwaukee. It looked like every other electronics store to Hal.

"Wait for me," Hal told the taxi driver. "I've got a plane to catch."

He went in the store and found a young clerk. He was a boy with long hair and a skinny face. He had acne and was chewing gum.

"Help you?" the boy said.

"I want the Internet," Hal said.

"Do what?"

"I want the Internet. I want to carry it with me."

"Oh," the boy said. "You mean wireless. A cell phone built into a palm-top computer. Is that what you're talking about?"

"All right," Hal said. "Let me see it."

"I've got the Nokia 9000IL Communicator. It's got a 386 processor, hands-free speakerphone, mobile Internet access, fourteen ounces, three-hour active battery life. That's my top-of-the-line model."

"Show it to me."

"It ain't cheap," the boy said. "Close to a thousand bucks."

"Show it to me now."

The boy took a longer look at Hal. Hearing the thing Hal could bring to his voice, the thing that made the boy's bristles stiffen.

"Yes, sir," the boy said. "Right away."

"And then you're going to explain it to me. How it works. How I find this place, *Deathwatch.com*."

"What's that, a Web page?"

"I guess so."

"Sure, no problem," the kid said. "I'll just see if we got the Nokia in stock. They're pretty cool."

"Good," Hal said. "I'll wait here."

The boy trotted away.

Hal stood at the counter and looked up at the televisions mounted high on the wall. Ten television sets and all of them were showing Hal. Hal Bonner, the main feature, a guy standing at a counter looking up at himself, like he was waiting for the man on the screen to do something. To smile or make a joke. But Hal did nothing. He simply waited and watched himself wait in each of the ten screens mounted high on the wall.

THREE

Hannah Keller had just passed the hundred-page mark in *Fifth Story*. Book number five, the most recent outing for Erin Barkley. Thirty-one years old, Erin worked as a PIO for Miami PD. But that's where the similarity between Erin and Hannah ended.

For one thing Erin had a rich and varied sex life. A new man every book. Sometimes two or three in the same book, as footloose and lecherous as any guy. While Hannah, on the other hand, had nearly given up on men. In the last year there'd been a cop, a lawyer, an accountant, and two realtors. All washouts. Lately, she'd begun to wonder if maybe she needed an aura-adjustment. Sending out the wrong signals, Angry Broad Alert. Don't Even Think About Flirting With Me, Asshole. Even after all these years she was still man-shy from her quick and disastrous marriage to Pieter Thomasson. Randall's father had turned out to be a philanderer of the lowest kind, and that betrayal left her scarred, brooding, overcautious. And now the bastard had reappeared, as if he were determined to destroy what marginal serenity she'd managed to achieve.

After six years as a single mother, six years living mostly inside her head, whatever adult social skills Hannah Keller once had were long gone. Ten hours a day she wrote the books, then spent what little free time she had with Randall. Most weekends she took one day off, coaxing her son out to a movie or the mall. Occasionally she managed to get him to go along on a bicycle ride into the Grove or out the long asphalt strip into Shark Valley, the edge of the Everglades. But it was such a chore to pry the boy away from his computer and out of the house that she'd all but given up trying to reignite Randall's youthful enthusiasm for the outdoors.

If it weren't for Erin Barkley, Hannah would've completely lost touch with adult pleasures. Erin was a childless single woman. She drove her car fast and stayed out till dawn, dancing, bar hopping, jumping in and out of bed with virtual strangers. She had a smart-ass mouth and a renegade view of justice and was a gifted marksman. Erin wasn't the least bit reluctant to pull the trigger when she needed to, and was willing to overstep the boundaries of the law if that's what it took to nail the thugs and psychos who managed to elude traditional law enforcement.

It was fantasy stuff, of course, Hannah indulging her vigilante yearnings, working off years of frustration from the job, and all that stored-up anger over her parents' unsolved murders. Using the novels to get some small measure of emotional vengeance.

In *Fifth Story* Erin Barkley was on the trail of the person who had twice attempted to kill twelve-year-old Jamie Newsome, a child model. A week after Jamie narrowly missed being struck by a speeding car, two high-powered rifle shots struck the wall of the fifth-floor balcony of her parents' Grove Isle apartment only inches from where Jamie sat doing her homework.

Of course, Hannah knew that Jamie was a stand-in for Randall. A kid in harm's way who teetered uneasily between childhood and maturity. All Hannah's anxiety about Randall's safety and his fragile mental health was submerged in this fictional character. What Erin Barkley was trying to accomplish was something Hannah could only dream of doing, pry aside the defiantly bland adolescent mask to see what shadowy and desperate emotions might be percolating beneath it.

So far, in those first hundred pages, Erin Barkley's investigation had led her to a small-time hood named Owen Band who ran a seedy strip joint on Miami Beach, a half block from the headquarters of the modeling agency that represented Jamie Newsome.

Hannah had no idea what Band had to do with the attempts on this young girl's life. In fact, she usually had no clear notion of what was coming next in any of her books. She didn't use outlines. She'd decided that she'd rather make a dozen wrong turns along the way than plan everything out so carefully that each day's writing was ruled by the predrawn map. She was a reader first and a writer second. Why in the world would she bother writing the book if she already knew how it was going to turn out?

Today, just before Hannah broke for lunch, Erin Barkley was questioning Owen Band in the office of his strip club when suddenly Owen lurched to one side and blood spouted from the side of his head. It was an amazing and totally unexpected moment. Hannah didn't know who shot him or why. Perhaps the shot was actually intended for Erin, or was meant to implicate her. Or maybe, given the nature of Miami, it was simply stray gunfire from some botched holdup going on nearby.

As Owen Band spilled his lifeblood onto the desk before him, Hannah got up, went to the kitchen, made a turkey sandwich, and took it out to the front porch table to eat.

The house she'd bought after her parents were killed was more than eighty years old, ancient by Miami standards, with a glinting tin roof and a screened-in porch that ran the full length of the front. Edging the property was a tall, solid wood fence overgrown with purple and orange bougainvillea, totally blocking from view the surrounding neighborhood. The old house had oak floors, a coral fireplace, a dozen ceiling fans, and its several French doors opened out onto a wide yard of neatly laid out avocado and mango trees, remnants of the grove that early in the century had spread all over that part of Dade County. Some mornings when Hannah sat out on the porch in one of the wicker rockers sipping her coffee, she could hear the faint echoes of those tenacious New England pioneers who had cleared and tamed that harsh subtropical tangle. And whenever she returned home after any sort of journey, just the sight of that shady two acres and the solid old farmhouse soothed the clatter in her pulse.

That afternoon the sky was clear and the last of the orange jasmine was still in bloom, cloying the air around the porch. As she finished her sandwich, she drew in a deep perfumed breath, feeling a ripple of energy and quiet pleasure. There were wild parrots squawking in the avocado trees and a blue jay scolding them in reply. She watched the birds fuss at each other for a minute, maybe something she could use, a little moment of atmosphere in her story.

She had about an hour and a half before Randall got home from school. If she was lucky that was long enough for Erin to check Owen Band's pulse, then run out into the alley behind the strip club and stumble on the next complication.

Misty was parked among the mothers. Their vans and sport utility vehicles lined the street outside Pinecrest Middle School. The mothers visited with each other or talked on their cell phones while they waited for the afternoon bell to ring.

Misty was in her powder blue Corolla with the peeling Naugahyde top. She was parked beneath a gumbo limb tree a half block east of the school. Nobody paid any attention to her. If they did, they'd probably think she was a maid, a housekeeper, someone like that, waiting to pick up young Travis or Michelle or whatever the hell cute names they were using this year.

One of her derringers lay on her lap. Small, but heavy. Its mechanisms were reliable and made firm, satisfying clicks. The derringer was loaded with two .38 slugs. It was Misty's belief that if you couldn't bring down your target with two shots, you shouldn't own a gun at all.

Out her windshield she watched the mothers. They were dressed in summery outfits, creamy beiges or pastels, or else bright-colored workout clothes. These women had nothing but leisure time. They had expensive hair and subtle makeup and they moved with slinky assurance. They were married to lawyers or accountants or bankers or stockbrokers. Misty knew their husbands, because it was guys like them who frequented the downtown Hooters where she worked, and drank draft beer and stared at Misty's breasts, always angling their heads to get a shot down her top, glimpse her nipples.

Misty didn't look like any of the mothers. First, she was very pale. Deathly white is how some people described her. She didn't mind that. It was kind of a compliment really. Set her apart. Her white skin was smooth, tight, but it simply wouldn't hold a tan. Her eyes were dark green, the shade of ripe avocados. Her hair was metallic red with a brassy orange undertone. It was her natural color, but it didn't look as natural as some of the bottle blonds waiting for their kids.

Compared to the mothers, Misty had a gawky body. Wide bony shoulders, long thin arms, pigeon-toed stance, hefty tits, and a little slump in her shoulders she couldn't seem to get rid of. She practiced sometimes in the bathroom mirror in her apartment, standing up on a chair so she could see herself. Pulling her shoulders back, lifting her head up, angling her hips this way or that, but everything she did looked phony, only made her seem more awkward.

After they brought their kids to school each morning, these yummy mummies spent the morning at their health clubs burning off their few remaining fat cells in front of floor-to-ceiling mirrors. Jazz dancing or doing karate moves, keeping themselves lean and taut. Then they went home, ate a stick of celery for lunch, had a sip of ten-dollar water, and came early to pick up their kids after school, and put on this fashion show for all the other mothers.

After school some of their kids played soccer. Some went to karate class or tennis practice or golf lessons. These pampered kids, their perfect lives.

Misty had been destined to be one of them. That was her birthright. To be married to a fast-track lawyer or a surgeon. Living in this part of town, or the Gables, or along the bay, a big boat bobbing out back. Waiting every afternoon at two-thirty for her cute blond kid to come rushing out of school and jump into her arms.

But that's not how it worked out. Not how it worked out at all.

When the school bell finally rang, the mothers began saying good-bye to their friends. Some kept on talking on their cell phones as they craned around searching for their child in the throng of kids who poured out the doors. There was a lady cop directing traffic. All the lights were blinking yellow. It was a clear, pretty day, no clouds. Monday, early October, low eighties, low humidity. There was a white dog waiting outside the fence, a Labrador. It was fat and had a sway back and it stared in through the fence wagging its tail, looking for its master in that mass of kids.

It took a minute but finally Misty spotted Randall Keller. He was wearing a black T-shirt and baggy blue jean shorts that hung below his knees. He had on red running shoes and a green backpack loaded with books. He was carrying his bright pink bicycle helmet. No other kids were talking to him. He wasn't looking around for anyone. He didn't seem depressed or happy or anything. He just walked over to the bicycle rack and rolled his bicycle out and got on it and started pedaling across the playground toward the gate.

Misty started her car.

She waited for a break in the parade of four-wheel-drive monsters, then cut out into the street. Going slow for the school zone. Staying back of Randall. Watching the blond hair sticking out from under his helmet. Watching him pump the pedals, not too fast, the pack heavy on his back.

He rolled through a four-way stop and kept going straight. Misty waited her turn, then eased through the intersection and cruised up slowly behind him. He was on the sidewalk, taking it slow. Looking straight ahead, his face was red from the exertion, sweaty. She drove with her left hand and held the derringer in her right. Her passenger window was open. She wasn't going more than ten miles an hour. Her speedometer was broken, but she knew it couldn't be any faster than that.

There was a big blue sports utility vehicle right on her ass. Tailgating mom with a car full of kids. Misty was out of the school zone now. Speed limit back up to thirty, but she held it at ten or so, creeping along beside Randall. Holding the derringer in her right hand. Thumbing back one of the hammers.

Raise the pistol, aim, then fire. That's all it took. A few seconds and it would be over, and the boy would be wounded or maybe dead, lying in the front yard of some stranger's house. People screaming, running to where he'd tumbled off his bike. Blood spilling out of his fragile body. His perfect childhood over. Then the poor kid's mother would spend the rest of her life grieving. Just like Misty was spending hers.

That's all it would take. Some kook. Some lunatic killer coming along and doing it like that. What was his mother thinking? Hannah Keller, sitting in her house ten blocks away, waiting for her boy to come home. Why didn't she get in her car and go down with all the other mothers and wait for him? She was home. She didn't have a real job. A fucking writer was all she was, sat in a room, made things up. Leaving her son to bike home on his own, vulnerable to any sort of disaster, to any kind of fucking maniac killer who might want to hurt him.

The big blue four-wheel-drive beast behind her tooted its horn.

Misty lowered the derringer. Eased the hammer back. She set the pistol on the seat beside her. Rubber foam was poking through the seat cover. She accelerated, headed up 124th Street, took the first right she came to, circled the block and came out onto 124th again, and there he was, Randall Keller, waiting for the light at Ludlam Road.

Misty pulled alongside him. She could call out, say hi. But she knew what he would do. He would look over at her, then duck his eyes, and point them back down the street where he was headed. He'd do that because that's what he and all the other little perfect kids his age were trained to do. Not speak to strangers. Like that would save them. Like that would make any difference.

And the really ironic thing was that Misty wasn't a stranger. She and Randall were old pals, intimate friends. Except that Randall didn't know what Misty looked like. Wouldn't recognize her sitting in her powder blue Corolla. And now wasn't the time to pull the curtain aside and step out into view. She wasn't ready for that just yet.

So she didn't say anything, but waited till the light turned green, then went on straight and turned down the street where she knew Randall was going to turn, and she went on past Hannah Keller's cute little wood house in the middle of a mango and avocado grove with the high white fence and the red and purple bougainvillea, and Misty went to the end of the block, looking for some place to pull off, somewhere in the shade, out of the way.

In the front yard of a big brown house at the end of Hannah Keller's street there were a dozen cars parked helter-skelter. A tea party going on inside. Or maybe a bridge club. Trays of tiny sandwiches without the crust. Some of the women in white gloves. Fresh from the beauty shop, smelling of gaudy perfume. Women saying catty things about women who weren't there. Whispering behind their hands.

Misty pulled in among the cars, Mercedeses, Cadillacs. She found a place on the shoulder of the road, in the shade of an oak tree. She shifted the Corolla around so it was facing back down Pinecrest Lane, Hannah and Randall's street. A good view of her driveway entrance. It would only be a half-hour wait before Hannah Keller and her eleven-year-old son headed out for Randall's weekly meeting with his shrink.

Misty's heart was fluttering. The air had a special tremble. Something was just about to happen. She could feel it— something big and ugly rumbling down the tracks. A freight train, with Misty, wild and crazy, at the helm.

FOUR

Hannah heard the back door slam.

She saved the chapter she was working on and leaned back in her chair, waiting for Randall to put his books down and come back to her study to say hi.

But he didn't come.

She waited, listened for his footsteps through the house, but she heard nothing.

So she pushed back her chair, got up and walked through her bedroom, out to the living room, then along a narrow corridor to Randall's room. She pushed open his door and stepped inside. Posters of *Star Trek* villains and all-girl pop groups covered his walls. His bed was neatly made and his closet door opened on a carefully organized array of clothes. A couple of framed math and computer studies awards hung on the wall and in the old metal birdcage that sat on the far edge of his desk, Spunky was curled up in his bed of shredded paper. A former lab rat, Spunky was black and fat, getting bulkier all the time. An insatiable appetite for pepperoni.

Randall was eleven years old and had his father's thick blond hair and liquid blue eyes and knobby cheekbones. Sometimes on a groggy morning, when Hannah shuffled into the kitchen to find her son at the breakfast nook reading the newspaper and drinking orange juice, her pulse stuttered hard and she had to take a deep, calming breath, for this son of hers was more than a rough approximation of his father. Randall was turning into his physical duplicate, as if Pieter Thomasson's Nordic genes had prevailed in all the thousand microscopic battles for supremacy. At the oddest times her ex-husband looked out at her from Randall's eyes, grinned at her from her son's lips, and sometimes he even haunted her sleep as the two of them, Pieter and Randall, appeared in her dreams as terrifyingly interchangeable.

Randall was wearing baggy jeans and a black T-shirt and his Marlins baseball cap was on backwards. He was tapping his right foot fast against the oak floor, probably keeping time to the infernal beat of his cursor.

Hannah smiled and shook her head and ducked down to give him a kiss on the cheek.

"Hey, pardner," she said.

"Hey." A listless voice.

"You didn't come say hi. What's wrong?"

"I didn't want to interrupt your writing."

"You can interrupt me anytime you want, Randall. You know that. I like it when you interrupt me."

A blade of sunlight from the west window cut across his desk and lit up the side of his face and she could see the faint dusting of peach fuzz on his cheek. He was going to have a beard as downy and inconsequential as his dad's.

"How was school? You do okay on that English composition?"

"I got a B."

"B's are fine."

"Not as fine as A's."

"And did Miss Mays like the drawing of the osprey?"

"She put it up on the board. I guess she liked it. Unless she was trying to make fun of me."

"Oh, she must've liked it. It was very good, Randall. Very realistic."

The assignment had been to draw one of the animals of the Everglades. Drawing was torture for him. So personal, so much exposure.

"Everybody else did alligators. There were a couple of deer. I was the only one who did an osprey."

"So you were original. That's good."

"I wish I'd drawn an alligator like everyone else."

She came up behind him, tried to keep her voice upbeat.

"You remember what day it is, right?"

"I remember."

"We have to get rolling in ten, fifteen minutes."

"Oh, Mom," he said. "Can't we skip it for once?"

"But you like Dr. English."

"She's okay."

"And we skipped two weeks ago, Randall."

"Once a month is enough. Cutting back would save money."

"Don't worry about the money. The money's irrelevant. What matters is for you to start feeling better."

He was using the computer mouse to flick through screen after screen, bright images coming and going almost instantly.

"What're you working on, Randall?"

"A project for computer science."

"Tell me again. What's it about?"

He looked up at her. His mouth twisted into a smirk.

"Go on," she said. "I know I won't understand it. But I like to hear the words."

"Cognitively self-modifying automata."

She nodded.

"And what's that in English?"

"Little bugs that live on their own inside a program. The longer they survive, the more they learn and adapt. They get smarter and smarter and harder to detect."

"That sounds like computer viruses."

"Viruses destroy things. These are just bugs. They're neutral. They're just there, learning, not hurting anybody."

"And they're teaching that in computer science?"

"They're trying to."

He smiled politely and his eyes strayed back to his screen.

"I really hate my clothes," he said.

"What?"

"Oh, never mind."

"Your clothes? Why? What's wrong with your clothes?"

"They're wrong. They're geeky."

"When did you decide that?"

"They're geeky and I hate them."

"Well, then we'll go shopping, find you some new clothes."

"I don't like when you go shopping with me. You watch me all the time. You smile and stuff."

"I make you self-conscious?"

"And I don't want to go to soccer anymore either."

"You love soccer, Randall."

"I only go because you want me to. But I don't like it. It's too hot out there, no shade, I get all sweaty and I can't breathe. The coaches scream at me. And I don't like the kids. I don't like getting kicked in the shins. I'm not doing it anymore."

"There's nothing about soccer you like, really? Now be honest."

"I don't like all the other people in the stands. All the parents and the little kids. Everyone hanging around watching, whistling and cheering. I'd rather be alone."

"You need friends, Randall."

"No, I don't."

"Of course you do. Everybody needs friends."

"*You* don't have any friends."

"Sure I do."

"Name one."

"There's Gisela."

"One friend, big deal."

"There's Max."

"He doesn't count. He's your book agent."

"But he's my friend too."

"He *has* to be your friend. You pay him. Anyway, he lives in New York. You see him like twice a year. That's not a friend."

"Randall, this is a ridiculous conversation."

"I have Stevie," he said. "I don't need any more friends. Stevie's plenty."

"Look, Randall, I like that you have an E-mail friend. But a real friend is someone you know face-to-face. Someone you spend time with. If you gave it half a chance, I'm sure some of your soccer teammates, or kids in your class would be thrilled to be friends with you. Isn't there someone you want to invite over? You could swim in the pool. Have a cookout."

"Yeah sure, Mom, sit around a campfire, roast weenies. Oh, boy."

"Come on now, Randall."

"I don't need anybody. I'm happy by myself."

"Remember how much you used to like to fish, go swimming, snorkeling? You need to get out of this room, away from the computer."

"Why? What's so good about being outside?"

"It's healthy. It's enriching."

"You get skin cancer outside."

"Oh, now you're being silly, Randall."

"*You* don't get outside. *You* don't do things."

"Of course, I do," Hannah said.

"All you do is write. You stay inside and you write. That's all you ever do. Turn on your computer first thing in the morning, sit down in front of it and type. Turn it off before you go to bed."

She drew a slow breath, let it out.

"I hate my clothes," said Randall. "They're stupid."

Hannah put her hand on his shoulder. She could feel the vibrations radiating from his body like the hum of a tuning fork buried deep in the bone, a low throb that had begun to pulse years ago, that morning when he found his grandparents dead.

The watershed moment. Everything forever different afterward. His startle reflex on hair-trigger. Now he was jumpy. Any little noise, a bird exploding into flight, an avocado falling from the tree would send him reeling. His appetite was erratic. He was depressed, quiet, stayed in his room. He had manic bursts, long hours lost in his programming language, deaf to the world.

"Have you been sleeping, Randall? Did you sleep last night?"

He pointed and clicked, pointed and clicked.

"Randall?"

"I don't know," he said. "I'm not sure. How do you know if you're asleep? You lie there in the dark, you close your eyes, how can you tell?"

"Have you stopped taking your medicine again?"

"I take it some of the time."

"Okay," she said. "Well, go wash your face, put on a fresh shirt. We're going to see Dr. English."

"Do I have to?"

"Yes, you have to. You always feel better afterward, you know you do."

"I feel better because the appointment's over."

"When you grow up, Randall, you should be a lawyer. You're so good at arguing."

"Do lawyers have to play soccer?"

"Not unless they want to."

"Then that's what I want to be, a lawyer."

She ruffled his thick mop, gave his scalp a gentle scraping with her fingernails, something that usually made him croon. Today he was silent.

"We're still pardners, aren't we, Randall?"

It was an old refrain. Single mother, only child, the mantra of their loyalty.

He lifted his hand from his mouse and turned to look at her. She gave his scalp another scratch.

"I'm not crazy, Mom."

"Nobody said you were."

"Only crazy people go to shrinks once a week."

"That's not true. A lot of people go to psychiatrists. It's because they want to feel better, because they want to understand how they can start enjoying life."

"I enjoy life."

"Do you?"

He moved his cursor around the screen, sailing across the electronic net.

"I'm not crazy," he said. "I'm not a wacko."

"Did somebody call you that? Somebody at school?"

"Never mind," he said. "Just never mind."

"Is somebody bothering you? Tell me his name. I'll talk to his mother."

"Oh, yeah, talk to his mother. Boy, you really know how it works, don't you?"

"Randall," she said. "If somebody's bothering you . . ."

"Nobody's bothering me. I'm fine. Just a little crazy, that's all."

"Oh, come on. Don't say that."

He settled finally on his own Web page. In a banner across the top, *Randall's World* glowed in a brilliant red. He had created the page a few months back as a school project and every week or so he redid it, another look, another motif. This week there were animated frogs swimming and flying over a purple bayou. Others perched on a floating log. Their long tongues unfurling, snapping flies out of the air. Silly and childish, something any eleven-year-old boy might like. Thank God, thank God, thank God.

"I'm sorry, Mom," he said. "I guess I'm just in a bad mood."

"Bad moods are allowed," she said. "As long as you give equal time to good ones."

He looked up at her, managed a smile.

"So we're pardners then?" she said.

"Sure, Mom," Randall said, looking back at the flying frogs. "Pardners."

FIVE

Monday, 4 P.M., hour sixteen of Operation Joanie. No sign of Hal Bonner.

Frank Sheffield was sitting behind the wheel of one of a dozen surveillance vehicles in play this afternoon, a brown UPS truck. He was idling at the stop sign on Seaview Lane, a side street off Old Cutler Road when Hannah Keller passed in a red Porsche convertible, a Boxster, if Sheffield wasn't mistaken. Hannah and her kid, with the convertible top up, windows down. The kid sticking his arm out the window, making a wing with his hand, riding the bumpy air currents.

Frank put the big truck in gear, rolled onto the roadway. He was wearing the UPS uniform, brown shorts and shirt, heavy black brogans. Wondering how the UPS guys stood it, the sticky synthetic threads, the sun-absorbing color. He was miked up, a black dot on his collar, and a flesh-colored receiver plugged in his left ear.

"I got her," Frank said. "Red Porsche Boxster. License AGP Five-Six-Six."

In his earpiece Helen Shane rogered that.

"I'm rolling now, four cars back. There's Hannah's Porsche, then a green Camaro, a blue late-model Toyota Corolla, a black Dodge van, then little old us. And there's some idiot on a red dirt bike riding my bumper. Maybe somebody could pull him over, write him a ticket."

"Frank, you stay with the Porsche only as far as Coplum Circle, then sixteen will take over. You hear that, sixteen?"

Sixteen rogered.

Forty agents, leapfrogging, falling away. Two choppers rotating positions, several hard-wired video cameras at the fixed locations. Yard-service workers along the route, mailmen, Rollerbladers, dog-walkers. It was a first-time thing for Frank. All the stops pulled out. Big-budget production, the full orchestra. Helen with the baton in her hand, keeping the beat, making sure everyone stayed on key.

She was back at the command post, a three-bedroom suite on the top floor of the Grand Bay Hotel. Big bank of windows with a sweeping view of Biscayne Bay and the Dinner Key Marina. Probably two thousand a night for a room like that. Though Sheffield wasn't privy to the deals, he assumed the room was comped to Senator Ackerman. Helen said the Grove was a central location, fifteen minutes from every venue on their game plan. Had to hand it to her, the lady wrote herself a nice part in the script.

"Did you say a blue Corolla, Frank?" It was Helen in his ear, her voice strained today. The plan unfolding. Sixteen hours down, fifty-six to go. Starting at midnight, due to close up shop midnight Wednesday. Helen was on hyperalert, as though Senator Ackerman was standing next to her, ready to promote her on the spot, or tear off her stripes.

"That's right. Blue Corolla, peeling fake leather top. Looks like just the driver, no passenger. Can't tell if it's male or female."

"Didn't we have an earlier sighting on a blue Corolla? Did you pick that up, thirteen?"

Thirteen came back with some static.

"Thirteen, go again," Helen said. "You're breaking up."

Thirteen backed down his squelch and a male voice that Frank didn't recognize said, "A blue Corolla was parked five houses down from the Keller house earlier this afternoon. Departed simultaneous with target vehicle."

Helen took a few moments to digest it. Maybe she ran it by the Senator or Charlie Pettigrew back at command central. When Helen came back on, her voice was steely.

"We're going to take the Corolla. This could be our target. Repeat, this could be target. All ground units in the blue team, and both our birds will converge. Wait till the other side of Cocoplum Circle. Corner of Poinciana and LeJeune Road. Twelve and fourteen get in position at Poinciana. Let the Porsche pass through, then intercept the Corolla at the intersection. Move the choppers. Three, five, and eight converge on the area immediately. One and four, you should be moving south on LeJeune. Everyone wait for my signal."

"Shit," Sheffield said. "We haven't even got going yet, we're already catching the guy. That's no fun."

Helen said, "No random traffic, Sheffield. If it's not critical, stay off the air."

"Yes, ma'am."

"And, Sheffield, disregard previous order. You're to keep target in sight. You stay with Hannah. We're taking down the Corolla."

"I hear you," Frank said.

It was supposed to be a kick in the nuts. A message from Helen. If Frank wasn't going to take this seriously, fine. But it meant he wasn't going to be included in the bust. Which would've pissed him off if he'd been an androgen junkie. But that wasn't Frank. He never tried to duck the action, he just didn't need to jack up his pulse rate on a regular basis like most of the other guys.

Anyway, since coming on duty this morning at 6 A.M., spending the first hour studying the case files in that Grand Bay Hotel suite, finding in the pile of paperwork a glossy photo of Hannah Keller, Frank had been taking this in a different direction. He was thinking how in a few days when this was over, he was going to have to call her up, see if maybe she wanted to come over to Key Biscayne, visit his favorite tiki bar for a margarita, watch the driftwood pile up on the shoreline.

The photo was a few years old, a publicity shot for her book jacket or something, soft focus, a lot of diffused light. Blond hair cut short, wide-set blue eyes that flickered with sass. Which brought it all back, the way he'd felt about her back then, a quiver in his chest. Knowing enough not to try to hit on her in her period of grief. Anyway he'd been involved at the time. A dark-haired girl named Darlene, or Arlene. He wasn't even sure of her name, but he remembered Hannah vividly. A rough-and-ready lady with an ironic take on things. No bullshit, straight to the point. And, he seemed to recall, she had a first-class pair of calves. As sculptured as a dancer's with narrow ankles. Not that legs mattered all that much, or any body parts. He'd just noticed. And remembered.

Now the caravan was moving through the tunnel of banyans along Old Cutler, a half mile till Cocoplum Circle. Pretty day, a good breeze off the water, golden sun rippling through the dense layer overhead. Traffic moving fine ahead of him. A little buildup of cars heading south, the other way, probably some business folks getting a jump on rush hour.

In his ear, Helen Shane was staying in touch with everyone, flitting back and forth between the two dozen units. The urgency in her voice rising. But Frank ignored her, keeping his eyes on the red Porsche. Nice car. The book business obviously doing well. He'd read a couple of them early on, liked them fine. She had a good ear for street talk, some good zingers about cops and bad guys. Her heroine, he seemed to recall, was one kickass broad. Quick with a comeback, fast on the draw. He hadn't kept up with Hannah's career, though. His reading tastes ran more toward the sports page, following whatever Miami team was in season.

The UPS truck entered Cocoplum Circle, rolling through the YIELD sign. Keeping Hannah in view on the other side of the fountain. The red Porsche, then the Camaro, then the blue Corolla. He heard the distant thump of one of the choppers. He steered the top-heavy truck around the tight circle, then took the second spoke off of it, north onto LeJeune Road, heading into the heart of Coral Gables. Hannah and her kid stopping at the light up ahead. The guy on the dirt bike was revving his engine in Frank's rearview mirror. Fucking Miami drivers.

Frank watched as the blue Corolla peeled off with most

of the other traffic onto Ingram Highway, heading for Coconut Grove.

Frank pinched the button mike that was fixed to his collar, lifted it close to his mouth.

"Corolla's heading east onto Ingram. Repeat, Corolla's no longer following the Porsche."

"Roger that," Helen said. "I hear you."

Frank waited for a moment. One car behind the Porsche. When the light turned green, he said, "So, Helen, you still going after the Corolla?"

"The Corolla's an anomalous sighting. Stand down. All units stand down. Let the Corolla go."

"It could be our guy," Frank said. "He might've seen us following and broken off."

"Thanks for the insight, Sheffield, but that bicyclist you just passed back on Cocoplum was one of our guys. He got a good visual and reported the driver of the Corolla to be a young white female."

"Maybe Hal is a master of disguise."

"It's anomalous," Helen said, clicking off.

"Anomalous," Frank said. "Man, tomorrow I gotta bring along my thesaurus. Stay up with you people."

"Cut the chatter, Sheffield. Keep your eye on the goddamn ball."

It was Senator Ackerman. His voice was hard and full of phlegm as if he'd been staring again at the photograph of his daughter.

Then it was Helen speaking, moving her men around the chess board. Sixteen here, twenty-three there. All the pieces still in play, the game moving forward. Fifty-six hours left.

Misty had the evening shift at Hooters. All the happy-hour idiots streaming down from the high-rise office buildings, loosening their ties, guzzling two or three quick ones before heading off to the suburbs in their fancy leased cars to join their skinny wives and coddled kids.

Misty parked in the covered lot and took a minute to stash

the derringers behind the backseat. A few thousand dollars of hardware. The only valuable thing she owned aside from her Radio Shack computer. Something she'd started doing a few years back, a hobby, collecting derringers. Saving up her cash till she had a couple of hundred extra bucks, then picking out another one at a gun show or pawnshop. Mostly used ones, each with its own smoky history. She liked the idea of a little gun like that. Tuck it away in a pocket, no bulge. Carry two of them or three and nobody would know what firepower was passing by. She scrimped on clothes, movies, eating out at restaurants, so she could add to her collection. With some women it was shoes or purses or jewelry. You had to spend your extra money on some damn thing.

In the rearview mirror she touched up her makeup, then walked across the lot to the Bayside Market. The place was busy as usual, teenagers and old folks, South Americans. Calypso music tinkling over the speakers, a strong breeze flowing off the bay. Out on the Intracoastal some big white yachts idled past, laughing gulls squawking overhead.

Misty had on the tight orange shorts and the white cotton Hooters T-top, shortened to expose her navel. Underneath the T-top was the pushup bra that laid her breasts out for display on an extra-reinforced white cotton shelf. An engineering marvel and requirement of the job. You wanted tips, you had to have tits.

Most of the girls had plastic ones, saline-filled or olive oil, or whatever they were pumping into them this year. Every week another girl showing off her new boobs in the kitchen, letting everyone have a squeeze, check how real they were. All the cooks standing in line, the dishwashers drooling. Misty kept hers natural. Not gigoondas, but big enough to get by. Though in the last year or two she had to admit they were starting to get a little gravity-challenged.

She walked in the big glass front door and right away she could see something was wrong. All the girls gathered at the bar, folding napkins. No one looked over. No one said hi.

Then Jesus Cardozo, the young manager with the sweaty

face and Hitler mustache, came bustling out of the kitchen, spotted her, and sailed right over to where she was standing just inside the door.

"Let me guess," Misty said. "You're about to fire my ass again."

Jesus just stood there inside a fog of cheap cologne. The other girls stopped folding napkins. They were out of earshot, but they were leaning toward her. She could feel the bra tightening around her chest.

"I been telling you, Misty," Jesus said. "I been asking you to try harder."

"Okay, okay, so I've been a little mopey. I've been going through a bad patch, that's all. What can I say? You never get down, Jesus? A guy like you, you're always up, happy-go-lucky, twenty-four hours every day? I don't believe that."

"You didn't think I'd hear about what you did, Misty? You think no one would tell me? You dump a glass of beer on a man's head, I'm not going to find out?"

"Hey, I was going to tell you about it."

"This is something we can't have, Misty. You ruined this man's fancy-ass toupee. We gotta pay for this goddamn thing. It's sixteen hundred dollars, this hairpiece. It's imported from Italy, the hair of some special order of nuns for chrissakes."

"It was an accident. I stumbled."

"That was no accident. It was on his fucking toupee, Misty. How's that an accident? Explain it to me, the accident part. I got eyewitnesses come talking to me, telling me what you did. You poured a beer on the man's head."

"Hey, the guy was sexually harassing me. He had his hand all over my butt. What'm I supposed to do, call over a lawyer, sue the guy on the spot? I did what I had to do. I cooled his jets."

Jesus shook his head.

"Doesn't matter he touched you, Misty. You're a big girl. That's part of the job."

"Asshole can do anything he wants to me, I got to stand

there and take it? You rewrite the Constitution, did you, Jesus? I lost my inalienable rights all of a sudden?"

"You have a problem with a customer you come talk to me. That's how it works."

"Oh, yeah. I've seen whose side you come down on, Jesus."

"Misty, you poured a beer on this man. He's sitting there doing business with his clients and you embarrassed him. You ruined the man's expensive fucking hairpiece. We gotta sell a lot of beer to make up for that sixteen hundred dollars."

"The guy should be happy I didn't slam him with the beer mug."

"Look, Misty. Maybe it's come time for you to look around for something you like better than serving beer. Some other line of work."

Misty looked over at the other girls. They'd gone back to folding napkins, chatting away like nothing was happening. None of them were her friends. They talked to her, shot the shit, but that was it. Not friends. Worked alongside a couple of them since she dropped out of community college her sophomore year. Five years and zero friends.

"Yeah, yeah, you're right, Jesus. I should've just stood there and let the asshole grope me. What was I thinking? I should've pulled down my shorts, made it easier on him, let him get way inside there."

"Look," Jesus said. "I could give you one more chance. I know you got problems, Misty. I could see if I can forget this. Put it behind us. I'm not a bad guy. Maybe we can make a bargain between us."

"Let me guess," she said, raising her voice so the other girls could hear. "Because you're being so nice and all, letting me keep my job, you expect to come over to my apartment again. Crawl in beside me, make me breathe your dead-fish halitosis for two minutes while you work up to one of your premature ejaculations. Is that the bargain you had in mind?"

Jesus looked over at the other Hooter girls. Everyone frozen, watching.

Misty reached behind her, worked her hands up under her shirt. She unclipped the bra, then shrugged her arms through the sleeves of her white Hooters T-shirt and slipped it free, and tossed the bra at him. Jesus caught it by one strap and held it away from him like a rotting animal.

"You know, Jesus, actually, I have to thank you. Last couple of months, I've just been delaying the inevitable. Now, because of the fuckhead in his Italian wig, I can start working full-time on my true calling in life. And listen, man, I want to tell you something. Thanks for the mammaries."

It was the same stupid joke the customers used all the time. Not the parting shot Misty would've wished for, but, hey, Jesus caught her by surprise. Next time she got fired, she'd do better.

SIX

There was never anyone waiting in Dr. English's waiting room.

Apparently Janet English was the one doctor in the western hemisphere who didn't stack her patients' appointments on top of each other. Gave herself a half an hour between sessions to have a cup of tea, clear her mind. Whatever the reason, Hannah was grateful for it. Never anybody to play eye-games with. Everybody wondering about everybody else. Afraid that one of the kids would erupt, start speaking in tongues or have a seizure, unzip his pants, flash his privates.

Or maybe Dr. Janet English only had one client per day. God knows, she charged enough to stay afloat on that.

There was one couch, gray nubby material. A green leather chair. A good magazine selection on the coffee table. The latest *People*, *Time*, then some weird ones you'd never look at otherwise. A tattoo magazine. A skateboarder monthly. A couple of teenage fashion rags and a couple for the computer crowd.

There were two Andrew Wyeth reproductions on the walls. The Bermuda scene. A pretty Key West house on the edge of the wind-tossed Atlantic, a single coconut palm along the seawall bending against pre-storm winds. The other Wyeth was done in muted whites and featured a golden lab curled up on his master's king-size bed. Tassels hanging from the edge of the bedspread. Late-afternoon light suffusing the room with a serene glow.

The waiting room always made Hannah feel relaxed,

which was a hell of a feat since every week when they came
here, she inevitably circled back to that July morning five
years ago when her parents were murdered, the second-by-
second unfolding of that day, and the days that immediately
followed.

They'd only been sitting for half a minute, Randall paging through the tattoo magazine, when Dr. Janet English
came out of her back office. She was barefoot, wearing blue
jeans and a black and red Miami Heat T-shirt. In her early
forties, she had close-cropped hair, not a buzz cut exactly,
but way too short for a part. It was black, graying around the
temples. No jewelry, no makeup. Cherub cheeks, gray eyes
that never seemed to blink.

Last week Gisela said she'd heard that Dr. English was a
lesbian. "Why should that matter?" Hannah said. "I'm not
saying it matters," Gisela said. "I'm just saying I heard she
was a same-sex lady." Hannah said, "But the implication is
that it's bad. That this woman with a medical degree from
Harvard is somehow compromised because of her sexual
orientation." "Hey," Gisela said. "That's your spin. I'm just
saying I heard from a reliable source, the child psychiatrist
treating your son for posttraumatic stress is not one hundred
percent kosher heterosexual. What's wrong with you? You
join the PC police or something? You been memorizing the
lists of things you can't say anymore? Look, Hannah, I'm
just passing along some information. Do with it what you
will."

Hannah was doing nothing with it. She liked Janet English. Liked the way she put her hand on Randall's shoulder.
Liked the way she smiled, and most of all liked the way she
talked. Which was a lot like the way she dressed. No frills.
Comfortable with the language of normal folk, not throwing
around a lot of medical jargon. At first, it'd worried her.
Seemed unprofessional. But Randall took to Janet immediately and that was good enough for Hannah.

"How we doing?" Dr. English asked. More to Hannah
than Randall, but including them both. "Everybody behav-
ing themselves?"

Hannah gave Randall a chance to respond. But he was staring down at the floor, eyes hidden.

"Randall's decided he needs a new wardrobe."

He shook his head, but wouldn't look her way.

"New wardrobes are important," Janet said. "Gotta have the right uniform or they'll throw you off the team."

"And I'm not sure we've got full compliance on the pharmaceutical front either."

"I know what you're saying, Mom." Randall lifted his head and gave her a reproving frown. "I'm not some little kid."

"So have you been taking your Xanax, Randall?" Janet had her hand on his shoulder. He was leaning lightly against her hip. A tingle of jealousy fluttered in Hannah's chest. The closeness, the familiarity between these two. "Have you been taking the pills I prescribed?"

"No."

"Why not?"

"Because."

"Oh," Janet said. "Because. Now there's the great all-purpose answer."

"I didn't take them because I shouldn't have to take medicine. Because I should be all right without any medicine."

Dr. English looked at Hannah. A small smile growing on the doctor's lips. Like, see how easy this is? This is how to talk to your son, how it's done. But Hannah didn't like it. Two adults double-teaming the anxious boy. It wasn't fair. Wasn't natural. And certainly nothing she could repeat at home alone.

"Good answer, Randall. Very good answer. And I totally agree. You shouldn't have to take any medicine at all. And that's what this is all about. Trying to get you to that place where not taking medicine is the norm."

She looked at Hannah again. A bigger smile now, like this had been a minor epiphany. A glimpse, for Hannah's benefit, of what went on behind the closed door of Janet English's office. She didn't allow Hannah to sit in. The doctor reserved ten minutes at the end of each session to go over anything that may have come to light during the forty minutes she was alone with Randall.

"I've got an errand up the street," Hannah said. "Shouldn't take more than half an hour. I'll be back before you two are done. Okay, Randall?"

"Okay," he said. But he wasn't looking at her. Sulking now. She'd embarrassed him again, made him self-conscious, treated him like a kid. One or the other of the litany of offenses she was continually guilty of.

"You do your errands," Janet said. "We've got to discuss Randall's fall wardrobe."

Hannah watched them walk into the dusky room. She waited till the door shut. Stood there a minute more, staring at the white dog curled on the white bed. That quiet bedroom where everything harmonized, everything made sense.

"It's called a petition for modification."

"He can do that? He can reopen the case? Snap his fingers, get a judge to reconsider."

"It's the law, Hannah. He has rights like anyone else."

"He's not even a U.S. citizen. He's a goddamn Norwegian. What rights does he have to come here and try to take my child from me?"

"Doesn't matter what color his passport is. He's the boy's father, Hannah. That gives him rights."

"Not in my book, it doesn't."

"Unfortunately we're not playing by your book."

Two blocks down Ponce de León Boulevard from Janet English's office, in the one-story white stucco office building, a cute Mediterranean restaurant on one side, more lawyers' offices on the other, she was meeting with Brad Cohen, her family-services attorney. Mid-thirties, pink shirt, green tie with spewing volcanoes on it, and a haircut so bad it made his curly black hair look like a cheap wig. He came with the highest recommendations. Big-time rep around the courthouse, the great white shark on domestic issues. Divorce, alimony, child custody. This was the number-one guy in Miami. Jaws for in-laws.

"Hey, I don't write the rules, Hannah, I just try to bend them in the right direction to suit my clients."

She'd used fifteen of her thirty free minutes trying to read and make sense of the document Brad had received from Pieter Thomasson's New York attorney. Pieter was safely back home in Oslo. Having fled the statutory rape charges stemming from his multiple encounters with a fifteen-year-old high school freshman twelve years ago, a period of time which coincided with his brief marriage to Hannah. A union that lasted all of eight months.

"This guy's got a warrant out for failure to appear in the molestation case. Unlawful flight to avoid prosecution."

"Even criminals have rights."

"You don't know the whole story, Brad. My father lawyered the divorce and the custody case too. At the custody hearing Pieter threw a violent tantrum in the courtroom, had to be restrained by a marshal, screamed obscenities at the judge, and got tossed out. Now, five years later, the asshole pops up, thinks he has a shot at half-time custody?"

"The court disposed of the statutory rape case. There's no more warrant for failure to appear or unlawful flight."

"Disposed of it? You're kidding. When?"

Brad tapped the document that lay on the table before him. The one Hannah had tried to read. Indecipherable legalese.

"Last week. An out-of-court settlement," Brad said. "Money changed hands, the girl and her family signed the papers. His record is clean, everything's whited out."

"He can do that? Drop some cash, walk away from something like that? He fucked a fifteen-year-old girl in the backseat of his Volkswagen bug. Tore her green plaid skirt, her goddamn school uniform, ripped her panties, deflowered this Catholic girl, and now he slips them a few thousand bucks and all is forgiven, come get your son, take him away to fucking Norway."

"I'm not saying we're giving up. All I'm saying is Florida law favors custody by both parents. Now that he's no longer a wanted felon, what the judge wants to know is: Has there been sufficient rehabilitation? Has the guy cleaned up his act?"

"You mean, has he raped any more kids lately?"

"Apparently he hasn't. At least no one's come forward to complain. Barring that, all we can really do is delay. Make the guy wait."

"That fucking bastard."

"I hear that a lot," Brad said. He leaned back in his chair, hands behind his head, showing her his armpit stains. "You wouldn't believe it, Hannah. Those three little words, it's like an echo in here. All day long. I open at ten, close at six-thirty, eight and half hours that's what I hear. 'That fucking bastard.' It's wormed into the woodwork now. 'That fucking bastard. That fucking bastard.' Those words, they're lurking in the bookshelves, hiding out in my silk palm tree over there. Like spider mites, the words are everywhere."

She sat there in the client's chair. Padded black leather. Probably a thousand dollars. Gold studs, beautiful shined mahogany. In the last month she'd paid for ten chairs just like it. Fending off Pieter Thomasson. Her major life mistake. Marrying her goddamn math professor at the University of Miami. Hannah, a freshman, falling for the tall blond Nordic prof with golden hair, deep blue eyes, enormous white teeth. And that accent. That suave European way he had. He carried a pipe, for chrissakes. He wore smoking jackets. He buffed his nails and boffed his students. Didn't let a little thing like a marriage vow change his mating rituals.

"That fucking bastard," Brad said again. Hands laced behind his head.

"Okay," Hannah said. "I get it, Brad. So give me a week, I'll work up something more creative."

On the sidewalk heading back to Dr. Janet English's office, still fuming, Hannah felt something tickle across the skin of her neck. The brush of eyes following her. She fought it for a few steps, this attack of dread, but it wouldn't cease.

In front of a delicatessen she halted abruptly and swung around. A couple of men in white shirts and ties passed by, neither of them looking her way. Lawyers talking shop. She peered across the street at the five-story parking garage. Nothing there either. A guy sitting at the counter in the deli with a motorcycle helmet in front of him was drinking a Coke through a straw. The traffic was light, the sky clear, a breeze was stirring the American flag planted in the small yard of an art gallery across the street. The scent of garlic and onions whisked down the block from Marco's Sicilian Restaurant.

The wave of uneasiness slowly subsided, but she stood a moment more, leaning against a parking meter, watching the traffic flow by.

She was having a minor flash about Erin Barkley in *Fifth Story.*

While tracking the would-be assassin of the twelve-year-old girl, Erin realizes she is being stalked herself. Someone who knows who she is, what she's been doing. Possibly the killer, who senses her drawing near, has decided he must kill her. Or was that a cliché? It felt good, but it also felt familiar. Well, she could call up Max Chonin, her agent. The guy had read every mystery novel ever written and he could quote the plots of any of them. She could ask him. He'd probably reel off half a dozen stories where the detective is being followed. The watcher watched. Still, she liked it. And she wasn't afraid of clichés. Everything was a cliché anyway. Boy meets girl, boy loses girl. A man goes on a journey, a stranger comes to town. There were only five plots. Or maybe six. It all depended on the words, how fresh they were. The language.

She looked back down the street in the direction she'd come. *That fucking bastard. That pus-sucking son of a bitch.*

Cursing had never been her strength. She'd ask Gisela. She'd have one suitable for Pieter Thomasson, something Hannah'd never heard. One of those good Cuban curses. May Jesus and his donkey defecate in unison on your morning oatmeal. One of those.

But for the moment, "that fucking bastard" would have to do.

She'd told Brad to prolong this any way he could. Stretch it out. Use Randall's fragile psychological condition as an excuse for delay if he had to. Anything to give her time to figure out some counterattack. Hell if she was going to let that child-raping son of a bitch spend a second with her boy. She'd hire a goddamn hitman before she let that happen.

Hal sat at the counter of the deli and drank his Coke. He chewed the crushed ice and looked out the window and watched Hannah Keller halt briefly outside the window and look around. She was blond. She was pretty. Hal wasn't stupid. He knew a pretty woman when he saw one. Like the ones in the magazines. The ones on television. That's how you knew, you compared the real ones to the ones on television. They had to be slender with smooth skin, straight noses, large eyes. These women were the most desirable. They attracted wealthy and powerful men who wanted to mate with them and create more blond children with straight noses. Powerful men gave these women money, they gave them fancy cars and big houses and lots of jewelry.

Hal understood how it worked. He wasn't mentally retarded. He knew things.

"Ready for another Coke?" the young woman behind the counter asked.

She had stringy brown hair and a large nose and her eyes were small and close together. She was fat. This woman would never be in a magazine.

"Have you heard of the kusimanse?" Hal said.

"The what?"

"Kusimanse," Hal said. "It is a West African dwarf mongoose, a small creature, not very strong. Not even strong enough to crack open an eggshell. But the problem is, this creature loves eggs."

"Yeah? So?"

"So what the West African dwarf mongoose does, when he finds an egg, he takes it, and he bends over like the center on a football team and puts his front paws on the egg and he hikes the egg through his back legs right into a rock or a tree. And he breaks the egg open and he eats it."

The woman looked at Hal like there was more to his story.

"There are many ways to accomplish a task," Hal said. "Even the weak can find ways to satisfy their needs."

"Ooo-kay," the woman said, lifting her eyebrows slightly. "That mean you want another Coke or not?"

Hal watched Hannah Keller pass by. He watched her go into a door across the street. She shut the door and was gone.

"I do not," Hal told the young woman. "I am finished."

The woman scribbled on her pad and tore off the sheet and set it on the counter in front of him.

"Have a nice day," she said.

But she didn't mean it. She did not care about him or how the rest of his day would go. She did not want to mate with him or ever see him again. He could tell this from her eyes and her tone of voice and the way she stood. Hal could see inside people. There was nothing difficult about it. He could read their bodies. He could tell who was dangerous and who was not. He could tell when someone was lying. He could tell who would be easy to kill and who would be difficult. Who would struggle, who would give in easily.

Hal tried to stay attentive to everything around him. He watched and listened and was aware. He wasn't stupid. He wasn't mentally retarded or demented. He wasn't an idiot.

He counted out the exact change and set the money beside the bill. This was how it was done. You gave a tip if the service was good. Fifteen percent. Hal decided that the service he had received was good. It was prompt and polite and nothing was spilled. He counted out more money so that the coins added up exactly to the bill plus fifteen percent.

He could do math. He could read. He wasn't learning disabled.

He sat at the counter and watched the door across the street. The door that Hannah Keller had entered. The door that soon she would exit.

SEVEN

The waiting room at Janet English's office was still empty.

Hannah sat down on the couch, set her purse beside her. She was thirsty, but there was no water fountain in the office. She could use something stronger than water anyway. Thinking more along the lines of tequila. That fucking bastard. Popping up like that out of nowhere, making a run at Randall. The man had no fatherly instincts whatsoever. The whole thing had to be about Hannah, getting even, making her sweat. Maybe he wasn't even serious. Just out to grind her a little. Christ, that fucking fucking bastard.

She had ten minutes before Randall's session was over. She needed to relax, calm down, not let Randall see her agitation. Like he didn't already have enough to deal with.

As she was shuffling through the magazines on the coffee table, she saw it. Lying right beside the tattoo magazine—a copy of *First Light*, the book that had gotten her writing career started.

She hadn't noticed it earlier. But then she'd been distracted.

Copies of *First Light* were rare these days. Only a two-thousand print run in first edition. Collectors starting to take an interest in her, snapping them up. She hardly ever saw one on book tour.

Probably Janet English had left it there, wanting it signed.

She plucked the novel off the table. The cover was wrapped in a clear plastic sheet, a book collector's standard practice. Beneath the plastic, the paper jacket appeared pristine. No nicks, no worn edges. She turned the book over and glanced at the photograph on the back. Half a decade younger with a defiant smile, that milky-skinned young woman was wearing faded jeans and a plaid cowboy shirt, arms crossed over her chest, her ash blond hair cut boyishly short with a part on the side and her shoulder cocked casually against a brick wall that had been tagged with yellow spray paint.

It was an image the rest of her book jackets had consistently imitated. Saucy blond with a hard-core police background leaning against crumbling urban walls marked with gang graffiti. Tough lady who'd done hard time in gritty back alleys, specialist in crime and grime. But a woman nonetheless, with ruby lipstick in her purse and four-inch heels back home in her closet.

The image wasn't exactly Hannah Keller, but what the hell. As images went, it wasn't as far off the mark as some she'd seen.

Seven days a week for two years she'd risen before dawn to tap out that book on the electric typewriter set up on the kitchen table. The rush she got each morning from reshaping her best cop stories into the plot of that first book kept her heart singing all day. In her literary innocence, the characters and dialogue gushed out in great effortless bursts. The coarse talk of the men she worked with, the heart-shaking savagery of the streets and grinding hours of monotony, the bloodstained carpets and shattered lives, all of it bathed by luxurious tropical breezes. Nothing she'd written since had come so effortlessly. Nothing ever again had been so raw or so true. It wasn't her best work, but it was a book she knew she'd no longer be able to write, composed as it was under that brief and luscious spell of innocence. Before she knew what the hell she was doing. Before she fully understood the depth of hurt, the confusion and rage an act of violence could produce in those who survived.

She settled the book in her lap and let it fall open to a random page.

And her breath caught in her throat.

The margins of both pages were littered with furious scrawls in a pinched script, the lettering as tiny as the print on the page. She peered at the scribbled words, studying them for a moment, but could make no sense of them. Then as she leafed through the rest of the book, her pulse began to flutter.

It was the same on every page. Passages frantically underlined, twice, three times, the pages nearly torn in places from the pressure of the pen. There was purple ink, red and black. Whole paragraphs highlighted in Day-Glo yellow and blue. Another phrase here, an entire sentence there. Cryptic clusters of scribbled words littered almost every blank space, verbs and unrelated nouns joined together like the garbled ravings of a maniac. Either the scribbler had been insane when he stumbled upon her book, or else the book had driven him mad.

Gathering herself, she flipped to the inside front cover and found several columns of numbers covering the flyleaves. The lettering was so small it was like the leavings of microscopic insects. The columns were made up of strings of one- and two-digit numerals separated by dashes as if someone had jotted down a long list of Lotto picks.

At the top of the list, someone had written: *"This is how to find me."*

On the back of her neck all the tiny hairs had prickled to attention. She drew a long breath and let it out. In her hands the book had suddenly begun to feel radioactive.

She shut the covers and pressed them tightly as if to keep the lethal fumes trapped inside. She lifted her eyes and looked across at the dog sleeping on its master's bed.

She took another long breath and let it out and managed to calm herself by a fraction. She was being silly. She was letting her imagination race. Later when she'd composed herself, it might be amusing to sit down with Gisela and examine the book with more care, try to decipher that crazy code. Something to joke about, another anecdote for the endless speaking engagements. Library groups, university women's clubs, the rubber-chicken dinner circuit. Maybe she'd take the book along, read some of the marginal scribblings to the audience, get an easy laugh or two. Say something pithy about the danger of taking her books too seriously.

She turned the flyleaf over and looked at the dedication page.

This time the air hardened in her lungs. Her heart began a long tumble.

> *To my parents, who taught me everything important I know.*
> *And to Captain Dan Romano, who taught me the rest.*

Beneath the dedication, in the same tiny script, was a signature that shook her heart.

J. J. Fielding

"Something wrong, Hannah?"

She forced down a breath and looked up at Janet English. Randall was standing at her side. They weren't touching. Randall was stiff, distant. Something had happened in his session.

"This book," she said, holding it up. "Is it yours, Janet?"

"What?"

Dr. English came over and took it from her hands.

"This is your first novel."

"That's right. I found it here, on the coffee table."

"Well, I didn't put it there, if that's what you're asking."

"Then who did?"

"I don't know. I'm sure it wasn't there this morning when I came in. I remember straightening up, putting all the magazines in nice neat stacks."

"Maybe one of your other clients."

"Monday I do my writing. Reports, all the crap I haven't gotten to. Randall's the only client I see on Mondays."

"No one else was in today?"

"What is it, Hannah? What's the problem?"

Randall was staring at her too. His face tightening in worry.

She drew a slow breath, tried to soften the strain in her face.

"Nothing," she said. "It's nothing at all."

"You can have the book if you want. It doesn't belong to anyone I know."

She handed the book back to Hannah.

"Could you come in for a couple of minutes, Hannah? A quick chat."

Hannah followed her into the back office. Her pulse surging. A stab of panic flashed through her gut. She looked back at Randall. He was sitting on the couch, paging through the tattoo magazine. Studying the lavish blue designs and the woeful bodies they were etched on.

She shut the door. Janet was sitting behind her desk, tapping a pen against her ink blotter.

"What's wrong?" asked Hannah.

"Randall's quite upset."

"Well, of course, he is. That's why we're here."

"No, this is something new. This is something that's just emerged."

"What? What is it?"

"Sit down, Hannah. Relax."

She had the copy of *First Light* in her hand. It was as heavy as iron. Her ears buzzed with static.

"I'll stand. I can't stay long."

Janet English said Fine, stand, sit, it didn't matter.

Hannah took another sip of air. Feeling her heart rolling around, a seasick wobble in her legs.

"What is it? Tell me about Randall."

"He's extremely agitated. As upset as I've ever seen him. But he can't articulate it. He talks around it, so I know its shape. I know it's large and I know it's scaring him. But he can't open himself to it."

"Soccer? His wardrobe? I know it can't be that."

"Those are manifestations. He wants new clothes because he wants a new identity. Soccer takes him outside in the open, makes him vulnerable, exposes him. He wants to hide, wants to disappear from view. He wants to stay inside where it's safe."

"Safe from what?"

"Think about it, Hannah. What would he fear the most? What began everything?"

"Finding his grandparents' bodies. The horror of seeing them dead. Of losing these people he loved in such a violent way."

"And what else?"

"Why don't you just tell me, Janet? If you know something, then please, just say it."

"The killers," she said. "He's afraid of the killers."

"What? Coming back for him?"

"That's right."

"But that doesn't make any sense."

"It does to Randall."

"So he doesn't want to go outside. He's frightened of the exposure. That's what you're saying? He literally thinks the killers are coming back for him?"

"Literally or metaphorically. It hardly matters to an eleven-year-old."

"Well, what set this off? Five years later, what's going on? Did he say anything about that?"

"These things can lie dormant. They're like land mines. We bury them, forget they're there. Come back later and stumble over one. Something trivial might have set this off, or something not so trivial. It's hard to say. Especially when he refuses to discuss the issue. We get close, he shies away, makes a joke, changes the subject. You know how he is."

"He's crafty, yes."

"Crafty, but very scared. Terrified, Hannah. Absolutely terrified."

"Jesus Christ."

"I don't want to alarm you. I just want you to be on alert. He's at a critical place."

"How critical?"

"Critical," Janet said. "Just stay aware. Keep on alert. Be there for him when he needs you. Even the slightest jolt could have serious consequences."

"Jesus," she said. "Jesus, Jesus, Jesus."

It was quarter after five and Hannah was caught in virtual gridlock on US 1. Trying to get over to the far-left lane to make her turn at Sunset Drive, but no one was giving an inch. Every time she left as much as half a car length in front of her, another hero cut into the space and pushed her farther back into the pack. She was focused on that, on the traffic and driving. Trying not to deal with these other things yet. J. J. Fielding's signature in her book, Randall's new elevated level of fear, the legal maneuverings of an amoral pervert who had fathered her son.

Randall had picked up the copy of *First Light* from the console and was looking through it.

"What's this?"

"It's my first novel."

"I *know* that. What's with all the scribbling?"

"I'm not sure. Probably one of my strange fans. He got carried away."

He leafed through it for a moment or two, then turned back to the front pages.

"'This is how to find me,'" he said. "Did you see that?"

"Yeah, I saw it."

"And these numbers right below it, that's code," Randall said.

"It is?"

"Yeah, some kind of code. Want me to crack it?"

"You're a cryptographer now? They teach you that at Pinecrest Middle?"

"If you want," he said, "I could try."

"Sure. Be my guest."

Randall took a ballpoint pen from the coin tray and busied himself with the book while Hannah inched through traffic.

Her pulse was jangling. A raucous clatter ricocheting inside her skull. Randall was making marks beside the list of numbers. Flipping through the book, counting words and lines, circling things.

Clawing for every inch, forced to be aggressive by all the super-aggressive assholes around her, she finally made it to the far-left lane. Ten minutes later, she was at the light at Sunset, waiting her turn to go left when Randall dropped the book on the floor at his feet.

He sat there looking straight ahead.

"So?" she said. "You figure it out?"

"Yeah."

"You're kidding."

"I'm not kidding. It's a simple code."

"Well, what's it say?"

He kept his eyes on the traffic. The light finished its cycle, turned yellow, then red. Five of the cars just ahead of her turned left after the red. She halted at the head of the line and the guy behind her leaned on his horn.

"It's not like it was very complicated. The first number in each set refers to the page, the second number is the line on that page and the last few numbers are the words on that line."

"Five minutes and you figured that out?"

"You could've figured it out, Mom. It was that simple."

"Thanks a lot."

Randall swallowed and licked his lips. He slumped deeper in the bucket seat.

"What is it, Randall? What's wrong?"

"I haven't written out the whole thing. But it's like a story. Whoever did it pulled out a few words here and a few more there, you know, like sentence fragments or whatever, and it's like, I don't know, like he's telling a story."

Hannah watched the traffic streaming across the intersection.

"Some wacko," she said. "Just forget about it."

Randall tucked his chin against his chest.

"What's wrong, Randall? Talk to me."

He took a deep breath and blew it out, fluttering his lips like a horse.

"I didn't read the whole thing. I stopped."

"Okay, so tell me what you read."

"Do I have to?"

"Not if you don't want to. Of course not."

"It starts out with three guys," he said.

"Three guys, okay."

She glanced up at the red light, then looked back at Randall. He lifted his eyes and met hers and the flesh on her arms rippled. The boy's face was rigid, lips pressed tight. Her son was terrified.

"What, Randall?"

He shifted in the seat, looking down at the toes of his shoes. His voice was far away.

She got the green arrow and immediately the asshole behind her honked. Hannah stayed put. Looking at Randall as he stared blankly out the windshield.

"Three guys dressed like house painters," he said. "They sneak into a house in the morning and shoot a man who's getting dressed for work and his wife making breakfast. That's as far as I got. Three guys dressed like house painters."

The man behind her continued to blast his horn through the complete cycle of the green.

EIGHT

"It's just some crazy fan," said Gisela. "That's all it is. A weird guy with a rotten sense of humor."

"No," Hannah said. "I don't think so. I think it's a lot more than that."

Hannah lifted her squat glass and swallowed more of the potent margarita. In the last few minutes her tongue had gone partially numb, but so far the drink had done little to relax the bear-hug pressure around her chest.

Eyeing her uneasily, Gisela took another sip of her margarita and set the glass on the plastic side table. Gisela had heavy eyebrows, dark drowsy eyes, and full lips. She was wearing white tennis shorts and a lime green shirt with avocado and mango slices printed on it. Leaning back in her aluminum chair, she propped her feet up on the chrome rail.

They were sitting on the roof of Gisela's houseboat, the *Margaritaville*, which was anchored in slip A-12 at the Dinner Key Marina. To the west the sunset's crimson sheen was spreading across the harbor like a gorgeous oil slick. All around them the halyards tinkled in the light breeze, while twenty yards off the bow of Gisela's boat laughing gulls plunged into the still water after a school of bait fish, then climbed back into the air and plunged again.

"Randall seems pretty upset."

"He's shaken, yeah. I told him it was just some kook, but I don't think he believed me."

Randall stood at the end of the dock staring out at the sunset. He'd been quiet ever since decoding the list of numbers. Eyes straight ahead. Answering in monosyllables. Now he had a hand on one of the pilings, keeping his back to her. But she knew he was probably sailing beyond the watery landscape, drifting back to that mid-July morning when he'd stepped into his grandparents' house and found their bodies, then tunneled into a pile of Hannah's clothes and waited for the police to arrive.

From the galley below, Gisela's tape deck pumped out Jimmy Buffett's mindlessly soothing voice, song after song celebrating pirates and booze and long torpid days. Gisela was a parrothead—a devoted follower of that simple-minded Key West blend of acoustic guitars and the jingly steel drums and plink-plonk of cruise ship reggae. A double margarita and Jimmy B. blaring from the tape deck was her evening antidote to her daily overload of sleaze.

Last month Gisela had had the *Margaritaville* painted a mustard yellow with cherry trim, and now it looked like a gaudy Haitian riverboat that sold jerked chicken from one village to the next. Brightly painted gewgaws were crammed on every shelf and nook throughout the cabin below, goofy paraphernalia from Key West tourist shops. Sculptures of macaws and purple manatees, giraffes and zebras, and a vast collection of fanciful animals formed out of blown glass. On her dining table sat a large sand-filled terrarium where a band of miniature pirates fought a never-ending battle against an array of plastic dinosaurs.

"Three guys dressed like house painters. They break into a house at breakfast time to shoot an old couple. All those words came from *First Light*?"

"They're my words, yeah. But he took them completely out of context. Like someone snipping up a newspaper to make a ransom note."

"Randall figured that out?"

Hannah said, "He took one look at that list of numbers, he knew it was some kind of code. I'm sitting there waiting for a red light and he solved it."

"He's some kind of whiz, isn't he?"

"Well, yeah, he's smart, but this didn't require any genius. Take a look at it. It's like some code from a second-grade puzzle book."

Hannah handed her the book and the scribbled page, a single paragraph she'd extracted from *First Light*, using the code. She'd pulled off in a Shell station and gone through the list of numbers, finding each word, adding to the paragraph. By the last sentence Hannah could barely hold the pen, her hand was quivering so badly.

Three men dressed like house painters enter the house early in the day. The wife is cooking breakfast, the husband is getting dressed for work. The tall killer aims and shoots the wife three times then goes after the husband. The old man has a gun but doesn't fire. He is wearing a white shirt, a tie with blue sailboats. Three shots kill the old man. Then the killer fixes his own face to the victim's face. Now he waits for you. 2649 Bayshore Drive, at nine tomorrow morning. Your name is the next key.

When Gisela finished reading, she took another sip of her margarita and waved hello to the guy puttering down the channel in an inflatable raft. The man wore a red bandanna around his throat and his miniature collie had a matching one tied around its neck.

"Yeah, it's pretty transparent," Gisela said. "So tell me, why the hell does somebody bother putting something in code, if the code's so easy to break, even idiots like you and me can see through it?"

"Good question."

"Okay, okay, so if it's not some wacko fan," Gisela said, "then what is it?"

Gathering her hair in one hand, Hannah lifted the hot mass off her neck and let the sluggish breeze move across her flesh for a moment. She took a breath of air but it didn't seem to fill her lungs. She blew it out and tried again with the same result. She let go of her hair.

"I think it's pretty obvious. Somebody wants to turn Fielding in."

Gisela snorted and brought her hands together in a T.

"Whoa there, girl. Time out, slow down." Gisela had a quick sip of her drink and set the glass on the table. "Turn Fielding in? How the hell you figure that?"

Hannah listened for a moment to the Buffett song, its bouncy beat, its studied gaiety.

"If there's another explanation I'd like to hear it."

Gisela was tapping her foot on the rooftop to the beat of the island music.

Randall had his arm around the piling and was gazing out at the western horizon where a small thunderstorm was hiding within a band of purple light, pulsing and sending flecks of red and gold into the stringy clouds above.

Hannah picked up her margarita glass and took the final swallow. She stood up and moved to the rail.

"Okay, so who is it? Who's sending you this secret note?"

"Either J. J. Fielding himself or somebody who knows where he is. Maybe one of his accomplices is feeling guilty and wants to see Fielding go to jail. Maybe Fielding screwed him out of his share of the money and he wants some kind of revenge. Who knows?"

"Hannah, Hannah. Any number of wackos could've read all that stuff about your parents' murder in the newspaper, then put it into that kindergarten code. Found out you go to see Janet English every Monday afternoon, snuck in there, and left it on the table for you to find."

"A lot of this stuff wasn't in the newspaper."

"Sure it was."

"Nothing about house painters. Nothing about the shooter being tall. Blue sailboats on my father's tie, no one knew that except the ME and a couple of homicide guys with Miami PD, but no one in the public. Even the thing about J. J. Fielding's news photo, that was never released to the press."

Gisela stared at her for a moment, then looked back at the page.

"Okay, what about this other thing? 'Your name is the next key.' What the hell's that about?"

"Part of the riddle, I suppose."

Hannah shook her head, staring up at the silhouette of a distant frigate bird hovering in the twilight sky like the blade of a black scimitar.

"In my limited experience," Gisela said, "somebody wants to give himself up, or turn somebody else in, he calls the police. He doesn't scribble in a book and leave it on some shrink's coffee table."

Hannah watched Randall lean against the piling. A laughing gull was strutting down the dock behind him.

"What you should do," Gisela said, "you should take this book down to the department, show it to one of the homicide guys, Dan Romano or somebody. Get some reality therapy. Dan would be like, 'Oh, you got a long column of numbers in a book you found in a doctor's waiting room, and now you're convinced that your parents' killer wants to talk to you.' Yeah, Dan would love to get his hands on this. He'd stand up on his desk, make an announcement to the whole squad room. Get everybody going."

"Yeah, he would."

"Damn right. And he'd get a hell of a laugh too. See what I'm saying, Hannah? This is just some kind of joke. A very bad practical joke. It's too screwy."

Gisela rose and walked over to the little table where she'd set the blender. Hannah leaned back against the chrome rail.

"So is that what you'd do, Gisela? Toss the book in the waste can, walk away, not even try to get to the bottom of it?"

Down below Jimmy Buffett was crooning a song about a girl he'd met in a bar, a sexy lady from Caroline Street.

Gisela shook her head in sad disbelief and poured herself more margarita.

Randall let go of the piling and sat down at the end of the dock. He hung his feet over the side and bent forward to stare down into the water.

Gisela said, "So tell me, girl, let's say for some totally freaking off-the-wall reason J. J. Fielding or one of his accomplices wants you to come looking for him. Then why the hell go to all that trouble, marking up your book, take it to a doctor's office on the off chance you might pick it up, and decode his little message? Why doesn't he just pick up a phone and give you a call, or send you a telegram?"

Hannah leaned against the rail and watched the purple bruise in the western sky grow darker by the second. A squadron of gulls drifted overhead with barely a movement of wing.

"Maybe he likes games."

Gisela looked over at her for a long moment before she spoke.

"Maybe what you need to do, you need to talk to somebody."

Hannah brought her eyes back from the sunset.

"I *am* talking to somebody."

"You know, like Janet English, somebody like that."

Hannah drew a long breath, held it for a second, then let it go in a rush.

Gisela wouldn't meet her eyes.

"All I'm saying is, maybe you should talk to a professional before you go launching off on something like this."

"What? To get the shrink's approval? Are you kidding? I'm not some fragile ego that needs protection."

"No," Gisela said. "But he is."

She lifted her chin and motioned toward Randall.

Down the row of boats someone turned on a television, the evening news. The long list of the day's horrors rendered in the glib voices of the professional news readers. Randall was still bent forward, communing with the water. Plinking pebbles into the still harbor.

"Listen," Hannah said, turning to her friend, and trying to calm the quiver in her throat. "I know this whole thing sounds nuts, but you have to understand, if there is even the slightest possibility this is for real, I'm going to have to follow it to the very end."

"Remember last time when you were so sure it was Fielding that murdered your parents? You were running all over town, looking here, looking there. In a real manic state. And remember what happened?"

"I stopped."

"Yeah, and why did you stop?"

"Because Randall asked me to."

"That's right. You were scaring him. You were scaring everybody. You nearly lost it, Hannah, you were so worked up, in a major lather. But because he asked you to, you stopped. You put it away and you went back to writing your books and your life and Randall's life got a lot better. Turned out you didn't need to find the people who killed your parents to be happy. You could be happy doing the things you liked to do. It was simple. And it's still simple. So I don't see why you'd want to risk everything you've got by starting all this up again."

Gisela looked at her for a moment, then her gaze wandered off to the fading sunset.

"All I'm saying is that you should consider Randall before you get in another uproar like last time."

"I am considering him. He's still afraid. He doesn't sleep. You know him, Gisela, the boy is in pain. He's never going to be a hundred percent secure until the killer is caught and put away."

"A hundred percent secure? Tell me, who do you know that's a hundred percent secure?"

"I've got to do this, Gisela. I have no choice."

"Okay," she said. "But don't kid yourself. You're not doing this for Randall. You're doing it for yourself. Because it's a bone stuck in your throat."

Hannah gazed into the half-light. A breeze tickled across her sweaty back. Out across the bay the twilight was losing its hold, darkness advancing quickly across the water, closing in like a dense fog.

The concentric rings Randall had made were widening out across the marina. Beautiful ripples spreading, one after the other, moving out toward the open water.

* * *

Hal was wearing a white Panama hat. He was wearing a yellow shirt with speedboats on it and a light windbreaker over that. Green-and-red plaid Bermudas that came to his knees and sandals. Clothes he'd bought at the airport when he landed. Everything still stiff, just a few hours off the rack. He had a camera and he was snapping pictures of the sunset. He was standing on the seawall looking out at the bay and taking photographs he would never develop.

The woman had a boy. She had a son and she took him with her when she went places. They were on the docks now. Hannah Keller was on the roof of a houseboat, big and square and painted bright colors. She was talking to another woman, dark hair and pudgy. The boy was standing on the dock, looking back toward the shore where Hal was standing. Hal took the boy's picture, then he turned and took a picture of a seagull.

Hal was not a dork. He was only dressed like one. A tourist dork. A pale Yankee sightseer down in Miami for a few days to get a tan and take lots of snapshots. That was the story his clothes were telling to anybody who looked his way.

The Keller boy was tossing pebbles into the water. Hal watched the rocks ruffle the smooth surface of the marina. Little waves from the rocks were headed right for Hal. He took a snapshot of one of them. The tiny wave ran into the rocks that were piled up next to the seawall, then it disappeared. There one minute, gone the next. Just like Randy Gianetti. Just like Hal. Now you see him, now you don't.

Hal took another picture of the sunset. It was purple and green and red and there were colored bands running high up into the sky like the streaks of fat that spread through meat. Hal had seen postcards with pictures of sunsets. People thought sunsets were pretty. They stood around and watched them. They sent people postcards with sunsets on them. Hal wasn't stupid. This was how you knew what the pretty things were. The things they put on postcards, the things that people stood and watched while they said nothing. It was possible to figure these things out, to learn from watching

people. To understand all the difficult things by being obser-
vant and putting two and two together. This was what Hal
did in his free time. He observed people. He watched and
learned what it was like to be human.

"Pretty, isn't it?" a woman said.

She had come up beside him while Hal was busy with the
camera. She had white curly hair and was slumped over with
a hump in her back. Bones gone soft. A lonely old woman
who wanted to talk.

"Pretty, isn't it?" Hal said back to her.

The woman took a look at him.

Hal raised the camera and snapped another picture of the
sky. It was starting to lose its colors. The dark leaking back
around the edges.

"The sunset is over," Hal said.

"Oh, it's only pretty for a second or two," the old woman
said. "I suppose that's why we like it so much. The ephemer-
ality, the briefness."

Hal watched as Hannah Keller walked down the dock
with her boy.

"Yes," Hal said. "That's probably why we like it so much.
The briefness."

The old woman peered at Hal Bonner as he turned and
ambled across the parking lot toward his red dirt bike. He
could feel the touch of her eyes on the back of his pale blue
windbreaker.

Across the parking lot Hannah was backing out of her
space. A white Ford started its engine nearby and Hal saw a
brown UPS truck parked by the office of the marina. Hal
watched to see if anybody followed Hannah out of the lot
and onto the street. He straddled the seat of the motorcycle
and watched as the white Ford pulled out of its space a few
rows over, then rolled slowly across the parking lot and out
to the edge of the main street. The Ford waited for a break in
the traffic, then turned in the opposite direction Hannah had
taken. The UPS truck was heading to the street too.

Hal sat still on his motorcycle, his eyes roaming the parking lot.

Something wasn't right. He'd not seen anyone else following Hannah Keller, but still, there was a twitch in his chest, the needle on his Geiger counter quivering uneasily. There was danger nearby. He wasn't sure where it was or what it was, but it was there. The twitch in his chest had never failed him.

He back-walked the bike out of the parking space, started it, and puttered slowly toward the exit. The big palm trees were turning black. The streetlights had come on. At the edge of the street, he leaned forward and looked east and he could just barely make out her small red car as it disappeared around a curve in the road. The thing in his chest was twitching faster. But Hal followed anyway. Staying well back. Cautious, alert, ready to pounce, ready to flee.

NINE

Frank Sheffield's porch at the Silver Sands Motel faced east toward the Atlantic. Tonight the dark water was restless, lots of noise down there, forty yards away through a stand of sea oats and coconut palms. More erosion shifting sand up or down the beach, never where they wanted it.

"So you bring your little girls here, Sheffield? This your love nest, is it?"

"I live here, Helen. This is my home. So, yeah, when I get lucky enough to have a girl, this is where I bring her."

"Jesus, I thought you were kidding. A dump like this. Does the Bureau know?"

"Hey, I got the surf pounding outside my back door. I got the breezes. I got stars. What the hell difference is it to the FBI where I live anyway?"

On the floor above them, there was a party in 206. There was always a party in 206. And they always played the same Moody Blues album, smoked the same cigars to cover up the odor of their potent dope. His tie-dyed neighbors.

Sheffield and Helen Shane sat side by side in the canvas directors' chairs which Frank left out in the elements on his small cement porch. The chairs had started out maroon, but in the ten years he'd had them, they'd weathered to a pale pink, always with a fine coating of sand on the seats. Usually he sat in one, used the other to prop his feet while he had his two evening rum and Cokes. Never more, never less. After the second Cuba libre he liked to lean back against the loose canvas and imagine himself as a movie director. Making a low-budget film about the people coming and going at a bro-

ken-down motel surrounded by monster condos. Two shots
of rum, and Sheffield became Cecil B. DeMille, all the gar-
deners doing his bidding, the maids smiling on his cue, the
endless stream of pleasure-seeking tourists happily playing
their parts. Everybody with a secret, a story bubbling inside.

Some nights when the booze hit him a little harder,
Frank imagined himself on the other side of the camera.
The star of his own show. No pretty-boy leading man,
Sheffield was forty-one and showed it, his skin a weathered
copper, deep wrinkles around the eyes from a lifetime of
squinting in the sun. He had straight sandy hair that was
thinning, the shine of scalp beginning to show. His eyes
were dark brown, and his mouth was usually relaxed in a
lazy grin.

He was an inch under six feet, and kept the fat off with
those ten-mile laps of Key Biscayne in his kayak. Too laid-
back to be a first-rate lady's man, still, Sheffield had become
quite adept at what he'd named the three-week romance. A
week of seduction, a week of passion, a week of drifting
back to earth. After ten years married to a woman whose
hostility seemed to grow with every year, Frank was now se-
verely gun-shy. And that was the part he'd play in his own
movie. Bogart in *Casablanca*. A single guy with a painful
past who'd made his peace with loneliness. Then, of course,
out of the blue comes his lost love. Ingrid Bergman, all pale
and fragile and queenly. The tale of a rekindled romance. An
ember that never died. That was the story that always got
Frank going. A second chance at love complicated by the
usual subplot. Because eventually, if the story's going to be
interesting, the lonely guy has to choose between doing the
right thing, the moral thing, or selfishly hanging onto the
woman. In *Casablanca* Bogart gives up the woman, surren-
ders her to a greater cause. Though Sheffield wasn't sure
that ending would play anymore. Because, hell, try to think
of a cause these days worth that kind of sacrifice.

Sheffield looked over at Helen Shane. She was fidgeting,
pulling her ring on and off. Tapping her foot against the ce-

ment. Not used to guys wandering off in their heads when she was around.

He had no idea why she was there. She'd showed up a half hour after his kayak workout. Frank was still sweaty, just about to step in the shower when she knocked three times, then three more right after it. A cop knock.

He'd asked through the closed door who it was.

"It's your boss."

"Which boss? I got so many."

"The one that pisses you off."

"That doesn't narrow it down much."

He slipped into a pair of trunks, opened the door, stepped out onto the porch. Barefoot, shirtless. Helen looking at his bare chest. Studying it, like she was counting the hairs, doing a masculinity calculation.

Now in the dark, two red wines later, she tugged off an earring. Then the other one. She kicked off her low-heel pumps.

"I'm surprised you're taking the evening off. Thought you'd be running with this the whole seventy-two hours. Popping amphetamines, staying at command central."

"I needed to get out of there. I was about to punch Ackerman."

"Yeah," said Frank. "Guy's a lot easier to take on television. Up close and personal his charisma is a little much."

Helen said, "They'll beep me if anything breaks. Just before I left, your friend Hannah was driving home from the shrink's office, out of nowhere she U-turns on US 1, drives back to Coconut Grove. Went to see a friend at Dinner Key Marine. Gisela Ortega. Lives on a houseboat there."

"I know Gisela," Frank said. "Miami PD. Took Hannah's place as media spokesperson."

"We're aware of that," Helen said.

"So why'd you come here? Things are happening. You should be back at the hotel pulling your puppet strings."

"Nothing's going down tonight. It'll be tomorrow when her boy's back in school. She's got the whole day free."

"But if she goes now?"

"They'll beep me. It's ten minutes back across the bridge."

Frank stared out into the dark. Listened to the swollen surf. The wind was stirring his hair, tickling across his chest. Mid-eighties, humidity dropping down low enough so he could take a decent breath. He wasn't sweating every second of the day and night. Best season of the year. Postsummer, pre-tourist.

"All this sand," Helen said. She stirred her bare toes through the grit sheeting the concrete porch. She had another quick sip of her red wine, stirring her toes some more. "How the hell do you stand it? You track it inside, it's gotta get in everything. The rug, the bedsheets. All the cracks."

"You come here to check my bedsheets, Ms. Shane?"

"Call me Helen."

"Call me Agent Sheffield."

"I like Sheffield better. Frank sounds so damn tightass."

"Call me Sheffield then, if it gives you a better feel for my ass."

She looked at him in the dark. He could see the sparkle in her eyes, reflections from the strings of red and green Christmas bulbs at the tiki bar. Three schoolteachers from Ft. Wayne over there. They'd been in town all week. Burned red, they'd picked up two Cuban Romeos, everyone having a hoot. A little cross-cultural education.

"Nothing's going to happen between us," Helen said.

"Fine by me."

"I can't get mixed up with the help."

"Oh, that's good, Helen. 'The help.' "

"I read your file, Sheffield. You haven't exactly distinguished yourself."

"Haven't extinguished myself either. Not yet anyway."

"You really don't care, do you? A lackluster job performance, not a single merit increase in twenty years, cost-of-living raises, across the board, that's all you've gotten. That doesn't embarrass you?"

"Oh, so that's the way you know if you're having a good life, you look at your paycheck?"

"You don't respect yourself, Frank. You've got no ambition."

"You come all the way out here to give me a career pep talk, Shane?"

She had another sip of wine. Slurring her words already, a little non sequitur creeping into the conversation. Maybe she was a quick drunk, or maybe not. With Helen it was probably dangerous to assume anything.

Frank took a bite off the top of his rum and Coke. Mostly Coke. He watched the schoolteachers and their new Cuban boyfriends swaying on the bar stools. They were all probably trying to figure out how to divvy up. Three schoolteachers, two Romeos. A little creative math. There was a laughing gull standing near their feet waiting for more popcorn to drop from the bowl on the bar.

"So now what do you think of my plan, Sheffield? You starting to see the beauty of it?"

"I don't like it, Shane. Putting an innocent civilian in harm's way."

"But she's on track. That's the important thing."

"Maybe."

"Like a good little detective, following the bread crumbs."

"No, Helen. Like a woman who wants to nail the son of a bitch she believes killed her parents."

"Think she'll go to Miami PD? Her old buddies. Try to get them involved."

"Not likely," Frank said. "She'd have to know nobody would take her seriously. A bunch of gibberish scribbled in the margins of her novel. What're they going to do, order up a SWAT team on the basis of that?"

"Even if she tries, it won't do her any good," Helen said. "We've taken care of it. Miami PD, the county people, the staties. Everyone's aware we're running a code-one operation. They're not to get involved. We've got liaison people there. Anything she tries to do, they'll squash it. So she can talk to her old buddies till she's red in the face, it won't matter."

"Blue," Frank said. "Blue in the face."

"Blue, red. Green in the face," Helen said. "It won't matter."

"My bet is she won't go anyway. She's a lone wolf kind of lady."

Helen gave him a careful look.

"Bingo, there it is. I knew it."

"Knew what?"

"What you just said. 'A lone wolf kind of lady.'"

"What the hell are you talking about?"

"There was a spike in your voice. A definite uplift."

"And what's that supposed to mean?"

"You have a thing for her, don't you, Frank? A case of the hots."

"I won't dignify that, Shane."

"Sure you do. It's written all over you."

"Jesus, 'the hots'? Nobody says shit like that anymore. Not even guys."

"Yeah, okay. Whatever you say, Sheff. Whatever you say."

"Okay, if I have the hots for the woman, how is it I haven't seen her or spoken to her in five years?"

"Don't protest too much, Sheffield. You'll give yourself away."

At the tiki bar somebody put a James Taylor song on the jukebox. One of the schoolteachers was dancing with one of the Romeos. Not touching, the woman dancing, the guy just standing close, swaying, some slow claps of his hands like some kind of half-assed flamenco. The others were watching, making cracks, giggling.

"So what about Hal?" Helen said.

"What about him?"

She set her drink on her knee. She had a nice knee. It was gold in the moonlight. Actually it was a superior knee, one of the best he'd seen. Too bad it was attached to Helen Shane.

"You think Hal's here?"

"Here, meaning Miami?"

She hummed a yes.

Maybe she *was* drunk. Maybe another word or two about bedsheets would nudge her inside the door. Though what he thought was, it would be safer from a purely physical standpoint to walk down to the beach, offer up his pecker to the first crab he found.

"My gut says no," said Frank. "This guy's been killing people for ten years with you people on his ass the whole time. I'm betting he's not dumb enough to fall for this bullshit."

"I know what you think of me, Sheffield. I know what you think of the plan."

"Then you should stop asking."

"I think he's here," Helen said. "I think Hal's in the vicinity."

"You picked him up on your radar, did you? Your personal antennae are all atwitter?"

"I *need* him to be here, Frank. I *need* this to work."

"To make Senator Ackerman happy. Career advancement. More merit increases."

"You think there's something wrong with that? Wanting to get ahead?"

"I wouldn't know."

"I know you don't like me, Frank. You think because I'm ambitious I have to be some kind of twisted bitch."

"Oh, here we go."

"What?"

"I must be getting slow. I kept wondering why you'd bother coming all the way out here. Now we're finally getting around to it. I'm this loser, lives in a dump, but I still bother you, don't I, Shane? You're not happy unless everybody's on your bandwagon. Every single one. It makes you uneasy."

"I have no idea what you're talking about."

"Sure you do, Helen. You came out here because you want me to know what a terrific lady you are. That's what this is all about, isn't it? For me to punch your ticket, validate you and your goddamn mission."

"Fuck you."

"Can't do it," he said. "I just ate."

She glowered briefly. Then she leaned back in her chair, reset her face like she'd willed herself to ease off. Her mouth softening.

"I'm taking that as a misfired joke, Sheffield. Because I'd bounce you off this operation in a second if I thought you meant to insult me."

"Well, then I'll just have to work harder."

Frank looked over at the tiki hut. He watched the schoolteachers giving the Cuban boys a lesson in Midwest hospitality. The biggest of the three was the dancer, a barrel-shaped woman, shaking all that corn-fed flesh, letting 'em look.

"I think you're the way you are," Shane said, "because of your father. His fame. The way everybody glorified him. Growing up in that kind of shadow, it must have stunted your ambition."

"Wow, look at me," Frank said. "I'm having a drink with Sigmund fucking Freud."

"Getting a little too close to the truth are we, Frank?"

"So if I lack ambition because of my terrific father, then hey, that would mean your old man must've been one hell of a loser."

She sat perfectly still. All the fidgets dead.

"What was he, Shane, a lush? Half in the bag all the time? Or maybe a wife beater. Or, no, I've got it. A molester, the old man came for visits in the middle of the night, showed you the one-eyed monster. Come on, Helen, tell Uncle Frank."

The wine spattered against his chest. Followed by the thump of the plastic cup against his sternum. She was on her feet. Fumbling with her shoes. She was making noises, huffing. Maybe it was tears, maybe it was acting. Who the hell cared?

He watched the Hoosier tourists. Taking a few days off to recharge the old schoolteacher batteries. God love 'em. Simple folks from Ft. Wayne, laughing and drinking on that lush tropical night. No agenda but getting laid. No need to kid themselves into believing anything was coming of it except one luscious memory.

Sheffield stood up. He turned and watched Helen Shane stalk across the parking lot. Watched her get inside her white Lincoln Town Car, start it up, flare on the headlights. Sheffield stood in the full beams. Stood there like that deer that gets blinded and freezes, only Sheffield wasn't any goddamn deer. He turned around and went back to the porch.

He bent down, turned on the hose, started spraying his green kayak that was leaning against one of the coconut palms. He'd already rinsed it off earlier, but hell, you could never get your kayak clean enough. All that salt crud could build up, start the rivets rusting. He sprayed it good. Sprayed it and sprayed it some more. He was going to stand there for half an hour and spray that damn thing till it was the cleanest kayak in all of south Florida. When he was done, he'd finish his drink, maybe afterward he'd go down to the tiki bar, have another, join the fun. After that, hell, he'd see what ball games were on TV. Fall asleep early.' Cause tomorrow was going to be a long day. And what he'd just done was only going to make it longer.

Frank was still spraying the kayak, watching Helen out of the corner of his eye, seeing her peel out of the parking lot, her tail lights disappearing, when across the lot a car door swung open. Away from the overhead lights, just a dull red gleam coming from the hood of the car. He shut off the hose, and watched as someone got out, stood there a moment uncertainly, then headed across the pitted asphalt toward him.

Ten feet away he recognized her, and he felt something shift inside his chest. He dropped the hose on the ground and took a step in her direction.

"Frank," she said. Coming into the motel lights. "Frank Sheffield."

"Hannah?" he said. Trying to sound surprised, which he was, only in a different way from what she would expect. Trying to remember his role. But he really didn't have one. This wasn't covered in the script.

"I didn't know if I'd find you here. Five years later, you're still in the same motel room."

"I find something I like, I stick with it."

She smiled, came closer.

"Plus they give me a deal. Seven-fifty a month, all the co-conuts I can pick."

Frank looked back over Hannah's shoulder into the dark lot. There had to be at least a half-dozen agents scrambling around somewhere out there. The night shift. By now Shane had probably gotten word on the radio and was circling back. Frank thrust into the spotlight.

"Something wrong?" She glanced back over her shoulder.

"No," he said. "Nothing's wrong. It's nice to see you. Been a while."

Hannah came close. She reached out and touched a finger to his bare shoulder, then brought the finger to her mouth and tasted it with the tip of her tongue.

"Cabernet?"

"No," he said. "Pinot."

"It's a little salty."

"That's probably just me."

"You have any more, or did she throw the whole thing on you?"

"You were sitting out there a while," he said.

"Yeah," she said. "Waiting for her to leave. What is she, a girlfriend?"

Frank considered it for a second.

"Somebody from work," he said.

"Oh, so that's some kind of FBI secret handshake thing, throwing wine on each other."

"Well, that," he said, "is a long story."

"The good ones usually are."

"So you want some pinot?" he said. "Or just stand out here in the parking lot and quip the night away?"

"Maybe a sip. I can't stay long. Randall's in the car. It's almost his bedtime."

"Bring him over. I got Coke, chocolate chip cookies. Unless that's too much sugar."

"No, he's finishing up a burger and fries. Anyway, I think he'd rather stay in the car. He's had a rough day. And FBI guys make him nervous."

Frank could still feel the place on his shoulder where her finger had trailed across the flesh. A tingle. First one of those he'd had in a while.

"You're still with the Bureau, aren't you?"

"Still plugging along," he said. "But I don't like the idea I make a ten-year-old kid nervous."

"He's eleven," she said. "And it's not just you. A lot of things make him nervous."

Frank nodded, wanting to take a longer look at her, but feeling bashful, keeping his gaze on the tiki bar.

"And the book career, how's it going?"

"Fine."

"I read a couple of them, you know. The first two."

"Then you stopped. Not your cup of tea."

"Well, yeah, I'm more of a *Sports Illustrated* kind of guy. But they were good. I liked that woman, what's her name? Sharon?"

"Erin. Erin Barkley."

"Yeah, Erin. She was tough. Real smart aleck. Quite a sex life, too."

"It's make-believe."

"Seemed pretty convincing to me."

"The cop part is factual, all that procedural stuff. But Erin's sexual habits, that's to keep my readers happy."

"Well, it worked for me. I remember that."

The flesh on Frank's shoulder was still prickling. Like she had acid on her fingertip, his skin peeling away, but in a pleasant way. He looked at her under the yellow porch light. Her blond hair was loose, tangling in the sea breeze. A dusting of hair on her cheek, a fine golden sideburn. She was looking out toward the ocean, but she must have sensed his stare because she turned her head and gave him a shy smile. With a woman as striking as Hannah it probably happened all the time, men's appraising looks.

"I'll get that wine," he said.

Sheffield turned and went inside the motel room, walked briskly to the kitchenette. He looked back at her through the screen door. She was standing there, peering through the dark at the tiki hut. Hannah Keller. Looking even better than the photograph. Better than his memory of her. He stood in the kitchenette trying to remember what he'd come inside for, why he'd left her alone out in the dark.

Then he saw the wine bottle on the counter. He poured some into a squat highball glass and took it back out to her.

Now she was sitting comfortably in the director's chair Helen Shane had vacated. There was a copy of *First Light* in Hannah's lap.

"So," Frank said. "To what do I owe this pleasant surprise?"

She took the wine, tasted it. Set it down on the cement porch.

"Somebody's screwing around with me, Frank."

"I'm sorry?"

"I said, someone's screwing around with me. They sent me this."

She took the book from her lap and held it out.

He looked at it for a few seconds. None of this in the script. At this moment he and Hannah were probably lit up green in night-vision goggles. 'She's handing him the book. She's handing Sheffield the goddamn book.' 'So what's he doing?' 'He's not doing anything, just looking at it.' 'All right. Just as long as he doesn't take it. Jesus, we can't have him getting involved. That'll screw up everything.'

"Frank?" Hannah said.

"Yeah?"

"Is there something wrong?"

Sheffield said, no, there was nothing wrong. Then he sat down beside her and reached out and took the book. He set it on his lap and watched as it spilled open to a random page.

TEN

She wasn't sure why Frank Sheffield was so tense. Maybe still worked up about the redhead who'd tossed the wine on him. Nervous she'd come back, find him sitting there with another woman. Hannah couldn't read him. He seemed different from the breezy beach bum she remembered. Kept his eyes down, dodging hers, fumbling with the book, looking at the pages, but not really studying them. She wasn't sure how she could tell, but he didn't seem to be paying full attention. Leafing too quickly, looking at nothing long enough to absorb it.

"Look at the front, the numbers in the front," Hannah said. "And the name."

Sheffield took a breath and blew it out.

He flipped to the front, tilted the book so it caught the full light.

"J. J. Fielding," he said.

He looked up at her. Holding her gaze for a couple of seconds, then his eyes straying off toward the tiki bar. Some folks over there dancing to a Phil Collins tune.

"Yeah, J. J. Fielding. His signature in a book that just happened to be lying in the middle of a table in the doctor's office where I take Randall every week. Imagine that."

"And you're saying what?"

"I think it's pretty obvious, Frank. Someone's sending me a message."

"Could be another J. J. Fielding entirely."

"Oh, yeah, the name is so popular."

"And what do you expect from me?" Still keeping his eyes from her. Sitting stiffly in his chair like he was on trial.

"Well, I thought you'd be intrigued. A little startled maybe. Some normal human response like that."

"I'm intrigued. Sure, I am."

He met her eyes. Smiling, but hiding something behind it. She couldn't tell what. Maybe he thought she was nuts. Scribbled Fielding's name in the book herself to get her parents' murder investigation cranked up again.

Hannah said, "The case is still open, isn't it? Fielding's money-laundering indictment, the embezzlement? You'd still like to catch this guy."

"Sure, we would," Frank said. "And so would a lot of other people."

"You mean the Cali cartel," she said.

"How'd you know about that?"

"It was in the paper."

"It was?"

"You should get off the sports page, Frank, maybe you'd learn something. Four hundred million and change, I seem to recall. I remember thinking, with that kind of money Fielding could hide anywhere. A penthouse at the Ritz, order room service till the end of time."

"Four hundred and sixty-three million is the exact figure. Largest embezzlement in U.S. history."

"But for some reason this doesn't interest you. J. J. Fielding. The name of an FBI fugitive written in a book, that doesn't arouse your curiosity."

"I didn't say that."

"What exactly did you say, Frank?"

"This is crazy. A copy of your book, Fielding's name in it. It's Looney Tunes."

She stiffened.

"Give it to me." She held out her hand. "The book. Give it to me."

He hesitated a second, then handed her the copy of *First Light*.

She stood up, crossing her arms over her chest, pressing the book tight.

"Look, I'm sorry I bothered you. Just go back to whatever you were doing, forget any of this happened."

"Wait a minute, would you?"

"I've got to get Randall home. It's his bedtime."

She turned and headed back down the sidewalk toward the parking lot. Then Frank was beside her, stride for stride. He put a hand on her shoulder and she halted.

"I'm sorry," he said. "You caught me by surprise, coming out of the dark like that. The book and everything."

"Look, it's nice to see you again, Frank. But I can take it from here."

"Hey, wait a goddamn second, will you? I said I was sorry. I didn't mean to imply *you* were Looney Tunes, I mean the book, the situation. This whole thing."

She could see Randall watching from one row over. Sitting in the same position she'd left him. Frank stepped in front of her, his chest blocking her view of Randall. The curly hair lit up golden by the parking lot lights.

"Don't you ever wear a goddamn shirt, Sheffield?"

He grinned.

"Only when it's required."

She took a step back, used her left hand to hold the hair off her face.

A white Lincoln caught them in its lights for a moment, then rolled on.

"You come out here, dump this in my lap, what exactly do you expect?"

"I guess I expected you to help," she said. "But never mind. It's after hours, you're busy with all this." She waved her arm toward the tiki hut and the beach.

"You want my help, like what, in an official capacity?"

"Official, unofficial. I thought you'd be interested."

"I am," he said. "I'm interested."

Frank was looking at her, his gaze steady and resolute. But Dan Romano had taught her to mistrust eyes. An expert liar could fool himself into believing what he was saying was true, and bring that sincerity to his eyes. What you looked at was the throat. The amount of swallowing. A tell-tale sign of a liar's dry mouth.

Frank's Adam's apple was bobbing. Every two or three seconds it moved.

"Look," she said. "Those numbers in the front of the book, they're some kind of half-assed code. Randall figured it out and it describes the murders, details only an insider would've known. And there's an address there too. An address on Bayshore Drive, and a time for the meeting. By nine tomorrow morning."

Sheffield nodded.

She said, "Randall is off to school at eight in the morning. I figure I can get to the Bayshore address by around eight-thirty. Maybe you'd like to drop by, we could see what this is all about. If you get lucky, you might even be able to make an arrest. You still make arrests, don't you, Frank? You haven't got so laid-back you don't do that anymore, have you?"

Frank swallowed again.

"I'll have to read my manual," he said. "Brush up on how it's done."

"Eight-thirty then. The address is twenty-six forty-nine Bayshore. You need to write that down?"

"Twenty-six forty-nine. My memory's still working fine." Another swallow.

"Sure there's not something bothering you, Frank? Something you want to talk about."

He waved away a night bug dancing at his ear.

"Twenty-six forty-nine," he said, mustering a smile. "I'll be there at eight-thirty. But if I'm a few minutes late, you'll wait for me, right?"

"I'll give you five minutes," she said. "Then I'm going in."

"Okay, okay, eight-thirty sharp," he said. "Scout's honor." And made a two-finger salute.

And another swallow.

* * *

Hal sat on his motorcycle in the large dark parking lot.

The air was different out here. It smelled like fish and seaweed. There was wind rattling through the palm trees. He watched as Hannah Keller got in her small car and started it and pulled out of the parking lot.

The man she had been talking to stood and watched her drive away.

Hal waited. He watched other cars pull out of the parking lot. They might be following Hannah Keller or they might not be.

Hal would ask somebody in the motel who this man was. He'd find out his name, what he did for a living, maybe even his relationship to Hannah. The man looked like a cop. That's how he stood, how he walked, like a lazy cop, a cop who drank too much, who sat around and watched TV. Worthless, slothful. A doughnut lover.

After he learned who the man was, then Hal had another person he wanted to talk to, somebody else he'd seen. Somebody he was curious about. He could let Hannah Keller go for the time being. She was taking her son home to bed. A good mother. Tucking him in, singing him lullabies. What good mothers did. He could pick her up again tomorrow morning. That would be soon enough.

From where he stood in the dark, Hal could smell the beach. He could smell coconut butter suntan lotion.

He'd been to the beach once long ago. Summer vacation, the eastern shore. Someone took him, he couldn't remember which one of his foster parents it was. Hal spent a while digging in the sand, then when he'd worked up his nerve, he walked down to the shore and stepped into the ocean. But the waves knocked him down and tried to drag him under. Like the ocean knew who he was, what an evil mind he had and the ocean wanted to kill him. Hal almost drowned.

A woman pulled him out of the water and carried him back to the beach.

The woman laid him on the sand and tried to press her mouth to his, but Hal pushed her away. He spit up water, then he got up and marched back down to the ocean and he walked into it and the ocean tried to push him down again. But Hal was ready this time. He kept his balance. He pushed back against the water. He slapped and punched and fought the ocean for a long time until the adult who had brought him to the beach yelled for him to come out of the water and go home.

By then Hal was exhausted. But he'd beaten the ocean. He wasn't scared of it. He wasn't scared of anything. He was seven years old.

ELEVEN

It was nearly midnight before the third cup of Tension Tamer tea finally began to take effect and Hannah felt drowsy enough to walk into the bedroom and lie down. She closed her eyes and almost instantly she was dreaming, drawn back into the shadowy images of her past.

She was eleven years old. Randall's age. She was a thin girl with thick blond hair that embarrassed her because everyone was always touching it as though it was community property, like the belly of a pregnant woman. Strangers standing behind her and her mother in the grocery store checkout line might reach out and stroke Hannah's golden curls. So lovely, they would say, like spun gold, the tresses of a fairy-tale princess. And Hannah cringed, wanted to hide, wanting to shave it off.

Seeing it now in her mind, part dream, part memory. The long-ago moment still simmered in her cells, unspooling before her now with all the detail of the actual event. Though she knew it was not real, knew she was dreaming it again, half-awake inside the dream, trying to interpret the images as she was seeing them.

Hannah was eleven years old, wearing pink pajamas, rising early on a Sunday morning in January, she went to her parents' room to see if they were awake. She pushed open the door and peered through the crack and saw her parents making love in the king-size four-poster bed, the same bed she slept in now, the same bed where she lay dreaming.

Hannah stood in the doorway and listened to the bed creak and watched them make love. She knew what they were doing. Martha Keller had already explained about sexuality. A straightforward talk with a pad of paper and drawings of a flaccid penis and an erect one. Both of them giggling at times, because it was funny, the whole thing, mother and daughter talking about that absurd object, that penis, how it changed, what it did. The big secret exposed. Hannah was fine with it. Ready for what was to come, her body's budding. Ready, eager, not shy at all. There were girls at school who were already there at eleven. Breasts, their periods. So when she saw her parents making love, the one and only time this happened, she was not shocked or upset.

But she stood there and watched because she had never seen her mother this way. Martha Keller on top of her father. Sitting up, her large breasts swinging loose from side to side as she rode up and down her father's shaft. Up and down again and again with her eyes closed. Controlling this lovemaking. And her father lay nearly still, his eyes also shut, head rocked back in the pillow. And Hannah could not stop watching.

For her mother was in charge, so obviously asserting herself in a way that she never did in public. Martha Keller was a quiet homemaker, willing to let Ed run the show, slow to reveal herself to strangers, quiet, holding back. Everything Ed Keller was not. Her wide-shouldered, athletic, tall husband, a federal prosecutor, an outdoorsman, brimming with confidence, maybe even a little arrogance. This man with enough strength to hold up a thrashing five-foot barracuda with one hand, a great sleek silver monster, holding it up beside the boat for the two of them to admire while he extracted the hook from its jaw with his free hand.

But there in the bed, her father was clearly powerless beneath Martha Keller's hips, grinding against him, pressing him down. Her father moaned and Hannah stood in the doorway absorbing this moment, this revelation of female power. This insight into her mother and into her father as well, their secret agreement, the thing that pleasured them both.

Then the dream changed, and Hannah at eleven became Randall at eleven. Her son was standing in her current doorway, watching her sleep, watching her dream in the big four-poster bed where long ago her parents had made love. Her son stood there for a moment staring at her, then he turned away from her sleeping form and padded through the dark house to his bedroom. The dream followed him like a camera watching from above. Watching Randall lie down in his own narrow bed and cover himself with sheets and blankets, lying face-up, peering into the blackness.

And this was no longer her regular dream, not the recurrent pleasure of visiting with her parents, witnessing again their secret dynamic, her mother's enthralling power. This was her son lying in his bed, where suddenly there was a dark angel standing above him, a faceless vampire with a wide cape spreading out like giant wings, a stranger hovering over her son, lowering himself closer and closer to his frail sleeping form.

Hannah knew it was a nightmare. Knew it as she swam upward to the surface of her sleep, kicking and clawing, and took a sharp gasp as she broke through into the air. Knew it was false, an image concocted by the phantom inside her, that creative maestro who spun together the day's anxieties with the powerful currents from her past. She knew all this, but that knowledge did not keep her heart from knocking out of rhythm or keep her from pushing herself up from her bed and hurrying through the living room and down the dark narrow corridor to Randall's room and throwing open his door.

He was at his computer. A blue halo surrounding him.

"Randall," she said.

His hands froze on the keys.

He turned his head and looked back at her.

"I couldn't sleep."

"What're you doing?"

"Talking to Stevie."

"At two in the morning, Randall?"

"Stevie doesn't sleep much either."

She came forward and stood at his shoulder.

Randall moved his mouse and clicked and the white panel that held a few dozen lines of typing disappeared.

"Why did you do that, Randall?"

"Do what?"

"You know what I mean. Why did you delete that screen?"

"We were talking about computers, that's all. Stevie's twelve. He's a lot better at programming than I am. He's a prodigy."

"Are you hiding something from me, Randall?"

"No."

His voice was shrill, uncertain. For of course he was hiding something. Just as every child concealed from their parents the secret kingdoms they inhabited, the universe they were convinced that only they fully understood.

She squatted beside his chair. In the metal birdcage Spunky dug deeper into the layer of shredded newspaper.

"Randall," she said. "Talk to me. Tell me what's bothering you. Can you do that?"

He shook his head.

"Nothing's bothering me."

"That's not what Dr. English thinks. She believes you're worried about something. Something very specific."

He stared ahead into the undersea screen-saver image. Big hammerhead sharks and dazzling schools of iridescent clownfish cruised by a forest of sea fans and elk horn coral. A stream of bubbles trickled up from the bottom of the screen.

"I want to talk about what's frightening you, Randall."

He got up from his chair and stepped around her, careful not to brush against her body, and he went to his bed and lay down. He was wearing his red-and-yellow-striped pajamas. There was a glass of water on the table beside his bed. Faintly glowing stars decorated his ceiling.

She stood up and went over to his bed and sat down on the edge.

Randall crossed his arms against his chest and stared up

at the greenish stars. There were a couple of moons up there too. Saturn with its rings.

"It's starting again, isn't it?"

"What do you mean?"

"The code in your book, the thing about house painters. It's beginning again. You went to see the FBI guy, you're going to start digging around, being a detective."

"Randall, I'm not going to lie to you. Yes, I'm going to dig around a little, try to see what this is all about."

He shook his head, clamped his mouth.

"Wouldn't you feel better if the killers were caught?"

"No!"

"Yes, you would, Randall. Because then you wouldn't have to worry anymore. It would all be over. Don't you want that?"

"It won't be over. It won't ever be over. You won't let it."

She reached out to comb a wisp of hair from his eyes but he wrenched away from her touch.

She sat still on the bed, hands in her lap.

"Sometimes, Randall, the only way for a wound to heal is to open it up, clean it out, disinfect it. And that hurts, I know it does. It seems like torture to touch a place so sore you can barely stand it. But that's the only way to cure some wounds. Otherwise they can go on festering forever, hurting and hurting all your life."

"You're not going to stop, you're never going to stop."

He rolled away from her, onto his side, and buried his head beneath the pillow and began to whimper.

She sat there for a long while, running her hands along his back, the knobby length of his spine. His sobs sent spasms through his body. Weeping with such force and abandon she could barely endure it. She spoke his name softly again and again until his crying finally tapered away to a few last hiccups, and she bent down and held him in her arms, rocking him until his breathing eased into the quiet regularity of sleep.

When he loosened his grip on the pillow, Hannah sat up and drew it off him, lifted his head and tucked the pillow beneath. She bent close and touched her lips to his damp, fevered cheek, the salt of his drying tears. She listened for a moment to his muffled snore, the sweet drone of his oblivion. Then rose and walked back to her bedroom where she lay down again and stared into the dark.

TWELVE

Misty was dreaming about a nipple. A nipple on fire. Not just any nipple. But her own, the left one. Burning. Flames rising from it. Dark licks of fire shooting out the puckered tip. Seeing that in her dream, the red nipple twisted erect, the spurt of fire, the white jet flame of a welder's torch. Blackness all around it like one of those surreal paintings, that guy with the clocks dripping off tree branches, a picture like that, only Misty's picture was a floating nipple in a sea of blackness, a thin spray of fire shooting out the tip. Hurting. Her left nipple aching so bad, burning so hot and stinging, the pain dragged her up from a dark spiraling cave of sleep.

She blinked, opened her eyes, stared up into the darkness.

Nude, lying on her back in her narrow bed, peering up at the ceiling, she could barely breathe from the pain. With great effort she lifted her right hand and reached up to pat her breast, soothe the ache. Somehow knowing what she was about to find. Feeling it now, the pressure, the tight grip.

She laid her right hand on top of the hand gripping her left breast.

It wasn't a dream anymore. She was wide fucking awake. Speechless. There was no air in the room. Dark as midnight at the bottom of the sea. She stroked the hand cupping her left breast, pinching her nipple, causing fire to spurt from it.

Her fingertips touching the back of his hand. Broad and cold and slick as marble, the hand of a statue in the park. She would've screamed if she could've filled her lungs. She would've twisted away, tried to scramble into the bathroom if her muscles would unfreeze.

She tried to pry the hand loose, but it wasn't like any hand she'd ever touched. She couldn't say why. Something about the skin. Something about the unmoving weight of it. Holding her entire body in place like that *Star Trek* guy with the pointy ears, the way he could pinch somebody by the shoulder, the Vulcan death grip, freezing them stock-still. Same thing. She was stiff against the mattress, the pain in her nipple so intense she was groggy, the bed starting to sink beneath her. She was writhing inside, deep down in her gut, but her body lay perfectly still on the mattress.

When he spoke, his voice sounded mechanical. Some kind of accent she didn't recognize. She was usually good with accents. Amazing her customers at Hooters. Wisconsin, Virginia, Alabama, New York, west Texas, east Texas. It wasn't all that hard. She had a good ear. You just had to listen, remember. But this guy spoke with no accent at all. Like he'd learned English from a machine, one of those tapes for foreign speakers, making you practice over and over. Hello, my name is Anne. I have a dog. My dog's name is Wags. He spoke like that, a machine. A deep, whispery voice.

"Who are you?" is what he said.

Her throat was swollen with pain. She couldn't reply.

She pointed at his hand, made a gargling sound.

He eased his grip, then slowly he moved his hand off her nipple. She felt his fingertip touch her throat. A sharp, cutting pain against the flesh of her neck.

"You're hurting me," she said.

"Yes," he said. "I know."

"Why? What have I done to you?"

"Who are you?" In that same mechanical tone. Like a doll she had once, pull the string, it says, "Please hug me."

"What do you mean, who am I? I'm a girl. I'm Misty."

"Who are you, Misty?"

"You're going to have to be more specific," she said. "You mean what do I like to do? My hobbies, favorite color, like that?"

Using the long, hard fingernail on his thumb, he began to draw a simmering line down her body. Starting at her throat, running between her breasts, her sternum, down her soft white belly, to her navel and below that, a straight line, all the way to the brim of her pubic hair. Stopping there. For the moment, at least.

Along the seam he'd drawn, the skin burned as if he'd been using a scalpel, opening her up. She could sense the moisture beside his thumb tip, although that might have been sweat. A straight, slow razory line back to her throat. Like he was dissecting her, going to peel back her flesh, climb inside.

Misty was paralyzed. Unable to look down at her body to see if it was sweat or blood she felt. Afraid of what she'd see in the dark, the gleam of her own fluids.

"Why are you following Hannah Keller, Misty?"

Misty lay very still as once again the man drew the hot line down her body, along the exact same seam.

"Why are you following her, Misty? What do you want from her?"

"Who the hell is Hannah Keller?"

"You're not good at surveillance, Misty. I spotted you easily. In your blue car with the peeling leather top, stalking Hannah Keller. I saw you on her street, I saw you follow her across Miami."

"What're you, a cop?"

"Do I look like a cop, Misty?"

"I don't know, I can't see you."

"Trust me. I'm not a cop."

"You see me driving around Miami, then you show up in my apartment. How'd you find me if you aren't a cop?"

"That's what I do," he said. "I find people."

"Yeah? And then what do you do, when you find them? You pull on their nipples? Big strong guy, got to show how tough he is."

"I find people, then I kill them."

Misty was quiet. Her heart was quaking. She snuck down a breath, let it out. Snuck down another one.

"Look, goddamn it," she said. "Nobody's stalking anybody. You broke into the wrong damn apartment."

But Misty could hear the quiver in her voice, the lie so obvious.

"When a polar bear stalks his prey across the ice, Misty, he covers his black nose with his white paw so he won't be seen. Even the polar bear knows more than you know."

"Polar bear?"

"Why are you stalking Hannah Keller? Tell me, Misty?"

The words broke from her like a belch.

"Because I hate the bitch."

The man was quiet for a moment, looking down at her.

"Why do you hate Hannah Keller?"

"Forget it," Misty said. "I'm not telling you a damn thing. You break in here, pinch my breast. Why am I going to tell you anything?"

"Why do you hate her, Misty?"

The guy didn't listen. He was touching her throat now, fingers spreading around it, tightening.

"Okay, okay. I hate her because she's living my life, the one I was supposed to have. She stole it from me. That's why."

"How did she do that, steal your life?"

"She just did. Don't worry about it. She stole it, take my word for it."

"Who are you, Misty?"

He started the incision line back down her throat, down between her breasts, the same exact line, all the way down. His thumbnail halting again right at the edge of her pubes. Like he was shy or polite, had his limits.

"For chrissakes, I'm Misty. Misty Anne Fielding."

"Oh," the man said, pausing for several moments. "You're the daughter."

A pale glow from the streetlight out on Flagler seeped around her orange curtains and lit up a portion of his face. She saw heavy eyebrows and a burr haircut. His lips were large, eyes with a dark glint. Beyond that, she couldn't tell much. Not enough to pick him out of a lineup later. That is, if she was still alive.

"And what is your father's name, Misty Fielding?"

"I don't have a father."

"What is your father's name?"

"I said . . ."

He gripped her left nipple again, just a quick pinch. Misty groaned.

"What is your father's name, Misty Fielding?"

She barely had breath for the words. Saying it in a burst.

"John Jackson Fielding. J.J. for short. But he's dead."

"Is he?"

"He's dead to me."

The man released her nipple and stood up slowly and she could see him tug something from his jacket pocket. Misty heard a plastic snap, then saw the gray glow of some kind of small screen.

"Is that why you are stalking Hannah Keller, Misty, because of your father?"

"Jesus," she said. "Who the fuck are you?"

"Who are *you*, Misty?"

"Okay, okay," she said. "You want to know who my daddy was. I'll tell you who he was. He was a banker. A good successful one. He made nice money. We lived in a nice house, I went to a good school, had pretty clothes. Then they came and tried to arrest him, the police, the FBI. They had their best guys going after him, but my old man was too quick. One night he didn't come home. Blink, he was gone. Emptied his bank accounts and ran off, left my mother and me with a ten-thousand-a-month nut and not a nickel to pay it with. That's what happened. That's what Hannah Keller's old man did. My daddy never hurt anybody. Just because he had some business dealings with a couple of drug dealers, they went after him, chased him into hiding. That's all it was, some banking bullshit. I mean drug dealers need to put their money somewhere safe like everybody else, right? Is that a crime?"

"Where is he hiding, Misty?"

"Hey, do you ever listen to anybody? You ask somebody a question, they answer it but you're off to something else, like I never said anything. Like the subject never came up.

You're back to this other thing. Man, it's not possible to have a fucking conversation like that. It's too twisted."

"Where is your father hiding, Misty?"

He laid his hand on her breast. Resting lightly, but she could still feel a slow shiver begin to take over her body.

"I told you, he's dead as far as I'm concerned. What do you want with him anyway?"

"Your father," the man said, "stole money. A great deal of money."

"Oh, Christ, I knew it."

"You knew what, Misty?"

"You're one of them, one of the drug guys."

The hand holding her breast was gentler now.

"Forget it," she said. "I told you people everything I knew back when it happened, which was a big fat nothing. I didn't know where he went back then and I still don't know. You think I'd be living here, a rattrap apartment like this, if I knew where that rich fuck was? Hell, no. He abandoned me. I was a month from starting my junior year in high school, and bang, he's gone. Not a good-bye kiss, see you later, it's been nice being your dad, nothing, not one word."

"And your mother? Does she know where he is?"

"Go pinch her nipple if you want to find out. I don't talk to my mother. We stopped seeing eye-to-eye some time back."

The man moved the gray glow down to her belly and rested it there. A palm-top computer with a black-and-white screen no bigger than a wallet. A tiny aerial sprouting from one edge.

Misty squinted at the thing. She didn't sleep in her contacts. So she had to bring her head off the pillow and squint hard to make out the tiny black-and-white screen.

"Where is he hiding, Misty?"

"Mother of Christ," she said quietly. "That's him. That's my old man."

"Yes," the man said. "And he looks very alive, doesn't he?"

"Where is he? What the hell's going on?"

"I would like to know this same thing, Misty."

She stared up into the dark at the man's half-illuminated face. She could see his left eye and his left cheekbone swimming in the shaft of streetlight. He looked like someone she knew. But she couldn't remember who or when or where. Somebody halfway cute, halfway scary. A little like the kind of guys she used to date in high school. Guys who spent all their free time souping up their cars, drag racing, smoking dope out in the parking lot. Guys going nowhere, but having a great time getting there. Only this guy didn't seem like he had a good time doing anything. At least not anything she wanted to know about.

"Are you going to kill me?"

"I don't know."

"You're not sure?"

"I haven't decided yet."

"Well, would you mind if I had some input on the issue? You know, make my case before you shoot me?"

"I don't shoot. I don't like guns."

"Aw, shit. Not knives. Don't tell me you're one of those, a blade guy."

"Guns are unnatural. I've never used one. Not knives either. Both of them are inhumane."

Misty lay back against the pillow.

"I would think, I mean, just as a philosophical point, if you wanted to kill somebody, a bullet in the brain would be fairly humane. It's like a second or two and it's over. That doesn't seem as bad to me as knives. You stick somebody with a blade, they could take an hour to die, bleeding to death. Flopping around. Jesus, now that's seriously inhumane."

"I use my hand," he said. "This one."

He held up his right hand for her to see. Turned it in the light like he'd just washed it and was letting it dry.

"You strangle your victims?"

"At first, yes."

"At first?"

"After they've blacked out, I reach inside."

"Reach inside their mouths? I don't get it."

"No," he said, "inside their chests."

"Jesus. You can stop right there. I don't want to hear any more of this."

"When I'm inside their chests, that's when I crush their heart."

Misty closed her eyes. When she opened them again, the guy was still there, still with his hand up in the air, looking at it.

"Oh, yeah, well, that's real humane. Crushing hearts."

The man lowered his hand.

"More humane than guns," he said.

"But you got to cut them open, right? You still need a knife."

"No," he said. "I use this."

He offered her his right hand and after a second's hesitation, she reached up and felt around until she came to his thumbnail. It was long and hard, filed down to a sharp point. A claw.

Misty swallowed. She took a long breath, then let go of his hand. It was cold and slick, that marble feeling again. Or maybe a reptile, some big thick snake that has to lie in the sun all day just to heat its blood to room temperature.

"Look, why the fuck are you telling me this shit?"

"Because you asked me."

"All right," Misty said. "Now look. Number one, I don't know where my old man is. If I did, I'd tell you in a flash. I would. I don't have any love for the fucker, believe me. And, number two, I haven't gotten a good look at you in the dark. So there's no reason you have to kill me. I couldn't identify you. Even if I did call the cops, which I'm not going to do. So if you're worried about doing the humane thing, well, it seems pretty clear to me that the humane thing in this instance is just to leave me alone. Go on your merry way."

"What are you planning to do to Hannah Keller?"

"Man, you don't listen, do you? A person could make the

best speech in the world, talk the birds down from the trees, but with you, it doesn't matter, you've got some kind of hearing dysfunction or something."

"You hate her. So you want to hurt her somehow. How are you going to hurt her?"

Misty lay there for a few moments wondering what to do. Just when she thought she was making headway, getting some connection going with the guy, bang, it's like nothing happened between them at all. Very shaky ground.

"That thing you got," Misty said. "That's a computer, right? You're on the Web?"

"The Internet."

"Okay, then," she said. "I'll show you what I'm planning to do to Hannah Keller."

She told him what to type in.

He used his first finger, pecking slowly, and entered the address. It took a few seconds to log on to the site.

She sat up and watched the screen with him.

When the page finally loaded, there were frogs perched on floating logs in the middle of a lagoon. They were snapping flies out of the air. Some of them were swimming past lily pads, their long froggy legs snapping through the water.

"What is this?"

"That's her kid," Misty said. "That's his Web page."

"Hannah Keller's boy."

"Yeah, that's right."

"Frogs on logs," he said.

"That's just what it is this week. He changes it a lot. He's a computer whiz, a smart little boy."

"What's his name?"

"It's right there, at the top. Randall's World. His name is Randall."

"What are you going to do to Hannah Keller?"

"Okay," she said. Going to give it another try. What did she have to lose, tell him everything, maybe that would do it, he'd leave. "I've been chatting up her kid, you know, over the computer. E-mail, instant messages. Seducing him, sort of. We're getting pretty close. One of these days, I'm going to bump into him somewhere. The mall, or on the way home from school. I'll let him know it's me, the girl he's been talking to. Girl who's been sending him pictures of herself. You know, sexually suggestive, showing a little skin, but keeping the face hidden. And then, what I was thinking, I'll talk the little guy into my car, and Randall and I'll drive off together. Disappear somewhere. Maybe go out west, California. I haven't thought out that part yet."

"You're going to kidnap her son."

"That's right. I'm going to steal her goddamn precious little boy."

"No, you're not."

"I'm not?"

He was quiet for several moments. He was watching the frogs swim. Watching the long tongues unfurl and snap the flies from the air.

"You won't do anything until I've told you it's okay."

"All right," she said. "Okay, sure. I can live with that."

"You'll do nothing."

"Sure, sure. Hold off a while. No problem, you don't want me messing up your plan, whatever the hell it is. I can see that."

The man snapped the tiny computer shut. He stood there a minute looking down at her. Breathing through his mouth.

"Sorry for the inconvenience," he said.

Misty smoothed a hand over her sore breast.

"Inconvenience? What? Breaking into my apartment, torturing my tit? I'd say that's a little more than a fucking inconvenience."

He looked at her for a few more moments. Not moving, just that slow breath through his mouth.

"You ever been in a magazine, Misty? Your picture?"

"What?"

"I think you could be in a magazine. You have the right nose. The eyes."

"I do?"

"Yes. You could be in a magazine."

"That's nice of you to say," she said. "That's sweet."

"And what is that?" he said. Motioning up toward her wall.

"Oh, that," Misty said. "It's one of my art sculptures."

Mounted on the wall a few feet over her bed was the crucifix Barbie. On a big brass cross Misty had glued a naked Barbie doll. In one of Barbie's hands was a miniature hair dryer, in the other was a derringer. She'd glued a triangle of green shag carpet to Barbie's crotch for pubic hair. There were five other sculptures on the other walls, hidden in the darkness. Her avant-garde phase.

"You are an artist?" the man asked.

"I used to be. I gave it up. Moved on to other things."

"I don't understand art," he said. "It's one of the things I don't understand."

"Well, you're not alone," Misty said. "I don't understand it either. It's just something I used to do. I glued a bunch of shit together and hung it on the wall. It pissed off my mother, pissed off my teachers, so I kept on doing it."

The man stared at her Barbie crucifix. He wasn't real tall. Wide shoulders, narrow waist, a slow, measured way about his movements like he thought everything through before he did it. He looked down at her again.

"From now on, Misty, you can call me by my name."

"Yeah? And what's that?"

"Hal," he said.

She pushed herself up onto her elbows, rubbed her eyes, and squinted up at him for a better look.

"Hal what?"

But he had already stepped backward into the shadows and was gone.

THIRTEEN

"No, Sheffield. It's absolutely out of the question."

Helen had her back to him, staring out the bank of windows that faced Biscayne Bay. It was ten to eight, Tuesday morning, hour thirty-two of Operation Joanie. One-third of the way. No sightings yet, no scent in the air. Everyone a little frayed. Out the windows it was a gray morning, the sun muffled behind low leaden clouds. In the distance the bay stretched before them like a platter of badly tarnished silver.

Helen wore a pair of khaki trousers and a blue-and-white-striped shirt, sleeves rolled up to her forearms. Her hair was fastened back with some sort of spring-loaded plastic clamp that looked like it doubled as a torture device. No counterfeit smiles this morning. The air around her was dense with bitter fumes.

"I told Hannah I'd meet her at eight-thirty at the Bayshore address."

"I don't care what you told her, Sheffield. You're not doing it. No way in hell. Tell him, Charlie."

Senator Ackerman was in the kitchen pouring himself another cup of coffee. Charlie Pettigrew sat on the gray leather couch, a mug balanced on his lap. In the master bedroom, hunched in front of an oversized computer monitor, Andy Barth tapped keys and fidgeted. Frank could see on the screen a color-coded street map of Dade County, Hannah's car was a glowing red dot. The other agents were green. A dozen of them moving in and out of contact with Hannah's car.

"She's approaching Pinecrest Middle School. Two blocks

east," Andy called through the open doorway. He was wearing red walking shorts and a yellow tennis shirt, purple flip-flops. Trying for Miami-hot-and-flashy, but getting world-class geeky instead.

Charlie Pettigrew had a sip of his coffee and set it on the end table.

"Why'd you do this, Frank? What were you thinking?"

"Charlie, I didn't do anything. She came to me."

"But you agreed to participate. Why, Frank?"

"This blows the whole scenario, Sheffield," Helen said, turning her head, speaking over her shoulder. "Was that your intention, to queer the operation?"

The senator wandered back into the living room blowing on his coffee.

"Nothing's happened," Ackerman said. "I think both of you need to calm down. If Hal was following the Keller woman last night and witnessed her meeting with an FBI agent, he would probably see it as perfectly normal."

"It wasn't in the script," Shane said.

"Well, maybe it should've been," said Frank. "Maybe you didn't design this as flawlessly as you thought."

Helen swung around, her lips drawn back, quivering on the edge of a snarl. The air around her was so combustible a stray electron could set it off.

"Do the two of you have some kind of problem I should be aware of?" Ackerman said. "This rancor."

Shane got control of her mouth, shook her head.

"A disagreement on strategy, Senator," she said. "Nothing more."

She moved out of the harsh gray light from the window and perched stiffly on the arm of one of the leather chairs. Bluish shadows were showing in the hollows beneath her eyes. Her raccoon genes starting to emerge.

"I'm glad to hear that," Ackerman said. "Because I'd hate to see dissension in the ranks sidetrack us from our mission."

"Look," Frank said. "In the first place, Hal Bonner can't possibly know every damn FBI agent in the U.S. on sight.

I'm in plainclothes, I could be anybody. And let's say he does make me, he asks around, finds out what I do. What's the harm? Like the senator says, it's perfectly predictable Hannah would seek me out and that I'd accompany her. It'd be more suspicious if she went in there alone."

"No," Shane said. "Absolutely not. You'll scare him off, the whole plan is jeopardized."

"My vote's with Frank," Ackerman said. "I think he has a valid point. He goes to the Bayshore address. Then afterward he drops away. It looks better that way. More natural. Frankly, I'm surprised you didn't think of using someone like Sheffield in the original plan, Ms. Shane."

"She's dropped the kid off at school, now she's circling back toward Old Cutler Road," Andy Barth called out. "Estimated ETA is eight twenty-eight. Traffic thickening ahead of her."

"Anything following?" Shane said. She was staring at the marble floor.

"Far as I can tell, only our people," said Andy. "But it's rush hour, it's hard to be sure."

Frank stood up, checked his watch.

"I'll get going, then."

Helen's glance was poisonous. She gave the senator a taste of it.

"I don't like this," she said. "Not one bit."

"So noted, Ms. Shane," said Ackerman. "But let's not forget Joanie, shall we? That's who this is all about. Not you, not Sheffield, not me. None of us. It's not about scoring points, it's about my daughter. What happened to Joanie Lynn Ackerman out on that snow-covered mountain slope."

Everyone stood in place, a moment of silence for Joanie, and for the senator's staggering, unrelenting grief, then Charlie Pettigrew stepped forward, put his hand on Frank's shoulder, and steered toward the door of the apartment, then down the hall to the elevator. He jabbed the button and gave Sheffield a hard stare.

"Okay, so what's really going on, Frank? Between you and Shane."

"We haven't exactly bonded."

"I can see that."

"Fact is, we're working on a pretty good personality clash. She came by my place last night, started talking trash about my dad. I threw some back at her and it got testy."

"Well, get over it, whatever it is. There's too much riding on this operation for a bunch of schoolyard name-calling. That clear, Frank?"

Sheffield nodded. He watched the elevator numbers count upward toward their floor.

"Senator's got a tight grip on your short hairs too, huh, Charlie?"

"Damn right he does. And he's got Director Kelly too. If we don't nail this asshole soon, believe me, a lot of dicks are going to get seriously shortened. And believe me, Frank, at this stage in life I can't spare an extra inch."

The doors slid open. Charlie Pettigrew reached out and held them wide. Randy Sanderson and Ronald Scruggs stepped off. His colleagues from the Miami field office, head-of-the-class poster-boys, there for a briefing. They nodded to Charlie Pettigrew, and both of them gave Frank a quick once-over. What the hell was this fuckoff doing with the big boys?

"Hey, Randy. Hey, Ron."

They made their curt hellos and walked on toward the suite.

"It's okay, guys, don't worry," Frank called. "Only reason they invited me along is for comic relief."

They shook their heads and kept on going.

"Look, Frank," Charlie said. "No more screwing around. Play this straight, okay? For old times' sake if nothing else."

Frank stepped aboard. Gave him the same two-fingered salute he'd used last night. Starting to like the gesture. Echoes of Bogart. Maybe he'd keep it in the repertoire.

On the way down he checked himself out in the mirrored stainless steel. He'd taken a little longer than usual dressing this morning. The tan slacks without the pleats, the Bass loafers, the black polo shirt. No jewelry, a light mist of some

Ralph Lauren aftershave one of the secretaries had given
him last Christmas. He hadn't used cologne in a decade. Not
since he was courting his ex-wife. Only woman he'd ever
met who actually liked Old Spice, which should have told
him something right there if he'd been paying attention.

He got a quick ride to the lobby and stepped out into the
marble luxury of the Grand Bay Hotel. Lots of mirrors, lots
of tall, slender beautiful people reflected in them. And whatever minor confidence in his appearance he'd enjoyed while
looking at his stainless steel reflection, departed in a sudden
rush.

This stretch of Bayshore Drive was filled with dignified old
mansions built up high on the limestone and coral ridgeline.
Most of the houses had large open porches and heavy tapered columns, staid, prosaic residences, more like something you'd find in a Chicago suburb than a neighborhood on
the edge of a subtropical bay. When they'd been built, about
the time Hannah's parents were born, there were no marinas
or restaurants or condos across the narrow highway which
meandered before them along the coastline. Back then, in
the thirties, these homes had sweeping and unobstructed
views of a bay as blue and pristine as a Tahitian lagoon.

But in the last few decades the nearby village of Coconut
Grove had swollen into a chic and noisy metropolitan center,
a playground for feral teens and South American tourists.
The narrow coast road had been widened to four lanes and a
stream of cars and throbbing motorcycles passed at every
hour of the day and night. All week long the Grove's clubs
and bars raved till dawn, so these elegant houses that had
once presided over a wide and tranquil panorama now
looked down on the blue haze of ceaseless Miami traffic,
and what had once been a treasured address in the city was
simply a row of faded villas with the moldy look of nursing
homes for the dispossessed.

Hannah drove slowly, counting down the numbers until
she spotted the address and swung her car onto the shoulder
of the road. The house she was looking for was a faded pink

stucco affair with two large dormer windows and a bleached-out red barrel tile roof. Its open porch ran the length of the front, and like its neighbors it was perched atop the high limestone crest. Craggy fissures of rock showed through the grass near the roadway. Sprawling oaks and banyans shaded the yard and obscured a large portion of the house. To the west a steep asphalt driveway mounted the bluff, then disappeared from view up on the plateau where the house stood.

She made a U-turn, cut sharply into the entrance, and held it in low gear as she rumbled up the steep asphalt drive. Frank Sheffield was already there, leaning against the door of a green Miata parked in the shade of an oak to the side of the house. His convertible top was down.

Hannah drew in behind him and turned off the engine.

As Frank approached, Hannah reached back into the jump seat and gripped her black leather bag. A few pounds heavier than usual, because of the loaded .357 Smith & Wesson in its suede holster. She hadn't handled the pistol for five years, not since that morning when she placed it on a high shelf in her bedroom closet. It had been her father's gun, the weapon he'd chosen that morning when the killers broke into his house, the unfired pistol Ed Keller was holding when he was killed.

She got out of the car as Frank ambled over. She was wearing jeans and a dark green cotton top, Nike running shoes, hair loose, no jewelry. Ready to rock and roll.

"Nice car," he said.

He took off his sunglasses and squinted at her through the dull gray light.

"Randall talked me into it. I'm not much of a car person myself. He chose the color and everything."

"Smart kid. He picks out his ride five years early, knows you'll have it broken in by the time it's his."

"I don't believe Randall has such a long view."

"You never know. Kids can be sneaky. Regular little connivers."

"Connivers?" she said. "Do you have kids, Frank?"

"No, but I *was* one."

"Yeah, well, my son is no conniver."

"That's exactly what my mother thought, bless her heart."

She looked at him for a moment, then glanced around the wide and empty lawn.

"So, is anybody home?"

"Not that I've seen."

"How long have you been here?"

"Couple of minutes."

The front porch was bare, the lawn was shaggy. In several of the windows the venetian blinds were in disarray, slats broken or twisted as if a recent storm had blown through the old place and left chaos in its wake.

"Anybody from work know you're here? What you're up to?"

"You mean like do we have backup?"

"Something like that."

Frank shook his head.

"You worry too much, Hannah. Even in the unlikely event that Fielding's here, the old guy would be close to seventy. Two trained law-enforcement types like us, that shouldn't be a problem."

"At least tell me you're armed."

He reached behind him and patted the small of his back.

Through a stand of Australian pines that ran down the east perimeter of the property, Hannah could see a lawn-service company at work. Men in yellow shirts mowing and weed-eating. But otherwise there was no sign of life anywhere around.

"I was wondering," Sheffield said. "You ever been in a kayak?"

She peered at him as if he'd spoken in tongues.

"A kayak," he said. "Long and slender like a canoe."

"I know what a kayak is, Frank."

"Well, I have two of them. One's a two-man, the other's one-man. I was wondering if you and Randall might want to come out, take a little tour across the flats. Around sunset you see lots of interesting stuff. Rays, sharks, crabs. A few inches of water, that's all you need, you skim across the surface like a water bug. It's very tranquil. Or if you wanted to leave Randall somewhere, a baby-sitter or something, it could be just you and me in the two-man kayak. That would work too. Either way is fine. I like kids. They usually respond to me."

"I bet they do."

"So, you want to come out?"

"What're you thinking, Frank? We're about to walk in a house where the killer of my parents may be hiding out and you're asking me for a date?"

"A kayak tour is what I was thinking. I guess you could call it a date. But that seems a little more formal than what I had in mind."

She shook her head and sighed. Truth be known, it was the best offer she'd had in a while.

"Listen, Frank. I appreciate the gesture, but we need to take care of this little problem before we talk about kayaking. Okay?"

"Sure," he said. "Okay, fine."

"So how do you suggest we proceed?"

"Ring the bell or break down the door. What's your preference?"

Frank was smiling at her, not taking this seriously. Only reason he was here was because she'd bullied him into it. What he wanted was to go kayaking. Skim across the surface. Be a water bug.

"Are you on the clock now, Frank? Or is this off time for you?"

The humor leaked out of his smile.

"Hannah, I'm at the stage in my career where that distinction has totally lost meaning."

"So you're not holding a search warrant?"

"We find something worth bothering a judge about, we can have a warrant in an hour."

"Meanwhile we violate the hell out of this guy's rights, give him a free pass out of jail."

"I truly doubt it will come to that."

She turned and marched across the pitted driveway and mounted the steep front steps. Red Cuban tile covered the stairs and ran the length of the porch. Perched on the railing near a rusty mailbox was a large gray squirrel. He eyed Hannah, unimpressed, and continued to munch on a seedpod.

The front door was a couple of inches ajar.

Frank was beside her. He reached out and nudged the door inward. Its rusty hinges creaked. Calling out a half-hearted hello, Frank Sheffield stepped over the threshold.

She followed him into a large high-ceilinged room, shadowy and dense with the mustiness of disuse. There was no furniture in the room. Simply a wide fireplace of quarried coral topped with an ornately carved mahogany mantel. The floors were dark, wide planks, probably old heart of pine from the days when such wood still grew in abundance throughout the state. There were dark, heavy beams stretching across the ceiling, and two wrought-iron light fixtures hung at either end of the big room, as round and large as wagon wheels with half the glass globes missing.

Frank called out another hello but his voice was swallowed up by the dark airless space.

"Looks like the banquet hall for a Viking warrior," he said. "Big and dreary. And decidedly vacant."

"We've just walked in the door, Frank. You want to give up already?"

She stepped over to the fireplace and ran her hand across its slick surface. The coral was etched with thousands of tiny squiggles, the unreadable hieroglyphs of its ancient biology.

She could hear the lawn mowers roaring next door, and the low drone of traffic from out on Bayshore Drive. And there was something else. Something on the lower register of her hearing. She made a quick tour of the two other rooms. A parlor with another small fireplace and a wall of built-in bookshelves, all bare. Then a large white kitchen with what looked an icebox from the previous century, and cupboards that ran from eye level to the fifteen-foot ceiling. The shelves barren, the refrigerator empty, electricity switched off.

Frank stood in the doorway and watched her prowl the room. Watched her open drawers and cabinets, peering in the cracks.

"I bet you were a good cop."

"I was okay," she said.

Wedged in a back corner of one of the tile counters was a white business card. Hannah turned her back to Sheffield and palmed the card, stepped away from the counter and slipped it into her hip pocket. It wasn't that she didn't trust Sheffield. Only that his passion for this enterprise fell so short of hers that she felt a need to safeguard any stray evidence. No telling if or when Frank would get around to analyzing them on his own.

"This is the kind of place," Frank said, rapping on a countertop with his knuckles, "everything's built so well, it makes you sad thinking about the plywood bullshit we live with nowadays."

"Let's try upstairs," she said.

"Right behind you."

It was a curved staircase, more white coral worn smooth by years of leather footsteps. The railing was an intricate wrought-iron filigree, a floral pattern, hibiscus blooms and a tangled vine. When she reached the landing, she heard that same noise coming from further down the corridor. And recognized it now, a quiet voice.

She dug her hand in her purse, came out with the Smith.

"Whoa," he whispered, and laid a restraining hand on her shoulder. "You're a civilian, remember?"

He'd drawn his nine-millimeter, a bluish Glock.

She followed two steps behind him down the narrow hallway past one empty bedroom, then another, until they came to a closed door at the end of the corridor.

Frank put his left hand on the knob, back to the door, pistol by his cheek. He looked at her and winked, gave her a quick wag of his pistol, signaling her to stand clear, then he laid his shoulder against the dark wood and shoved it open.

He entered in a rush. Hannah lost sight of him briefly,

then she brushed the door aside and charged forward into the unlit chamber, stumbling to a sudden stop.

Heavy curtains were drawn against the light on two sets of windows. For a moment her eyes were dazzled by the sudden darkness, then a second or two later she began to make out the blue shimmer of a large-screen television.

"Jesus," Frank said. He was beside her now, a hand on her back.

For a moment Hannah saw only the fuzzy snow of faulty reception, then the image gradually resolved into slightly better focus. A desiccated man in a white nightgown was propped up in what looked like a hospital bed. Beside him several plastic IV bags dangled from a chrome rack and an array of tubes ran from the bottle to his forearm and chest.

The picture was grainy and had a halting slow-motion feel, and though she had only seen his face in a handful of photographs, there was no doubt that the withered man in the bed was J. J. Fielding. He had a long, narrow face, grown gaunt in the last five years. His hair was extravagantly full, a bright silver, and he wore it swept back on the sides and pomaded into place, as crudely out of style as the hairdo of some oafish Russian diplomat. He had a deep crease in his chin and the fleshy lips of a sybarite and deep-set eyes that seemed both cold and anxious to please as if this were a man who took no great pleasure in the cruelties his appetites required him to commit.

Beside him, wearing a blue surgical gown, was a tall, potbellied gentleman with windblown Einstein hair. He was scribbling with a ballpoint pen, paging through sheets clamped to a metal clipboard.

The television was a new model, a Sony. It sat up on a metal rack, the kind with rollers that you might find in the visual ed room of a high school.

When Fielding spoke, his lips seemed to be a second out of synch with the amplified voice that filled the room.

"So at this point, I'm told there's nothing further they can do," he said. "Nothing but painkillers, morphine, Demerol.

They're letting me self-administer the drugs, but I'm trying not to use too much because I want to stay clear-headed as long as possible. The good news and the bad news are the same. Pancreatic cancer is quick. Dr. Mau tells me I've only got a few days left. When I heard that, I decided I couldn't wait any longer. I needed to do this. To let you hear from me. There are so many things I need to explain."

The old man's voice was a squeaky tenor, a warped violin, badly out of tune.

Hannah stepped closer to the television. The picture was framed with the familiar white border she saw every day on her own computer screen. Hannah touched the edge of the screen, running a finger along the cool glass as if to make certain it was real.

"This is the Internet," she said. "The guy is broadcasting over the goddamn Internet. See? Right there, that line—*www.Deathwatch.com*. A Web address and everything. Can you believe this shit?"

On the screen, Fielding took a sip of clear liquid from a tall glass and handed the glass back to his doctor.

Then he craned forward in the bed and peered into the camera.

"I've sent you something, Hannah. I sent something to you. A secret message. I believe you've received it by now and that you're watching me. I want you to come to me. I need to see you, to talk to you in person. Please, Hannah, I have something terrible to confess. It's about your parents. The terrible things I've done. Please come, Hannah. Right away. There isn't much time left. Look at the message I've left for you and do what it says. Please, Hannah. Please, I beg you."

FOURTEEN

"That bastard," Hannah said. "That goddamn worthless son of a bitch. He wants to confess. He wants absolution. The big come-from-behind finish. Well, screw him."

They were on the front porch. Frank glancing around the empty lawn. Before Fielding drifted off to sleep, he'd repeated his plea to Hannah twice more. The same speech verbatim, as if he were giving it over and over, not knowing exactly when she might show up before the screen. When finally Fielding began to snore, Hannah stalked from the room and Sheffield followed her outside.

"So what're you going to do, Frank?"

"I'm going back to the office, get busy on this."

"You have computer people, right? They can track down his Web address, locate him."

"We have computer people, yes. I'm not sure what they can and can't do. Or how quickly. But we'll see."

"And what about me?"

"What about you?"

"Where do you see me fitting in?"

"Where do you want to fit in, Hannah?"

"I want to be involved, of course."

"Then I won't try to stop you."

"Don't you want the book? You heard him. It's got more code. More messages."

Frank glanced away, stared out at the traffic. He shook his head.

"You hold onto it for the time being. Read it over, see if it makes any sense. I'll run this by Rosie Jackson, the SAC, maybe he'll want to put some of our crypto people on it."

"But there's something wrong. What is it, Frank? Level with me."

He flinched and looked away.

"You still don't believe this, do you? What do you think, this whole thing is some kind of fabrication, something I invented?"

"No, I don't think that," Frank said.

Hannah looked out at the lawn where three white ibis with long orange beaks were poking in the grass.

"But you're just going to send me off with the book? Is that FBI procedure now? Let civilians handle evidence?"

"I think of you as more than a civilian, Hannah."

"But still . . ."

"If you'd like me to confiscate the book, I will. Is that what you want?"

"I didn't say that. But I don't understand your reaction. You're being so blasé."

"Hey, I'm an easygoing guy. I think we've already established that. And anyway, you broke the first code, you can probably handle this one just fine."

"Okay, if that's the way you want it."

Frank said, "All you have to do is promise you'll stay in close touch. You figure out anything, you're going to let me know. A lead, no matter how slight it might look, you call me. Can you live with that, Hannah?"

"I know about teamwork, Frank. I keep you informed, you keep me informed. It flows both ways."

"And, Hannah, I don't want you poking your nose in something, drawing your weapon, any of that."

"This isn't about embezzlement anymore," she said. "You understand that, don't you, Frank? Fielding wants to make a deathbed confession. Like I'm the one he thinks can pardon him."

He took a small swallow. Eyes scanning the open yard. Looking for something out there, something he didn't see.

"I'll give you my cell number," he said. "You've got to promise me you'll call if anything develops."

"Like old times. Me pestering you every hour of the day."

"Yeah, like old times."

"I knew it," she said. "I knew it all along. That bastard killed my parents."

"Yeah," he said. "It appears that way."

The dense bed of gray clouds had burned away and Frank was squinting through the glare.

"*Appears*, Frank? You heard him, the guy wants to spill his guts."

He nodded. Something going on behind his eyes she couldn't read.

"I'll write down that cell number."

He walked back to his car and got a pad and scribbled his number and brought it back.

"And listen, Frank. I don't care if the son of a bitch has only five minutes to live. If he killed Mother and Dad, I want him in jail. He can die on a goddamn prison cot. He might be looking for forgiveness, but I'll be damned if he's getting it from me."

"I know," Frank said. "I know."

Men were mowing the lawn. There were four of them in yellow shirts. Their company was called He-Man Lawn Service. They didn't look like he-men or bodybuilders. They were smoking and they had earrings and tattoos. They mowed the lawn quickly with fast sit-down machines.

Hal Bonner stood in the shadows of the Australian pines holding a weed-eater he'd taken from the back of the lawn truck. He ran the weed-eater back and forth along the fence line and watched Hannah Keller and the FBI agent leave the large empty house. A few feet away in the pines he'd parked his dirt bike. A brand-new Kawasaki he'd picked up after he arrived in Miami. He had a rental car and now he had the bike. Using one, then the other when it suited him, stashing his clothes and traveling gear in the trunk of the car. Leaving the car in a shopping-center parking lot across the street from where he'd bought his motorcycle.

He'd used some of Randy Gianetti's money to buy the bike. Randy would've liked it. It was a flashy red and it was fast and had knobby tires. It could go from zero to sixty in less than five seconds. He'd bought a red helmet too. A black sunshield. He liked the way he looked. Like a space warrior.

Hal used the weed-eater on the thick grass and watched the FBI agent stoop down next to Hannah Keller's car, talking to her through the window. He was in love with her. Hal could see this from the way he stood. He could see it in the way he hung around and watched her car as it drove down the steep hill. He could tell that this man wanted to have sex with Hannah Keller. Wanted to marry her and give her children.

Hal watched the FBI agent get into his small green sports car and start it. He watched him drive away. He stood there in the shadows and watched the house. This was not where J. J. Fielding was hiding. He didn't need to go inside to be sure of that. He could see what was happening on his palmtop computer. He watched the computer and he used the weed-eater, then he watched the computer some more. The old man he was seeking was in a hospital somewhere. He was sending Hannah Keller on a chase. From one place to another. To make sure she wasn't followed.

Hal wasn't stupid.

Once when he was young, his IQ had been measured, and on the morning when he was sent to the guidance counselor, the woman looked across her desk at him and then looked down at the sheet and then looked at him again and shook her head sadly like she couldn't bring herself to say the number out loud. She just kept shaking her head.

Finally Hal stood up and told the woman that it didn't matter whether the number was high or low. All that mattered was that Hal could kill the woman with his bare hands if he chose. He could strangle her right there, right then, and she was helpless to prevent it. That's all that mattered in the world, not numbers on a sheet of paper, whether they were high or low. He told her that. And she sat frozen behind her desk, staring up at him.

That night a social worker came to talk to his foster parents. A big black man who brought along two uniformed cops. The next morning Hal was put on a Greyhound bus and shipped to another small town in Indiana. Only because of some words he spoke to a woman across a desk.

This was before he had killed anyone. This was before he had used his hands the way he'd learned. He had only imagined killing at the time. He pictured it and with time the pictures grew clearer. They became so clear that finally he knew how to do the thing even though he had not done it yet. He could see it perfectly in his mind. And then he was doing it in real life. Seeing it in his mind and doing it exactly as he'd pictured.

He stood in the shadow of the pines and watched the house for another moment. Then he dropped the weed-eater and walked over to his motorcycle, and climbed on it. He kick-started it and rode through the dense stand of pines down to the road. He could see Hannah Keller's car up ahead. She was stopped at a traffic light.

The old man in the hospital bed was clever. He was playing a game. Being careful so Hannah could find him but no one else could. He was sending her secret messages, telling her what to do next. Hal could try to intercept one of the messages and go where it told him to go, get there before Hannah Keller, or he could simply continue to follow her. He had decided to follow her. That was his decision. Track her till she led him to the man who had stolen four hundred and sixty-three million dollars of his employers' money. His employers were impatient with Hal. They were giving him this one last chance to find Fielding, then they would fire him and hire someone else to do it. Hal had been searching for Fielding off and on for five years but with no success. This was as close as he'd come. The man sending messages to Hannah Keller, playing some kind of game.

Hal Bonner didn't play games. He never had. Not board games or sports, none of it. It was a waste of time. All that mattered was eating food and drinking water and staying strong so you could kill when it was necessary. Everything else was a waste of time.

People played games to have fun. He wasn't dumb, he understood that. Over the years he'd tried to figure out what fun was. He'd asked a lot of different people. Tell me what fun is. And they'd say things like, fishing is fun. Lying in bed, reading a good book on a rainy afternoon is fun. Sex is a lot of fun. But that didn't mean anything to Hal. He didn't believe there was such a thing as fun. He'd tried to watch games on television, but he usually fell asleep. Maybe he would ask Misty about fun. Hal believed it was a lie, one of the things people told themselves so they could keep on living. Like God. Like those things they told you in school. If you work hard, you will succeed. But it was a lie. Some people worked very hard. They shoveled coal or they welded, but they didn't succeed like the people who sat around in offices not working hard. It was a lie. Like God. Like fun. Like love. He'd ask Misty about it. She would know. At least she'd have something to say about it. She was a talker.

Misty was sticking in his head. The way her face looked. The way her voice sounded. Sassy and blunt, the way she hated her father for leaving her and she hated Hannah Keller for living the life she was supposed to live. The way she tried to talk Hal out of killing her, giving him reasons, one, two, three.

Hal was on his dirt bike riding down the street two blocks back of Hannah Keller's car and he was thinking of Misty Fielding. Seeing her in his head. A girl, her face, her body. It was the first time that had happened to him. First time he'd felt the thing in his chest, something burrowing down inside him, digging a hole, a small narrow den where it would curl up and be safe.

Hal was zipping through traffic. A red helmet, a red bike, black sun visor. And something small and warm nesting in his chest.

FIFTEEN

Hannah fired two quick shots, then, with four more squeezes of the trigger, she emptied the cylinder. To her right and left other handguns answered back, their concussions shaking the air.

She set the empty pistol on the shelf and stepped back. A suffocating pressure was tightening around her as if she had sunk to the ocean floor, the relentless press of gravity stealing her air.

It was eleven-thirty, and the firing range was busy. A half-dozen cops and a clean-cut gang at the far end that looked like FBI trainees, and a few other moms and pops keeping their skills honed for neighborhood crime watch.

This was her first time at the range since leaving the force. Until today it'd been five years without so much as fitting her hand around the grip of a pistol. Only a few moments earlier, as she'd unholstered Ed Keller's .357, she felt the panic begin to build. Looking out into that bright, fluorescent room, the pistol sagged in her hand and she had to marshal all her resolve to raise it and begin to fire.

With her heart still knocking out of rhythm, Hannah Keller raised the yellow shooting goggles to her forehead and mashed the button on the wall beside her station, and the paper silhouette slid toward her along its stiff wire.

As the target drew near, Marcus Shoenfeldt leaned around the partition from the adjacent firing station, lifted his ear protectors, and shook his head in wonder. There were no perforations in Hannah's target. All six rounds had sailed wide.

"A little rusty," she called out.

"I'll say." Marcus showed her a tight smile. "They find out about this, they're going to take back all your marksmanship medals."

These days Marcus Shoenfeldt had trimmed down to around four hundred pounds. Two hundred off his peak, when he was forced to spend most of his days reclining in a specially reinforced bed.

Back in high school before he'd bulked up, he and Hannah had been friends. They'd even dated once or twice, Marcus a shy kid, tongue-tied and clumsy. But a latent hunk nonetheless. All the girls could see it. He had the potential to turn into a matinee idol, a TV star, one of those square-jawed, dark-eyed men who haunted their girlish dreams.

By the time they met again, Marcus had tripled his weight and was barely able to navigate the halls of the Miami Police Department, where he did consulting work for the Crime Scene Division, a graphology technician. When she'd called him last night Marcus told her that Tuesdays were his gun days. It was part of his new regimen. On medical leave now, he'd adopted a rigid diet and an equally rigid schedule. For two hours on Tuesday mornings he did his target practice, then headed for the café a few doors down at the same shopping center and had a single cup of beef bouillon. She could come along if she liked.

Hannah slipped the .357 into its leather holster and she shook out her shooting hand, tried to massage away the bruising jolts from the deep tissues of her palm. Two booths down a uniformed Metro cop began firing a semiautomatic pistol and Hannah watched the flakes of paper flying from his target as the cop's bullets riddled the torso of the silhouette man.

Marcus stepped around the edge of Hannah's booth.

"Is that it?" he said, motioning at the copy of *First Light* that lay beside her leather holster. The novel was sealed inside a plastic Ziploc bag like a piece of crime scene evidence.

"Yes," she said, "that's it."

Marcus turned the book over to look at the jacket photo.

"You've aged," he said without a trace of humor.

The man with the semiautomatic was reloading, and the gallery was momentarily quiet.

"It happens," she said.

He shrugged—a man who'd long ago come to peace with his lack of social grace.

Marcus gave her a quick look, then picked up the Ziploc bag and held it up to the light and squinted as if it contained some rare and lethal specimen. His curly black hair was in a ponytail and ran halfway down his back. He wore a long-sleeved white T-shirt and denim dungarees and heavy brogans. The man who had been emerging those last two years from the husk of fat was darkly handsome, a Byronic dreamer that might adorn the cover of some historical romance novel. But it would probably take at least two more years of steady discipline before that handsome man stepped free of the corpulent giant before her.

"Thought you didn't believe in graphology," Marcus said. He turned the book over and studied Hannah's photograph again. "Hocus-pocus, I believe you called it once."

"I don't remember that."

"Oh, you said it. You told a goddamn reporter for Channel Six that a lot of people considered handwriting analysis hocus-pocus. And then he asked you if you were one of those people and you just smiled. That's the same as saying you believed it."

"Marcus, I need your help. That's why I called. If I thought it was hocus-pocus, I wouldn't have bothered."

"It's impulses in the brain," he said, "the little twitchy electrons that give you away. Stuff you can't control that reveals to the trained professional eye all sorts of things about what's going on inside you. Like body language. You can't control your tics, your gestures. Everything that's hidden away inside you, your thought patterns, your character, your criminal tendencies, it's always leaking out in subtle ways. Like the way the hand moves when it's writing. There's a scientific basis for this, Hannah. Yeah, sure there's a certain amount of subjectivity in analyzing handwriting. But god-damn it, it's not magic. It's not hocus-fucking-pocus."

"If you were so angry over what I said, why'd you agree to meet me?"

Marcus smoothed his palm across his cheek as if he were checking his shave.

"You don't like this place, do you?"

She asked him what he meant.

"This place, the gun range. All this shooting."

"I used to like it fine."

"But not now. This place gives you the creeps, all the bullets flying."

"Maybe not the creeps," she said. "But close enough."

"But you came here anyway to meet me. Whatever this is about, it's that important."

Hannah glanced down at her paper target riffling in the air-conditioned breeze.

"Yes," she said. "It's that important."

The patrons of Garcia's Café were mostly Cuban and they were in high spirits, eating and talking with the boisterous gusto of a fiesta crowd. Marcus withdrew a tiny sugar spoon from the breast pocket of his overalls and dipped it carefully into his bouillon. He brought the spoon to his mouth and inhaled the fumes rising off it, then with his eyes going dreamy, he closed his lips around the broth.

Hannah dabbled with her Caesar salad and watched Marcus as he pored silently over the pages of *First Light*, making noises in his throat that sounded like the moans and grumbles of a sleeping dog. Out of his pants pocket he fished a leather pouch and opened it and withdrew what looked like a jeweler's magnifying glass. He bent to various pages and peered at the mad scrawl. After a while, he came to the inside front pages where the numbers were written. He studied the scribbles for several moments, then drew a long breath and lifted his eyes and stared at her.

"What?" she said.

Marcus Shoenfeldt set his magnifying glass down next to his saucer. His gaze roamed the café for a moment as if he were surveying the place for eavesdroppers.

For a moment Marcus stared down at his steaming cup of bouillon, then he suddenly bent forward, leaning his heavy forearms against the small wooden table and glowered into Hannah's eyes.

"This some kind of trick?"

Hannah drew back in her chair.

"What're you talking about?"

"I'm talking about this." He thumped a thick finger against the cover of her book. "I'm talking about loops and tilts, pressure, size, width of margins, crossing *t*'s and dotting *i*'s, rhythm and regularity. I'm not some amateur, Hannah. This is what I do for a living."

"What's going on with you, Marcus?"

"Is this some kind of test the department put you up to? Somebody wants to put a turd in my file, so they send you out here with this little joke. Test my reflexes, see if I'm still sharp."

"No, Marcus. This is me and you. It's no setup. This is a book I found with some strange writing in it. And it's very important to me. I want to know everything I can about the guy who wrote this. Anything that might help me find out where he's hiding."

He sat back in his chair, not fully convinced.

"A guy didn't write this," Marcus said.

"What?"

The waitress came to the table and asked Marcus if his bouillon was okay.

"Terrific," Marcus said. "Best damn bouillon I ever had."

The waitress gave Hannah a pitying look and stalked away.

"Talk to me, Marcus."

He peered into her eyes with a cagey look. Then he stared at the waitress hurrying between tables.

"It was written by a woman, a badass woman," he said.

"From the tiny size of the script, the intense pressure, the extreme rightward slant of the letters, it's clear she's agitated, defiant, probably intensely disturbed."

"Disturbed as in unstable?"

Marcus looked at her with a hint of a smile.

"I'd say this lady is about as stable as a gyroscope on its last revolution."

"What else?"

"The buckle on her uppercase *K* indicates a strong ambition. A woman who's tough and resourceful, and willing to do whatever it takes to get where she wants to be."

"All that from the *K*?"

"Don't mock me. Not just the *K*. It's her full, clean lowercase *e* loops, the openness of the *o*'s and *a*'s. And the big hooks on the *H* and *E* show a hypersensitivity. A woman who can be badly wounded by destructive criticism. A dangerous combination, warring sides of her personality. Tough and ambitious, but hypersensitive. Insecure."

"A woman," Hannah said.

"That's right," said Marcus. "A hateful woman. Not much sympathy for others. Very smart, very cold."

"But why did you think this was some kind of trick?"

"Because this isn't real," he said.

"Isn't real?"

"The handwriting. It's faked."

"I'm not following you, Marcus."

"A person who writes something like these numbers, say, they'll have certain characteristics in their handwriting, certain things that show up over and over. And there's some of that here. That's how I can tell you a little about the woman who wrote this, because despite what she did to conceal herself, some of it leaks through. But there's a lot more of this that's artificial. It's inconsistent, like she was writing it for effect, trying to create an illusion."

"What illusion?"

"Like maybe she wanted you to think she was in a highly agitated state. But this wasn't written that way. It was composed very carefully. Written slowly and thoughtfully. If you ask me, someone's trying to con you, Hannah. Dupe you into believing something that's not true."

Hannah turned her head and looked at the next table. A heavy woman in a flowered dress was sitting with two young girls in pink frocks who appeared to be her granddaughters. All three were eating roasted chicken, laughing between bites, their hands greasy.

Marcus picked up his sugar spoon, licked it off, and dropped it back in his breast pocket. He slid the magnifier into its leather case and stood up.

"Well, I've got to go," he said.

"Already? We just got here."

"I should've told you when you called. I don't get out in public much. I can only take it for an hour or two, then I get these attacks. Panic things. Something happens in my belly, my timer goes off, I start getting dizzy and weird. I need to go home."

"Well, sure, okay. I understand."

"I'm trying to get better, but it's not easy."

"It's all right, Marcus. Really, it's fine. I need to go pick Randall up after school anyway."

"How's the little guy making out?"

"Randall's fine."

"He's talking now?"

"He's talking, yes."

"He's a good kid. It's sad he got traumatized like that."

"It was pretty bad," she said. "But he's just about over it now."

Marcus took a deep swallow and smiled at the back wall of the restaurant.

"I'd watch out if I were you, Hannah. The woman who wrote that shit in your book, she's serious trouble. She's one tricky customer."

"I'll be careful, Marcus. Thanks."

Without looking her way, he nodded mechanically, then turned and trudged toward the door.

SIXTEEN

Hal was in the waiting room of a dentist's office. Armando Lopez-Lima, DDS. Over the years he'd discovered that doctors' offices were good places to wait. No one bothered you. No one cared if you were there or not there.

He was sitting with five other people, all of them with toothaches. No one looked happy. Everyone was reading a magazine except for one young woman who was on a cell phone, talking in loud Spanish. He sat next to the window of the dentist office so he could see the door of the restaurant where Hannah was eating lunch. She was eating with a fat guy. A very fat guy. They had been in the gun range down at the shopping center and then they went to the restaurant and now the fat guy was walking out the door of the restaurant and heading across the parking lot.

Hal had been looking at the pictures in an issue of *National Geographic* he'd picked off the dentist's magazine rack, an article about bees. About a dance the explorer bee did when it returned to the hive after finding a patch of flowers. Bees had two different dances. One to tell the other bees that the flowers were nearby and another dance to tell the bees that the flowers were a long distance away. Inside the hive the other bees were arranged in a circle, all facing inward, and the bee with the flower information did his dance in the center of the circle with all his bee friends watching.

It was called a waggle dance because the dancing bee waggled his rear end in a certain way and made certain movements that told the other bees exactly which direction they should fly to find the new nectar. The dancing bee

showed them in his dance where the flowers were in relation
to the sun. The exact angle they should take to find them.

While waiting for Hannah Keller to finish lunch, Hal read
the article about bees three times. It took him that long to
understand everything. He still wasn't sure about how the
waggle dance worked, how that one bee told the other bees
the exact angle to take to get to the flowers. He was about to
read the article a fourth time when he saw the fat guy waddle
out of the restaurant.

He sat there a minute more watching the fat guy wedge
himself into his blue Ford. Hal didn't know what to do. He
wanted to know who the fat guy was. But he didn't want to
lose sight of Hannah either.

He also wanted to read the article about bees a fourth
time. But work came first. His job. To find J. J. Fielding and
recover the money. So he stood up and looked around the
waiting room at all the unhappy people waiting to see the
dentist.

A couple of them looked up at Hal, then looked quickly
back at their magazines. Hal decided to follow the fat guy.
He knew where Hannah Keller lived, and he was fairly sure
she would be going to pick up her kid at school and take him
back home, so that gave Hal a little while to follow the fat
guy and find out who he was. Plus, it occurred to him that he
could take the copy of *National Geographic* with him and
read the article about bees a fourth time later on. The recep-
tionist was behind a frosted glass window and hadn't even
noticed him when he came in and took a seat, so she probably wouldn't see him steal the magazine.

He walked to the door with the magazine in his hand.

Hal was proud of himself. Proud he'd figured out a way
to do two of the things he wanted to do. Two out of three.
Follow the fat guy, learn more about the dance of the bees.

Hal didn't care for bees in real life. He'd been stung a few
times and it hurt like hell. But he liked reading about them.
There were lessons to be learned from reading about
wildlife. Hal Bonner was a slow reader and had to read
things over and over before they finally sank in. But that was

okay. He didn't waste his time on other subjects, Hollywood stars or singers or athletes or current events. He was a specialist. He just read about animals and insects and birds. There was a time long ago when he'd been illiterate. In school he couldn't read much more than a few words here and there. None of it made much sense. He might've spent his whole life that way if he hadn't found that book with pictures of animals in it ten years ago. He was on an airplane, flying from one place to another, and the skinny book was in the seat pocket in front of him. Somebody had left it behind. It was a book for kids with big print and not many words, but Hal enjoyed it. The animals were brightly colored and some of them looked dangerous. Hunting, slinking low through the grass, pouncing on their prey. Hal studied the pictures carefully, but he wanted very much to read the captions below the pictures. He wanted to know about these golden animals, these red-faced creatures, these large winged birds. So right then he started to teach himself to read. He sounded out the words in his head like they'd tried to get him to do in school. He put his finger on each word until he'd brought it into his mind and knew what it meant. And now, ten years later, he didn't need to use his finger anymore. He knew a lot of words by sight. He was still a slow reader, but he could usually figure out most of the articles he wanted to figure out. It took him a while, but he could do it.

Sometimes he watched the nature shows on television, but he preferred reading, even though it was difficult. In books the pictures held still. You could study them, look at them as long as you liked, put yourself right there with the animal. On television everything happened too fast.

With the magazine in his hand, Hal walked out the door of the dentist office, and went down the walkway of the shopping plaza and got on his motorcycle. He tucked the magazine under the bungee cord on the seat. He watched the fat guy back out of his space and head out of the parking lot toward the main street. Hal kick-started the dirt bike and pulled on his helmet and flipped his dark visor down.

He thought about that bee coming back to the hive all excited by his discovery. Flowers, flowers, flowers. They're out there a hundred yards, just a little to the right of the sun, a bunch of daisies. He'd like to tell Misty Fielding about the bee dance. He thought she might like to know about the way they waggled their stingers in a certain way to communicate with the other bees. She would probably make a joke about that. She made jokes. Hal wasn't always sure what was funny and what was not, sometimes he laughed at the wrong places, but he liked that Misty had a sense of humor. She'd like the bee stuff, that one bee waggling in front of the other bees, shaking his stinger in their faces. He'd tell her about that later and she'd make a joke. He was almost sure of it.

Hal shifted through the gears. He kept the fat guy's car in sight. The motor racing between his legs, buzzing like a bee.

Just after noon on Tuesday, hour thirty-six of Operation Joanie. Thirty-six to go, and Frank didn't think he could make it till midnight tomorrow without strangling the whole idiotic bunch of them.

Frank, Helen, Andy Barth, Ackerman, and Roosevelt R. Jackson were in the back of the UPS truck being used today as the mobile headquarters. Rosie Jackson was Frank's boss, Special Agent in Charge of the Miami field office. First African-American to hold that post. Twenty-odd years earlier Rosie was starting quarterback for Coral Gables High when Frank Sheffield, outsized and outweighed by every lineman he faced, was Rosie's center. He snapped the ball into Rosie's hands, then dropped back to block the mean dumb linemen who were determined to tear off Rosie Jackson's helmet with his head still inside. Two seasons together and Frank didn't allow a single sack. Now it was Rosie's turn. For the last decade he'd been running interference for Frank. Among other things he composed Frank's yearly reviews with as charitable an interpretation of Sheffield's performance as one could hope for. They had a silent understanding. Frank wouldn't let his lack of ambition turn into gross negligence, and Roosevelt Jackson would do his best to see that Frank made it through to retirement, four more years.

Rosie wore dark cotton Dockers, a white button-down shirt, red tie. Sweating heavily as he usually did when he was out of the air-conditioning. He had a mountain of paperwork he should've been attending to back at the office, but apparently he wanted to have a firsthand look at the high-profile shenanigans taking place in his district. Helen, Andy, and the senator were coolly polite, but basically ignored Jackson. And after ten minutes or so, he was shooting Frank Sheffield looks. How the hell do you put up with these people?

Andy and Helen were both wearing their one-ear headsets, listening to the street chatter from the fifteen other agents scattered throughout the parking lot, the adjoining streets. Both choppers were aloft again, hanging back at a two- or three-mile distance. Even a motorcycle today, a big black Harley. Andy Barth sat at the computer console, tapping keys, changing screens.

"His name is Marcus Shoenfeldt," Rosie Jackson said. "He's with Miami PD, a handwriting technician, graphology. I believe he's on medical leave at the moment. Nice guy, a little weird around the edges."

"Handwriting expert?" said Helen. "Would someone please tell me why the hell she's having lunch with a handwriting expert?"

"She's being a good cop," Frank said. "Following the leads she's been given."

"What can she expect to learn from the goddamn handwriting?"

"Doesn't matter," Ackerman said. "If she wants to vary from the scenario, there's nothing we can do about it. Anyway, we're looking for Hal, remember? We're not concerned if Ms. Keller follows the program in lockstep fashion."

"Well, *I'm* concerned about it," Helen said. "Our locations were chosen very deliberately because they all have good, safe perimeters, we can see anyone coming or going, block all avenues of escape. Now this is getting too fluid, too chaotic. We need to get her back on track."

"You're something else, Shane," Frank said. "You cook up some cute little scheme in your quiet D.C. office and expect it to unfold on the streets just like you dreamed it up. That's a bit unrealistic, don't you think?"

"I know what I'm doing, Frank."

"Do you?"

"It's called Virtual Paradigms, Sheffield," said Andy Barth. "You wouldn't understand it."

"That complex, is it? Would go right over my head."

"You know anything about gaming theory, artificial intelligence programming?" Andy said.

"Gaming theory?" Frank said. "What, like video games?"

He glanced at Rosie Jackson. The big man was staring up at the roof of the UPS truck summoning his patience.

"Simulations," Andy said. "The Bureau has been using them for years. I guess they haven't made it to the boondocks yet."

"Oh, sure, simulations. The kind where you chase cartoon monsters down those narrow hallways, splatter their guts against the wall."

"A little more sophisticated than that, Sheffield."

"Jesus Christ. You people are a bunch of depraved tenyear-olds. You should be hanging out at a video arcade somewhere, not working the streets."

"Their success rate is more than ninety percent, Frank." Ackerman was rolling up the sleeves on his blue work shirt, watching the parking lot through the dark tinted window. "The program is a proven winner."

Helen gave Sheffield a barracuda smile.

"Frank fancies himself a humanist. Doesn't believe behavior can be reduced or explained. Isn't that right, Frank? Everyone's so complicated."

"Some people are."

"Wrong, Frank. Once you know the inner dynamics, what makes someone twitch, the one thing in their personality that overrides everything else, the rest is easy. Write them a part they can't resist, the one thing that motivates the hell out of them, then plug them into the scripts and away we go."

"Like dead frogs," Andy said. "Zap the right nerve, the leg jerks."

"Doesn't look to me like Hannah's playing along so neatly."

"Oh, sure, she's a little off track at the moment, but she'll get back to it. I'm not worried. She'll be back in the groove in no time. Just watch."

"Why riddles, Helen?"

"Riddles?"

"Yeah, why the bullshit riddles like some kind of high school scavenger hunt?"

"Think about it, Frank. You're a shrewd investigator."

"Why don't you just tell me, Shane? Save me the energy drain."

"She's a mystery writer, isn't she?"

"So?"

"So she likes puzzles."

"You ever bother to read one of her books?"

"I looked at them. Enough to get the idea."

"Well, I've read a couple, all the way through, and I could've told you, Helen, her books are about people, not plots. Not riddles."

"And your point would be what?"

"Well, what I think she's doing, Shane, and this is funny, this is very very cute, Hannah's not solving the riddle. She's not going after Fielding at all."

"Okay, hotshot, so what's she doing?"

"She's coming after you, Helen. The woman's tracking your ass down."

Helen met his eyes, gave him one of her death ray blasts. Frank got his shield up in time, deflected it back at her with a grin.

"Hey, Sheffield," Andy said. "When you were driving the UPS truck yesterday, didn't you have a guy behind you on a motorcycle? Agent Scruggs wants to know."

"Yeah," Frank said. "A tailgating asshole on a red bike."

"Scruggs is on the west end of the shopping center. Says a guy fitting Hal's general description just got on a red dirt bike and drove out of the parking lot. You want to track him, Helen?"

"He's leaving the scene?"

"That's right. Going east on Bird Road."

"Where was he? How long was he in the vicinity? I need more information."

"Scruggs said he came out of a dentist's office."

Helen scowled at Sheffield for a moment, then shook her head.

"Forget the motorcycle. Guy had a cavity filled, that's all."

"Target has left the restaurant," Andy said. "Hannah's outside, walking over to a pay phone. Looks like she's going to make a call."

Helen kept Frank in her glare for a second or two longer, then turned away, raised her binoculars, and focused them out the tinted window.

"Christ," she said. "Now what?"

"We should put somebody on that dirt bike." Frank was trying to bring the image back, the guy he'd seen out his big rearview mirror. But he was pretty sure the biker had on a dark visor.

"He's leaving the scene," Helen said. "He's not our boy."

"Unless he made us," Frank said.

"He didn't make us."

"I say we put somebody on him. We can spare one guy. Use one of the choppers."

"Drop it, Sheffield. This is my call."

"And you're making the wrong one."

"All right, you two," Ackerman said. "Put a lid on it. Keep your focus."

Helen strafed Sheffield with another look, then turned her binoculars back to the scene.

Frank stepped behind her, watched over her shoulder as Hannah looped a strand of hair over her ear and pressed the phone to it. At this distance it was a little hard to see, but it looked like a lovely ear. A guy could whisper into an ear like that. Sweet nothings. The mumbo jumbo of romance. Not something Frank was particularly good at, but with a woman like Hannah, he might find the inspiration. He could even see pushing the envelope of his three-week romance routine. Maybe extend it to a month, two months. What the hell. His shoulder was still tingling from last night. That had to mean something.

SEVENTEEN

The business card Hannah found at the Bayshore house belonged to an Anna Marie Salvano, a broker for Weber-Sloan Realty. Hannah called her from the pay phone outside of Garcia's Café. Got Anna Salvano's voice mail. She left her name, her cell phone number, said she was very interested in some property Anna had listed.

Then she called local information and asked for the number for Maude Fielding and was told that there was no such listing.

"Anything close?" Hannah asked.

"There's an M. A. Fielding on Flagler Street. And a Martin Fielding in Hialeah."

Hannah got the number for M.A. on Flagler.

After seven or eight rings, ready to hang up, she heard a drowsy female voice answer. Too young to be J.J.'s wife.

"I'm looking for Maude Fielding," Hannah said.

The young woman was silent.

"Are you there?"

"I'm here," she said. Irritable, suspicious. "You got the wrong number, lady. There's no Maude Fielding here."

"I'm sorry to bother you."

But Hannah kept the phone at her ear. Something in the girl's voice wasn't right.

A second or two went by, then the girl said, "So whatta you want with her?"

"Is this her number or not?"

"I want to know who the hell I'm speaking to."

"I'm an old friend of hers. Trying to get back in touch."

"What old friend? Give me a name."

"Hannah Keller."

The girl cleared her throat. It sounded like she was fumbling with the receiver. When she spoke again her voice was tense.

"I asked you what you wanted with Maude Fielding."

"I want to talk to her, ask her some questions."

"About what?"

"It's a personal matter. Is Maude Fielding there or not?"

After a few seconds of silence, the girl hung up.

Hannah stood there for a moment looking at the receiver. She was just putting it back on the hook when her cell phone rang.

Hannah stepped beneath the awning of Garcia's Café, out of the harsh midday sun. As she opened her phone, she looked through the large plateglass window at the two young girls in pink frocks. They'd finished their lunch and now their grandmother was talking to someone at an adjacent table. One of the little girls grinned at Hannah and waved her fingers. Hannah waved her fingers back.

"You're interested in seeing some property?" Anna Maria Salvano said.

Hannah said yes she was and gave her the Bayshore address.

"Oh," Anna Maria said. "That one."

"Is there a problem?" The little girl in the restaurant was winking at Hannah. Her left eye, then her right. Showing off a new skill.

"Well, I can't get you into that house till Friday."

"Friday? Why Friday?"

"That's when it's available again."

"It's rented till Friday?"

"That's right. A short-term rental. Just a few days. A movie or commercial or something. I'm not sure."

Hannah was feeling giddy. It'd been so long since she'd conned an honest citizen out of information. She was out of shape, winded already.

"I need to act today," she said.

"Today? No, I don't think that's going to be possible."

"Why not?"

"Well, beside the fact that it's rented, I have two closings this afternoon. Even if we could get permission from the client to let you see the property, I can't get away from the office."

"Well, that's too bad," Hannah said. Scrambling, putting herself in Erin Barkley's head for a moment, a quick hit of her audacity. "Because, you see, Ms. Salvano, I'm representing a gentleman from Zurich and I'm only going to be in town today. The Bayshore house is exactly what he's looking for. What're they asking for the place anyway?"

The little girl was pressing her nose against the glass, mashing it flat for Hannah's amusement. Her grandmother was still turned to the nearby table.

"A million two," Anna Maria said. "But I think we can get them down from that. The house needs considerable updating, a little TLC, if you know what I mean."

"A million two is within my parameters," Hannah said. "Perhaps you could give me the number of the woman who's renting it and I can speak with her directly."

Chancing that it was, in fact, a woman. Possibly the same woman whose handwriting was in her book, the woman apparently aiding J. J. Fielding with his plan. Maybe Maude, maybe someone Fielding had met since going on the run.

"Oh, I couldn't do that," Anna Maria said. "Our clients' confidentiality is quite important to us."

"Listen, I spoke to her today," Hannah said. "I was at the Bayshore house. We hit it off nicely. She offered me her phone number, but I said no, I'd rather speak to the realtor first. The normal protocol."

"You met her? You were at the house today?"

"That's right. All I need is a quick look inside, make sure the layout's right. I would've done it this morning but she was on her way out and couldn't let me inside at the time. If there's a movie being made there I didn't see any evidence of it. The place was dead quiet."

Now the other little girl was smushing her nose against the windowpane. Two greasy streaks against the clear glass.

"I was told we couldn't show the house again until Friday."

Stubborn woman, sticking with the rules. But a little crack was showing in her voice, wiggle room.

"Well," Hannah said, "I'm pretty sure the lady would be willing to let me walk through with her. As I say, we had a nice rapport. If you give me her number, I'd be willing to call her, try to set something up for this afternoon."

"I don't know," Anna said. "It's certainly not standard practice."

"Come now." Hannah, playing her part, a brisk business-woman with major money to spend. Not going to dillydally with underlings. "If I like what I see, I can leave a written of-fer at your office by six this evening. How would that be?"

Anna took another moment. Probably doing the math on her commission, six percent of a million two.

"All I have for her is a cell number," Anna Salvano said. "It's not local."

Hannah waited. Let her silence do the work.

"I should really be the one to call her," the realtor said.

"Listen, Anna. I'm looking at one other property, maybe I should just concentrate on that one and let this drop. Frankly, the realtor for the other listing was a lot more re-ceptive."

"Okay, all right then," Anna said. "If you want to call her, I guess it wouldn't hurt." And she gave her the number.

Hannah said, "The young woman told me her name, but I forget what it was. Judy, Margaret. I'm so bad with names."

"Helen," Anna said. "Helen Shane."

Hannah thanked her again and promised to call back as soon as she'd met with Helen.

Behind the plateglass window the grandmother had turned back to her misbehaving girls. She was lecturing them sternly. One of the girls was crying, the other grinning at Hannah.

Hannah punched Helen Shane's number into her cell

phone. It rang once, then there were a series of clicks, some
kind of elaborate forwarding system, then a woman's
brusque voice said, "Go."

"Helen?"

There was a second's hesitation.

"Who is this?"

"I think you've been trying to get in touch with me."

Slipping into Erin Barkley mode, ballsy, fast talker, quick
with the bullshit.

"I said, who is this?"

"I thought maybe we could just forget this Internet bullshit. You and I could just talk directly. Doesn't that make
more sense? Woman to woman. Tell me where J. J. Fielding
is hiding out. Maybe we could work out a deal."

Hannah was fully prepared to offer a spectacular bribe, or
threaten the woman with jail time for aiding and abetting,
whatever it took. Winging it, rolling along in high gear.

But the connection clicked off.

Hannah dialed the number again but it was busy. She
waited a second, redialed, still busy. Everyone hanging up
on her today.

She'd probably been too direct, stayed too close to the
truth. Probably should have given them an alias, a better
cover story. A little out of practice, not as quick and nimble
as Erin after all.

She snapped her phone shut and was turning away from
the window when out of the edge of her vision she saw the
grandmother lurch backward in her chair and tumble to the
floor, and then inches from Hannah's face, the smeared pane
of plateglass splintered into thousands of diamond sparkles.
The glass hanging in place for a second, then collapsing in a
sheet of glittery chaos. Beautiful and strange and so utterly
surprising that Hannah simply froze before the shattered
window trying to absorb the scene, standing there for several
dizzy moments until a few inches from her head another
slug blasted the wood siding and sprayed splinters onto the
front of her blouse.

Then she was crouched behind the hood of a green

Lexus, old habits finally switching on. She had the .357 out and was tracking it slowly back and forth across the parking lot. Tires squealed on the asphalt, men stumbled out of shops up and down the plaza. Inside the restaurant there were shouts and shrieks, china broke, tables overturned. A UPS truck moved slowly across the lot.

Hannah squinted along the barrel of her pistol, inching it from left to right, then back again. But she heard no more shots, saw no one with a weapon, no one at all. Behind her, through the splintered glass, the two girls were huddled around their grandmother. One of them was staring at Hannah, her lips drawn back into a snarl of anguish and blame as if she believed this horror was somehow Hannah's fault. Which, almost certainly, it was.

"Stay right where you are, Sheffield."

When the gunfire began Ackerman didn't hesitate. He marched directly to the rear of the van and took up his position, blocking the door. In his khakis and neatly pressed work shirt, his arms crossed over his chest, he looked like the bouncer at some preppy dance. Ackerman outweighed Frank by fifty pounds, and it looked like he meant to use every ounce of it to keep him from getting by.

"You can't go out there," Helen said. "You'll blow the whole thing. This could be Hal testing to see if Hannah's got protection. We can't show ourselves. It's absolutely crucial."

Frank was staring into the senator's hard brown eyes. The glower he used so often to frighten generals wasn't having much effect on Frank.

"Jesus Christ, she's pinned down, Shane. Your people aren't doing anything."

"She's okay. She's not hit. The show's over."

Helen was at the tinted window, scanning the lot with binoculars.

"You're just going to let this go down? Christ, you got a woman out there drawing fire, innocent civilians in harm's way, and you're more concerned about safeguarding your goddamn operation?"

"That's right, Frank," Ackerman said, pointing a stubby finger at Sheffield's chest, then jabbing him once. "We have higher concerns. Now calm down and step back."

"The police can handle this," Helen said. "They're on their way."

"The guy could still be out there, working his way in for a kill shot. You're just going to leave her hanging in the wind."

"It may not even be about her," Helen said. "It could be stray gunfire for all we can tell."

"A white Chevrolet Caprice," Andy called. "That's the shooter's car. We got a visual on the plates. It's left the scene, going west on Bird Road."

"You see, Frank? There's nothing to worry about. Your precious Hannah is safe."

"Rosie?" Frank gave him a fierce look.

"It's not my call, Frank."

"They're on your turf."

"I'm outranked."

"Jesus Christ, you got fifteen people on the ground, all in this one-block area, and no one's going to try to stop this guy?"

"They have their orders," Helen said. "We'll pass the ID onto the local cops, let them handle it."

Frank took a step toward the door.

"Whatever the shooting was, it's over now, Frank." Ackerman poked a stiff finger into Sheffield's chest. "I can't let you go out there. The integrity of the operation is our only concern."

"Fuck the operation."

Frank snatched Ackerman's right wrist and swiveled hard, wrenching the big man forward. And all that kayaking must've done something for his arms and shoulders, because the senator came sprawling toward him, a large, ungainly mass of machine-tightened muscle stumbling across the narrow space of the van.

Sheffield was dodging past him when Ackerman slashed a wild right hand toward Frank's face, trying for an eye-gouge. Some ancient football cheap shot they must've taught at Notre Dame back in the old days.

Frank ducked away, but the senator's fingernails still clawed his neck. A scalding gash. Then purely out of reflex, with absolutely no malice, Frank swiveled and dug a right hand into the senator's gut. Not as muscled as it looked. A doughy inch or two before Frank's fist met any resistance.

Rosie Jackson, Special Agent in Charge, jumped forward, caught the senator by the shoulders, kept him from pitching headlong into the side wall, then settled him onto the floor where he sat gasping. Roosevelt shook his head.

"Not good, Frank. Not good at all."

Frank swung back to the door, but now Shane was in his way. She'd drawn her weapon, aiming the Glock at his gut.

"Stay put, Sheffield. You step out that door and the whole thing comes crumbling down."

"Come on, Helen. Don't give me an excuse to hurt you too."

"If you want to go down in flames, fine. But I won't let you take the rest of us with you. You go out there, you put Hannah in serious jeopardy."

"You already put her there. I'm going to try to get her out."

"No, Frank. I can't let you do it."

"You people aren't going to leave her alone till she's played this out every step of the way. So I'm going to be her escort from here on. Don't worry, I'll make sure she stays inside the dotted lines, plays out the rest of this bullshit scenario. Now get out of my way."

Frank reached out and nudged the pistol aside, opened the door, and stepped past Helen Shane into the parking lot. He looked back at her.

"That was her on the phone, wasn't it? That was Hannah."

Helen tried to keep her face empty. But Frank could see a twitch in the corner of her mouth.

"You guys need me more than you thought."

"Do it the way it's written, Sheffield. You step outside the program, there's no guarantee we can protect you."

Frank gave her the two-finger salute.

"I'll be out of radio contact, so don't bother trying to give me any orders. So long, kids."

And he turned and sprinted through the cars and innocent civilians toward the spot where he'd seen Hannah drop.

EIGHTEEN

When she saw Frank Sheffield coming across the parking lot, tan slacks, a black polo shirt, ambling along casually as if he were headed to Garcia's Café for lunch with nothing more serious on his mind than fried plantains and black beans and rice, Hannah closed her eyes and shook her head to clear the image, certain it was some kind of panic-induced mirage.

Then Frank was there, standing over her, giving off a faint whiff of cologne, a musky lime.

"Let's get out of here before the cops come and we're stuck all afternoon."

"Jesus Christ, Frank. Get down."

"The shooter's gone."

She peered out at the lot. People hustling to their cars. Others ducking behind shelter.

"You're sure of that?"

"He was in a white Chevy Caprice. He's gone."

"You saw him?"

"I saw the car. Called it in. Come on, Hannah, let's move."

With a hand on her elbow, he helped her up from her crouch.

Sirens had begun to wail in the distance. The two girls in the pink frocks were both crying now, people bent over their grandmother.

"Where's your car parked?"

She motioned with her chin along the front row. He

steered her toward the Porsche amid the tire-squealing turmoil in the lot.

"You've been following me."

He hesitated a moment, watching a skinny man on a big black Harley rumble past. Then took her elbow again and hustled her on toward the car.

"Okay, yes. I was tailing you."

"You didn't trust me. You thought I'd manufactured this whole thing."

"I was concerned," he said. "Concerned for your safety."

She gave him a disbelieving frown. They were at the car. She clicked the locks open.

"Can you drive?" he said. "Or should I?"

"What? You're going to leave your car here?"

"Don't worry about it, Hannah. Can you drive?"

"I can drive. Of course I can drive. You think I'm some fragile flower, a couple of bullets whizzing by my face is going to make me too weak to drive?"

"So drive," he said.

She got in the car and he eased into the passenger seat.

They passed the EMS truck on their way out of the lot.

She swerved into traffic, headed east to the Palmetto Expressway, gunned it up the ramp faster than she needed to, burning some rubber. Frank looked over at her, tightened his seat belt, but said nothing. She jumped into the speed lane and stayed ahead of the traffic till the expressway ended and emptied out onto Dixie Highway.

"Okay, okay, so you're a tough cookie. I'm convinced."

"Am I scaring you, Frank?"

"Scared isn't the word I would've chosen. I was thinking more along the lines of terrified."

She slowed, cutting into the shady neighborhoods of Pinecrest, large ranch-style homes on acre lots, taking them south, then east, until they hit the flashing yellow lights of a school zone and she pulled off onto the shoulder amid a throng of vans and big SUVs. She parked, turned off the engine. They sat in silence for a moment.

Frank said, "You're the only Porsche."

Hannah's pulse was still staggering. Breathing off the top of her lungs, unable to get a full breath.

"I'm not exactly the soccer-mom type. Thirty years in Miami, I haven't needed four-wheel drive yet."

"So you buy a two-seater," Frank said. "No room for a third party."

"Randall can squeeze into the jump seat."

"But you see my point. You pay all this money for a car, it's a pretty blatant statement. Two seats, that's all I require. Just me and my boy, no room for anyone else."

Hannah glanced at Frank. His smile was faltering around the edges.

"Suddenly you get serious."

"Just making conversation," he said. "Distracting you a little with my psychological acumen."

"I like two-seaters, Frank. I like sports cars, always have, something I inherited from my father. He always wanted a Porsche, but he could never afford one. So now that I can, I decided to indulge myself. Nothing more complicated than that. It's not symbolic, it's not a statement to the world. It's just a car."

"A nice car."

"Yeah," she said. "A damn nice car."

"With only two seats."

A Pinecrest police cruiser pulled up a half a block ahead, and switched on its flashing blue lights. The female officer got out and stood on the edge of the road watching the traffic pass slowly in front of the school. Going to let it flash for the next hour, slow down speeders.

"Was the guy in the white car shooting at me, Frank?"

"Hard to tell. But I doubt it."

"Two shots, both of them close. I'd say it's a pretty safe bet."

"In this town, who knows? He could've been signaling for a left turn."

"Both shots missed me by less than a foot."

"Yeah, well. Could be a coincidence."

"You're a big believer in coincidences, are you?"

"We'll know something when the plates get back."

"They'll be stolen," Hannah said. "They always are."

"Man, you're glum."

"I think I've got something to be glum about."

"You're alive. The shots missed. *Carpe diem*."

"*Carpe* your own *diem*. I'm dealing with it the best I can."

The school bell began to blare and almost immediately a sea of kids broke from the side doors, pouring into the playground. Hannah bent the rearview mirror down to look at her face, rubbing at the skin around her eyes to smooth away any remaining traces of panic.

"You look fine," Frank said. "Kind of tight around the edges, but other than that, Randall won't know what happened unless you tell him."

"No one's going to tell him anything."

"And what's my cover story? Why am I here?"

"You're helping me find J. J. Fielding."

"You told him about that? He knows what's going on?"

"Randall's the one who decoded those numbers in the book. He knows. I couldn't hide it from him if I tried."

"Whatever you want," Frank said. "You're the parent."

"I certainly am."

On the other side of 124th, Randall was waiting with a group of children and mothers for the crossing guard to stop traffic. He wasn't talking to anyone. He wasn't looking around. Frank got out of the car just as the group was crossing.

Randall was wearing baggy blue jeans and a green long-sleeve shirt, the tail hanging out in the sloppy fashion of the moment. He walked with the same loose-gaited stride as the other boys, the cocky strut of the ghetto, a don't-fuck-with-me insouciance that seemed sadly comic in this privileged neighborhood.

Frank stood beside the car, holding the door open.

As Randall approached, Frank put out hand for a shake or high-five, but Randall gave him a distrustful once-over, then dipped his head down to take a look at Hannah.

"You okay, Mom?"

"Fine," she said. "We're just working on something, Frank and I. He's coming over to the house for a while."

Randall sighed, then he let the front seat down and climbed into the narrow jump seat.

Frank got in, buckled up.

Hannah cranked the engine, eased out into the traffic.

"You're an FBI agent," Randall said.

"Twenty-one years," Frank said. "And counting."

Randall leaned forward.

"So how many people have you killed?"

Hannah stopped at the four-way street, waited her turn.

"That's not polite, Randall, asking something like that."

"Why not?"

"It's okay," Frank said. "The answer is none, a big zero. I stepped on a few cockroaches around my motel room, but beyond that, no, it's been a pretty nonviolent career."

"I thought that was why people became cops, so they could shoot people."

Hannah took a long breath and let it out. Wincing at the acid in his voice.

"Oh, yeah," Frank said. "Now I remember, there was this one guy I killed a few years ago. It almost slipped my mind. The guy was so short."

"Short?" Randall said.

Hannah slowed for the light at Ludlam Road, waiting behind a UPS truck.

"Yeah, this guy was incredibly short. Fantastically, amazingly short. This guy was so short if he stood in water up to his waist he'd drown."

Randall craned forward to get a look at Frank's face, see if he was smiling.

"He was so short," Frank said, "he could drop his wallet and pick it up without bending over. This guy was so short he used to get armpit stains on his shoes. In fact, the guy was so damn short he had to climb up on a ladder just to eat a pancake."

"That's goofy," Randall said.

"Yeah, that's what I thought too," Frank said. "So I shot him. Man, this guy was so short, when I shot him, he didn't even fall down."

"That's not funny," Randall said. "You shouldn't make jokes about shooting people."

Frank turned in his seat, gave Randall a quick look.

"Now that, young man, is the first sensible thing you've said."

Hannah looked over at Frank. He turned back around and stared straight ahead out the windshield. In her rearview mirror she could see her son's face. She knew the look. Randall was pissed. Thinking hard of some rejoinder, some slashing irony. But after a moment his face went slack. He'd given up. He knew he'd been outwitted, something Hannah rarely managed. Outmaneuvered by humor, joked into submission by an FBI agent.

She drove silently the five remaining blocks to her house on Pinecrest Lane, feeling the strain in the air, the unspoken alpha dog tension between these two males.

"Pretty day," she said, as she was pulling in the brick driveway.

Frank hummed his agreement. Randall was silent.

Frank got out first, held the door open for Randall, but he stayed in the jump seat until Hannah opened her door, then he climbed out through her side. He marched past her up to the back door, used his own key to let himself in, and stalked through the kitchen and dining room heading back to his computer. Frank followed Hannah into the house and watched her as she set her purse and keys on the kitchen table.

"Well, I certainly made a good impression," he said.

"You were fine."

"Was I? I thought maybe I was a little brusque."

"You were fine. Funny and fine. Exactly brusque enough."

"I say things sometimes, I don't know how it's going to sound till it's already out there. Low impulse control. Works okay at parties, but it's not exactly a treasured skill in day-to-day life."

"You thirsty, hungry?"

"Hey, this is some house. Oozing with character. Tin roof, wood siding, you don't see that much anymore. Nice kitchen, that old-fashioned country look, oak floors, cherry cabinets."

"Charm is my middle name."

"A Coke would be nice, or a sandwich if you got one. I missed lunch."

"Yeah, too busy standing around parking lots spying on people."

Hannah opened the refrigerator, took out some sliced turkey, Swiss cheese, lettuce, tomato, pickles, mustard, a can of Coke.

"Who was the big guy? The one you were having lunch with."

"Marcus Shoenfeldt's his name. I wanted him to look at the handwriting, see what he could tell me. He does graphology for Miami PD, an old friend."

"And?"

"Toasted or regular?" She held up the loaf of whole wheat.

"I don't care, surprise me."

"Marcus claimed the handwriting was done by a woman. A somewhat unbalanced woman. Mentally unstable."

Frank grinned. He leaned his elbows on one of the counters. She watched him as his gaze prowled the room, the row of brightly colored Ball jars lining the tops of the shelves. A couple of philodendron vines running around the window.

"Why is that funny?"

"Not funny, it's just that I like your style. You don't let Fielding dictate the shots. He's trying to get you to follow the stuff in the book, solve the riddle, go from point A to point B, around the Stations of the Cross or some bullshit, and you're off at the gun range analyzing the handwriting. That's good independent thinking."

"Marcus said the handwriting is fake. Meant to look one way when actually it's another."

"Fake?"

"The woman who wrote it wanted to appear agitated but in truth she was very deliberate. Like some kind of con."

"All that from the handwriting?"

"This guy is good."

"Well, he's big. I saw that much."

"Big and good," she said.

Hannah put the bread in the toaster oven, got out a plate. Took a handful of ice from the freezer and dumped it into a glass.

"Okay, you're all set," she said. "Here's the stuff. This is a make-it-your-own-damn-self household."

"Great."

Frank moved over to the counter and started assembling the sandwich. Heavy on the mustard, an inch of turkey slices. Big eater. Of course it had been a long time since she'd had a man in her kitchen. Her dates were usually the fancy-restaurant type, trying to impress her. None of them had gotten as far as making sandwiches back at her house.

"Listen, I should go check on Randall. He's taking this hard. Doesn't want me chasing after this stuff 'cause it brings back all the bad memories."

"And all of a sudden there's this big bad FBI agent hanging around," Frank said. "He's not exactly rapturous about that either."

"I'll be right back," she said. "Then we can sit down with the book, go over the code, figure out the next step."

"It's a date," he said.

Hannah shot him a look. Frank with an innocent twinkle in his smile.

"I didn't mean date-date. I meant like it's a deal. You know, like that."

"This is not social, Frank. I'm one hundred percent dead serious about this."

"So am I, Hannah. As serious as I get."

"You gave Fielding's Web address to your computer jocks?"

"I did."

"I suppose you haven't heard anything yet."

"Apparently it takes a while to track this back to its source. It's a good deal more complicated than a phone trace. They're working on it. Top priority."

"We should go back on-line," she said. "Keep monitoring Fielding's site. I just hope he doesn't die before I can get my hands around his throat."

Frank poured his Coke and as the foam died he took a bite of his sandwich. A layer of pickles, Swiss cheese, lettuce, a thick slice of tomato. Having a guy like this around would double her grocery bills. He tore off a sheet of paper towel and wiped the mustard off his mouth.

"Something worries me," she said.

"Yeah?"

"Fielding mentioned my name."

"So?"

"It was only my first name, so it's not that important. But who knows how long he's been on the Net, broadcasting his bullshit. He might have mentioned my whole name before. Might've mentioned Miami. Given out my street address, for all we know."

Frank took another bite of his sandwich and gave her a so-what shrug.

"In case you've forgotten, Frank, other people are after Fielding. If they found out about that Web site, that Fielding was sending some woman secret messages about how to locate him, they'd be on my tail in a second."

He set the sandwich down, wiped his mouth again.

"You mean the drug people."

"That's right, the drug people. Those happy-go-lucky fellows from Cali."

"I doubt they pay a lot of attention to the Internet down there. Not much surfing going on in Colombia."

"You're sure of that, Frank?"

"Not sure, but I think it's a pretty safe bet."

"There must be a way to check previous transmissions on a Web site like that. Randall would know how to do it. If I could bully him into it."

Frank took a long breath, lowered his eyes to the floor as if he were hiding his reaction.

"Maybe it's my imagination," she said, "but I've had the feeling in the last couple of days that I was being watched. Maybe followed."

He lifted his eyes.

"Yeah? Why do you say that?"

"I saw a guy yesterday and then again today."

"What guy?"

His lips were tightening.

"Yesterday in the Gables, walking down the street I got a glimpse of this guy in a deli, he had a motorcycle helmet sitting up on the counter next to him."

"Motorcycle helmet."

"Bright red with dark visor."

"Yeah? What else?"

"I was a little spooked at the time, had a little prickle on the neck like I was being spied on. This guy with the helmet just caught my eye for a second and I passed on. I forgot all about him until this morning after I left the Bayshore place. Then I saw a guy behind me in traffic, a few cars back on a dirt bike, and he was wearing a red helmet. He came and he went, but he was back there for a good while."

"No other description of him?"

"What? Do you know this guy, Frank?"

"Did you get a look at him, Hannah? In the deli when you were passing by. Did he have a beard, long hair, what?"

"Close-cropped hair, I think. Other than that, no. I just got a quick glimpse."

"Listen, can I use your phone?"

"Sure. But what's going on, Frank?"

"Probably nothing. But maybe you're right. Maybe some Cali guys have come to town. I just need to check in, pass this along. Have them put it on the street."

"Put what on the street? A guy on a motorcycle, buzz cut. What good's that going to do?"

"Look, I'll just be a minute."

"Is someone trying to kill me, Frank?"

He looked at her for a long moment and said nothing. His lips twitched as if he was struggling to give her a consoling grin but couldn't manage it.

"Phone's in the living room," she said. "Take your time. I need to talk to Randall anyway."

Frank said, "Nobody's trying to kill you, Hannah. Those shots, they weren't about you."

"You're sure about that?"

"I'm sure. Absolutely."

He nodded and after a second she nodded back. But he wasn't sure. She could see it in his naked eyes. For a career FBI guy, Frank Sheffield was one lousy liar.

Shane answered with a quick, "Go."

"Those plates on the shooter's Chevy Caprice. You get them back yet?"

"Is that you, Sheffield?"

"The plates, Shane. Tell me."

"Stolen from a hotel parking lot on Miami Beach. A rental car registered to a tourist from Europe."

"You got an all-points on the car, right?"

"The shooter dumped the car two blocks from the shopping plaza. Miami PD is working the area right now, checking for witnesses."

"You should've chased him, Shane. We had the manpower."

"Miami PD is doing the fiber and prints now. If there's anything in the car, we'll know in a few hours."

Frank said, "So are you guys still mad at me?"

She paused a second or two, then said, "You assaulted a United States senator, Frank."

"I believe what happened was a civilian was trying to interfere with a federal agent in the performance of his duties."

She said, "I think you better start planning your retirement."

"The guy on the motorcycle," he said. "Hannah's spotted him twice. Yesterday in the Gables and this morning leaving the Bayshore address. Probably the same guy we saw at the shopping plaza."

Helen was silent.

"But he left the scene," she said finally. "A long time before she did."

"Like I said, Helen, he probably made us. But that's our guy. Close-cropped hair. Red helmet, dark sun visor, red dirt bike."

Helen covered the receiver and spoke to someone. He couldn't make out her muffled words.

When she came back she said, "All right, we can run all recent purchases or reported thefts of red dirt bikes."

"Sure," Frank said, "for all the good it'll do. The guy's not that dumb."

"You got some other idea?"

"I'm hanging up, Shane. I've got to get back to work."

"What're you doing now, Frank? Where are you taking this?"

Frank leaned around the door, peered down the hallway, but it was empty. Hannah was still back there with Randall.

"I'm going to get Hannah back to your script, Shane. Point A, point B. Will that make you happy?"

"Frank, you're fucked, any way you look at it. If you think going back to the plan will get you out of this, you're dead wrong. When this is over, there's going to be a full review at the most senior level. Believe me, Frank, you're totally fucked. Kiss your pension good-bye. You'll be lucky to dodge jail time."

Frank saw Hannah appear in the doorway of Randall's room. Standing there talking to the kid, a few last words.

"Nice talking to you, Shane. Oh, by the way, the handwriting guy, he analyzed your scribbling. I got the skinny anytime you want it, your full profile. Sounds to me like the guy's got a pretty good handle on you. The short version is, he thinks you should probably increase your visits to the shrink from two times a week to three."

"Fuck you, Frank."

"I'll be talking to you, sweet pea."

She clicked off before he had a chance.

NINETEEN

Hal Bonner followed the fat man's dark blue Ford through traffic a few miles east of the shopping center to a neighborhood of two-bedroom houses with red tile roofs, and one-car garages. A big shady tree out in the front yard of every one. Sidewalks, fences in the back. Dogs barking. Some tricycles and swing sets and statues of Catholic saints inside glass domes. People off at work doing whatever people at work did.

Driving through traffic, Hal decided he hated Miami. In most ways it was the same as Milwaukee and Atlanta and Chicago, same burger places, same pizza places, chicken and pancake places, same gas stations, same Wal-Marts. But there was something different here. It was hotter, stickier than anywhere he'd been. Even South America. The air smelled like melting asphalt and concrete. His skin couldn't breathe. His lungs wouldn't fill. And the way people drove their cars. Everyone angry, everyone swerving left and right, looking for any gap, any advantage. Hal felt his heart beating. The thump of it against his ribs. Something he'd not felt before in any other town. The heat, the pushy drivers, the brightness in the sunlight. Hal's heart was beating. It was loud in his ears. It didn't usually beat. Usually it was silent inside him.

Ahead of him on the shady street, the blue Ford swung into a driveway and Hal drove on past the house and stopped at the next intersection and turned his bike around and headed back slowly. Two doors down from the fat man's place there was a house for sale. The blinds were drawn, no car in the drive. Hal parked the bike in the driveway of the vacant house. He took off the helmet and set it on the seat of the bike.

Hal headed down the sidewalk. Feeling the pressure come into his veins, the electric spark in his heart muscle. All the glands opening, pumping out their drugs, giving Hal Bonner that edge, that high, hot chemical advantage.

He ambled down the sidewalk like he belonged there, not darting from tree to tree, hiding in the shadows. Walked like it was Sunday afternoon and the neighbors were all outside, mowing grass, throwing sticks to their dogs, cutting flowers, whatever normal people did on Sunday in their cute yards.

He wondered if the fat guy had a wife. He wondered if he had a daughter or son or a big dangerous dog. Hal Bonner didn't mind dogs. He'd dealt with them before, snarling, fur standing up, teeth snapping. Hal just had to look them deep in the eye and they'd start backing away, their snarl quieting, sometimes becoming a whimper. They could smell who he was, knew instinctively what he could do. Hal hadn't met a guard dog yet that wanted to find out for sure.

Hal stopped in the driveway of the small stucco house with a red tile roof. It was painted white with brick-red trim on the shutters and front door. There was a security light mounted high on a pole in the side yard. There was a sticker on the front window that warned of an armed response from the security company. There was the blue car in the driveway, an old Ford Galaxy. Two trees, some bushes near the front windows, three steps up to the front porch, a wide picture window with orange blinds closed against the early afternoon light.

Hal opened the gate to the backyard and walked to the garbage cans. He lifted the lid on one, picked up one of the white plastic sacks, and tore it open. He had to paw around for a minute till he came to some discarded mail. A credit-card statement in the name of Marcus Shoenfeldt. It was a strange name. He'd never seen it before and had to sound it out several times, saying all the syllables to himself before he thought he had it right.

Hal put the garbage back in the can and pulled the cell phone out of his pocket and called information and got the number for Marcus Shoenfeldt. He walked to the front porch as he punched Marcus's number in. Just as he pressed the front door bell, he heard the telephone ringing inside Marcus Shoenfeldt's house.

On the second ring an irritated voice answered the phone. Hal heard it in stereo. One voice traveling out to the stars and back to the little piece of plastic at his ear, the second voice coming from the other side of the front door.

Hal said, "Marcus, is that you?"

"Yeah, and who is this?"

"It's Hal. Your old buddy."

Marcus hesitated, then said, "You must have the wrong Marcus."

Hal pressed the bell again.

"That your doorbell?" Hal said. "Go ahead and answer it, Marcus, I'll hold on."

"I'm hanging up," Marcus said. "I don't know any Hal."

"You do now," Hal said.

Up close the man was even bigger than Hal had thought. He filled up the doorway. Long black hair that he wore in a braid down his back. Blue bib overalls over a white long-sleeved T-shirt. But he wasn't a dangerous man. Hal could see that in the first second. The man was mush. Sad blubber in a big sack.

He tried to close the door in Hal's face, but Hal put a shoulder against it and shoved it aside and nearly knocked Marcus off his feet. He was through the door and in the foyer and he turned and closed the front door and bolted it.

"What the hell you think you're doing?"

Marcus was backing across the living room. He had bookshelves made of concrete blocks and yellow pine planks. A stereo and a small TV were squeezed in among the books. A jumble of pizza boxes filled one corner of the room. A lot of plants, little indoor trees and ferns. Against one wall was a long leather couch, black. Magazines scattered all around.

"Why don't you sit down?" Hal said. "I want to ask you a few questions."

Marcus was looking around the room like he was searching for a weapon.

"It won't take long. Three or four quick questions, that's all. Sit on the couch, make yourself comfortable. You want, I can put on some music."

"This is breaking and entering," Marcus said. "You'll do time for this."

"We're just having a conversation. Do you see me breaking anything, Marcus, or entering anything?"

"Man, you're in some deep shit here."

Hal backed him across the room till Marcus was at the couch.

"All right, big fellow, why don't you sit down?"

Marcus pushed some of the magazines aside and let himself down onto the black couch. Hal could hear the wood frame heave under his weight.

Hal came over, stood across the coffee table from him. He looked down at one of the magazines lying on the glass-topped table. There was a handsome man on the cover with his arm around a beautiful woman. Both of them were smiling. They were smiling because they were beautiful and they knew it and because they were on the cover of a magazine.

Hal picked up the magazine and paged through it. More beautiful women, and handsome men on every page. All of them smiling.

Hal dropped the magazine back on the table.

"I like pictures of animals better than pictures of people."

"Yeah, well, each to his own."

"I like bees a lot. Do you know anything about bees, Marcus? You know about the waggle dance?"

Marcus stared at him uncertainly.

"Look man, I don't know what the hell you want, but if you're looking for money, you're out of luck. I got about ten dollars in my wallet and some change in a jar in the other room. You want my collection of nickels, hey, it's yours, but that's the only thing I got of any value. I'm on disability pay.

You know what that is? It makes welfare look like winning the Lotto. So go on, take the TV if you want. Take the couch, everything. Just get it done and get out of here."

"Yes, I want money," Hal said. "Four hundred and sixty-three million dollars. Is that number familiar to you?"

Marcus stared at him, his lips quivering. All that tough talk had just been air fluttering across his larynx.

"Man, you're mixed up. You broke into the wrong house this time, bud."

"Where is J. J. Fielding hiding, Marcus?"

"Never heard of him."

"Where is J. J. Fielding?"

"Like I said, you've made a mistake. You broke in the wrong house."

"Why were you talking to Hannah Keller, Marcus?"

He held Hal's gaze for a moment, then closed his eyes and looked away.

"Hey now," Marcus said. "I don't know anything about this shit. It's none of my business."

"Were you talking with Hannah about J. J. Fielding?"

"Hell, no," Marcus said. "You want to know what we talked about, we talked about some handwriting in her book, that's all."

"What handwriting in what book, Marcus?"

"A copy of one of her novels. There's all this scribbling in it. She wanted me to tell her who wrote it, what they were like, give her a profile. That's all I know."

"You can do that? Look at handwriting, tell about the person who wrote it?"

"That's my job," he said. "That's what I do for a living."

"What did you tell Hannah Keller about this handwriting?"

"Whoever wrote it was a woman. And she was some kind of psycho. That's all I know. A dangerous woman. Which I guess is kind of redundant."

Marcus smiled at him. It reminded Hal of Randy Gianetti of Detroit, Michigan, the way he smiled in the Milwaukee hotel room. Trying to get Hal to smile back. But it didn't work that time and it didn't work this time either. Hal didn't smile a lot, not that he was aware of.

"Where is J. J. Fielding hiding?"

"Listen, man. I swear, if I knew who this guy was, and I knew where he was hiding, I'd give him up in a second. But I don't know. I never heard of him. Hannah didn't say anything about any J. J. Fielding or anybody else. I did most of the talking."

Hal studied the man's dark, nervous eyes for several seconds. The man was telling the truth. He didn't know anything that could help Hal. This was a wasted trip.

"Do you have any friends or family, Marcus, people who stop by your house and say hello from time to time? Now tell the truth. Don't lie to me. Do you have friends who stop by?"

"No," he said. "Unless you count the postman. Why?"

"That's good."

"Yeah? And why's that good?"

"Could you look at my handwriting, Marcus, and tell me about myself?"

"Hey, man, what the hell is this? I told you what I know. I'm not doing some damn parlor trick for you."

Hal walked over to the kitchen and found a pencil lying on the counter. He came back to the coffee table and picked up one of the magazines, opened it to a page with a beautiful woman holding her beautiful child in her arms. He scribbled some words in the white border of the page.

"Read this," Hal said. "Tell me who I am."

"All right, but Jesus, I told you everything I know."

Marcus took the magazine from him and glanced at what Hal had written. He read the words over again and then one more time. Then he dropped the magazine on the floor and stood up. He was wobbling a little, his eyes were wide open and watery. He was breathing through his mouth.

Hal had written these words. "Now I am going to kill you by crushing your heart."

The big man stood there for a moment longer, staring into Hal's eyes, then he lunged to the left and broke for the bathroom. But he'd eaten too many doughnuts and potato chips, too many beers and cheese sandwiches, too many Christmas cookies and apple pies and pizza pies and all the other goodies that fat people filled their fat selves with. Stuffing and stuffing and stuffing more food inside themselves, stretching out their skins until they couldn't run anymore, they couldn't flee the charging predator. No way to escape the fingers that reached out and grabbed his hair and yanked backward, bringing him down. An earthquake against those wood floorboards.

No way to squirm free. Too slow and too big. No way he could pull loose from the fingers. Hal's thick, strong fingers around his throat, choking off his air, kneeling on Marcus Shoenfeldt's chest, strangling him till he wallowed beneath Hal and gasped and closed his eyes and his body sagged.

When the big man was quiet beneath him, Hal unbuttoned the straps of his overalls, and pulled them down. Then he rolled his shirt up over the swell of his belly. Hal squatted down over the man and used his thumbnail to gouge an opening in the flesh below his chest plate, breaking through the tough hide of Marcus Shoenfeldt. The blood began to seep, pumping with each beat of the big man's heart.

Hal leaned over the big man and used both hands to tear the skin wider. Then he unbuttoned the sleeve of his shirt and rolled it up to his elbow. Hal squeezed his right hand into a small shape and sunk it deep into the meaty folds of Marcus Shoenfeldt. Wedging his hand through the wet, greasy layers, deeper and deeper, up to his wrist, then his forearm inside Marcus, under the bone and past the stomach, until Hal felt the big solid quivering muscle of his heart. Beating and beating and beating. And Hal Bonner spread his fingers wide around the biggest heart he'd ever held, huge, the size of a cantaloupe. It beat, it beat. And Hal closed his fingers around the living thing, the muscle, the pump. He squeezed. He clamped the man's heart muscle inside his hand until he could feel it stumble and surge and cramp and wriggle. Blood on Hal's arm. Blood on his pants. Blood everywhere on the floor. But Hal held on, slowing the man down till the heart beat one more time, one more after that, then was silent. And the big man lay with his eyes open. Looking up at Hal. Looking through Hal, through the ceiling, into the sky, into that place that dead men can see, the place they speed away to.

Hal needed to take a shower. He needed to wash his clothes.

He was a mess.

He walked into the big man's kitchen. The sink was full of dirty dishes and roaches scrambling. Hal found a sliver of soap and ran hot water over his hands and washed himself, then he used some paper towels to dry off. He was leaving DNA everywhere, traces of himself, but he didn't mind. They could have his DNA, for all the good it would do them.

After some of the blood was washed away, he searched the pantry until he found a gallon bottle of bleach and a roll of silver duct tape.

He went back to the hallway and took hold of Marcus Shoenfeldt's heels and dragged the man into his bedroom. He pulled the blue bedspread off the big man's bed and laid it over his body. He pulled the sheets off the bed and draped them over the body as well. Then he took hold of Marcus's shoulder and turned him slowly, wrapping him in the sheets and blankets until Marcus was a mummy. A very fat, bloody mummy. Hal opened the bleach and poured it over the sheets and blankets. He would have preferred lime, but lime was not available.

He used the duct tape to seal around the edges of the two windows. Then he went to the bedroom door and shut it and stood in the hallway using more duct tape to seal up the edges. When he was done, he ran his finger over the duct tape inch by inch all the way around the door, mashing it flat against the wood frame, fixing the seal.

He stepped back. A good job.

Two or three days would go by before Marcus began to stink and the mailman smelled him. Hal thought that would be enough time. Two or three more days before anyone found out that Hal Bonner had been a bad boy again.

TWENTY

While Frank Sheffield finished his sandwich at the picnic table and Randall disappeared again into his computer, Hannah went to her bedroom, shut the door, leaned her back against it for a moment, lifting her hands and watching them quiver. She took several slow, deep breaths, willing the tremble to cease, but her hands continued to defy her. The cold palsy of panic.

She pushed away from the door, marched into the bathroom, and turned on the shower full blast, as hot as she could stand it.

A few minutes later, standing naked under the spray, running her soapy hands over the familiar contours of her body, she felt an odd flush of awareness. A man in the house, changing the chemistry, the vibrations in the air, giving this simple act of hygiene and renewal a sensuous cast. Without intending it, her own nervous hands became Sheffield's hands, a flicker of fantasy. Frank in her shower, naked beside her, stroking her, touching those places that no man had caressed in years. The whisper of another's flesh across her flesh, bringing the sleek skin alive with a creamy warmth, a glow. She cocked her hip against the shower wall, touching herself with another's hands, touching and touching until her legs were soft and the shiver in her flesh finally stilled.

Then she was back in the shower alone, the hot spray in her face, feeling silly, feeling juvenile and vaguely ashamed.

She finished her shower, toweled off, gave her hair a

quick blow dry. Minimal makeup. Considered, then rejected
a dab of perfume.

She put on beige walking shorts, a pale blue cotton jersey
with three-quarter sleeves, black leather sandals. She looked
at herself in the bathroom mirror, still feeling foolish, a little
out of breath from her reverie.

The house was quiet beyond her bedroom door. It was not
yet three o'clock. She walked to her study, sat down before
her computer, and clicked her way quickly back into Erin
Barkley's world.

She knew it was crazy to tinker with the story at a time
like this, so much going on, so much unresolved, but it had
become an automatic response to emotional turmoil, turning
on the computer, slipping away into that clear, sensuous par-
allel universe. A world of order. Where she could neaten the
edges, go from rough draft to second draft and third. Paring,
shaping, eliminating the superfluous, the bothersome irrele-
vancies. Edit out the banal. Control the uncontrollable.

But this time as she stared blankly at the words on the
bright screen, she felt nothing but a great sense of detach-
ment. Suddenly the bodiless people on the page seemed ab-
surdly irrelevant. Their struggles trifling. For years she'd
been wasting her time in that vaporous world, resolving
nothing, discovering not a single thing that mattered.

With an angry rap on her mouse, she exited the novel and
hooked up with her Internet provider. When the opening
browser page came up, she punched in the Web address,
www.Deathwatch.com and in a few seconds she was staring
at the scratchy, color image of J. J. Fielding in his hospital
room. He was still napping, his adjustable bed cranked up to
nearly a sitting position. The room was bare except for the
IV stand and a small wood bedside table. On the table was a
stack of magazines. Hannah recognized the top one, a copy
of *People* from a week ago, a cover photograph of the
teenage British prince hand in hand with one of the Kennedy
girls, a giddy smile on the young royal's lips. A paparazzi's
wet dream.

She glared at J. J. Fielding, watching his tranquil, dreamy

face, feeling her blood warm and her airways tighten. Before she knew what she was doing, she reached up and pressed a finger to the screen, grinding it against Fielding's face, smothering him, then bearing down hard against the glass as if to crush the old man's skull.

"You cocksucker," she said. "Hang on a little longer. I'm almost there."

When she could stand it no longer, she drew her hand away and killed the screen. She sat there a moment more, taking long gulps of air, then she pushed away from the machine, got up, and walked back into her bedroom. The house was still quiet. The two males had not yet come to blows, no hand-to-hand, no furniture overturned, no glass breaking.

She settled on the edge of her bed and opened the copy of *First Light*, took out the folded typing paper where she'd written the decoded message. "Your name is the next key."

She knew what it meant. She'd known it almost from the first instant she read it, though her knowledge had remained vaporous, hovering in the back chambers of her mind. She had solved this puzzle as she solved most things, in that wordless, intuitive zone where impossible knots were unsnarled and crucial decisions took shape.

Hannah got up and walked out to the living room, and found Frank Sheffield still on the screened-in porch, still at the picnic table with his empty plate before him.

"You've got parrots," he said.

"What?"

"Parrots. I've seen about ten of them so far. They land in that big tree there, they squawk at the other birds, then they fly off. Ten minutes later they're back squawking again."

"It's a rosewood, an Indian rosewood, that tree."

"We don't get a lot of parrots out on Key Biscayne. What we get a lot of is tourists dressed like parrots, but not many of the birds themselves."

She set the book down on the table and took a seat next to him on the bench. She drew out the sheet of typing paper and unfolded it and laid it before him.

"I figured it out. 'Your name is the next key.'"

He examined the sheet a few moments longer, looked up at her.

"Can't we just stay with the parrots? Forget all this."

"If you want to, Frank, you can forget it, run along home. But I can't."

"I'm sorry. You're right. Don't pay any attention to me, I was just doing some wishful thinking. So tell me, what'd you figure out?"

"My name is a palindrome. H-a-n-n-a-h."

Frank's eyes flicked away from hers, following the squawking flight of another parrot sailing low through the branches of the avocado trees.

"And a palindrome would be what? I know I've heard the word. Something from high school if I'm not mistaken. Is it chemistry? I was never very good with science."

"No, it's from English class. A palindrome is a word or phrase that can be read the same way frontward or backward. Rats live on no evil star."

Frank repeated it slowly to himself, looking out at the yard, the avocado trees.

"Okay, I get it. Backward and forward. Like kayak."

She smiled, gave his arm a playful thump. "Yeah, like kayak."

"So that tells you what? A palindrome."

"Well, think about it. When Randall read through the list of numbers, he naturally read from top to bottom. But what if you read the list backward, starting at the bottom, going to the top, what would you come up with?"

"Gibberish probably."

"I don't think so."

"Well, there's a simple enough way to find out."

Hannah got a pen and a scratch pad from the kitchen, came back to the picnic table and Frank started tracking down the words, going from the bottom of the long list of numbers this time. Page number, line number, the words on that line. Hannah wrote them one by one, a sentence, then another. When they were finished she set down the pen.

"Somebody was pretty clever," he said. "Says one thing

going down the list, says another going back up. That's amazing."

Hannah read from the scratch paper.

"Next you travel to the west house with the red shingles. It is on stilts in the water looking out to sea. There you will find what will lead you to me. One step at a time. One after the next, one, two, three, four. But please you must hurry, please be quick, come now, there's not much time, hurry, hurry, hurry."

"Stiltsville," Frank said. "The westernmost house."

"Seems that way, yeah."

Stiltsville was the small community of simple wood homes built in the fifties and sixties. The houses were erected on pilings, planted in about ten feet of water on the edges of the flats of northern Biscayne Bay, a mile or two offshore of Cape Florida. Fishing shacks, weekend party retreats built by some of the early Miami movers and shakers. By now the stilt houses had passed on to the descendants of the original owners or to other lucky souls, but after numerous hurricanes and severe zoning restrictions forbidding any remodeling, only half a dozen of the houses remained standing, and those were under seige by the U.S. Park Service, which considered them eyesores in the serene and natural surroundings of Biscayne National Park. The owners of the houses and their supporters had been fighting to win historical designation as a way of preserving their little enclave, claiming those remaining structures were a crucial part of Miami's colorful legacy. But their position was weak. It was hard to argue that any building less than a century old was historically significant, even in Miami, a town that reinvented itself every five years. Hannah valued the past as much as anyone, but was finding it harder and harder to justify the whole idea of grandfathering in all the shady bargains and cushy arrangements of the past. Just because it was old and colorful didn't make it worthy. Didn't make it right.

"Doesn't this strike you as odd, Frank?"

"Which part?"

"All of it. The Bayshore house, a place in Stiltsville. This idiotic code. I mean, if Fielding wants me to come to him, why the hell make me jump through these hoops? He could've just laid it out. Such and such address at such and such a time. Meet me there, we'll talk."

"Well, like you said, maybe he's worried about the Cali guys. All the hoops are meant to keep them at bay. He wants to be sure it's you and not them showing up at his door."

Hannah shook her head, not buying it.

"If he's worried about them, why is he on the goddamn Internet, broadcasting like that for the whole world to see, saying my name out loud? If he wanted to get me to his bedside, a simple discreet message would've done it."

"I think it's pretty obvious, Hannah. Fielding wants to make sure you're not being followed. He has these locations staked out; if no one's tailing you, he shows himself. Like the classic kidnapping payoff scenario. Same thing, running you from phone booth to phone booth around the maze he's invented. You don't know exactly where you're going next. I mean, maybe the guy watched too many movies, this is the way he thinks it's done."

"Still there's no need for all this code bullshit."

"Who knows, maybe he likes playing games."

"That's what I said to Gisela, but now I don't know. This doesn't feel kosher."

Frank looked at her, tried a grin, but couldn't sustain it and his face grew serious.

"Why not just stay with the program? See where it leads?"

She gave him a careful look.

"My, aren't we getting conservative all of a sudden."

"It just makes sense, Hannah. Time's running out on this guy. He's about to croak, for godsakes. Why flail around looking for some other way to find him when he's laid out the bread crumbs for you already?"

"Because that's not who I am. I don't take orders very well, especially from the guy who killed my parents. If this son of a bitch is so damned determined to have me barge in through the front door, then that's reason enough right there to find some way to break in through the back."

"You're not going to make this easy, are you?"

"Easy? What's that supposed to mean?"

Frank shook his head, staring out at the empty yard. No parrots now. Quiet out there, just a sea breeze rattling through the avocado leaves.

"So what do you have in mind?"

"My boat's docked at Dinner Key Marina," she said. "Fifteen minutes from Stiltsville."

"Okay?"

"That would be the natural, predictable thing for me to do. Go this afternoon while there's still enough daylight, take the boat and check it out."

"Okay," he said. "So let's get going."

"No, I'm not going to do it the predictable way."

"So what do you do? Skydive in at midnight?"

"What I was thinking, Frank, I'd like to take you up on your offer."

"Which offer is that?"

"A little outing. You, me, a kayak."

Frank looked at her. A faint smile beginning to dawn.

"Man, you're something else."

She managed a small smile.

"You, too, Frank. You, too."

Misty was sitting at her Radio Shack computer watching her father nap. Her heart was flailing, whipsawed by current events. Things happening so damn fast she couldn't get down a full breath of air. Last night this guy Hal coming out of nowhere to bruise her nipple, then her old man appearing out of the same nowhere, then that fucking Hannah Keller calling her up on the phone asking who she was with that flat cop voice.

Goddamn tilt-o-whirl.

Misty was barefoot, wearing jeans, a white sleeveless T-shirt, and a black baseball cap turned backward. Toying with the idea of calling Hannah Keller back on her cell phone. She had the number on her Caller ID box. She could scream at her, get it all out of her system, tell the bitch she'd stolen Misty's life, then hang up and get the hell out of Miami, point her car north and just drive till she saw something that caught her eye. Start over, a new identity. She was sitting there watching her old man snooze away in his hospital bed, having escape fantasies, when she heard the tap on her apartment door. She froze.

Way things were going it was probably the Miami SWAT team coming to bust her, ship her off to Raiford Prison. She sat there and listened to the tap on the door. Not moving, not even a breath.

When the tapping finally stopped, Misty slowly inhaled and let it out. Probably the landlord wanting to snarl at her about her rent. Ten days late already. She waited another half a minute, listening to the silence. Then she sighed and settled back in her chair again. And a second later the lock jiggered a couple of times and the door swung open behind her.

She popped to her feet, grabbed the double-action derringer she kept on the desk, and swung around.

He was already inside the apartment, shutting the door behind him, locking it. Hal, the nipple pincher. Wearing black jeans and a blue work shirt and carrying a yellow magazine in one hand.

"Hello again," he said.

"Jesus, I thought I was done with you."

Hal walked over to the computer, reached out and took the pistol from her hand, and set it on the desk. Then he bent forward and peered at the screen.

"Your old man been doing anything interesting?"

Misty shook her head in wonder.

"You break into my apartment twice within twenty-four hours and I'm supposed to just say hi, how you doing? Man, you've got a reality problem."

"Your old man been doing anything interesting?"

"Jesus," she said. "Here we go. Old one-track mind."

"Your old man . . ."

"Okay, okay. He's been sleeping mostly. He called out for

that bitch Hannah Keller a couple of times, but that was a few hours ago. Mostly what he does, he sleeps."

"Do you know about the waggle dance, Misty?"

"Waggle what?"

Hal had opened the yellow magazine and was paging through it. It was a copy of *National Geographic*. Her mother used to subscribe and Misty remembered looking at the glossy photos, naked natives from New Guinea or the Amazon. Imagining herself among them, those topless warriors, spears and shields and loincloths. Hunting lions and rhino, taking shit from nobody.

"Bees do it," he said. "It's how they communicate."

"You broke into my apartment to talk about bees?"

"It's called the waggle dance," he said. "Where's your bathroom?"

He held the magazine out to her and she took it. The cover was coated with a brownish sticky film.

"Where's your bathroom?"

She hesitated a moment, shaking her head.

"First door to your right."

"You'll like it, Misty. The waggle dance, it's very interesting. You can read, can't you?"

"I can read."

"Reading's important. I get a lot of good ideas from reading."

He walked past her, then halted and stared at her Barbies. Four of them lined up side by side on the wall near the bathroom. The dildo Barbie, one rubber cock in each hand, a battery-operated dildo glued between her legs; and the condom Barbie with lubricated, nipple-end Trojans unrolled over her arms and legs and one covering her face like a robber's mask; the crucifixion Barbie, her arms spread, her body pierced with jackknives and steak knives, a darning needle and straightened paper clips poked into each eye socket. And the one Misty liked the best, the disemboweled Barbie. Sawed in half from the top of her skull to her crotch and hinged open, the empty spaces inside filled with miniature replicas of T-bone steaks and lamb chops, a tiny red

Maserati sports car, and a plastic Jesus in his manger and the Three Wise Men and all the donkeys.

"These are weird," Hal said.

"I'm surprised you can tell."

"You ever think about selling these? Go into business, open a shop somewhere."

"You think there's a big demand for Barbie sculptures, do you?"

He squinted at her for a moment.

"I like you, Misty. I like your jokes."

"Oh, yeah, I'm a regular comedian."

"I can only stay a few minutes, then I have to get back on the job."

"Don't let me keep you."

"Hannah Keller is going to lead me to your father. I have to get back over to her house and start tailing her again."

"Is that right? And how the hell is she supposed to find him? All the cops in the world looking for him, all the drug guys."

"Your father's sending her secret messages."

"Oh," she said. "Is that what he's been doing?"

"Yeah, he wants to see her."

"Why? Why the fuck does that dying old man want to see her, of all people? Not his wife, not his own daughter."

"I don't know. He just does."

"Look, I don't want any part of this," Misty said. "Just use the bathroom and hit the road, okay?"

"You know, we have things in common, you and me."

"No, we don't."

"We both want the same thing, Misty. We both want to find J. J. Fielding."

"No way. I don't want to find him. He's dead as far as I'm concerned."

"Oh, yes you do. You want to find him. You want to hurt him like he hurt you. I know how that is. That's how I got my start. Going back to see my father, hurting him like he hurt me. I was in a lot of pain before I did it, but once he was dead, the pain went away. I cured myself."

Misty looked at the computer screen. Her father sleeping. Maybe there was a grain of truth to what Hal was saying. Maybe that *was* what she wanted. To hurt the old man. To get her revenge on him, not Hannah Keller after all. Maybe that would set everything right, kill the old bastard, then she could get on with her life.

"You got a nail file?" Hal was still looking up at the disemboweled Barbie.

"Nail file?"

"I need to put the edge back on."

He held up his right thumb.

"In the medicine cabinet," she said. "First shelf on the right."

Hal looked over at her for a moment as if he was waiting for her to make another sarcastic remark. Then he turned and disappeared into the bathroom and shut the door. A few seconds later the shower water started to roar.

She picked up the double-action derringer from the desk and aimed it at the closed door. Whipsawed again. Things happening so fast she couldn't keep track. Bing, bing, bing. Tilt-o-whirl spinning out of control, an earthquake rattling the ground beneath it.

She set the pistol down and looked at the magazine. The sticky stuff was all over her fingers now. It had a smell. Strange but familiar. She brought her fingers to her nostrils and inhaled the scent, then touched her fingertip to her tongue. She recognized it from somewhere but couldn't place it.

She sat down at the computer again. Her daddy was still sleeping.

She opened the magazine to the dog-eared page. An article about bees. She listened for a minute to the shower run. The steam was seeping out beneath the door and her coconut bath soap was filling the air. She read a couple of paragraphs of the bee article, then took a sharp breath and leaned back in her desk chair.

She'd just remembered what the sticky stuff smelled like. That time five years ago, a week after her father disap-

peared and it was obvious he wasn't coming back, and Misty
and her mother were sitting there with about a hundred dollars in the bank, not enough to pay the mortgage, grocery
money disappearing fast. She'd come home from school one
afternoon, went into her bathroom, filled the bathtub with
hot water, and she'd stripped naked and slipped into it and
she'd scooched low in the water for a long time thinking
about her life, about the hopelessness of it, the dead, empty
feeling she'd had as long as she could remember, only now
even deader and emptier. A father who'd abandoned his family and took every last cent, a mother who'd become catatonic. Lay in her bed all day staring at the ceiling, not
crying, not talking, nothing. And Misty couldn't think of a
single reason to keep on living in the world, not a single one.
So she picked up the straight razor her father used to shave
with, and she laid the blade against her left wrist and she
drew a long slice against the white skin. Then quick, before
she even felt the pain, she drew the blade across her other
wrist.

   That's what the sticky stuff on the magazine smelled like.
The scent of fresh blood.

TWENTY-ONE

On the phone Gisela said sure, no problem, she wasn't busy tonight, she'd be happy to take care of Randall. It just so happened she'd rented a couple of movies that might suit him. *Star Wars.* The first two. They could have a special-effects orgy, sit there in the galley of her houseboat, make some old-fashioned popcorn in an iron skillet.

Gisela said, "I'm not even going to ask where you're going on a school night. I don't want to know. What is it, a date?"

"You remember Frank Sheffield?" Hannah said.

"The FBI guy? You're kidding. He's cute."

"I hadn't noticed."

"Oh, yeah, right."

"It's not like that anyway. We're working on the J. J. Fielding thing."

Gisela was quiet for a moment, Jimmy Buffett moaning in the background.

"Is this a sleep-over, Hannah? Am I supposed to take Randall to school tomorrow?"

"I doubt it'll come to that."

"But it might?"

Hannah leaned into the doorway of her bedroom, watching Frank out in her front yard. He was staring up into the Indian rosewood. Through the open French doors she could hear him. Apparently he was trying to mimic the squawk and screech of a large green parrot roosting there. Like some overgrown Boy Scout working on his birdsong merit badge.

"I don't know," Hannah said. "I guess there's some remote possibility it could turn into an all-nighter. Could you handle that?"

Gisela let the question hang there a moment. Hannah could feel her smiling on the other end of the line.

"Look, I'm off Wednesday and Thursday. I could take him to school tomorrow, pick him up, bring him back here, maybe the two of us will tool around the bay, snag our dinner."

"He'll go into withdrawal without his computer," Hannah said.

"Hell, I'll keep him so damn entertained he won't have a chance."

"You're a peach, Gisela."

"Hey, I'm the boy's godmother, for chrissakes. This is the international godmother's job description. And, anyway, if I can help you get laid, hey, it's my sworn duty."

"It's not like that," Hannah said. "Really it's not."

Tuesday night, ten o'clock, Operation Joanie was in hour forty-six. A little more than twenty-four hours left. And Frank Sheffield was fairly sure he was on his own for the moment, separating from surveillance when he slid the two-man kayak into the dark, foaming surf just south of the Silver Sands Motel. Not that he was worried about losing contact. Let them scramble, figure out how to keep the surveillance active, give them a little challenge. And he certainly wasn't worried about deepening the hole he'd dug for himself. It was a cinch he'd already moved well beyond the limits of Rosie Jackson's power to save his ass. That fist in Senator Ackerman's gut wasn't going away. But Frank had to say, it was a hell of a way to resign from the Bureau. Nice flourish. Knock the air out of one of the most powerful men on earth. Something he could share with his grandchildren, or, more likely, the way his procreative life was going, he'd have to settle for bragging about it to some old geezer buddy in the nursing home.

"Am I holding the paddle right, Frank?"

"You're fine," he said. "Just keep stroking at your own pace, I'll stay in time with you."

"I can't see where we're going."

To the east the moon was smothered behind a thicket of cumulus. They were already passing beyond the reach of the lights from the motel and tiki bar, just a smear of dim color rode the surface of the Atlantic.

"Don't worry, Hannah, I'm steering. Anyway there's nothing to run into out here. Water's not more than five, six feet deep. You can swim, can't you?"

"I can swim fine. It's just so damn dark."

"Well, hang on, once we get to the other side of the is-land, it's going to get even darker."

They stroked across the swells, Frank keeping them on a heading around the tip of Cape Florida, the old lighthouse, the barren point of land where until a few years ago a dense and shady forest of pines had stood. Hurricane Andrew had changed that, sweeping the land clean, taking away all those fast-growing, shallow-rooted trees and shrubs that had flour-ished for decades, untested by a real storm.

Frank eased back in the tight cockpit seat. He was enjoy-ing being downwind of Hannah. Looking at her back, at the stray flickering in her gold hair. It was arousing him, catch-ing her scent like this, the flowery taste of her bath soap, the deeper pungency of her rising perspiration. She'd found a nice rhythm with the paddle and was digging the water past them and Frank fell into her pace and the narrow craft slid forward across the dark sheen. Frank mirrored her actions, harmonized with her. A kind of sexual intimacy, like danc-ing very close without touching. Filming this in his head, Bogart and Ingrid out in their kayak, the silky water, the soft air, the swell of watery distances opening up around them.

"You see why I like it out here?"

"At the moment, Frank, I can't see anything."

"Well, of course, it's even better around dusk. When the sun gets low, you can see right down into the water, but the angle of the light confuses the fish, they're not spooked when you pass by. It's amazing stuff you see. Leopard rays, good-size hammerheads. Paddle right over the top of them, you can reach down, pet their fins."

"Stop it," she said.

"What? You squeamish?"

"I'm not fainthearted, it's just that I'm used to being a little higher out of the water, that's all. A little less exposed."

Frank matched her stroke, steering them around the point, twenty yards out, picking up some wind at their back as they came around the jut of land and started off into the dark bay. It was sweaty work but she didn't falter, didn't ask for a breather, nice wide shoulders working the water past them.

"So what's going on with Randall? He seemed particularly pissed on the drive over. He doesn't like staying with Gisela?"

"Like I said, he's threatened by this, Frank. He's afraid I'm stirring things up, putting us in danger."

"Well, he has a point."

Hannah took a deep stroke on the starboard side, then raised her paddle and settled it on the hull before her, and they coasted through the dark.

"He said he hated me."

"Yeah? When'd he say that?"

"This afternoon, while you were on the phone. He looked me straight in the eye and said he hated me and wished he had someone else for a mother."

The kayak drifted sideways, carried along by the incoming tide, bumping toward the flats north of Stiltsville. A mile in the distance he could see the dim glow of an outdoor light fixed to the nearest of the stilt homes, running off solar-powered batteries.

"Every kid says that to his parents at one time or another. I know I did. There was a stretch when I told my old man almost every day how much I hated him. Hell, I was twenty-nine at the time."

"Not me," said Hannah. "I never said it, never felt it. And it sure as hell isn't easy to hear."

"He's just a kid. What does he know?"

Hannah swiveled and peered back into the dark.

"Did you hear that?"

"What?"

"Like a splash."

"Mullet," Frank said. "Or a barracuda having a midnight snack."

"Listen," she said.

He strained to pick up anything out of the ordinary, but all he could hear was a distant marine engine.

"We keep paddling, we'll be there in fifteen minutes. As long as we can ride this current."

"I heard something, Frank. Something human."

He reached down to his feet and patted around the inside of the hull until he found the Maglite clipped to the side. He switched it on, then he used his paddle to turn the kayak in a slow circle, focusing the light out about ten to fifteen feet into the dark. Nothing but the ruffled crests of small waves showing in his beam. Frank made two complete revolutions, then switched it off.

"You're spooked," he said. "There's always a lot of sloshing out here."

A mile or two toward the west, coming out of the channel for the Rickenbacker Causeway, was a fast-moving boat with a bright beam swinging back and forth across its path. But beyond that, the bay was empty. Frank knew Helen Shane had to be busting a gut. No way under present circumstances to keep surveillance both active and out of view. A chopper would be too obvious, and any kind of marine engine would be impossible to conceal out on the dark, uninhabited bay. They were probably ganged up back there at the Silver Sands, pacing around, debating what to do.

"Frank, I hear something back there." But the conviction wasn't in her voice anymore.

"Mullet," he said. "The last few weeks they've been running like crazy through this pass."

And he picked up his paddle and straightened them out, then began his stroke, a steady pull toward the faint gleam of Stiltsville.

* * *

Hal wasn't much of a swimmer. A dog paddle was the only stroke he knew. That's why he'd stolen the surfboard from the beach as Hannah and the FBI guy left in their kayak. Paddling now, flat on his stomach, water splashing in his face as he tried to stay up with them.

It was a tortoise and the hare situation. The story his first foster mother had told him over and over. Eloise Bonner, a big woman, twice her husband's size. Trying to comfort Hal with that fairy tale, knowing he was slow, but trying to find the virtue in that. Telling him over and over that the long march was what mattered. Sticking to it. You didn't have to have talent. You didn't have to be quick and bright and strong. Endurance was better than anything else. And endurance was something you could control. It was just a question of mastering pain. Not paying attention to the muscles burning. You stroked and stroked through the ocean, a tortoise, dragging its heavy shell along for three or four steps, pausing for a breath, then trudging on, his eyes always on the hare.

Hal had never been so far out to sea before. It was hard work. But he wasn't afraid of the water. He wasn't afraid of the dark. The ocean was warm and it was quiet, didn't try to knock him down or pull him under. He paddled along behind the kayak, a hundred yards in its wake, stroking quietly. He guessed there were fish out here, maybe big fish with ragged mouthfuls of teeth staring up at his legs as he swam overhead. He was in his underwear and a T-shirt, his clothes lying in a heap back on the beach. He wasn't afraid of sharks. There was nothing Hal Bonner was afraid of. He wasn't sure why. But it probably had something to do with not being afraid of death. He'd been around it, seen it, looked into its eyes from an early age, and it didn't frighten him or amaze him or make him wonder. It was just death. The end of living. The body switched off the same way a TV shuts down when you punch the button. A crackle of electrons and then it's dark.

He paddled the surfboard through the warm water, keeping his eyes on the dull shine of the kayak. The two of them were going somewhere in the dark. Hal had to follow. This could be the moment he'd been waiting for. This could be where J. J. Fielding was hiding out, in one of those houses that stood up above the water. The houses looked like hide-outs. No way to approach them without being seen. A place Hal might have chosen to hide out, if he ever hid out. But he didn't. Only people who were afraid had to hide. And Hal was not afraid. Not of sharks, not of the dark or water or death.

Hal Bonner's first father was a mortician. An old man. An undertaker. People are just dying to make me rich, he used to say to Hal. He made Hal watch him work. There was something wrong with the man's sperm. He couldn't have a real son, so he'd chosen Hal from the orphanage. He wanted someone to take over his business one day when he died, someone who could embalm him with the same skill he used on others. He wanted to teach Hal everything he knew about the dead. He wanted to show off his knowledge, bask in Hal's admiration.

His name was Harry Bonner. He'd given Hal his name and Hal had kept it out of laziness. Harry was short and wiry. He had white wispy hair and a mustache, and his eyes were dark and small. His lips fleshy, his jowls quivering when he sucked on his teeth.

Harry and Hal worked alone in the cool rooms of the mortuary. The smell of embalming fluid. The dizzy reek of formaldehyde.

Harry Bonner specialized in the obese. He could charge twice as much for embalming the fat ones. The relatives of the plump corpse always went along with the higher rates, not aware that a fat man's thoracic cavity was not much larger, if any, than that of a skinny man. One gallon of arterial solution for every seventy-five pounds of body weight. Sixteen ounces of concentrated 50 index was what Harry Bonner used for cavity chemical. And high pressure was required for the fat ones, anywhere from 100 to 140 pounds while implementing the intermittent rate of flow.

Harry made Hal assist him in the embalming room.
Teaching him a trade, showing him the mechanics. How to
use the right carotid artery as the main injection site, how to
drain the body's blood from the jugular. Covering bed sores
and cuts and wounds with towels soaked in cavity fluid. Re-
lieving the bloating pressure by opening up the anal vent.
Packing the nostrils with cotton saturated with insecticide
to prevent insects from entering. Sewing the mouth shut
with needle and fine catgut and coating the lips with soft-
ened wax.

Hal paddled through the dark water of Biscayne Bay and
thought about death. Thought about his first father, Harry,
thought of the embalming room, the smells, the harsh lights,
harsh smells, the glitter of the surgical instruments. He kept
his eyes on the kayak and he did his dog paddle and he re-
lived those years. Ten, eleven, twelve, thirteen years old. A
young boy, curious about death. Eager to please his father.
Every day another dead body, and another one. Naked
women, naked men, and children lying on the steel table.
Their blood flushed into the sewer system, Hal, standing on
a stool so he could reach the surgical table, had the chore of
washing their bodies with germicidal soap, every crevice,
every fold.

His father, Harry Bonner, explaining it all to Hal. Showing him the secrets of human anatomy, the hairy, hidden
places in women, the large and small breasts and penises,
testicles of every size. The strange formations, the humps,
the goiters, and lumpy tumors. He made Hal look, made Hal
touch and smell and sometimes touch the tip of his tongue to
a nipple or a navel. Often Harry Bonner unzipped his pants
and pulled himself out and stroked his skinny penis beside
the gleaming steel table where the women lay. Showing his
son how to enjoy his work. Harry sometimes put his hands
inside them, or fondled their empty breasts. He touched their
wounds, inserted his fingers into the ones with deep gashes.
Moved in and out, closing his eyes.

He was a small man with a musty smell and a glass eye.
And he would remove that eye sometimes when the body

was a particularly attractive woman. He would touch the cold marble to her body, roll it across her nipples. He would tell Hal about sex, what women enjoyed, the pain they secretly hungered for. Showing the boy how to enter a woman, her limp legs dangling over the edge of the surgical table while he moved his long thin penis in and out of the corpse. As the formaldehyde pumped, the tubes squirted with blood. He shaved off their pubic hair with a straight razor and hoarded it in shoeboxes. Black hair in one box, and blond in another, red and brown coils of hair brimming to the top of the boxes that lined a shelf in the basement of their house. Harry Bonner used surgical scissors to snip off the women's nipples, then suspended the oily coins of flesh in glass jars filled with formaldehyde. Small nipples and large, puffy ones and dark ones. Harry loved the women, hated to give them up to the earth. He saved as much of them as he dared. Some afternoons Harry Bonner would corner the boy, and force a clump of pubic hair beneath Hal's nose and slap the boy hard if he could not recall the woman's name from the fragrance she had left behind.

Harry Bonner gave Hal a trade, a craft. Something that would serve him well when he became a man. People were dying to make Harry Bonner rich. The living gave their loved ones to him and Harry used them for his profit and his pleasure. He taught Hal everything he would ever know about the human body, about the empty eyes of the dead, the inevitable fate of all living things, and the hollow chill of the human heart.

Harry Bonner was Hal's first victim.

When he was fifteen, Hal returned one day to the mortuary, surprised the small man. He didn't say a word to him, just reached out and took him by the throat and strangled him, lifting him off his feet, and watching his eyes roll back, Harry Bonner, his first father, the man who taught him about death. He couldn't remember why he'd done it, why he murdered the man he thought of as his father. The idea had simply formed in his head, taken shape out of the mist that usually filled his head. He wanted to bury those nipples and penises and all that pubic hair. He wanted to hide it in the earth where it belonged, so he wouldn't think of it anymore, wouldn't see it when he shut his eyes.

Over time, passing through other foster homes, the murder of Harry Bonner had become so clear and pure in his imagination that he had no choice but to do it. It lay before him, a movie that he had watched a thousand times until he had memorized his part, knew every action, every event exactly as it would unfold. Then he did it. Played out his role. Simple as that. See it, then do it. As though his mind was a film projector, throwing the light out his eyes onto the screen of the world. Seeing what to do, then doing it. He strangled his father in the embalming room, then dug a hole in the backyard and buried the nipples and penises and hair. Harry's large wife, Eloise, caught Hal dropping the last shoebox into the ground. She screamed at him. She hit him with the handle of her broom. She ran into the house to call the police. So he strangled her too.

Hal's arms were getting tired. Heavy and slow. His muscles were burning. He was a tortoise. Slow and steady and unyielding.

He paddled the board across the black water. He watched as Hannah Keller and the FBI man came to a house and then one of them, then the other, stood up carefully in the kayak and hauled themselves up the ladder that dangled down to the water's surface.

Hal's arms were so tired, he was starting to think he might not make it back to shore. He might have to do something radical if he was going to survive.

TWENTY-TWO

From halfway up the ladder, Hannah turned and watched Sheffield lash the bowline to a piling, then haul himself up to the first rung. It was tricky work. Between the wobbly kayak and the bleached and pulpy wood of the ladder, Hannah was expecting any second to go crashing back into the bay. But somehow she kept her balance, got her feet moving up the last few rungs, and though the ladder shifted and creaked beneath her weight, it held.

Frank hung back, waiting for her to reach the top and wriggle through the small hatch door and step onto the deck before he tested the ladder's strength. She stooped down and watched him scuttle up toward her, moving fast across the bars of frail wood. On the top rung, he hesitated a half second, giving her a quick smile of relief. But as he was taking his last step the wood cracked beneath his foot and he lost the grip, whirled his arms, tipping backward. Hannah shot out a hand and grabbed the collar of his shirt. She levered her legs hard against the railing and with a short grunt and heave, she hauled him upright.

Sheffield got hold of the ladder again, stepped over the broken rung, and whispered his thanks as he emerged through the hatch.

They moved silently to the railing, leaning against it, catching their breaths, staring out into the black breeze.

After a moment, Frank turned to her and was about to speak, but she shushed him with a finger to his lips. Then pointed below at the dark unsettled water.

She thought she'd heard the splash again, but now as she

listened, she wasn't certain. It could be the tide jostling against the pilings of the house, or the awkward bump and gurgle of the kayak on the shifting current. It could be a mullet leaping, or the plop of a stilt-house rat bailing out of its nest. Her jitters magnifying every sound.

Hearing nothing more, she turned from the water and surveyed the house. From what she could see, the deck wrapped around the entire structure. Above the front door the tattered remains of an awning fluttered in the rising wind. Off to the east a pulse of lightning brightened the sky miles out to sea, a small thunderstorm riding up the Gulf Stream.

The sea's fertile scent was everywhere, and a wilder fragrance was filtering in from farther out, riding the onshore breeze. A teasing mingle of scents. Odors carried directly from the islands, lobsters grilling over charcoal, the hard sweet fragrance of sunbaked sand, and the quiet hint of nutmeg and cloves and rum and fresh green mint. Scents that were possible only out there on the edge of the ocean, borne by the freshest winds.

The last time she'd smelled that perfumed blend, she was a child, standing on the porch of one of the ghostly, long-gone houses of Stiltsville, a two-story affair that once stood somewhere off to the east. Her father had brought her along with him to a party. It was someone's birthday, a judge, a state senator, someone with an old teak yacht that was anchored in the nearby channel. They'd used rowboats and skiffs to ferry people back and forth between the yacht and the stilt house. Everyone was giddy. The sun was bright, and she remembered how clear and blue the water looked and how cool it was, jumping from the deck of the house, twenty feet down into the sheer streaming bay, kicking back up from the white sandy bottom. She was the only kid that day, twelve or thirteen at the time, on the brink of adulthood, watching her father drink beer from a bottle and smoke cigars and trade jokes and stories with policemen and lawyers and those rich judges and politicians. A glorious day. Permitted a glimpse into a world she'd never seen. Adults acting like schoolkids.

certain about the underpinnings of the world, that it was as if Hannah were staring through an interstellar peephole, given a quick glimpse of the inhabitants of some utopian moon, orbiting off in the deepest reaches of the cosmos.

"There she is," Ed Keller said. "There's my princess."

She wore a simple yellow dress tufted with white nubby flowers. She was gripping a white patent leather purse that matched her shoes, a strap across her arch. One of her white socks had rolled down below her ankle. Her blue hat was as small and round as a robin's nest. She stood for a moment next to her father, posing for the camera, a smile of artless pleasure. He had his arm around her back, bending down so their cheeks were brushing.

She'd forgotten that look of his. That impish smile, that wink he gave Martha, their secret joy exposed.

"Okay, then," he said. "Come on, Martha. Your turn."

"No," she mumbled, and the camera wobbled.

"Come on, you shy goose. Let's get one of you for a change."

He left his daughter's side and walked directly toward her. Martha, filming him, protested all the while.

"Come on, Mother," Hannah called out. "It's your turn."

And as Ed Keller reached out for the camera, his hand approaching the lens, the film went dark and there were the X's and O's and coarse gray light of badly spliced film.

"That was your parents," Frank said.

"Yes. That was them."

"Those fuckers."

She looked at him.

"Who're you talking about?"

"Whoever did this," he said. "The sons of bitches."

When the film resumed, the color was more vivid, the focus precise.

J. J. Fielding reclined in his hospital bed, staring into the lens. His shrunken face was gray beneath his outsized silver pompadour, all that hair balanced atop his head like some ill-fitting helmet.

"Is it on?" he said. "Yes? Okay, then."

The camera jiggled, then jerked to the right, giving a quick glimpse of the rest of the room. A television mounted high on the wall, the open door of a sterile bathroom, a visitor's green leather chair, nothing more than a basic hospital room interchangeable with all other hospital rooms. Then the camera panned slowly back to Fielding and jiggled a few more times as if someone was locking it into place on its tripod stand.

"We're a little low-tech here," Fielding said. "Good equipment, bad operators. But we're doing the best we can on short notice."

He coughed and the rattle in his chest sounded papery and wet. He continued to hack for several minutes, a breathless seizure. Finally he grew still, settled himself beneath the sheets, smoothing them over his lap and thighs. Eyes down as if summoning his strength, taking a last run through his speech before he began.

"Well then," he said, lifting his head and peering into the camera.

Hannah inched closer to the wall, studying Fielding and his room. As far as she could tell everything was identical to the Internet image. But something was bothering her, a small detail she couldn't identify.

As Fielding dissolved into yet another spasm of coughing, she saw it. On the old man's bedside table was the same stack of magazines she'd noticed before. Only now the copy of *People* was gone, replaced by a *New Yorker*, its cover showing what looked like a snowy skyline of Manhattan, and a silhouette of Santa steering his sleigh through the gauntlet of skyscrapers. An issue that had to be at least ten months old.

Fielding wiped his mouth with the back of his hand.

"All right then," he said. "So, what I wanted to do was to speak to you directly, my dear, tell you exactly why I fled. Although you probably believe you know the reasons for my disappearance, I hope you realize there is more to the story than what you read in the newspapers and what little the police shared with you. Please hear me out, my dear. Please be

patient with me. There is so much you don't know. So much
I need to get off my chest."

In a sudden crackle of light Fielding's image disappeared
and the bedroom wall went white. Behind them the loose end
of the film began to slap against the housing of the projector.

As she stared into the bright square of light, Hannah's
eyes were blurry with swelling tears. She wiped them an-
grily.

"Look," Frank said and stepped past her. Pointing at the
letters framed by the projected light. Hidden while the
movie image ran, the careful printing in black Magic Marker
was now fully visible.

See page 276.

Hannah nodded. She rubbed the last of the blur from her
eyes, then walked over to the projector. She yanked the cord
free from the wall, and lifted the bulky machine off the
dresser. She raised it above her head, held it a moment, then
hurled it down against the floor.

Hannah stood in the dark and felt the sift of ocean breeze
through the leaky walls, the warm air passing across her bare
legs and arms. Beneath the floorboards she could hear the
nervous dance of the bay.

Frank touched her back, steering her gently toward the
living room, then out to the deck. They came to a halt at the
railing facing back toward the shore. The glimmer of houses
and condos.

"You've seen that piece of film before? You and your parents."

She stared out into the dark breeze.

"I haven't watched it since I was a kid. I thought it was in
an old Army footlocker of my dad's, along with a lot of
other paraphernalia of his. Someone must have stolen it
from my attic. God knows how or why."

"To motivate you, pump you up," he said. "In case your
spirits were flagging. To keep you on the chase, remind you
why you care."

She turned her face and looked at him.

"It was a shitty thing to do," he said. "Unnecessary."

"This whole thing is shitty, Frank. Start to finish."

He was quiet for a moment, shifting beside her, then settling his weight against the rail.

"It's almost over," he said. "Just a little more."

"You sure of that, are you?"

"You saw him. The old guy's about to die. Tomorrow night this time, he'll be gone."

She studied his profile for several moments.

"How do you know that, Frank? Tomorrow night this time?"

"Trust me," he said. "Twenty-four hours, it'll be all over."

"It's over for me right now. This is it, Frank. I've had it."

"You can't quit. You're so close."

"I'm giving up," she said. "The old guy can die and rot in hell for all I care. This is too hard on Randall. It's too hard on me. I'm quitting, Frank. As of this moment, I'm finished with this bullshit."

Hal was sitting in the front compartment of the kayak. He was floating directly below the stilt house listening to them talk. Listening to Hannah Keller resign. But she couldn't resign. Hal had been chasing J. J. Fielding for five years and this was the closest he'd come. His employers were unhappy with him. And when those people grew unhappy, they sent others to replace the ones they were unhappy with. Men who disappointed them were not fired, they were executed. Hannah Keller couldn't quit. Hal Bonner wouldn't let her.

Frank saw it first, a dull gleam about twenty yards out in the dark.

"Jesus Christ!"

Hannah followed his gaze and saw a shimmer of moonlight on the narrow hull of the kayak, a wide-shouldered man paddling off into the dark.

Frank was at the top of the ladder, staring down.

"Somebody's stealing our goddamn boat?"

Frank said yes, and in the next instant he was climbing over the rail.

"What the hell're you doing?"

"I'm going to get it back."

He pitched forward into the dark and she heard the splash, then a few seconds later heard him rise to the surface.

"You okay, Frank?"

"Fine," he shouted. "Just fine."

And she could hear his fleet flutter-kicking and saw him in a stray glimmer of moonlight taking long powerful strokes toward the kayak. In the next moment she was over the rail and perched on the edge of the deck. As a ragged flash of lightning tore through the western sky, Hannah picked a spot on the shimmering surface and dove.

Resurfacing quickly, she swam, keeping her head above water, following the sound of Frank's thrashing kick. It was thirty yards or so through the rising chop before she caught up with him.

Treading water, she struggled for breath. Behind her a strobe of lightning pulsed through the sky and in that instant she saw Frank struggling with the wide-shouldered man who was hunched low in the kayak.

Frank and the man were grappling for the paddle. Another flare of lightning lit the sky, followed instantly by a blast of thunder. The sky rumbled for half a minute while Hannah circled the kayak, looking for an opening, a chance to seize the attacker. But the two of them were whirling unpredictably. Frank snorted and heaved for breath as he ducked the savage swings of the paddle. The other man worked grimly in silence.

Then it was over. A blow she didn't see, some lung-emptying whack. Frank was suddenly floating facedown in the water. The man made a threatening wave of the paddle in Hannah's direction, then plowed away into the dark.

She stroked to Sheffield's side, pulled his head up, turned him onto his back, and got her right arm around his chest and side-stroked a few feet to the bottom of the stilt house.

Behind her the man in the T-shirt paddled steadily into the darkness. A double slash of lightning framed him for a half-second and she saw his broad back, narrow waist, the blunt shape of his head.

Hannah could haul Sheffield back to the ladder, but she knew that was no good. The bottom rung was within reach, but there was no way she could haul the two of them up. Even if the rotten wood could hold their weight, she simply didn't have the strength to muscle him all the way to the deck.

Frank coughed. He puked up a half-cup of seawater, then went slack again in her arm. He was breathing, but he was clearly far too weak to make it to shore on his own.

"Frank?"

He mumbled something, eyes shut. He made a strangled, whistling sound as he drew breath.

She looked back at shore, the dim twinkle of lights.

Pushing off from the nearest piling, she tightened her right arm across his wide chest, took a grip on the slab of pectoral muscles near his armpit. His butt jounced lightly against her right hip, his legs trailing. She scissor-kicked and made a short stroke with her left hand. High school Red Cross water-safety training. They moved through the water, two feet for every stroke. Two feet and two more.

Frank coughed and hacked up more watery phlegm.

She spoke his name again but he remained limp in her arms. The air temperature dropped a sudden five degrees and as the storm swept in off the sea, the water was churned to froth around them. She kept her head above the chop and stroked another two feet, then another.

TWENTY-THREE

Misty was packing her green Samsonite. She was trying to hurry, but trying to do a thorough job too. Leaving this place where she'd lived for five years, she didn't want to forget anything she'd be sorry about later.

She had all eight derringers and her extra ammunition tucked in among the blouses and jeans and T-shirts and panties. She'd taken down all the Barbies, laid them out on the bed side by side, but then decided no, she didn't want them anymore. They belonged to some other girl. Some sappy young thing who'd thought that expressing herself artistically was a way to be admired and respected, maybe even loved. But it hadn't worked that way. People just looked at the Barbies and shook their heads.

Misty took down all her cosmetics and put them in a Ziploc bag. She chose a handful of cassette tapes, Hole, Kurt Cobain, a couple of Megadeth. She was moving quickly but not in a frenzy. A cold, shivery speed to her actions. She didn't know how long she had before Hal came back again.

The icy shudder in her belly was spreading through her limbs. There was a clammy smell of blood tainting the air and the tackiness on her fingertips wouldn't wash off. But it wasn't the blood that worried her. It wasn't the fact that this man was a killer. What frightened her was that she kept hearing his strange, awkward voice, seeing his intense eyes, his full lips. What frightened her was that she wanted to stay and wait for him to arrive, see what was below his surface, what the two of them would be like together. She knew it was crazy. Knew it was death. She had to run. She had to get away.

She made another pass through her closet, found an old Dolphins sweatshirt she'd always liked, and laid that on top of all her blouses and jeans. She snapped the case shut and carried it to the door. She should probably take apart her computer and put it in the trunk of her car. But when Misty tried to picture her future somewhere out in America, she didn't see a computer anywhere. What she saw was a cheap motel room and a diner where she fried hamburgers and popped the caps off Budweisers. What she saw was the desert of west Texas, tumbleweeds rolling down the streets and lanky cowboys wandering in to buy a Bud and stare at her tits. What she saw was doom.

She stood at the door and took a last look at her apartment. On her computer monitor, her father had awakened and a nurse was taking his blood pressure. She watched the screen and felt the prickle of cold radiating through her arms and legs. He was saying something. Her father was speaking.

Misty set her suitcase down beside the door and walked over to the computer and turned up the volume. Her father was moving his lips but the words coming from him were inaudible. She had to roll the volume knob all the way up. His eyes were half-open. He seemed dazed. Not the cocky man he'd been only yesterday.

With the volume all the way up, his words were filled with static from her cheesy speakers, but she could hear him now.

"Our Father who art in Heaven, hallowed be thy name. Thy kingdom come, thy will be done . . ."

Then he halted. He took a long raspy breath and began again, slower this time.

"Our Father who art in Heaven . . ."

Misty had never heard him pray. The Fieldings hadn't attended church. Sundays they used to sleep in, get out of bed in the afternoon, toast bagels, and read the *New York Times*. Misty was surprised the old man even knew the words to the prayer. But there he was, getting a little of it right, then losing his way, starting over again.

"Thy kingdom come, Thy will be done . . ."

Misty said, "On earth as it is in Heaven."

Her father lay there squinting into the camera trying to talk to God. Death was shriveling his body. Death was eating his organs, swallowing his tongue, sucking the juicy marrow from his bones. His skull beginning to show through, the shape of it so much like her own. Her father, J. J. Fielding, was peering head-on into the eye of the camera. Saying the words over and over, what he knew of the prayer, what he could remember.

The poor fucker. Dying alone like that, nobody to talk to but a camera. Driven into exile by Assistant U.S. Attorney Ed Keller, sent running from the two people on earth who cared about his ass. And now look at him. Lost, lonesome, and hopeless, calling out to a God he'd never believed in before. That poor old man who'd thought that four hundred million dollars would substitute for what he had, the love of his wife and child. A man who thought he could do the impossible, escape his own destiny. As if anybody could. As if running from it ever worked.

Misty stood there for a long while watching him fumble around with the Lord's Prayer. Then she went back to the doorway and picked up the suitcase and turned around and carried it to the bed. She opened it and began unpacking it, piece by piece, putting everything back where it belonged.

Hal made it to shore by eleven-thirty. He climbed out of the kayak, left it bobbing in the surf. He tramped down the beach and found his clothes beneath the curved palm tree where he'd left them. In the shadows he peeled off his sopping underwear and buried them in the sand. He slipped on his jeans and the dark T-shirt and his white Nike running shoes, then he cut through a patch of scrubby grass and headed to the parking lot.

The thunderstorm he'd paddled through had blown away and now the asphalt lot was glistening and full of puddles.

There was steam in the air. Raindrops trickled off the tips of the palm fronds.

Back inside his rental car, Hal sat watching the big parking lot. There were people arriving and leaving, walking to the thatch-roofed tiki bar, stumbling back to their cars after too many drinks; some were leaving the little glassed-in restaurant down by the beach.

Hal watched a white car over near the motel. Two men sitting in the front seat. The men wore dark shirts and sat without moving. In the next row over, there was a woman standing behind a brown panel van. She was talking on a cell phone. He saw two men in tie-dyed shirts go into the motel unit above the FBI agent's, then a little later a mother and father and their little girl arrived in a car and walked down to the beach. He saw two slender men with short hair holding hands near the tiki bar.

When the woman on the cell phone was finished with her conversation, she tapped on the back door of the brown van and it opened. She climbed inside.

That was all Hal needed to see. The needle in his chest had been quivering. Now he had seen a woman climb into a van and two men sitting in a parked white car. He had all the information he needed. It wasn't conclusive, but it was enough for Hal. Someone was shadowing Hannah Keller. They were waiting in the parking lot for her to return. They were either hoping she would lead them to J. J. Fielding so they could recover the stolen money, or they were hoping Hal would appear and they could catch him. Or maybe they wanted to do both things at once.

He sat there a while longer, slumped down in his car behind the steering wheel. He would stay there all night if he needed to. He wanted to watch, wanted to see what was going to happen when Hannah and the FBI agent finally made it back.

The motel tiki bar was busy. There were people dancing in the glow of the Christmas tree lights. It was more than two months until Christmas but they'd hung strings of colored holiday lights already. Just like the last foster home Hal lived in. He was fifteen. In that foster home outside of Evansville, Indiana, his mother left her Christmas decorations up all year long. A plastic Santa Claus sat on top of their yellow trailer, blinking through the summer nights. The trailer was planted on a small lot beside the main highway and Hal's foster mother decorated the yard for every holiday. She said it cheered up the travelers, particularly the long-distance truckers. His foster mother loved long-distance truckers. She'd married one of them and she slept with others when her husband was away from home. A lot of truckers honked as they passed by on the highway. At Easter his foster mother filled their yard with plastic bunnies and poked cutouts from Styrofoam egg cartons onto the tips of their tree limbs. At Thanksgiving there were cardboard replicas of pilgrims and lots of plastic turkeys spread around the yard.

When Hal's foster father was off on the road in his own eighteen-wheeler, Hal never knew who was going to come walking out of his mother's bedroom in the morning. Sometimes it was a trucker in his underwear. Sometimes it was a trucker with another woman. Sometimes it was two truckers. Once or twice one of the truckers tried to get Hal to join them.

When Hal came back to the trailer in Evansville to kill his foster mother there was a trucker sleeping late in her bedroom. She was frying eggs and bacon. In the year he'd been away she'd gotten old. Hal had already killed Harry Bonner and his wife, Eloise. He'd killed Sarah and Johnny Mitchell and Trudy and Simon Shallows. Now there was only his last foster mother left. Her husband had died in a highway accident, so Hal didn't have to kill him. When this last foster mother was dead, no one would know Hal had ever existed. He would be free to come and go as he pleased. He would be completely unrooted, no longer existing in anyone's mind.

Hal was fifteen years old and he'd been surviving on the road for a year. Run away from school, run away from the trailer beside the highway with the blinking Santa Claus on the roof. Judy Terrance's trailer.

Judy was standing at the stove frying eggs in her pink see-through nightie when Hal came into the trailer. She turned and saw him and something in her eyes went very still. She seemed to know exactly why he was there but she couldn't make herself scream or run away or anything. She stood there with a spatula in her hand. The bacon was sizzling and the sunny-side-up eggs were almost done in the big black iron skillet.

Her hair was gray and her old breasts hung loose, dark nipples staring down at the linoleum floor.

Hal took the spatula from her hand. He turned off the burners.

"I did the best I could," she said. "You was the way you was when I took you on, and there wasn't any changing it. I tried the best I knew how."

"You did all right," Hal said. "You did fine. I was a handful."

Then he reached up, spread his hands around her throat, and he strangled her. She stood there looking into Hal's eyes until she was unconscious. He laid her on the kitchen floor, then he lifted her nightie and tore an opening in her chest below her sternum, then he put his hand inside her soft old body and squeezed her heart till it was quiet.

When Hal looked up he saw the trucker had come out of the bedroom and was watching him from across the breakfast nook. His name was Hector Ramirez and he'd been visiting Judy Terrance for as long as Hal could remember, bringing her the white powder that got her through her empty days. Cocaine usually, but when he could get it, Hector gave her heroin. The man always had plastic bags of the powder in his truck, tucked among the lettuce and corn. He didn't use the stuff himself, but he sold it to other truckers and to people along his route. That's how he paid for the jewelry he wore, the diamonds on his hands and in his earlobe. Hector was a big man with a mustache that curved around his mouth and ran down to his chin like a Mexican bandit. He had a large belly and his tattooed arms were big and thick. Hal had seen the man wrestle the giant tires off his truck, so he knew how strong Hector was.

That morning Hector was naked. He came close to Hal while he was stooped over Judy's body, his right hand still inside her warm chest. Hector was a foot taller than Hal with big snaky muscles in his neck and shoulders. He bent close to see what Hal was doing. Hal drew his hand out of Judy Terrance's body.

"Now I gotta kill you, too, Hector."

"You could try, boy, but there's not a chance in hell it'll work out in your favor."

"I gotta do it, Hector. I can't let you live."

Hector stepped back, pulled out a chair from the kitchen table, and sat down in it. He fondled his long penis and studied Hal.

"What'd you do, reach in there and grab hold of Judy's heart?"

"I squeezed it till it stopped," Hal said. He was looking at Hector's big chest, wondering if his arm was long enough to reach all the way inside him.

"You seem to know what you're doing, boy."

Hal nodded.

"I'm guessing this isn't the first time you killed somebody that way, is it?"

"No, sir. This is my seventh. You'll be number eight."

Hal rose to his feet. He wiped his bloody hand on the leg of his blue jeans.

"I know some people," Hector said. "They might be interested in talking to a boy like you."

"What people?"

"You got a trade? Some kind of work you do to make money?"

"I know about embalming," Hal said. "Preparing the dead."

Hector smiled. He looked over at Judy, lying on her back in her pink nightie.

"She was a good woman, old Judy, but she was starting to

dry up a little. I liked her, though. We had some laughs. When she wasn't stoned out of her gourd."

He fiddled with his penis, not making it hard, just stretching it, scratching his balls. Hal watched him and said nothing. His hands were sticky with blood.

"So tell me, boy. You think you could kill somebody you didn't know? Some complete stranger? You think you could do that? Kill somebody without the heat of passion driving you to it."

"I guess so."

"Well, if you want, I'll make a phone call, see if these people I know might be interested in talking to you. There could be a future in it, boy. There's always somebody needs killing. And you seem to have a knack for it. There'd be a lot of travel, I'd expect. How you feel about traveling?"

"Traveling is okay," Hal said. "I don't mind traveling."

Hector made his phone call and Hal went to work a month later. By the time he was fifteen, he'd killed fourteen people, the first seven for free, the next seven for pay. Most of the ones he was hired to kill were people like Randy Gianetti, men who'd stolen money from the drug dealers, men who thought they were smart. There were a couple of women, too. Hal made good money. Enough to live in motels wherever he was, order room service, watch whatever movies were on the pay-per-view. The number of people he'd killed was much higher now. He'd stopped counting. Keeping score made it seem like a game, and it wasn't a game. Hal didn't play games.

In the dark motel parking lot, Hal watched those Christmas lights twinkle. Green and gold and red and blue. Little Japanese bulbs like fireflies trapped in plastic. Same kind Judy Terrance liked, only she always set hers so they'd blink. Two seconds, then a blink. Two seconds, then another, as regular as a heartbeat.

Hal sat in his rental car and watched the motel until somewhere around two-thirty he saw Hannah Keller and the FBI agent come walking past the tiki bar. The agent had his arm over Hannah's shoulder like he was too tired to walk on his own. Both of them were hunched over, trudging. It was a long swim back from the stilt house. Hal's arms were still tired from the trip out and the paddle back. There was probably a bruise on the FBI agent's throat where Hal had chopped him with the paddle.

Hal Bonner waited in his car till the two of them went into his motel room and closed the door. He waited a little longer, then a little longer after that. She didn't come out. A while later the gray van pulled out of the lot and then the white Ford left a while later. A silver Taurus with two men in it pulled in right afterward. Neither of the men got out of the car.

Now Hal knew he needed to act. To do something to distract the men who were following Hannah Keller. And he needed to do it pretty quick before J. J. Fielding had a chance to die and the money he'd stolen disappeared forever. He sat there for another few minutes hatching a plan. He put Misty Fielding into the plan, then took her out, then once more he put her back in.

When he could see the whole thing in his head, all the details bright and clear and perfect, he started his car and backed slowly out of the space, and pulled out of the lot. He was going to visit Hector Ramirez, his old friend. Hector would be just the distraction he needed. If these men in the parking lot were searching for Hal, trying to trap him, his plan would lure them away.

Hal started the car and pulled out of the parking lot. His mind was tired. He'd been thinking more than he ever had before. He had never been involved in an assignment that required so much of him. It was a challenge, perhaps too great a challenge. All he'd ever had to do in the past was locate someone and kill them. But this was far more complicated and Hal was starting to tire. Starting to feel a knot of muscle tighten inside his head. Then he thought of Misty Fielding, and he felt the knot relax. He thought of her some more and the pressure continued to ease.

All the way across the city of Miami, Hal saw Misty's green eyes staring at him out of the dark.

TWENTY-FOUR

Hannah took a long, hot shower in Frank's tiny bathroom. After drying off and slipping into a pair of his fleecy sweatpants and a white sweatshirt, she was still shivering. Her hair was damp but at least the sticky, salty feel was rinsed away. Her legs were weak. She felt faint and dizzy, as if she were hovering out-of-body a foot or two in the air above herself. The marathon swim had totally drained her, pushed her beyond any limits she'd ever known.

She opened the bathroom door and stepped back into the efficiency apartment. Frank was brewing coffee. He was barefoot, wearing jeans and a plaid shirt, his hair in a madman's tangle.

"How's the throat?"

"Great." His voice was a painful croak. "Just great."

"You sound like you've been smoking three packs a day for twenty years."

"I must've swallowed a half gallon of seawater." He poured them each a mug of coffee. "Black or what?"

"Black's fine."

She took the mug and sat down at the small dinette table. She blew on the coffee, then had a sip.

"I should go, let you rest."

He had a sip of his coffee, came over, patted her on the back, and pulled out the chair across from her and sat down.

"You saved my life."

"It was nothing."

"I respectfully disagree."

"You should probably stop talking, Frank. Save your voice."

"I probably should."

He downed half his coffee, grimacing as the hot liquid passed through his throat. He set the mug down between them.

Hannah was still hovering near the ceiling, watching herself. Her stomach wobbling. Something clenching and unclenching deep in her gut.

"That guy," he said. "Did you get a look at him?"

"Not much of one."

"Same guy you saw at the deli? One with the motorcycle helmet?"

"It was dark, Frank. I didn't get that kind of look."

"He had a buzz cut, though."

"You saw him better than I did. You were in his face."

"Well, he was one strong little weasel, I know that much. Jesus, if you hadn't been there, Hannah, I'd be floating face-down about now, drifting with the tide. I'd be in the morning paper, another body washes ashore."

She finished her coffee, stood up, and took the mug to the sink and rinsed it.

"What the hell's going on, Frank? Somebody's taking shots at me. A few hours later, this guy steals our kayak, leaves us out there to drown."

Frank shrugged.

"I thought you'd quit. You were just going to walk away."

"I'm still considering it."

"I wish you'd hang on a little longer. We're almost at the finish line."

"Look," she said, leaning against the sink. "I'm going to need to go."

"What? You gotta pick up Randall?"

"Randall's okay. He can sleep over with Gisela."

"Really?"

"Yeah, he'll be fine there."

"You made arrangements for that, a sleep-over?"

She shrugged.

"So, were you planning to spend the night with me?"

Frank leaned back in his chair. He seemed to be fighting off a grin.

"I didn't know what was going to happen, Frank."

"Well, well," he said.

"I'm going." But she didn't move from the sink.

Frank pushed his chair back, stood up.

As he approached, he raked a hand through his hair, got some of it unsnarled.

Even as tired as she was, as emotionally wrenched from seeing the film of her mother and dad, it wasn't an unpleasant prospect, cuddled with Frank Sheffield in that queen-size bed filling the adjoining room. Except for the gnawing uneasiness, something about Frank that kept bothering her, a series of slightly off-key notes that kept jangling the air between them.

"So, what you're saying is, there's really no reason you need to go home." His eyes were on hers. He tilted his head to the side with an easy grin.

She reached out and pressed her palm flat against his chest. About to grab a handful of his shirt and draw him to her or fend him off, she wasn't sure. He looked down at her hand, trying to read this moment, the ambiguous heat of her gesture.

Then he reached up with his right hand, gripped her wrist and slowly drew her hand down his chest, smoothed it across his flat stomach. Eyes on hers. At waist level, Frank hooked his right arm behind his back, like some ballroom dancer's slinky move, tugging her into his embrace.

His head tilted to the side, tipped down, lips softening against hers, finding the mesh. She kept her eyes open, looking at his lids and his cheek, trying in this way to stay aloof, but her lips betrayed her, the kiss deepening, mouths coming slowly apart, resettling. And she shut her eyes and gave herself to this moment, the hunger and urgency. His hands rising to cup her head, guide the pressure of the kiss, and

Hannah could feel the distance melt, the breathless merger begin.

But she couldn't let it happen. She wasn't sure why. She snaked her right hand up, pressed her palm against his chest, and pried herself away. He relaxed, let go of her head. He blinked at her like a man emerging from a pleasant sleep. For a second or two his hands still held the airy shape of her skull, then he let that go as well.

She took a deep breath, tried to hide her gasping.

"What is it?" His whisper was hoarse. "What's wrong?"

She stepped back, got another foot of distance between them.

"Would you tell me something, Frank?"

"If I can, sure."

A shy smile flickered on his lips as if he were reliving the kiss a few seconds more. Hannah's hand wandered in the air between them, fumbling for the right gesture, something emphatic, something to snap him out of his erotic drowse. She pointed a finger in his face. It was all wrong, but she held it there. Stubborn, on the edge of inexplicable tears.

"Tell me, Frank. Why the hell should it take so long for your FBI computer geeks to trace a Web site back to its source? Is it really that complicated?"

His quiet smile dissolved. Hannah, the mood killer.

She said, "Here we are, we're playing ring-around-a-rosy with the bastard who killed my parents. I'm getting shot at. We were almost drowned out there tonight. When all we need is for your computer people to do their job and we could get off this merry-go-round, go arrest this son of a bitch, and be done with it. Why's it taking so long, Frank? Can you answer me that?"

He shook his head, nothing to say. His smile was in ruins.

"Whose side are you on, Frank?"

"Yours," he said. "Yours, Hannah."

"That's not how it feels, Frank. I'm sorry, but that's not how it feels."

And the sexual tension that had been gathering in the air vaporized.

Ten minutes later Hannah was on her way back across the Rickenbacker Causeway, headed home. Her face flushed, her lips still plump with blood.

Misty lay on her bed in a pair of white panties and one of her old Hooters shirts watching Hal circle the room, then come over to the bed and sit down on the edge. She sat up, puffed the pillow, and leaned back against it.

"I didn't know if you were coming back."

She'd set the lights low, just the one in the bathroom with the door mostly closed, a dim halo surrounding them.

Hal took a break and let it out like he had something to say but didn't know how to begin. His hands were in his lap. He was looking at a place on the wall just above her head.

"What is it, Hal?"

"I don't know," he said.

"You don't know what?"

He brought his eyes down and gave her a thin smile. She was getting used to him now, seeing him better than the first couple of times. He wasn't like anyone she'd met, Jesus from work, the dozen other guys who'd been in her bed, mauling her, using her body roughly like it was some kind of gym equipment.

Hal was calm and quiet and serious. A guy who actually saw her when he looked, glimpsing some of what lived behind her eyes. That's how it felt anyway. She might be wrong. But the fact was, she'd never experienced that before, a guy looking at her, penetrating a few inches below the surface.

"I came back because I wanted to give you something."

Misty was quiet, not moving. He kept studying her but she didn't feel invaded or violated or any of that male-pushy stuff. A guy trying to force his advantage. None of that. Just his eyes prowling around inside her, seeing some of the stuff she kept hidden there.

"What?" she managed to say. "What did you want to give me?"

Hal looked off at the wall, his eyes getting fuzzy. A moment passed, then he looked back at Misty, blinking as if to clear the vision. He leaned forward, dug his hand into his pocket. He came out with something in his closed fist.

He gazed at her, making up his mind, then he opened his fist.

Lying flat in his palm was a shiny brown glass marble with a black dot in its center.

"What is it, Hal?"

"It's all that's left. An eye. One eye. I wanted you to have it."

She watched as Hal took another long breath, then another.

"I don't understand, Hal. You're going to have to talk to me."

Hal shook his head, swallowed a couple of times. When he spoke again, his eyes were hazy, and the words seemed awkward in his mouth, like he was uttering a language he'd never used before. Having to work hard to fit the clumsy words together into complete sentences.

"I see you in my head," said Hal. "I close my eyes and I can see you. When I'm driving around, when I'm off somewhere else."

"Well, that's good, Hal. That's a good thing. I've been seeing you like that too. Shut my eyes and you're there. Same thing."

He looked at the wall again. He blinked a couple of times, then he spoke.

"From when I was little till I was fifteen years old and went off on my own, I lived in one place after another. Different houses, different parents. Some of them were okay, some weren't. It didn't matter either way, because I knew they'd get sick of me eventually, ship me to the next place. On to the next, then the next, then the next after that. The only thing I managed to hold onto all those years was some stupid stuffed animal. I had it from the time I was a little kid. I always figured it was something my real mother stuck in my crib when she sent me off to the orphanage. It was a little toy animal. A silver wolf."

Misty reached out and rested a hand on his thigh.

"Sometimes, I talked to the thing. I told the wolf what I'd dreamed the night before, which bully at school was pushing me around, what I was going to do to him, stupid stuff like that. During the day, when I left for school, I'd stuff the wolf under the mattress. At night I'd get it out and I'd talk to it some more. And sometimes the wolf talked back to me."

"Jesus, Hal."

He flicked a look her way, then slid his gaze back to the far wall.

"Then the wolf started falling apart. The seams split, the stuffing started leaking out. I didn't know how to fix it and I couldn't ask any of the women to sew it back together because I didn't want anyone to know I had the thing. They might take it from me or make fun of me, use it against me somehow. I got so I didn't want to touch the thing anymore. More I touched it, more stuff leaked out. I tried to break the habit, just stop touching it. But I couldn't. Until finally all the stuffing was gone. It was just a rag with glass eyes."

Misty looked again at the brown half-marble in his palm.

"Now that's all that's left."

With her breath tight in her chest, Misty said, "And you want to give it to me?"

"Yeah, I do."

He handed it to her and Misty took it and let it lie in her palm.

"Why, Hal? Something means so much to you, why would you give it away?"

"I don't know."

"I think you do know, Hal."

"I do?"

"Yeah, I think you know. But I think it's hard for you to say the words."

She reached out with her right hand and trailed her fingers across his cheek. Hal's breathing smoothed out, deepened. She felt the bristles of his heavy beard and the muscles in his jaw starting to relax.

Misty traced the outline of his lips.

"You know the two of us, we have something in common, Hal."

"We do?"

"Yeah, think about it. We're orphans, both of us. Abandoned by the ones who were supposed to love us. No wonder we're so fucked up. So needy and lost."

"I never felt like this," he said. "I don't know what's wrong with me. It's like I'm sick. Dizzy and weird."

"It's okay. It's just a new thing, a new feeling. It's normal for it to feel weird. You've always been a lone wolf. Like your toy animal. A loner, going your own way. So it's a little strange to be thinking about someone else, seeing them in your head, including them in things."

"It is. It's strange."

"But perfectly natural," Misty said. "Two people, a man and a woman, having these feelings. It's the natural way."

"I don't know," he said. "It feels weird."

"How about animals? You know all about animals. Aren't there some that take mates, stick with them? Like a family."

"Some."

"Well, see. It's natural."

"It's called pair bonding," Hal said. "Most birds just do it for one season, then the next spring they have to start all over again, do the whole mating thing. All the dancing around, special songs, fighting the other males."

"But there are some, aren't there, they take a mate and never let go?"

"Swans and cranes," Hal said. "Gibbons too. And macaws."

"Macaws, they're what, like parrots?"

"Parrot family, yeah. They fly in pairs. You see an odd number of macaws, it's because one of them has lost its mate and won't ever remarry. Swans, cranes, gibbons, macaws. There's a few others too, but I can't remember them right now."

Misty watched the steady rise and fall of his chest. She could hear the air filling his lungs, hear it leaving.

"There's something else," Hal said.

"Yeah?"

"Something I need to ask you, something you could help me with if you were willing."

Misty leaned back against the pillows.

"I know," she said. "You want me to help you kidnap the boy."

He looked at her for a long moment.

"How'd you know that?"

"Because that's how it is between people like us. We can read each other's mind. We're blending together, becoming one."

"You'll help me, then?"

She looked again at the glass wolf eye, cold in her palm.

"Just tell me what to do, Hal. Just tell me what to do and I'll do it."

"Hannah Keller wants to quit. She's going to give up trying to find your father, and just walk away. But I can't let her do that."

"So we steal her kid," Misty said. "Then she has to do what we say."

"That's right," said Hal. "You're very smart."

Misty looked him deep in the eye to see if he was being ironic. But he looked back at her, a hundred percent dead-on sincere. Hal Bonner didn't know how to be ironic. And Misty liked that. Misty liked that a lot.

"Thanks," she said. "You're sweet to say it. You're very sweet."

TWENTY-FIVE

Back on the mainland, Hannah took Old Cutler Road south through the Gables and South Miami. The narrow road meandered along the coast, mirrored its irregular contours, just two lanes cutting through a tunnel of overhanging banyans and oaks, past the big pink Mediterranean mansions. It was one of the first roads in Miami, the one the settlers had used to push farther south, hacking another mile and another after that through palmetto and buttonwood and black mangroves, tying bandannas over their mouths to keep from choking on the clouds of mosquitoes, all the while looking out for Indians and alligators and con men. Hannah's mother loved that road, describing again and again its marvelous history, an anecdote at every crook, how it looked when she was a girl growing up in Miami, a twisty path fringed with gumbo limbo and the snarl of mangroves. Tonight it was haunted, eerily empty, so late, so dark. That Easter home movie replaying as she drove. Her father's smile, her mother's shy voice. Hannah standing primly in her new dress and hat and purse, the unbearable serenity of that place and time.

Hannah passed the Gables fire station, turned onto Red Road, only five minutes from home. A mile farther on, she suddenly gripped the wheel hard and veered off Old Cutler Road, an impulsive left into Gables by the Sea. Drawn down the darkened streets, the very neighborhood she'd avoided for years. Going slow, she turned left again and headed up the narrow lane along the edge of Biscayne Bay, the street

where her parents lived. The place where everything started
to go wrong.

When she came to the end of the cul-de-sac, she put two
wheels up on the shoulder across from the old house. She
lowered her window, switched off the lights, turned off the
motor.

She drew a long breath and released it. She listened to the
wind sifting through the pines. A spectral moan. From the
nearby canal she could hear the slosh of water, and halyards
clinking, and she could smell the sulfurous decay wafting
off the tidal flats. A child's bicycle lay in the front yard of
the house across the street.

Drawing the scented night air into her lungs, Hannah
slipped back into a flutter of ancient images. Seeing a girl in
Bermuda shorts learning to ride her first bicycle on this same
street while her father and mother followed Hannah's orders
not to watch or embarrass her in any way as she mastered
the birthday gift. The two of them out in the front yard pre-
tending to obey. Ed mowing the lawn and Martha clipping
sprigs of bougainvillea, purple and yellow blossoms fluttering across fresh cut grass. Both of them sneaking glimpses
of their daughter, smiling at her success, holding themselves
back when she tipped over, tumbled to the asphalt, then
stood up, dusted off her scuffed knees, and climbed back on
that bike. Then another image replacing that. Six-year-old
Randall with a blond mop, cranking his spinning rod out on
the seawall. And then the loop of film she'd watched a thousand times began to play—three men dressed as house
painters walking into the kitchen door. One tall, two short.

Hannah closed her eyes, opened them again, blinked
away the vision.

She looked across at the dark house. Strangers lived there
now. She didn't know their names, and they probably knew
nothing of the history of that house. The horrors that happened there.

She craned forward, peered down the driveway.

Then she opened the door and got out. She walked slowly

into the middle of the street, stood there lining up the angle, then stepped a few feet to the right, a few more feet.

"Christ!"

She marched down the brick driveway and opened the chain-link gate and stepped into the backyard. For all she knew the current owners could be heavily armed paranoids with a flesh-eating Doberman. This was, after all, Miami. But she pushed on, stepping lightly across the back lawn toward the seawall. No dogs barked, no sirens went off. On the seawall she turned and looked back at the house. She moved left until the seawall ended in a heap of boulders, then went all the way to the right perimeter until she reached the neighbor's fence. Nowhere along the entire path could she see the driveway.

If Randall had been fishing on the concrete seawall like he claimed, he couldn't possibly have seen three men going into the kitchen door. His view was blocked by the east wing of the house. There's no way he would have been able to describe the men as thoroughly as he did. House painters. Two short, one tall.

But no one had thought to check out that part of his story. No one had done the simple, skeptical, routine thing. To stand where Randall said he'd stood and look back at the driveway to see if what he described could actually be seen from that vantage point. No one bothered to double-check, or to question the boy because he was so badly traumatized. He was mute and withdrawn, under psychiatric care. And what's more, he was the son of one of their own. He was a cop's only child, so he got that extra leeway. They left him alone. Didn't double-check his story.

For after all, the boy had absolutely no reason to lie about what he'd seen.

No reason at all.

It was nearly four in the morning by the time Hannah sat down in front of Randall's computer and switched it on. Alone in the house, still she was feeling guilty, as though he would walk in any second and find her snooping on him. She had never done it before, never prowled through his drawers or poked in the back corners of his closet. She trusted her son completely. And even now, with this troubling revelation pulsing in her mind, she felt deeply uneasy about invading his privacy.

All she really wanted to do was get Stevie's address. His E-mail friend. A boy, according to Randall, who was a world-class computer prodigy. Someone she might be able to enlist to trace Fielding's broadcast back to its origin, the exact location of his hospital room.

Of course, this whole thing could wait till daylight. Hannah should go to bed, try to get a little rest, then after Randall got home from school tomorrow she could simply ask him for a way to reach his friend. But as Hannah navigated through the opening screens, then began to prowl the folders Randall had created to store his files, she felt the pang of guilt subside. Apparently her son had misled the police and her about what he'd seen. Something horrifying had sent him into shock back then and now that she had begun a fresh investigation of the events of that morning, Randall was suffering another wave of torment. If that wasn't permission enough to do all the snooping she wanted, she didn't know what was.

She scanned quickly through his school assignments. Essays she'd helped him with, a few he'd tackled on his own. There was another folder of Web pages he'd downloaded from the Internet. Scanned photographs of animals and comic book heroes and a couple of all-girl groups in slinky, revealing costumes. His computer address book was empty and she quickly exhausted his other personal folders. No E-mail addresses anywhere she could see, no old mail stored to his hard drive. She opened some of the general program files and read the file names but nothing struck her as suspicious.

Hannah sat for a while staring at the screen. If Randall wanted to conceal something from her on his hard drive he certainly had the ability to do it. It wouldn't even represent a

challenge for the boy. In only five minutes Hannah was close
to exhausting her computer skills.

The only other possibility she could think of was his Internet service provider's storage system where Stevie's old
E-mails might be saved. She clicked through the steps and
the modem dialed into the system. Fortunately he'd stored
his password and in a few seconds the opening page appeared.

Welcome Randall.

As Hannah was locating Randall's E-mail log, an electronic trill sounded from the speakers. She stiffened.

In the corner of the screen a small white box appeared.
An instant message from Stevie. Apparently some kind of
buddy system alerted him that Randall Keller was on-line.

"Hey Randall. Where you been?"

Hannah sat there for several moments staring at the
empty message box below Stevie's welcome. The cursor
pulsed inside the box, waiting for a response.

She settled her fingers on the keyboard and typed.

"Hey Stevie."

She waited but no reply came. Thirty seconds, then a
minute.

Finally the trill of another message.

"You're not Randall."

Hannah didn't hesitate.

"I'm not?"

"No. He doesn't talk that way."

"Okay," she typed. "That's true. I'm not."

"You're Hannah, his mother."

"Good guess," she typed.

"I've read your books."

"Really?"

"Yeah, I like Erin Barkley. She's a real tough lady. And
sexy."

"Thanks."

"I'm ready for the new one. What's taking so long?"

"You sound like my editor."

"So where's Randall?"

Hannah considered it for a moment.

Then she typed, "He's sleeping over with a friend tonight."

"Gisela? The houseboat."

"That's right."

"So how come you're on his 'puter?"

"Just playing around. I couldn't sleep."

"I know the feeling."

"I was wondering," Hannah typed. But then she hesitated, not sure where to take this. How much she could trust this kid. If he was indeed a kid.

"Yes?"

What the hell. Frank had failed her, his buddies at the FBI were fumbling or stalling for reasons of their own.

"I was wondering if you could help me with something. A computer problem."

"I could try."

Hannah sat there a minute more, debating it. Then finally, she began to type, telling this total stranger what she needed to know.

When she was done she waited for several minutes before his reply came back.

It was a street address on Star Island. And below it he'd typed, "Stop by before noon. I'll show you what I've dug up."

"You don't go to school?"

"Home schooling," he replied.

"I'll be there," Hannah typed back.

"Now you should probably get some sleep," Stevie said.

"You too," she responded.

"Fat chance."

Hannah sat there a moment more after Stevie had signed off. This was her first instant message conversation and she was shivering at the strangeness of it. Disembodied words passing back and forth through the black vacuum of cyberspace. It was nuts, laying out this private matter for some complete stranger. It was something only a totally reckless, totally desperate woman would do. Someone like Erin Barkley. Someone like herself.

Spunky rustled in his shredded newspapers. He poked his nose through the thin bars of the birdcage. Hannah took down the carton of food pellets and dumped a few in his feeding dish. Spunky wriggled his nose at her and went to work, munching ravenously on the brown pellets.

She turned back to the computer and just as she was beginning to run down the list of Randall's recent E-mails, she noticed that in the corner of the screen, the red flag on his mailbox was popped up.

Hannah hesitated a moment, then moved the cursor and clicked on the mailbox.

The message was from someone calling herself Barbie-girl. Another insomniac pal of Randall's orbiting the electronic void.

Hannah clicked open the mail.

Barbie-girl had typed, "Hi, Rando. Here's a recent snap so you have a better idea what I look like. Better shred this when you've finished looking. Wouldn't want Mommy to get the wrong idea. Barbie-girl."

There was a file attached to the mail. Hannah double-clicked to download the attachment.

Slowly, a photographic file resolved into view, a girl's face filling the seventeen-inch screen.

She had metallic red hair and very pale skin, maybe twenty-one, twenty-two years old. She had dull green eyes and used a garish array of blues and browns in her makeup. She had a longish nose and was squinting back over her shoulder into the camera lens. Her chin rested on her shoulder blade in a Marilyn Monroe cootchie-coo pose. The smile on the girl's narrow lips was probably meant to be coquettish, but it had all the subtlety of a hooker's come-hither leer.

Hannah sat still. It was half a minute before she managed to draw a breath. She got up from the desk and paced back through the house to the kitchen. From an open bottle in the refrigerator she poured herself a glass of Chardonnay, gulped it down, and poured another. She carried it back through the silent house and took her place again at Randall's desk.

She had another sip of wine, then set it aside and went back to the E-mail log and clicked on the icon to open the folder. Three other folders were stashed inside. Once was titled **Stevie**, one called **Barbie-girl**, and the last one **Dad**.

Hannah fumbled with the mouse, nearly knocked it off the desk.

"That fucking bastard."

When she regained control of her faltering hand, she guided the cursor to the **Dad** folder and clicked. There were a couple of dozen files inside, each one dated, starting back in January, ten months ago. About the same time Randall had created his Web page and hung it out on the Internet, a virtual post office box. Making himself available to anyone searching for the name Randall Keller. Which is how his father, Pieter Thomasson, that goddamn son of a bitch, must have located him. And for the last ten months the bastard had been courting her son, engaging him in some kind of E-mail relationship, no doubt trying to plant seeds of discontent or betrayal.

Hannah chose the first file, a message dated the seventeenth of January.

But when she clicked it twice, the file wouldn't open. A small gray box appeared instead, asking for her password. She tried typing *Randall*, but that wasn't it. She tried *Keller*, then *Spunky*, but was refused. *Pieter* was rejected and *Thomasson* was as well.

She sat back in the chair. A screech owl was hooting in the neighbor's yard. The sea breeze had stiffened and she could hear the rattle of the palm fronds outside Randall's window, and the quiet tick of the wood house resisting the steady pressure of the wind.

In the middle drawer of his desk she found a box of floppy disks. She punched one of them into his disk drive and in a few seconds she'd copied all the **Dad** E-mail files to the floppy. She backed out of the **Dad** folder and then opened the one named **Barbie-girl**. Twenty-odd files starting back in July. The Barbie files were password-protected as well, so she exited the folder and copied it to the same floppy disk.

The **Stevie** files did not require a password. But it only took her a couple of minutes, scanning through the first four or five, to see that the conversation that passed between these two was innocuous, the talk of boys who shared an obsession for computers and the arcane intricacies of software programming.

She got up slowly from the desk and carried her wine through the dark house. In her bedroom she switched on the small reading lamp perched on her bedside table. She opened the top drawer. Beside the .357 Smith & Wesson lay the copy of *First Light*. She plumped the pillows and propped herself against them and opened the book to page 276.

There was only a single phrase underlined.

She closed the book, lay it on the bed beside her and reached over for the phone.

Frank Sheffield answered on the first ring.

His voice was husky, as if he'd been screaming at the bare walls ever since she'd left him.

"Are you all right, Hannah?"

"I'm fine."

"You don't sound fine. What's wrong? What happened?"

"I'm fine."

The line was empty for several moments.

"I looked up page 276."

"And?"

"Fifty-yard line at the Orange Bowl."

"That's all it says?"

"That's all."

He was quiet for a second or two, then said, "So does this mean you're back on the case?"

"I'm back."

"Good. I'm glad to hear it."

"How about noon, Frank?"

"The Orange Bowl at noon. Okay, sure. I can be there."

"You starting to see the pattern?"

"Pattern?"

"The Bayshore house. Stiltsville. The Orange Bowl. A place in plain view. Exposed. Easily monitored."

"Yeah, that's true."

"Frank?"

"Yeah."

"Does the name Helen Shane mean anything to you?"

She thought she heard him swallow.

"Helen Shane?"

"Never mind, Frank. I'll see you at noon. North entrance. We can go in together."

"Fine," he said. "Noon, north entrance. And listen, Hannah."

"Yeah?"

"I'll get on those computer guys. Crack the whip. I agree, it shouldn't take this long to locate the source of a Web address. They may even have something by now."

"Good, Frank. You do that. Crack the whip."

She hung up and sat there for a while staring at the phone, listening to the push of the steady breeze against that old wood house.

TWENTY-SIX

Hal Bonner was changing planes in Atlanta. It was six in the morning and the plane that was to take him to Nashville was parked at the gate just about to start boarding. Hal was talking to a man in a brown corduroy suit. The man was red-haired and gangly and he had huge feet inside his huge wingtip shoes. His portable computer was perched on his lap and his fingers were still resting on the keyboard, but a few minutes earlier he'd stopped working on the memo he was typing. The man wasn't looking at Hal. He wasn't looking at his computer screen. He wasn't looking at anything at all. The gangly man hadn't so much as twitched since Hal started letting him know about the feeding practices of the bearded vulture of Eurasia.

How it lives on a diet of bone and marrow. How it spots a carcass from above, and circles in and lands, then waits patiently near the carrion while all the other jungle scavengers strip away the meat and gristle and lick up all the blood. When they're finished with their meal the bearded vulture hops forward to take his turn, and consume the skeletal remains.

But the femurs of antelope or gazelle are not easy for a bird to crack open. So the bearded vulture had to discover a way to take advantage of the one skill that is his greatest strength—flying.

With a bone grasped in its talons, the bearded vulture flies around till it locates a slab of rock. Then after it gains a little altitude, it dives at the rock at speeds of more than fifty miles an hour, turning away at the last second and letting the bone go so it smashes against the boulder. The vulture might have to repeat the trick two dozen times to pulverize a single bone. Though the splintered parts don't have to be all that small because the bearded vulture can swallow a ten-inch piece of bone without any trouble.

"Like a sword swallower," Hal said to the businessman. "Only this bone goes in, but never comes out."

The man wiped his mouth with the back of his hand and after a moment he turned his head to take a look at Hal.

"I think it's time to board," Hal said.

By 6 A.M. Central Standard Time Hal was in his rental car going west past the Grand Ole Opry. Using a different credit card than he'd used in Miami. One of the dozen or so he got in the mail every month from South America. Nice new credit cards with nice new names.

Fifteen minutes later he passed Vanderbilt University and kept on heading west till he came to a small road on his right that led up a hill to a neighborhood of large white houses with big columns across their fronts.

He'd been there a few times before. Just parked down the block to watch the house and the comings and goings of Hector Ramirez. The trucker who'd gotten Hal started in the murder business wasn't driving a truck anymore. These days Hector owned a white Cadillac and he lived in a big Nashville house with seven white columns across the front.

Two years earlier the DEA had tried to throw Hector in jail on an interstate transport of narcotics charge, but Hector hired the best lawyer in Nashville and beat the case. That's how Hal found him. Just by chance, seeing Hector's picture in the paper, him and his lawyer standing on the Nashville courthouse steps holding up their hands in a victory celebration.

Hal had forgotten all about the guy until last night, sitting in the parking lot watching the guys who were watching Hannah Keller. That's when he had the idea. Hector Ramirez was going to be Hal's distraction. His old friend helping him out one last time.

Hal drove up Hector's driveway and parked in front.

He was wearing his Florida tourist clothes. The yellow shirt with speedboats on it and a light blue windbreaker over it. Blue jeans and tennis shoes. Hal walked up the stairs and rang the doorbell.

The man who answered the door was an African-American. He was tall and had wide shoulders and long arms. He was dressed in a black shirt and black pants. He had a gold tooth in his smile.

"I'm here to see Hector," said Hal.

"Everyone wants to see Hector," the man said. "But only a few get to."

"Tell him it's Judy Terrance's boy," Hal said. "He'll remember."

The black man slanted his head and peered at Hal for a few seconds. Then he stepped back and shut the door in Hal's face.

Hal waited. He stared at the white paint on the door. It was glossy and looked like it was many layers thick. Someone had spent a lot of time painting the door. Over and over and over until the door was thick with glossy white paint.

Hal could feel someone looking at him through the peephole. Then he heard a voice behind the door and a moment or two later the door swung open and Hector Ramirez was standing there in a white robe and a black cowboy hat. He was wearing shiny gold slippers.

"Hey, kid."

"Hello, Hector."

"Tell me right now, no bullshit. Is this a business call? 'Cause if it is, then I can tell you flat out, it isn't going to happen. I got serious protection right inside this door."

"You mean did they send me to murder you?"

"That's what I mean, yeah."

"No," Hal said. "I just wanted to see you again. To say hi."

"Is that right?"

"Sorry for the inconvenience," Hal said.

Hector looked at Hal for a long time, then he turned his head and looked to his right and nodded.

Hal saw the big black man step away. He was holding a large automatic weapon. Hal didn't recognize it or know its brand name. He didn't care about weapons or their names or calibers. He had his thumbnail and his hand and that's all he needed.

"You wanted to see me again? What, like to reminisce about the good old days in Judy's roadside trailer?"

"I brought you something. A present."

"What're you talking about, Hal?"

"I owe you, Hector, for getting me started in this business. It's turned out to be very lucrative."

"Yeah, I heard they're keeping you busy. I should've taken a referral fee, or a cut on your future earnings, boy."

"Well, I brought you something. It's something I found in my travels and when I saw it, I thought of you, Hector. I thought of how much I appreciated your help, getting me started."

"What kind of bullshit is this, Hal?"

Hal turned around and walked back to the rental car. He sat down in the driver's seat and he honked the horn. Then he honked it again and again and then held it down for several seconds. Hal waited there, looking across the street, until he saw a woman in a blue dress and white hair come to her front window, a neighbor concerned about the noise in this expensive neighborhood. Hal continued to tap the horn.

As Hector came down the sidewalk, he screamed at Hal to stop that fucking racket.

Hal continued to honk.

Hector came up to the open door and ducked down and reached out to pull Hal's hand away from the horn.

Hal turned in the seat and with one hand he grabbed Hector by the throat and with the other he reached inside Hector's robe. Hector's cowboy hat tumbled off his head and fell to the asphalt.

Hector tried to push Hal's hand away. He tried to scream for his black valet. None of this succeeded. Hector Ramirez's eyes blinked several times like the Christmas tree lights, like the Santa Claus on the roof of the trailer. They blinked and then they closed.

Then the black man was out on the porch. He was waving his weapon. He was yelling at Hal to step back. But Hal held Hector as a shield between him and the black man until he had entered Hector's body and done the deed.

Then he let Hector fall to the pavement. As he pulled onto the quiet street of that hillside neighborhood, he looked over at the house across the way and saw the woman in the blue dress was still at the window, a telephone pressed to her ear.

By seven-thirty in the morning the temperature in Miami was already in the mid-eighties. Misty Fielding wore denim overalls over a shorty white T-top, showing a little midriff, the curve of her waist. She wore white Keds and a baseball cap with the Miami Heat's logo. In her right pocket was the wolf eye. She could feel it through the material of her overalls rubbing against her thigh. As she got out of her car at Dinner Key Marina, she reached into the pocket and touched the glass eye. A good luck touch.

She was nervous but pumped. Following Hal's plan, the two of them were a team now. Feeling the blood fizz in her veins, the pleasant breathless tingle of nervous energy. This was the day everything came together, all the random story lines of her life intersected into one. Misty and Hal. Misty and Randall. Misty and Hannah. Misty and her father. All the strands braiding.

She carried a straw bag with five derringers in it, and she was wearing her wraparound shades. Trying for a nautical look, though she wasn't sure if she was close or not. She'd never spent much time around marinas or boats or the water, but as she crossed the parking lot and saw the way some of the other people headed toward the docks were dressed, she relaxed. Apparently any scruffy thing would do.

There were several entrances through the high chain-link fence, but Hal had told her which one to take, the one on the far left. She passed an old man with white hair who was sitting on a bench having a breakfast beer. He had a grizzled Ernest Hemingway beard and bleary eyes that he turned on her as she passed.

"Tight lines and good fishing." He raised his beer can in salute.

Misty marched down the dock past the big white yachts and the long sleek sailboats. She was almost to the end of the dock, starting to think she'd taken the wrong entrance after all, when she saw Randall Keller sitting on a bench in front of an open slip. He was plinking rocks into the water.

She walked up behind him and looked down at the top of his head. His blond hair was thick and uncombed. He was wearing a blue-and-white-checked shirt and blue jeans and black basketball shoes. She caught a hint of his shampoo, something with a strawberry flavor. A cute kid. Cuter up close than he'd seemed at a distance when she'd followed him home from school those times.

He was drawing back his hand to toss another pebble into the harbor when Misty spoke.

"You do your homework, Randall?"

He stopped his toss, then slowly craned around and looked at her.

"You get that photo I sent?"

"Who are you?" he said.

"Think hard. You'll probably be able to figure it out, Rando."

The boy swallowed. The rock fell from his hand onto the dock.

"Barbie-girl?"

Misty came around the bench and sat down beside him. He gave her a stiff smile and inched away.

"What're you doing here?"

"I thought it looked like a nice day for a boat ride."

"You have a boat here?"

"No, but I understood your friend does. The one your

mother dumps you with when she wants to be alone. Dark hair, a little pudgy."

"You know Gisela?"

"No, but I'd like to. Which boat is hers?"

Randall looked across at a red and yellow houseboat with several purple life preservers hooked along its rail.

"The *Margaritaville*, huh? You think she'd mind if I came aboard?"

Randall swallowed again and said nothing.

"Oh, come on, Randall. Why're you being so shy? You're not shy on the computer."

"Gisela's getting dressed," he said, "then we have to go to school. I don't think it's a good time right now."

"What's wrong, Randall? You don't seem pleased to see me. After all the intimate conversations we've had, you're so cold. Do I scare you?"

The boy frowned and looked down at the water.

Misty said, "I'm really hurt, Randall. I thought we had something nice. Is that the kind of little boy you are? Rude, unkind?"

"What do you want?" His voice was meek. "Why are you here?"

"I told you. I want to go on a boat ride. It's such a pretty day. Don't you think it's a pretty day?"

Randall looked up at the empty blue sky, then turned his gaze back toward the houseboat.

"I have to go," he said. He rose and started around the bench.

Misty hopped to her feet and followed him. Down the dock Ernest Hemingway was coughing loudly as he popped open another beer.

At the ramp that led to the *Margaritaville*, Misty reached into her straw bag and chose one of the derringers at random. The .38 Mighty Midget. She kept her hand inside the purse, taking a firm grip on the pistol.

She stepped onto the deck of the houseboat, a couple of paces behind Randall. The boy shot a quick look back at her, then headed for the door.

He was in the main cabin only a step ahead of Misty.

She shut the door behind her and turned just as the small dark-haired woman came out of the other cabin. She was running a brush through her hair when she saw Misty.

Randall dropped down on a small couch and hunched his head low like a turtle trying to disappear into its shell.

"Who the hell are you?"

Gisela pointed the hairbrush at her as if it were loaded.

"Hey, I know you," Misty said. "You're the one from TV, the cop lady who's always in an uproar about some 7-Eleven robbery or something. That's you, isn't it? The TV cop lady?"

"That's right, I'm a police officer. And who are you? And what the hell do you think you're doing in here?"

Gisela took a half step to her right. Closer to the little kitchen with its drawers full of knives. Maybe even a gun hidden in there somewhere.

Misty withdrew the derringer from her purse and showed it to Gisela.

Randall looked up, saw the gun, and sank lower on the couch.

"Okay," Misty said. "So let's crank this baby up, see what she'll do. The three of us, we're going for a little boat ride."

TWENTY-SEVEN

At just after eight Hannah swung her Porsche off the Julia Tuttle Causeway onto Star Island. The sky was polished a milky blue, with a strong breeze off the water, traffic inexplicably light.

Almost a century earlier Star Island and several other perfectly oval dollops of land had been scooped from the bay bottom and distributed along the edge of the causeway to Miami Beach so that the moderately rich might have a waterfront way station to enjoy until they amassed sufficient wealth and could afford to move an hour north to the true luxury of Palm Beach.

It took her only a few minutes to locate the correct gold numerals on the stucco column. Behind the heavy brass bars of the front gate, the house was a three-story sprawling Mediterranean mansion that confronted a blue expanse of Biscayne Bay like a fortress of culture and good taste. It was protected from drive-by gawkers by a high pink stucco rampart backed by a fifteen-foot sculptured hedge.

At the head of the driveway Hannah spoke her name into the speaker box, prepared to give a long explanation about the E-mail relationship between her son and the boy who lived behind those walls, but only a second after she'd uttered her name, the heavy gate rolled open.

A slim Japanese woman in a white dress and white leather shoes greeted her at the front door and admitted her into a cool, shadowy foyer. To the right a small waterfall rustled inside a screened atrium. Two garish parrots squawked and fluttered their wings. On the whitewashed wall to the left hung a small dark painting signed by Marc Chagall.

The slim woman waited serenely for Hannah to take in the surroundings.

When Hannah turned back, the woman's slender hand fluttered up toward the stairway.

"Stevie is expecting you, Ms. Keller. He's in the studio."

"Are you Stevie's mother?"

"No. Mr. and Mrs. Brockman are in Provence for the week, buying wine. I am Yoshia, Stevie's nurse."

"The boy's ill?"

The woman smiled graciously.

"I'll let you be the judge of that."

Hannah followed Yoshia up a wide spiral stairway flanked by narrow slotted windows that looked out on the rose garden and pool and clay tennis court and a pool house that was a small replica of the main house.

Stevie Brockman's bedroom was as spacious as the lobby of a fine hotel. From what Hannah could see, the room occupied most of the third floor. A single bed was stashed in one corner of the room, but the rest of the space was taken up by long benches heaped with electronic paraphernalia. Several units with small screens filled by pulsing green lines like a dozen heart monitors lined up side by side. Meters and motherboards and soldering irons and pliers and screwdrivers were scattered across the workbenches. Two TVs sat in the far corner, both on, both tuned to the same channel. One was in black-and-white, the other color. Hovering in the background was an insistent hum that sounded like the drone of an overturned hive.

The boy sat in a black leather swivel chair in front of a sleek computer terminal. He was wearing khaki shorts and a blue polo shirt, like a prep-school uniform. He had curly black hair and round cheeks and chubby arms and his shoes didn't reach the floor. He glanced over his shoulder, nodded a quick hello, then went back to his screen.

Yoshia moved up beside him and stood with reverential

stillness as if the boy were performing the last difficult passages of a piano sonata.

Hannah stepped closer and leaned in to see the screen.

Stevie Brockman was using his mouse to scroll through columns of computer language. Line after line of hieroglyphs rolled past so quickly Hannah couldn't catch a single letter. She watched him click the mouse, apparently inserting lines of code into the streaming list.

"Hannah's a writer. She writes mystery novels," Stevie explained to Yoshia. "They're good. A little gory in places, but I like all the whackos. My favorite was *Third Time Out*. Very lyrical nature descriptions. And I liked the baseball stuff. That Erin Barkley is one tough lady."

"You seem a little young for my books."

"I'm twelve, almost thirteen," he said. And continued to speed through the column of runic symbols, adding here, subtracting there. "I'm allowed to read anything I want. Last week I read *Ulysses*. Do you know *Ulysses*?"

"I know it," she said.

"I liked that woman. Molly Bloom. I liked how it ended, that long sentence, it went on for twenty pages or something. The sex was good, too. I like sex in a book."

"Stevie's quite a reader," Yoshia said.

"I'm very interested in sex," he said. "Of course I'm too young for it in real life, but what the heck, I can read about it, can't I?"

Yoshia gave Hannah an indulgent smile.

"I'm trying to learn to write," Stevie said. "But it's tough. Getting it all down, making sense. Something can be clear in my mind, but as I start to put it into words, it just seems to go away."

"I know the feeling," Hannah said. "It's like telling a dream. No matter how vivid it is when you wake up in the morning, as soon as you begin to tell it, the images seem to decay."

"Yeah, yeah, that's good," Stevie said. "Have you read Robert Frost?"

Hannah smiled. Grilled by a twelve-year-old.

The kid was clicking the mouse, using the pointer, cutting and pasting large sections of computer code, doing it all with effortless speed and certainty.

"Yes," she said. "I know a little Frost."

"What I like is how he can change tone so quickly, go from humorous banter to passionate expressions of tragic feelings."

"You have a good English teacher."

"I don't take English," he said. "I just like to read. Books are old-fashioned, but they make me think about stuff I wouldn't otherwise. Like just recently I was thinking how there's a big difference between writing code and writing a book. If you write code all day, and you get it right, you can change how something works. Make it run smoother or quicker. But when you write a book, it's like you change yourself. Rewire your brain. It's weird. Like just by telling your story in a certain way, using *these* words instead of *those* words, you change how you feel. You understand things in a new way. You can change."

"Unless you're one of those who tell the same story over and over," Hannah said.

"Why should anyone do that?"

"Maybe it's the only story they know. And until they tell it right, they can't let go of it."

Stevie processed that for a moment. Flicking his mouse, flicking, flicking.

"Stevie's trying to write a book about his run-in with the law," Yoshia said. "The law and the FAA, Federal Aviation Administration."

"You hacked into their computers?"

Stevie stopped. He lifted his hand from the mouse and sat for a moment staring at the screen.

"I don't hack," he said finally. "Hacking is for morons. Time wasters."

He turned his head and looked back at her with a disappointed frown.

"A year ago," Yoshia said, "when Stevie and the Brockmans flew into LaGuardia, they wound up having to circle the airport for half an hour. A backup on the ground. That's what got him started. Isn't that right, Stevie?"

The boy went back to work. Once again the script flew past.

"It's a stupid waste of time, all those people just waiting to land, flying in circles. It doesn't make any sense."

"So when Stevie got back home, he went into their computers and fixed things."

"Their timetables were completely wrong," Stevie said. "Paths of descent too moderate. Their tolerances were ten degrees off all the systems they were running. I just streamlined a few things. Cut out the waste, the garbage. Their programmers were like high school dropouts or something. They had absolutely like zero security."

"No one even knew he'd been there," Yoshia said. "Things ran smoothly for a day or two, planes coming in early, getting out right on time, no stack-ups, nothing. Until LaGuardia started to throw things off downstream. Other airports were using the same old systems, a certain percentage of planes leaving late, so eventually LaGuardia started causing synchronization problems all down the line. At one point Denver almost had to shut down."

"The unintended effect," Stevie said. "It's hard to debug a system so totally botched up."

"I'm sure it is."

"So they undid everything," said Stevie. "Put it all back the way it was. Instead of looking at what I did, seeing how they might apply it to other airports."

"People in Washington wanted to talk to him."

"I would think so," said Hannah.

"Oh, I'm used to it," Stevie said. "You think you're doing somebody a favor, the Secret Service gets all bent out of shape because I didn't use the right protocol. Didn't say please and thank you. Supposedly I violated Section 1030 of Title 18. An act of computer intrusion."

"So Stevie," said Hannah. "Did you get a chance to look at that thing I told you about?"

"*Deathwatch dot com*," he said. "Yeah, I looked at it."

"Can you tell me anything?"

"Tell me what you want to know, I'll tell you if I know it."

Hannah said, "I need to know where the broadcast is originating from."

"The thing about the Internet," Stevie said, still pruning the moving lines of code, "it's just all these billions of connections. It doesn't really exist as one single unit. Not like the plumbing in your house or something. When somebody ships something over the Internet, it isn't like water coming through a pipe. You turn on your tap, the water finds the one and only way to fill the vacuum. Point A to Point B.

"But the Net has a billion ways the water can get from the source to tap. It could've come through Asia or Guam or zigzag from one side of America to the other and back again. You send something across the street, it might travel five thousand miles to get there. Whatever works. Whatever's fastest. The Pentagon designed it that way because they wanted the Net to survive a nuclear war, for people in the military to still be able to communicate even when large parts of the system were down. But it's a lot more than that now."

"So what're you saying, Stevie, it's not possible to locate the source?"

"Sure it's possible. Every data packet that goes across the Net has a history. An IP return address. Hackers disguise their IPs, or they'll route them through Australia or China, some country that has no reciprocal agreements with the FBI. So if someone's backtracking the trail, it'll stop right there. That foreign country won't help them.

"And even if you're able to finally nail down the service provider, most of the time it's still a big step to figure out where the personal computer is that's sending the message in the first place. Someone really paranoid will use cell phones to bounce their signals around, before it gets to the service provider, or multiple modems set up at different locations, or they'll Telnet to another host, log in there, and then access the Internet from that other host location. That's a trick called looping and weaving. It can completely confuse anyone trying to get a hard-line trace back to the point of origin."

"So you tried and couldn't do it?"

"Oh, no, I did it. Took me an hour. I had to get into a couple of phone-company systems, some billing files, check their switching stations, their routing records, but I didn't leave any trace I was there, so I don't think Jesse's going to come looking for me."

"Jesse's his parole officer," Yoshia said.

"He's not the smartest guy," said Stevie. "But we have a good time."

"So where is it, Stevie? Where's it coming from?"

"Washington, D.C. Our nation's capital."

"Fielding is in D.C.?"

"Well, it's more complicated than that."

Hannah could take it no longer, talking to the back of a twelve-year-old's head.

"Would you mind," she said, "taking a little break from the computer, turn around, talk to me face-to-face?"

"Oh," Stevie said. "Sorry. Was I being impolite again?"

"Only slightly," Yoshia said, and patted the boy on the shoulder.

He let go of his mouse, swiveled around, and looked at Hannah.

She drew a hard breath.

The boy's bare legs were covered with sores. The flesh reddened and peeling off in damp welts. Dark blisters the size of pennies covered his thighs like ticks fattening on his blood.

"It's a viral thing," Stevie said. "I got it when I was a baby, they had to do a blood transfusion and it was tainted. But don't worry, it's not contagious."

"I'm sorry, I didn't know."

"Oh, it's okay, Ms. Keller, don't worry. It doesn't hurt that much. You'd think something fatal would hurt like hell.

But this doesn't. I stopped taking the drugs, the painkillers, 'cause they make me dopey, so sometimes it flares up at night, but otherwise, basically I'm fine."

"No medicine, no cure?"

"Oh, they're working on it," Stevie said. "Some experimental drugs in the pipeline. Going to do some trials pretty soon. But you know, it looks like it'll be a little too late for me."

"God, I'm sorry."

"At least my brain works fine. The virus just makes me push a little harder, you know, before I have to check out."

Hannah looked out the wide window, a view of the lawn, the sprinklers shooting high, glistening arcs. Beyond the high wall she could see the wrinkled crawl of the bay. Out on the street a stream of cars drove slowly past, people at their windows, trying to peer into the perfect kingdoms beyond the shrubs.

"So is Fielding in Washington or not?"

"The signal is originating in D.C. But the whole thing looks hokey to me."

"Hokey?"

"You ever heard of dithering?" Stevie said. "I have an example over here, all set up so you can see."

Stevie got down from his chair and walked over to one of the far benches. His stride was bowlegged and labored as if even the touch of moving air across his legs was torment.

"What I did, I looked at Fielding's site like you asked, and something didn't seem right. Oh, it's a pretty sophisticated attempt, but there was just something a little off, so I grabbed a single frame of the broadcast and checked it out on another system. You freeze on a frame, like on your VCR, you zoom it out, then you have to eyeball it to be sure. Kind of old-fashioned, really."

Stevie touched a finger to the monitor screen that was perched on a long work table. The image was scrambled and to Hannah it was as unreadable as a photo enlarged a dozen times too many.

"See what I'm talking about?"

Hannah said no, she didn't see anything but a row of specks.

"Yeah, that's right. A row. But what's wrong with the row?"

"I don't see anything wrong."

"Those are pixels," Stevie said. "Those are the building blocks of the image. This is a shot of a magazine cover on the nightstand next to Fielding's bed."

"*People* magazine," Hannah said. "Yes, I noticed it."

"Yeah, well, this is the edge of the cover as it merges with the wall. See that, right there."

He touched his finger to a slight zag in the row of pixels.

"That's dithering. The horizontal rows don't mesh, and the tints of gray don't match either. Which means the pixels didn't transition correctly across the screen. Which means this magazine was inserted into the frame. Like they do with movies, virtual-reality stuff. Pretty sophisticated programming, you don't see it much outside of Hollywood. So what they did, they wrote the magazine cover into the packet of information they sent over the Internet."

Hannah stared at the screen.

"You realize, don't you, that it's not a continuous feed? The video image you're seeing on the computer monitor, it's not like television. With computers you have to send packets of data. Two minutes of video time. It plays, then the next packet comes and it plays. They're working on a better video network. It's operational already, much better quality video, but the people broadcasting this Fielding thing decided to use the data-packet method. It's a little antiquated, but it works."

"You follow all that?" Yoshia said.

"Vaguely."

Stevie said, "I thought Fielding's voice was kind of weird too. They distorted the timing, took the words and the movements of his lips out of synch to disguise what they did, but when I dial it back to a correct timing, those words you hear aren't always the same words coming out of his lips."

"Really?"

"For example, when he says your name, Hannah Keller. His lips aren't saying that. That's been inserted."

"Oh, Christ."

"So," Stevie said. "Apparently someone wants to make people believe this image is current. That's why they put in a recent issue of *People*."

Hannah looked around at the workshop, the quiet buzz of current humming in her ears like a low-grade fever. She waited a moment for everything to suddenly make sense, but it didn't happen. Nothing but the hum.

"Do you have a rough location in Washington, an address or something?"

"Better than that," Stevie said. "I can give you the exact building and the room number within that building. I can even give you the name and beeper number of the contact person who's in charge of this whole operation."

"Operation? What operation?"

"Federal Bureau of Investigation," Stevie said. "I got in through their main site. Twenty minutes and I was in, no sweat. Government agencies are the leakiest places on the Web. Their budgets don't allow them much security."

"You're saying J. J. Fielding's broadcast, *Deathwatch dot com* is part of an FBI operation?"

"Code name Operation Joanie," Stevie said. "The contact person is a special agent out of the Washington, D.C., field office. Helen D. Shane. I got her Social Security number if you want it."

Hannah shut her eyes and drew a long breath.

When she opened them Stevie was smiling at her.

"You know, what you said about dreams, that was interesting. Decay. That's such a nice word for a very difficult thing to express."

Stevie pulled himself up on a stool. There was yellow ooze leaking from one of the sores on his knee.

"A lot of hackers make fun of the FBI. Dumping on them, calling them dull and bureaucratic. But what's that? All it means is, they have rules they have to follow. Like that's bad. Like that makes them dumb. Unlike a hacker who has no rules, he thinks he's so hot because once he figures out the rules someone else plays by, he can beat them at their game. That gives him an edge, because he doesn't have rules. He doesn't believe in anything or care about anything. Sure he can foul up somebody's system, shut them down. But that's stupid. It doesn't prove anything. Rules are what makes things work. If there weren't any rules, nothing would make sense. Nothing would work."

Hannah rested a hand on the boy's shoulder. He turned his head and peered at her fingers. Then he reached up and patted her hand, gave her a consoling look.

"Is there anything else I can help you with?"

The boy was feasting on Hannah's eyes. Soul mate in training.

"I can't think of anything," she said.

"Well, you could always tamper with that broadcast, if you wanted. The same way they inserted the magazine cover and your name, you could insert something into that video. Break into their site, make alterations, make it look like it belonged there. An image, a voice, whatever. And that altered image would be broadcast over the Net."

"You could do that?"

"It might take a while, but, yeah, I could do that. It's all just code, plus and minus, yes and no. I know most of the browser loopholes, defects in their programs. I just go in, exploit the flaw, write a file so big it causes buffer overload. Once you get inside the site, you open the door wide, it's no problem, you can tamper all you want."

Behind them Yoshia cleared her throat.

"I'm sorry to intrude," she said. "But it is time for Stevie's injections."

Stevie's smile dimmed briefly, then revived.

"So you want me to do that, Hannah? Alter the site?"

"I can't think of anything I'd want to insert."

"You're the writer. I'm sure you'll think of something. I'll try to break into the site, get it ready in case you come up with something."

He eased down from his stool and reached out a hand to

Hannah. She smiled and took it in hers. Stevie Brockman's grip was light and knowing, more alert than any hand she could remember.

"There *is* one other thing you could do for me, Stevie."

"Yes?"

She took the floppy disk out of her purse and handed it to him. Stevie looked at it for a moment then turned and popped it into the slot on his computer. When the directory came up, he clicked on one of Randall's E-mail files. A message from Barbie-girl. The password protection box came up.

Stevie swiveled around slowly, and shook his head.

"No, I'm sorry," he said. "I don't do that kind of thing."

"It could be important, Stevie. It could be very important."

"These are Randall's files?"

"That's right."

He kept shaking his head.

"You mean you'll break into the FBI's site, or the FAA, but you won't decode the password on my son's E-mail file?"

"I have my values."

"Well, can you at least give me a clue, something I could try?"

He shook his head some more.

"He's your son," Stevie said. "You're the expert on him. Most people use passwords that mean something to them. A special word of some kind."

Hannah turned back to the video screen on the workbench. She ran her fingertip along the dithering line of pixels.

"So, tell me, Stevie, what was Fielding really saying when they substituted my name?"

The boy settled into his chair again and used his mouse to switch his screen to J. J. Fielding's hospital room. The old man was sitting upright in his bed. It was the same scene that she and Frank Sheffield had watched together in the Bayshore house, Tuesday morning. Fielding calling out to Hannah.

Stevie double-clicked his mouse and Fielding spoke.

"I need to see you, to talk to you in person. Please, Hannah, I have something terrible to confess. It's about your parents. The terrible things I've done. Please come, Hannah. Right away. There isn't much time left. Look at the message I've left for you and do what it says. Please, Hannah. Please, I beg you."

Stevie wiggled the mouse, tapped it, then tapped a couple of keys, and the voice sounded again.

"There isn't much time left. Look at the message I've left for you and do what it says. Please, Maude. Please, I beg you."

Stevie turned in his chair.

"You know a Maude?"

"His wife," said Hannah. "Maude Fielding."

"Maybe you should talk to her. She might know something."

"I don't know how to locate her. I've tried. At least I know she's not in the phone book. I could call my friends at Miami PD, see what they could come up with, but that might take days."

He looked at her for several moments.

"You think Maude drives a car?"

"A car?"

Then a slow smile dawned on Hannah's lips.

"You mean you could break into the Department of Motor Vehicles?"

"I could try."

TWENTY-EIGHT

Senator Ackerman wasn't making eye contact with his constituents this morning. In his one-of-the-guys uniform of khakis, blue work shirt, and highly polished Weejuns, standing at the picture window that looked down on the marina and the bay, he sipped thoughtfully from his FBI coffee mug as Frank Sheffield summarized his last few hours of work.

"Amazing as it sounds, there were no reported thefts of red dirt bikes in the last two days in either Dade or Broward County. So I ran a list of all transfer of titles of for the same time period, and found twelve. I cross-referenced those twelve new motorcycle owners against arriving airline passengers in the last forty-eight hours. And there were no hits. So either he's using multiple IDs or he came to town by bus. Or else that's not him on the red dirt bike. I'm leaning toward the multiple-ID theory. All of which, of course, get us nowhere."

"If you're trying to impress me with your industry, Frank, I think it's a little late."

Ackerman's frown was pinched around the edges. His complexion seemed to have soured overnight, a yellow haze in his eyes.

When he spoke again, it was with the measured cadence of a professional orator forced for the moment to address an unworthy audience of one.

"I'm deeply disappointed in you, Frank. The childish way you've behaved. I think your father would be ashamed of you as well. I think he would be deeply saddened by your insubordination."

Sheffield tried to muster a smile but it wouldn't take hold.

"Hey, I'm sorry, Senator. Apparently the charisma gene skipped a generation. What can I say? I wish it were otherwise."

He could hear Helen Shane talking on the phone in the back bedroom. A tense question now and then, but mainly listening. Andy Barth was nowhere to be seen, and in the adjoining room his computer had been shut down.

"I'm meeting Hannah at noon at the Orange Bowl. There's still a possibility Hal will show. We've got almost sixteen hours left."

"Not anymore," Ackerman said. "The mission is dead. We're finished. We're folding up our tents, pulling out."

"Why? What happened?"

Ackerman turned back to the window. In the harsh morning light his face appeared bloated and his eyes had the defeated, empty glaze of a sleepless man.

"You want to know what happened, Frank? What happened was that you chose to personalize this. You decided at some juncture to let your own trivial needs preempt the goals of the mission. Willfully and for your own self-gratification, you drove a stake through the heart of Operation Joanie."

"I didn't want to see Ms. Keller get hurt."

Ackerman swung back around.

"Frank, do I have to remind you who we were dealing with? A man who has killed dozens of human beings, a man whose method of murder is so ghastly, so obscene as to challenge the very definition of evil. And for some reason, Frank, you let your own petty personal interests supersede our goal of catching this monster."

"Your daughter's gone, Senator. Sacrificing Hannah Keller won't bring her back."

The mist in Ackerman's eyes cleared instantly as if burned away by a sudden flare of the sun.

"You stupid, stupid boy," Ackerman said, taking a half step in his direction, his hands balling. "You have the unrestrained impulses of a spoiled adolescent. As soon as I get back to Washington I'm going to see to it that your career in law enforcement is terminated. I won't have you enjoying the respect and benefits of a profession you so clearly disdain. You're finished, Frank."

He heard Helen Shane slap the phone down. A second later she hustled into the room, slinging the strap of her bag over her shoulder.

"Hal Bonner is in Nashville, Tennessee," she said. "Field office there has two eyewitnesses and the body of one Hector Ramirez, heroin distributor. His chest has been punctured, heart stopped manually. It's Hal's signature, no doubt about it."

"Wait a minute," Frank said. "Nashville?"

"That's right, Frank."

Ackerman gulped down the last of his coffee and set the mug on an end table.

"The rental car Hal was seen driving away from the scene was found parked outside a Holiday Inn near the airport. SWAT teams have already set up a perimeter and they've agreed to wait till we arrive. But if Hal moves out before we get there, they'll take him down themselves. Your plane is waiting at Opa Locka, Senator. We've got to move."

Frank headed them off at the doorway. Helen halted, bringing the voltage to her eyes.

"Look," Frank said. "Something happened last night out on the bay. A guy stole our kayak, paddled away. Out at Stiltsville."

"Stand aside, Agent Sheffield." The senator raised his right hand as if he meant to stiff-arm Frank backward through the wall.

"Do you hear me? This guy tried to drown me. He had a burr haircut like the guy Hannah spotted earlier, the one on the motorcycle. It was dark, so I didn't get the greatest look, but from what I could tell, he fit the description."

Helen gave him a small smile.

"You're pathetic, Frank. Truly sad."

"You think I'm making this up?"

"Whatever you're doing, Frank, it hardly matters anymore."

"Get the hell out of the way, Sheffield."

The veins in Ackerman's temple had squirmed to the surface and looked like they might be about to rupture in unison.

Sheffield stepped back and followed them out the door and down the hall to the twin elevators. An elderly Japanese couple was waiting by the stainless-steel doors, smiling up at the numbers.

"Maybe this guy in Nashville, he's a copycat of some kind."

"Bullshit," Ackerman said.

The Japanese couple smiled more brightly at the numbers.

"I'm sorry to disappoint you, Frank," Helen said. "But we've got a positive ID. Hal Bonner is in Nashville. If he was ever in Miami, he's not here anymore, and I think we all know the reason why. Because a certain FBI agent decided he'd rather shack up with a certain second-rate hack writer than follow his assignment in a professional manner."

"Shack up?"

"You heard me."

"What're you talking about? She was in my room last night, yeah, she took a shower, ten minutes later she left. I don't call that shacking up."

"You two deserve each other, Frank. A cop who lost her desire and a federal agent who never had any."

Both sets of elevator doors parted at once. Ackerman and Helen stepped aboard one car. The Japanese couple smiled at them and chose the other.

Hannah nailed the brakes, lurched to a stop, put the shifter in reverse, and backed up three car lengths. She'd driven right past it. A brick house, rare for Miami, wedged between two shabby apartment buildings.

She was in North Miami Beach, a part of town that had

been a fashionable suburb when Hannah was growing up, but like much of this part of town, it had begun a long slide into third-world fragmentation, a melting pot where nothing melted anymore. Up and down these desolate avenues, there were dozens of ethnic markets representing every exotic corner of the planet, but the main economic staple of the neighborhood was bought and sold on the street corners, hot zones controlled by dead-eyed boys in baggy clothes.

Hannah drew up to the address Stevie pulled from the DMV computer. Maude Marie Fielding, age sixty-six, five foot three, one hundred and thirty pounds, a safe driver. Hannah parked behind a yard-service truck that years ago had been stripped of its tires and left hunkered on its rims at the curb.

In the front yard a small oak tree sprouted from the barren soil, its branches bearded with strands of smoky gray moss. Two empty bird feeders swayed from its branches and an overturned tricycle rusted in a knee-high stand of weeds.

Hannah got out of the car and stood by the door for a moment. The sky had turned to pewter and the humidity and trapped fumes of the city were mingling in an airless brew. She looked across the roof of the car and gave the two teenage boys across the street a warning look. They were eyeing the Porsche as if calculating its resale value.

Hannah walked down the broken cement sidewalk to the front porch. With her eyes on the boys across the street, she knocked on the front door. She waited for a moment, hearing no noise inside the house. She was raising her hand for another try when the square peephole behind a rusty grill snapped open.

The eyes that peered from the opening flinched against the gloomy light like some half-blind cave dweller.

"What do you want?"

"Maude Fielding?"

"Who are you?"

"I'm Hannah Keller. I don't know if you remember me, but I spoke with you a number of years ago about your husband, J. J. Fielding. My father was Ed Keller, Assistant U.S. Attorney."

"Well, well. Don't you have some nerve?"

"I need to ask you a couple of questions. It won't take long."

"I don't believe I have anything to say to you."

"Please, Ms. Fielding. Your husband is dying. He's crying out for you."

The woman craned forward until her nose mashed against the grillwork.

"Can I come in, please?"

The old woman studied Hannah for another moment, then slapped the peephole shut. A second later, the door swung inward and Maude Fielding stood with one hand on its edge as if she was still debating slamming it shut. Frail and humpbacked, Maude wore a blue smock with oversized red hibiscus blooms printed on it. Her hair hung limply to her shoulders and was dyed jet black except for the two-inch silver roots. In her other hand she held a half-eaten sandwich on white bread.

"He's crying out for me, is he? Well, now that would be a trick."

"Can I come in?"

Without reply Maude turned and headed back into the gloom.

Hannah stepped quickly across the threshold.

Underfoot she felt the crunch of sand, as if the white terrazzo had not been swept in years. Lying heavy on the air was the smell of old tuna fish and sour towels. Dark damask drapes blocked the windows, and as Hannah shut the front door, the murky room became even murkier.

The woman stood silently a few feet away, then Hannah saw her turn and disappear into the shadows of the room. There was only the chafe of the old woman's sandals against the gritty floor as she shuffled deeper into her house.

Hannah followed the trail of noise.

A few feet away she heard Maude Fielding come to a

stop and in the next second the room was suddenly blazing with light. Hannah squinted into the harsh fluorescence and when her eyes finally cleared, she sucked in a quick breath. Maude Fielding was standing behind a breakfast counter, the sandwich in her left hand, a .45 automatic in the other.

"Now," she said. "Just what kind of game is this?"

"There's no reason for the pistol, Ms. Fielding. I mean you no harm."

"No, ma'am, I'm not going to be one of those pitiful old ladies gets dragged off to a nursing home 'cause she can't protect herself anymore. No, ma'am, I'm not."

She took another bite from her sandwich and waggled the pistol at Hannah.

"Ms. Fielding, please. Put the gun down."

Maude blinked twice, and the tension began to drain from her face as if her paranoia had suddenly quit whispering in her ear. With a bewildered smile, she peered down at her right hand as if the pistol had just sprouted there. She slapped the weapon down on the countertop and stepped away from it.

"I hate guns," she said quietly. "I hate them."

Hannah eased forward and nudged the pistol farther out of reach.

Maude glanced over at the kitchen where an array of open jelly jars and stacks of dirty plates covered the counter-tops. Her mood seemed to dip and surge every few seconds, an uncertain light fluttering in her eyes. Synapses starting to misfire, the short circuits of a faltering nervous system.

Her gaze lit on Hannah and a quiet smile flickered to her lips.

"Care for a sandwich? I have peanut butter, crunchy or regular. I have strawberry preserves or blackberry jam and there's some cherry left too, if you prefer that. I just love a good peanut butter–and–jelly sandwich on Wonder Bread, don't you? Bread with absolutely no redeeming nutritional virtues. Oh, but it's soft and chewy and wonderful. Sure I can't interest you in one? I was just having a little snack when you knocked."

Hannah said no, she wasn't hungry. Maude Fielding took another bite of hers and without another word she turned and padded down the hallway toward the back of the house.

Hannah followed.

Crowding the walls of the narrow corridor were dozens of family photos in color and black-and-white. J. J. Fielding had been a dashing young man and Maude was once a silky, dark-haired beauty. Sleek and handsome, the couple stood smiling together on the prows of sailing yachts and in formal dress at ballroom dances. In one they held up strings of fish, kneeling side by side in rustic camps. In another they gazed up insouciantly from the bucket seats of a low-slung British sports cars, Maude in a scarf, J. J. in a sporty hat.

Three quarters of the way down the hall, a baby appeared. A girl with mousy brown hair and sad, distant eyes. Maude and J. J. were late-in-life parents. Maude in her early forties, J. J. apparently approaching fifty. The daughter aged quickly as Hannah came to the end of the corridor. In the last few photographs, the girl was in high school looking sulky, and garbed in the angry black uniform of the rebellious teen of half a decade before. Spiky hair, grotesquely shadowed eyes.

At the end of the hallway was a final portrait of the girl frowning into the camera. Hannah halted abruptly and stared at the photo. Beneath the bad makeup and the butchered hair, Hannah recognized the girl. Maude Fielding's daughter was the same young woman whose coquettish smile she'd seen the night before on Randall's computer. Barbie-girl. One of Randall's E-mail pals.

"Your daughter," Hannah said. "What's her name?"

Maude stood in the doorway of the back bedroom, munching her sandwich.

"Misty Ann," she said. "Why?"

"Where is she? Where does she live?"

"Here in Miami."

"M. A. Fielding," Hannah said. "Does she live on Flagler Street?"

"Last I heard, yes. Why do you ask?"

"I believe I spoke to her on the phone yesterday. I was trying to locate you and I got her. No wonder she nearly dropped the receiver when I told her my name."

"Be careful with Misty," Maude said. "She's a very unhappy young lady. She's never recovered from her father leaving."

"She's been sending my eleven-year-old son E-mail."

"Misty has?"

"That's right. She calls herself Barbie-girl."

"Well, I don't want to tell you what to do, dear," Maude said. "But if my Misty is sending notes to your son, I would find a way to put a stop to it. I don't like to say it about my own flesh and blood, but that girl is just brimming over with maliciousness."

Maude turned and shuffled into the bedroom, Hannah two steps behind.

The small room was jammed with furniture. She was barely able to move among the crush of chairs and tables and couches. In one corner was a tall, ornately carved secretary with a glass case filled with Hummel figurines and silver-framed photos. A red satin-covered couch was wedged against one wall and a cherry coffee table and matching end tables and entertainment unit lined the other. Large, dark oil paintings of mostly pastoral scenes in heavy gold frames hung on the walls. It was as if Maude had rescued these few tokens from the lavish life she'd known, and carted them off to this dreary prison cell so she might sit among these sumptuous pieces and dream herself back to the glory days.

Maude took a seat across from the TV set where a morning game show played soundlessly. Hannah pried her way through the tangle of furniture and found a perch on the arm of a green leather wingback chair.

"And do you have more than one child?" Maude asked.

"No, just the son."

"Well, I wish you better luck with yours than I had with mine. Misty was born angry. Nothing I ever did seemed to satisfy her. Her life has been one long tantrum. I always thought she must have felt like an outsider, coming into our life so late. We were close, J. J. and I, at least I thought we were. And Misty must have felt it was two against one. That J. J. and I loved each other more than we loved her. And maybe we did. Maybe I simply didn't have enough love in me to spread around to one more person."

"Children aren't easy," said Hannah. "Even under the best of circumstances."

"You probably think I'm very sad," Maude said. "Living like this, in such squalor. And I suppose I am. Sad and sick at heart. Maybe some other woman my age and circumstances would have bounced back after her husband abandoned her. Maybe I should try harder than I do. I don't know. I just don't seem to have the will to do much beyond the basics of surviving."

"It's okay," Hannah said. "You don't need to explain."

She frowned and shook her head. This was a speech she'd been harboring too long. It needed saying.

"Your father was simply doing his job," Maude said. "I don't blame him for what happened. For this." She waved a hand at the cheerless room. "You should feel no guilt whatsoever. He was doing his job and J. J. was undeniably in the wrong, using the bank to launder money. I didn't realize what he was doing. I had no idea. He had a secret life, a second personality he never showed me or Misty. With us he was simply J. J. Fun-loving and full of mischief. A good husband, a father who tried the best he could to give guidance to a wayward, difficult daughter. But he was living another life none of us knew about. He consorted with those people. Took trips down to South America to visit his friends, the drug lords. I think he must have been so impressed with their wealth and power that he lost his way. That was J. J.'s weakness. He was easily dazzled. Money impressed him so."

Maude was quiet for a moment, holding the remains of her peanut butter sandwich in her lap.

"Now what was it you wanted, young lady?"

Hannah began to explain about the Internet broadcast. She told Maude everything, about the copy of *First Light* with the scribbled notes, the house on Bayshore, the house at Stiltsville, her appointment at noon at the Orange Bowl. She told her about Stevie and about dithering pixels and Operation Joanie and Helen Shane.

Maude sat quietly through the recitation with her eyes on a painting across the room. A richly colored oil of an elegant southern belle in a gold satin dress seated with aristocratic calm on an outdoor garden bench. Looking at the painting seemed to relax her, bring some brightness to her eyes.

When Hannah was finished with her story, Maude continued to stare at the painting with a dreamy concentration.

"Ms. Fielding?"

The woman smiled. She blinked her eyes and drifted back.

"Did you hear what I said, Ms. Fielding?"

"I heard you," Maude said. She gave Hannah a quiet smile.

"I could show you the Internet broadcast. Your husband is very ill. He's in a hospital somewhere. Maybe you'd be willing to look at it and tell me if you recognize the place."

"That won't be necessary," she said.

Hannah stood up. She angled through the furniture and sat down beside Maude Fielding on the couch. Maude reached over and patted Hannah's leg.

"I've already seen the film you're talking about," Maude said.

"You have?"

She nodded.

"But this isn't a film," Hannah said. "It's a broadcast over the Internet."

"It's a videotape," Maude said. "J. J. sent it to me just before he died."

"Before he died?"

"Back in August," Maude said. "He sent it because he wanted me to forgive him, to soothe his guilt. To make his dying easier."

"August? Are you sure?"

"Oh, yes, I'm sure. I'm not so far gone I've lost all track

of time. J. J. made the tape over his last three days. For his final seventy-two hours, he recorded everything he said or did, every medical procedure done to him. He claimed he wanted to reconnect. He wanted me to exonerate him. But I couldn't. I sat and watched him die. Then I rewound the tapes and sat and watched him die again. I've watched him die a dozen times and not once have I been able to cry.

"Because there are simply some things you can't forgive. I'm not a saint. I wish it was in me to pardon the man, to say it was all right that he simply disappeared and left his wife and child without a dime and with no idea where he went or what was in his mind. For a long time I believed he committed suicide. That when his money-laundering scheme was discovered, he couldn't bear the public shame and he went off somewhere and ended his life. That's the story I told myself. That's the way I learned to cope. And then this tape came in the mail. This terrible tape."

Maude picked up a remote and aimed it at the TV set and punched a button. The VCR began to roll and the morning game show disappeared, replaced by the dreary image of J. J. Fielding in his hospital bed. It was a scene Hannah had already viewed. J. J. and his white-haired doctor in a blue surgical scrub.

"Your husband sent you this tape in August?"

"That's right. Five tapes in all, wrapped in Christmas paper."

"And did you show the tapes to anyone?"

Maude drew her gaze from the screen. Her eyes were muddy. Maybe she hadn't forgiven her husband, but she hadn't hardened herself to him either. She looked at Hannah.

"They told me if I ever heard from J. J., I was to get in contact with them immediately. So I did. I'm a good citizen. I'm responsible and public-spirited. That's the way I've always been. I sent them a note and they came and got the tapes."

"Who?"

Maude looked down at the last of her peanut butter sandwich. She brought it to her lips and popped it into her mouth.

"Why the FBI, of course. They sent a man by and he took the tapes away and then after I called and called, they brought the tapes back."

"Those bastards."

Maude set her sandwich on her lap.

"You haven't asked about the money."

Hannah was looking at the tape of Fielding in his hospital bed.

"The money he stole, you mean?"

"Yes, yes. J. J. transferred the money to an account in my name. I got a letter in the mail after he died from a bank in the Bahamas. Four hundred million dollars, just sitting there waiting for me to collect. But I don't want it. It's evil money. He only sent it to me as a payoff, so I would think kindly of him. That poor sad fool. He thought money mattered. He thought if he had enough, he would be immortal. But look at him. It didn't help. It didn't help one bit."

Hannah sat for a while longer with Maude Fielding and together they watched her dying husband plead one more time for forgiveness.

TWENTY-NINE

"What's wrong with him? Why isn't he talking?"

"Because he's upset, you imbecile," said the lady cop.

"Hey, there's no reason to get nasty," Misty said. "I just asked you a simple goddamn question."

Randall sat at the dining table staring into the aquarium that was filled with sand and little alligators dressed in pirate outfits. There were rubber dinosaurs in there too. The kid hadn't spoken a word since they left the marina. Just sat there with his zombie eyes. All the way across Biscayne Bay, nothing Misty could say or do got any response.

Gisela sat in one of the blue-and-white-striped galley chairs, patches of sweat darkening her orange shirt. Her ankles and wrists duct-taped.

The plan was simple. She'd take the kid and the lady cop out on the bay somewhere private, anchor, and wait. She'd leave her cell phone on and when Hal got back from his trip, sometime around noon, he'd call her and then Misty would make the call to Hannah Keller's cell phone. We'll give your kid back when you tell us where J. J. Fielding is. Simple as that. If the old man dies first, then the kid dies too. Say that and hang up. Nothing fancy.

The houseboat was anchored in a narrow canal on the edge of Key Biscayne. Skyscrapers visible just over the top of the bushes. The city seemed very close, though the boat was hidden so well, they might as well be in an Amazon river a thousand miles from city lights. Misty had rammed the houseboat so deep into the dense branches, they didn't even need the anchor.

Outside the tinted windows a dozen white birds were roosting in the high branches, their guano streaking the leaves below. In the distance Misty could hear motorboats speeding here and there, and a few feet away there was the squawk and flutter of the birds as they resettled on their perches.

She looked out the window, feeling groggy now that the adrenaline rush was over. Hal Bonner and Misty Fielding were pair-bonded now. She was helping Hal do his job, at the same time she was getting her chance to even the score with Hannah Keller. Two birds, one stone. Like maybe that was what love was all about. Two people using the same rock to kill what each of them needed to kill.

"There something wrong with Randall?" Misty said. "A mental problem I should know about?"

"You're the one with the mental problem," Gisela said. "Kidnapping a police officer and an eleven-year-old boy."

"Hey, I'm trying very hard to be courteous with you. But you keep insulting me."

"Listen to me, young lady. You need to let the boy go immediately. He was badly traumatized once in his life already. For three months afterward he was nearly catatonic. There's no telling what harm this might be causing him."

"Catatonic?"

"He didn't speak, he barely ate. It's a dangerous, life-threatening condition."

"Bullshit," Misty said. "Don't try to trick me. The kid's a little upset, so he's clamming up, that's all. Don't bullshit me. A person stops talking, that isn't going to kill them."

"It's more than that," Gisela said. "It's emotional shock. Like his system is shutting down."

Misty eased into the chair beside Randall. She inched it close to his. She ran her hand through his blond hair and ruffled it. He didn't move. Didn't look her way, just kept staring into the glass case with the dinosaurs and pirates.

She tried to get some sugar in her voice.

"It's going to be fine, honey. I'm not going to hurt you. There's nothing to worry about, Randall. Not a single thing.

Your mother cooperates and gives us the information we want, you'll be home in no time. I promise."

The boy just kept staring into the glass case.

"Would you like some ice cream, Randall? A candy bar maybe?"

Randall didn't move.

Misty looked over at Gisela.

"What're some of his favorite foods?"

Gisela shut her eyes and shook her head.

"Come on, goddamn it. Help me out here. I've got to do something to comfort the boy."

"Let us go," Gisela said. "That's the only way he's going to be all right."

"Nobody's going to let anybody go, so you can get that idea out of your head."

The lady cop was very still. Staring at Misty from across the cabin, giving her the thousand-watt evil eye.

"All right," Gisela said. "I'll tell you how to comfort the boy, but first you've got to cut my ankles loose. My feet are numb."

"Bullshit."

"Hey, you've got the gun," Gisela said. "And we're out here in the middle of nowhere. What're you worried about?"

Misty knew it was cop talk. Angling for every advantage. Always looking for a way to improve their situation, find an opportunity to make a break. But it didn't matter. She needed to get the kid talking, break the spooky silence. The way Randall was acting was making her start to doubt the whole plan. If she couldn't get him to open up pretty soon, how the hell was she going to get the kid to say something on the phone, let Hannah know they'd kidnapped him?

At the moment about the only real comfort Misty had was her derringers. One in each pocket of her overalls. The Legendary Model 1, .45-caliber Colt in her right pocket, the LM5 .32-caliber magnum in her left.

Misty walked over to the kitchenette, dug through a couple of drawers until she found a steak knife. She drew out the .32 derringer and kept it in her right hand while she went

over to Gisela and with a quick stroke, sawed through the
tape on her ankles and waited while the woman bent forward
and rubbed the life back into her feet.

"Make any kind of move to get out of that chair, you're
dead. You got that?"

"Listen," Gisela said. "I can guarantee you immunity
from prosecution. You could just walk away from this now
before you get in any deeper, no harm, no foul."

Behind Gisela, out the dark-tinted window, one of those
big white birds landed on the chrome rail and stared down
into the water.

"Forget it," said Misty. "I don't want any goddamn plea
bargain."

"The boy goes back to his mother, you walk away. We
forget this whole stupid thing happened. Think about it,
Misty. Weigh it for a second before you decide."

Misty didn't answer. Outside the window, just beyond the
white bird, there was a motorboat idling up the canal. Gray
hull with large blue lettering on its side that said MARINE PA-
TROL. At the wheel was a tall, serious-looking guy in a gray
uniform. Short pants, short-sleeved shirt, a gun on his hip.

"Aw, shit."

Misty watched as the boat circled around the houseboat,
the guy craning around his console for a better look.

"All right, you stay quiet," Misty said. "I'll take care of
this."

Gisela turned and looked out as the boat circled closer.

"Now look, Misty. You can turn yourself in to this marine
patrol officer. Let him know what's going on, and the deal I
offered you would still apply. You walk."

Misty spun around and jammed the pistol to Gisela's
temple and ground it hard against her flesh. She got her
voice down to a harsh whisper.

"Goddamn it! You just sit here and be quiet while I'll get
rid of this guy. You make a peep, everybody dies. Everybody."

Misty gave her a last jab with the pistol then left the
cabin.

She went out onto the deck and moved over to the chrome rail. She felt the calming weight of the two-shot der-ringers in both pockets of her blue overalls.

"Hey there, officer. How's it going?"

He idled his boat up closer. Blond hair cut in a flattop, dark aviator glasses. Curly blond hair on his hammy arms and his muscular legs. The guy's sidearm looked like a .45. Big fucking cannon he must've needed to bring down all those ocean-going rhino.

The guy slid up alongside the houseboat, and slung two white boat bumpers over the side, pressed his rail to the side of the houseboat, then lashed a thick line to one of the cleats that ran along the gunwale. His big Yamaha outboard was grumbling at idle.

"Could I see your boat registration, please, ma'am?"

"What's the problem, officer? I know I wasn't speeding."

"Ma'am, are you aware of what kind of trees those are behind you?"

Misty turned and looked at the green bushes covered in guano.

"They're not palm trees," Misty said. "I know that much. But I'm no big devotee of plants. I know the names of a few constellations. But bushes, no. Bushes aren't my strong suit."

"Those are mangroves," the man said. "They're a vital part of the aquatic ecosystem and they're protected under environmental law."

"You got laws to protect bushes?"

"Ma'am, the way you've anchored your houseboat, you've done considerable damage to several of those man-groves. I'm afraid I'm going to have to write you a citation."

Misty was looking at the bushes, shaking her head.

"What's so damn special about these bushes they need the police to look after them?"

The marine patrol guy pulled out a pad and a ballpoint pen from his pocket. He clicked it a couple of times, giving a closer look at the houseboat as if he were trying to find other infractions.

"I'm going to need to see your registration, ma'am."

"So you can give me a ticket for bumping into some fucking bushes."

The guy took off his sunglasses and folded them into his shirt pocket. His eyes were pale blue. He came closer to her and put a foot up on the side of the houseboat, setting his pad on his knee.

He was peering straight ahead through the tinted windows, trying to see into the cabin.

"Hey, look, officer. How about if I just pay my fine right here? Give you the twenty bucks or whatever it is, you pass it along to the appropriate parties, or whatever."

The man was silent, leaning closer to the window.

Misty slid her left hand into the pocket of her shorts, felt the cool, heavy presence of the .32-caliber derringer. Her heart was knocking hard.

"To tell the truth, I've always considered myself a bush lover," Misty said. "Just because I don't know all their names doesn't mean I don't love the little buggers."

The man shot her a quick look, then brought his face even closer to the window, cupping his hands to shield his eyes from the glare.

Misty heard Gisela say something, her voice muffled by the glass.

"Don't mind her," Misty said. "That's my mom. She's had one too many cocktails for breakfast and had to lie down. She's got a drinking problem."

The marine patrol officer lowered his head and looked up at Misty again.

"Old Mom's had a hard life, lots of things she's trying to forget. You know how it is. All those husbands leaving her, boyfriends beating the hell out of her. Booze is about the only thing that's stuck by her. Booze and me."

The marine patrol officer drew away from the window.

Misty's hand tightened around the .32 in her pocket.

He gave her a long, steady look, then said, "I'm going to need to go into the cabin, make sure your mother is all right."

"I don't think so. This isn't a real good time for visitors."

"I'm sorry, ma'am, but that's what I'm going to have to do."

"Look out!" It was Gisela calling from the cabin. Her voice muffled and hoarse, but loud enough to be heard. "She's got a gun!"

The marine patrol officer hesitated a half second, then jerked his hand to his sidearm, but by that time Misty already had her derringer aimed at his chest. Their eyes held for a second, the marine patrol officer with his .45 halfway out of his holster but frozen in that position.

"Take it out real slow," she said, "and drop it over the side."

The cop glanced down the empty canal. He looked back at Misty, took a deep swallow of air. Then he feinted to the right, lunged to the left, drawing his pistol as he moved.

Misty fired the .32. Winged him in the left shoulder, spun him around.

Behind her a few dozen birds exploded from the mangroves and sailed off into the blue sky. The marine patrol officer was stumbling to the side, still trying to dig his .45 out of his holster so Misty had no choice but to fire a second round, this one clipping him in the right shoulder and sending him floundering into his console.

A strangled noise came from his throat, then he slumped over the throttle and his big gray boat lunged forward. The line he'd tied to the cleat of the houseboat went taut and the *Margaritaville* reeled to the side, and felt for a moment like it was going to tip over. Misty lost her footing and a second later she was sprawled on her back, slipping across the slick deck toward the edge.

Twisting onto her stomach, she snatched hold of a chrome rail, dragged herself back away from the edge, got to her knees.

The Yamaha was revved up, water churned wildly at the props, the big gray patrol boat dragging them out of the mangroves toward the main canal.

Misty heard things crashing down in the cabin, glass

breaking. The marine patrol boat plowing ahead, ten feet, fifteen into the wide center of the canal. Its bow rose high out of the water, which sent the officer toppling backward off the controls.

He was still alive, arms flailing for balance. Misty could see the bullet wounds in both shoulders, the blood running down his arms, staining his gray shirt. He floundered against the leaning post and somehow got lodged there.

There was nothing Misty could do but pull the .45 derringer from her pocket and sight at the rope that was binding the boats together. But with the houseboat shuddering and rocking so hard, she couldn't get any kind of aim.

And now the marine patrol officer had gotten hold of the microphone for his VHF radio. He punched the button on the side and was just bringing the mike to his mouth when Misty fired the .45. The slug struck him in the left thigh, near his crotch, knocked him to the side and he dropped the microphone.

The throttle was still mashed flat, engine roaring. Both boats were plowing toward a piling in the center of the main canal, a creosote-soaked telephone pole sticking fifteen feet out of the murky water. They were moving fast enough, ten, fifteen miles an hour, if they hit that marker head-on there was a good chance it might split the houseboat in half.

Misty tugged on the rope, tried to unhook it from the cleat, but it was as rigid and unyielding as iron. When she looked up again the marine patrol boat was brushing hard through the mangrove branches. The boat wallowed to the side and sent the officer staggering toward the rear of his vessel.

He waved his big muscular arms like a tightrope walker, then he tripped over the transom and tumbled headfirst onto the top of the outboard motor. He grabbed at it, tried to hug it to his chest, his feet kicking. But his hands slipped on the slick plastic housing and he began to slide headfirst into the foamy water.

As his shoulders were just disappearing below the surface, one of his boat shoes snagged on a rear cleat and his body was slung hard against the lower unit.

The motor shuddered and almost died, like a blender that's overloaded. Then the big Yamaha surged and the bubbles sputtering out behind the boat turned to red froth. The propeller twisted the officer, once, twice, with his boat shoe still snared on the cleat.

Ahead of them the piling was less than ten feet away, dead ahead of the houseboat. Misty pulled herself up to her knees and crawled to the rope, got out her .45, and fired into it. Her first shot just nicked the outer strands. She pressed the barrel to the rope and squeezed the trigger again, but the derringer was empty.

The marine patrol boat roared on, dragging the *Margaritaville* sideways into the pole. Misty dropped flat to the deck and gripped the chrome rail but when the boat crashed, her body was pitched forward and her chest slammed against a flag stanchion, the air knocked from her lungs.

Dazed and reeling, Misty raised her head. She felt the deck listing hard to the left. The big Yamaha had stalled out and for a moment the canal was silent. A breeze filtered through the branches. Two white butterflies danced around the leaves. Out in the middle of the canal a patch of bloody foam floated on the surface.

Misty lay back against the deck trying to catch her breath. She'd kidnapped a cop, then murdered another cop. All in the same day. She squinted up at the sky and listened to the hot rasp of her breath and felt the houseboat sinking beneath her.

Bloody foam on the canal. A hacked-up body floating in the bushes.

Behind her eyes, the burn of tears began to build. She was wiping at her eyes with the back of her hand when she heard the two splashes.

Misty stood up and hustled to the front of the houseboat.

Gisela and Randall were swimming side by side into the dense mangroves. The kid must've cut Gisela's hands free and now the two of them were flailing around, searching for somewhere to hide.

Misty scrambled down the chrome ladder to the lower deck, found her blue gym bag on its side near the transom. The houseboat was tilting hard to the right, the sound of water rushing below deck.

She unzipped her bag, chose the M-4 Alaskan survival two-shot .410 and the Model 4 with the rosewood grip. She tucked one in each pocket. Then she crab-walked down the narrow side deck, reached up, and yanked down the long aluminum boat hook. She went forward to the open front deck, flattened onto her belly, and stretched out as far as she could, reaching with the boat hook until she snagged the bow rail of the marine patrol boat and dragged it over.

When it was near enough, she got to her feet, steadied herself on the edge of the gunwale, then hopped from the *Margaritaville* to the patrol boat. She untied the line, then slid behind the console, turned the ignition key, and after a couple of cranks the motor revved to life. She swung around, went back to the stern, unhooked the marine officer's shoe from the cleat, and let it fall into the dark water.

Then she put the boat in gear, cut it hard to the left, and idled up the canal toward where Gisela Ortega and Randall Keller had headed off into the thick tangle of mangroves.

It only took a minute to find them. They'd gone right into a dead-end canal and were treading water side by side, holding onto the stalky roots of the mangroves.

Misty idled closer. When the patrol boat was ten feet away, she shut down the engine and let it coast.

Gisela was shaking her head sadly, one arm around the boy's shoulder, one holding onto the mangroves.

"Let the boy go," Misty said. "And move away from him. Do it now."

Gisela continued to shake her head. Misty walked up to the bow of the boat and aimed the pistol at Gisela's face.

"I told you what I was going to do if you tried to get away. Now move away from the boy. If you don't move away, I might accidentally hit him. You wouldn't want that on your conscience, would you?"

Gisela looked at Randall. The boy was crying soundlessly.

She pushed away from him and started to breaststroke out into the open water. Randall shrieked and grabbed at her blouse.

"Stay there, Randall. Stay there. She won't hurt you."

Gisela swam ten feet from the boy. The sun was shining on her black hair, giving it a bright sheen.

"Okay," Misty said. "Now turn around, look back that way."

Gisela continued to tread water, facing her, Gisela's dark eyes holding to Misty's.

"Okay, then," Misty said. "If that's how you want it."

Misty Fielding leaned over the bow of the marine patrol boat and brought the pistol close to Gisela's face. The cop lady made a lunge for the pistol, splashing her arm through the water. But it was too late. Misty had already fired.

The woman's head snapped back in the water and then she slowly sank below the surface. A slick of blood bloomed on the water and a couple of birds squawked at the noise. But beyond that Misty didn't observe much about the moment. She was inside her head. Off in a drowsy haze, seeing Hal's face and seeing her father lying in his hospital bed praying to God.

Misty sucked down a breath. She watched the water where the cop lady had disappeared. She could still see her floating a few inches below the surface like a ghost that's left its body but is still hovering nearby.

"Okay, Randall," Misty said. She motioned with the pistol. "Swim on over here, kiddo. Hurry up now, we've got a real big day ahead of us."

That's when her cell phone rang. Hal calling.

"Everything okay?" he said.

"Oh, I hit a couple of snags," Misty said, still waving her pistol at Randall. "Nothing I can't handle."

Misty made a show of cocking the hammer back on the derringer. The boy let go of the mangrove root and started swimming slowly toward the boat.

"So go on and make the call," Hal said. "You got her cell phone number, right?"

"Yeah, off my caller ID from when she called yesterday."

"Okay," he said. "Then I'll meet you along the causeway where we said. You just run the boat up on the beach, I'll be there."

"Hey, Hal."

"Yeah?"

"Can we say the words now?"

"Which words?"

"You know which words."

Hal was silent.

"I need to hear them," Misty said. "I just need to hear them coming out of your mouth, that's all."

"You first," Hal said.

"Okay," she said. "I love you, Hal."

He was silent. She could almost hear him cringing, teeth clamped.

While she waited, Misty helped haul Randall over the side of the marine patrol boat. He was shivering and he wouldn't look at her. He dropped down on the deck and hunched his back against the transom.

"You still there, Hal?"

"I'm here."

"Well?"

"I'm at Miami International Airport right now," Hal said. "If traffic isn't bad, I should be over there in about twenty minutes. I'll be driving a blue Taurus. Can you make it in twenty minutes?"

Misty watched as the cop lady bobbed to the surface, face-up, eyes wide open, staring through the bright skin of water up at the violent blue sky.

"Yeah, Hal, I can make it in twenty."

"So I'll see you."

"Yeah," Misty said. "See you."

The line was dead for a moment and she was about to hang up. Then his voice was there again. Quiet, in the same mechanical way he'd spoken from the beginning. All words uncomfortable in his mouth. But especially these.

"I love you," he said. "I love you, Misty."

THIRTY

When she entered the Orange Bowl, there were two souped-up lawn mowers racing up and down the bright green pasture with the precision of a military drill team.

Hannah passed through the maintenance gate and walked up the circular ramp for Section H. She kept following it up until she came to the opening at Level 3 where her father had owned season tickets to both the Dolphins and the University of Miami Hurricanes. For as long as Hannah could remember, she and her parents religiously attended all the home games. Sitting out in the baking heat or huddled beneath ponchos in those wonderful subtropical downpours. Cheering national champions one year, bumbling losers the next.

She found their old seats near the thirty-yard line on the west end of the stadium. In the center of the field, Frank Sheffield was talking to one of the men on the mowers. Frank was wearing jeans and tennis shoes and a white polo shirt and a khaki baseball cap. Hannah sat down in her old seat and took out her cell phone and dialed Gisela's number. Still busy. Had been since eight this morning when she'd called before leaving home. The phones at Dinner Key were always on the blink, but, still, she was concerned. She dialed the number again. And again it was busy.

Out on the field the man on the mower went back to his work and Frank turned in her direction. He stood there a minute staring up at her without moving, then he lowered his head and trudged across the field to the cement stairs.

As he approached she saw the grim strain in his face, his

eyes dodging hers. Saying nothing, he took the seat beside
her, Ed Keller's place, and together they looked out at the
mowers working up and down the green plain. Gulls circled
the sky above the stadium. The dense gray clouds had broken up and now the sky was the tangy blue of sapphire.
Frank shifted uneasily beside her, wouldn't look at her.

"You have something to say to me?"

He eyed her for a second, then looked away.

"Well," he said. "You ready for a confession?"

"I know," she said. "The film of J. J. Fielding is a hoax.
He's been dead since August. You and your buddies at the
Bureau fiddled with the tape, made it seem that Fielding was
calling out to me. You set me on this wild goose chase, point
A to point B. For some reason you called it Operation
Joanie."

He gave her a rueful smile.

"You're good."

"So tell me, Frank. What was I going to find here at the
Orange Bowl? Were you going to put my next clue up on the
scoreboard lights? Where were you planning on sending me
now?"

"Does it matter?"

He glanced at her, then looked back out at the field. He
took off the baseball cap and crumpled it in his hands.

"What I don't understand, Frank, is why? What was so
goddamn important you'd jerk me around like this? Throw
my son into an emotional tailspin? Why, Frank?"

"You know Abraham Ackerman, the senator?"

A white gull landed at the fifty-yard line and stood
watching the mowers crisscross the field.

"Democrat from New York. That one?"

He nodded. Then he told her the rest. His meeting in New
York last weekend, the hired killer who murdered the senator's daughter Joanie, the same killer who would be dis-
patched to murder J. J. Fielding. Hannah as bait.

When he finished they sat for a moment in silence. Hannah's face was hot and tingling. She could feel the prickle on
her neck, hairs standing stiff.

"Did you do this, Frank? Set this up?"

He shook his head.

"I was invited along for the ride at the last second, an afterthought. I'd worked the Fielding case, I knew you, I know Miami, they thought I was a good fit."

"I see."

One of the mowers was headed for the gull, but the white bird just stared at the big red machine and didn't move.

Frank said, "Helen Shane put it together. About the same time Ackerman started making a fuss, stomping around in Director Kelly's office, those videotapes from Maude Fielding arrived in the mail. They wound up on Helen's desk, and I guess she was intrigued. So she took a closer look at the file we had on J. J. Fielding and apparently she found some letters you wrote back then to the Bureau, complaining about me, that I hadn't followed through on all your suspicions about Fielding. Those letters were in the file and Helen saw how passionate you were, how certain you were it was Fielding who killed your parents. So, bingo, she came up with the idea of hooking you into the operation. Dangle Fielding in front of you, and you in front of Hal Bonner. The operation runs exactly seventy-two hours, the length of the tapes. Bonner sees Fielding is dying. He gets desperate, afraid he's going to miss his last chance at the guy and the money. Then when he makes his move, we step in and nab him."

"Only he didn't make a move."

"Oh, I think he was here and we didn't recognize him. He got scared off, now he's gone."

The mower came to a halt a yard in front of the white gull. The man revved his engine but the gull refused to yield his spot on the green field. The man waved his arms but still the gull did not budge. The man on the other mower stopped nearby and was laughing at the spectacle.

"And you went along with all this, Frank? You thought that was a fair trade? Risk the life of a civilian and her son so a U.S. senator could have his revenge? You thought it was okay to bring this monster, Hal Bonner, into my life and my son's life?"

"I went along with it, yes."

"And the person who took a shot at me? What was that about?"

He shook his head.

"I don't know, Hannah. The car was a rental. It was stolen from some tourist, a European."

"Which country?"

"I don't know. Norway, I think."

"A tourist from Norway?"

"Yeah, I think so."

"Do you have a name for this tourist?"

"I didn't ask for a name," Frank said. "Why? Why's that important?"

"It probably isn't. Probably just a coincidence. My ex-husband is from Norway."

"Randall's father."

"That's right. His name is Pieter Thomasson. We're in the middle of a messy legal fight over visitation rights."

"How messy?"

"Not messy enough for him to take a shot at me. He's a coward anyway. A bully with no guts. His specialty is preying on underage girls."

Hannah stared at the field for a moment.

"What about the guy last night, Frank? The one who tried to drown you, was that the killer Ackerman's looking for?"

He shook his head again.

"He fit Bonner's description. But no. Hal murdered someone this morning in Nashville, Tennessee. Apparently he never took the bait. Operation Joanie is closed down."

"As of when?"

"This morning."

"I was just watching Fielding on the Internet a couple of hours ago."

"I suppose they haven't gotten around to shutting down the broadcast site. Everyone rushed off to Nashville."

The man on the mower inched forward until he made the gull hop aside, then he mowed the patch of grass where it had been standing. As soon as he passed on, the gull hopped back and took possession of his plot of earth again. Territorial stubbornness. Must have been an alpha gull.

"And how was I, Frank? Was I good bait? Did I do my part as expected?"

"You vastly exceeded expectations," he said.

"I'm so glad I could help."

She stood up.

"And last night, that little intimate moment in your room, was that part of the operation? Was that your role, Frank, seducing the bait?"

Frank stared off at the field.

"If you couldn't tell that was real, nothing I could say would make any difference."

She squeezed past him and headed down the stairs.

In the movies, he would have called out to her and she would have stopped and turned around and they would have had a parting exchange, something poignant or enigmatic, some last dramatic milking of the moment. But as she descended the stadium stairs, all she heard was the mowers, those big blades shaving the grass to perfect flatness, so that next Saturday boys in sharpened cleats could gallop up and down that field and have their fleeting chance at glory.

It was two-twenty when she pulled up to Pinecrest Middle School and parked the Porsche behind a big blue SUV. A couple of mothers waved at her and Hannah waved back.

She got out of the car and marched up the sidewalk, scanning the line of vehicles for Gisela's white Bronco. But she didn't see it anywhere. Gisela was supposed to pick up Randall after school and take him back to Hannah's and wait there till Hannah arrived. Gisela Ortega was always fifteen minutes early for every appointment, always had been. But not this afternoon. Hannah walked to the east end of the school and didn't see her Bronco anywhere.

She was heading back to her car when the dismissal bell

rang and the children began pouring out of the side doors, racing across the playground. Hannah walked back to the main gate, boys and girls swarming around her, the crossing guard halting traffic so the first wave of children could cross the street.

Inside her purse, her cell phone rang.

Hannah stood at the front gate watching the children whoop and skip and run toward their afternoon freedom. She dug the phone out, flipped it open.

Her hello was met with silence.

She was about to snap it shut when the voice spoke in her ear. She recognized it, but couldn't place it for a second.

"Hannah Keller?"

"That's right."

She thought she saw Randall coming across the playground. A blond boy about his size hidden among a crowd of slightly taller kids. She moved in his direction.

"We have your kid," the girl's voice said.

Hannah was craning to her left, but the blond boy wasn't Randall. He was shorter, thinner, happier.

"You hear what I said? We have your fucking kid and you're not going to see him alive again unless you tell us where J. J. Fielding is. Did you hear me?"

Hannah pressed the phone hard to her ear. She stood still among the streaming children.

"Did you hear me, Hannah Keller? You hear what I said? We have your goddamn precious little boy. You go to the police, he's dead. You don't tell us where Fielding is, he's dead. If Fielding dies before we get to him, your kid dies. You got that?"

She couldn't seem to fill her lungs. Her knees were spongy. All around her was the chatter of children, reunions between mothers and children.

"Let me speak to him," Hannah said. "Let me speak to my son."

She continued to scan the sea of children. The rush was dwindling now. Maybe this was another part of the hoax, Operation Joanie's final phase. Maybe Randall was there among the last children straggling out the doors. But it was a short-lived thought. The voice in her ear said, "He's not talking. He's gone mute on us."

"Put him on," Hannah said. "Give Randall the phone."

Hannah heard the girl muffle the receiver and speak, and she could hear a male voice answer. She couldn't make out the words but the man's accent sounded stiff and foreign.

"All right," the girl said. "I'm giving him the phone, but like I said, the kid's not talking. He hasn't said a word in six hours."

Hannah listened as the phone was passed from hand to hand.

Then she heard the quiet rasp of breath against the receiver.

"Randall? Randall, is that you?"

There was only silence on the line. But it was *his* silence. It was impossible to say how she knew this to be true, but she was utterly certain.

"Randall, now listen to me. You're going to be all right. I'm going to get you away from these people. Please believe me, Randall. You're going to be fine. You just need to be brave, to hang on, don't panic. Can you do that for me, Randall? Can you be brave?"

More silence.

"We're pardners, right, Randall?"

She waited, listening for the chafe of his breath.

"I love you, son. Be strong. I'll see you very very soon."

She heard the man's awkward accent again and then the girl was speaking in her ear.

"So, okay, you satisfied? That was him."

"Where's Gisela? What have you done with her?"

The girl did not reply.

"Where is she?" Hannah said. "I want to speak to her."

"The question is," the girl said, "where the hell is J. J. Fielding hiding out? That's the only thing that matters."

Hannah watched the last of the kids wander out of the school. Some heading for their bikes, others for the last vans and cars still parked along the shoulder of the street. Her thoughts were whirling. Trying to piece together a plan, a strategy. The very thing she'd been doing for the last five years, creating clever maneuvers, Erin Barkley's quick-witted schemes. But those fictional moments took hours to compose, sometimes days or weeks to polish to a flawless sheen. This required seconds. Less than seconds.

"I don't know where Fielding is," Hannah said. "Not yet."

"What the hell does that mean, not yet?"

"I mean he's about to tell me. That's all I can say right now. In the next few hours, he's promised to reveal his location."

"The next few hours?"

"Now listen to me," Hannah said. "That man you're with. Is his name Hal?"

The girl was silent. Two seconds later the phone clicked off.

"You did good," Hal said. "You're a natural-born kidnapper."

"She knows your name, Hal."

"She does?"

They were in his rental car driving down Bayshore Drive, heading into the Grove. Hal at the wheel, Misty and Randall in the backseat. She had one of the derringers in her hand, out in the open where Randall could see it, so he wouldn't try anything stupid like jumping out into the street, screaming for help.

"She asked me if I was with a guy named Hal. She fucking knows your name."

"Doesn't matter," he said. "What'd she say about Fielding?"

"She said he was about to reveal his location to her. He was going to do it in the next few hours."

"Is that right?"

"That's what she said."

"You believe her?"

"She sounded too scared to lie or make something up."

"Good," he said. "Then take this."

Hal craned around in his seat, holding out the small portable computer.

"What am I supposed to do with that?"

"Turn it on," Hal said. "I'll tell you how to work it. We gotta keep watching your old man. If he lets something slip, we might not need Hannah Keller at all."

Misty took it and popped open the lid. She looked out the window at the Grove. Busy today. Shoppers and lots of high school kids. The sidewalk restaurants nearly full, people sipping wine in the middle of the afternoon. There was a time Misty might've been out there among them, killing time, looking for hot guys. But all that seemed like kid stuff now. Like a little girl's aimless existence.

"Where we going now, Hal?"

"I thought we'd swing by your apartment."

"My apartment?"

"Sure," he said. "So you can run in, pack some things."

Misty looked over at Randall. He was peering at the screen of the little computer, watching it come alive, go through its start-up routine.

"Yeah, I guess there's a few things I'd like to take with me."

"One bag, that's all," Hal said. "In this business you have to travel light."

Misty leaned forward and laid a hand on Hal's broad, muscular shoulder. He turned his head and looked at her fingers. Then he reached up and laid his hand on top of hers. The sunlight glinted off his sharpened thumbnail, a golden barb, as beautiful as the talon of an eagle.

THIRTY-ONE

As she raced through traffic on the Palmetto Expressway, Hannah called Lieutenant Dan Romano from her cell phone. She had to bully her way through three layers of secretaries before she finally got him on the line.

"Hey, stranger," he said. "Long time, no hear."

"Randall's been kidnapped, Dan. I'm on my way to her apartment right now."

"Whoa, whoa, Hannah. You're on your way to what apartment?"

"The woman who kidnapped my son. I recognized her voice. I know where she lives."

"Hey, back up a second, tell me what the hell's going on."

She gave him a quick rundown of the situation, a little garbled maybe, but the best she could manage. When she was finished Dan Romano was silent.

"Did you hear me, Dan? Are you there?"

"Hey, look, I'm sorry, Hannah. But I'm afraid there's nothing I can do."

"Nothing you can do? Dan, you need to send a SWAT team over here right now. Seventeenth and Flagler. They've got Randall. This girl and a man named Hal Bonner, a professional killer."

"I can't interfere," Dan said. "We've been briefed on this."

"Briefed on what!"

"I'm sorry, Hannah. I'll pass the word on to the right people, but our hands are tied on this one."

"You mean the FBI? They told you to disregard me if I called?"

"Something like that. I can't go into it, Hannah. I have to work with these people."

"My son has been kidnapped, Dan. Did you hear me?"

"I'm sorry, Hannah. I really am. I'll call them right away. That's all I can do."

She stormed off the exit for Flagler, swerved into the emergency lane to pass a slow-moving truck.

"Jesus, listen to me, Dan. The Bureau's operation has been shut down. Check with Frank Sheffield. Talk to him, tell him Randall's been kidnapped. Do that much for me, will you? I need your help. I've never needed it more."

Dan was silent for a moment.

"Sure," he said. "I'll give Sheffield a call. I'll do it now."

Three minutes later she screeched into the parking lot of the Desert Rose apartments. It was a two-story building wedged between a strip club called The Party Girls and a pawnshop with more bars on its windows than Raiford Prison. The apartment building was a cement block rectangle designed in a Santa Fe adobe style. There were low, rounded walls with metal grates, a small, withered cactus garden near the manager's office.

On Hannah's first knock the manager jerked open his louvered door, and stepped out of his apartment in a white undershirt and a pair of baggy gray gym shorts. He was a beefy American with a salt-and-pepper military crew cut and marine tattoos on both arms. A ring of keys jingled at the waistband of his shorts. In the apartment behind him, Hannah could see a thin Cuban girl half the man's age. She was barefoot and wore a white slip and her hand was cradling her jaw as if she had a toothache. In the crook of her other arm she held a white miniature poodle.

"I'm Misty Fielding's aunt."

"Well, now isn't that interesting."

"You know Misty, right?"

"What do you want, lady? I'm smack in the middle of something."

There was booze on the man's breath and the faint trace of cigar smoke clinging to his flesh. Behind him the delicate woman had picked up a phone and was hunched around it, speaking in hushed tones. The dog leaned its snout close to the mouthpiece as if it meant to corroborate her story.

"Misty had to go out of town for a few days," Hannah said. "She asked me to look after her place, but I've mislaid the key she gave me."

"Look after her place, huh?"

"That's right. Water her plants, feed her cat."

"She has a fucking cat up there?"

Hannah said, "I'll only be a minute. I'm sorry to bother you."

Behind the man's back, the slender woman had put the phone down and was standing by a side window, holding an ice cube to her right jaw. The water glistened on her chin. Without moving her shoulders, she wept silently, her tears, bright in the sunshine, were running down her cheek, mingling with the trail of melted ice, a steady drip of water off her chin. The tiny white dog was licking the drops one by one off the point of her chin.

"That little bitch never told me about any fucking cat. We got a pet deposit. One month's rent, five hundred fifty dollars."

"I could give you something toward that," Hannah said. "And Misty will pay you the balance when she gets back. I'm sure she just forgot to tell you about the cat."

"Oh, sure she did. She forgot."

A red pickup truck roared into the parking lot and lurched to a stop in the handicapped space at the head of the sidewalk.

The old marine lifted his head and looked at the truck and smirked. He took a quick glance back into the shadowy apartment and shook his head sadly.

Hannah got out her wallet and slid out five twenties and handed it to the man. He counted the cash, then counted it again.

"How do I know you're the bitch's aunt? You could be some thief."

The door of the pickup slammed and a tall Latin man jumped down from the cab then reached back inside and came out with a baseball bat. He was barefoot and shirtless, wearing only a pair of soiled white jeans.

"Is that what thieves do in this part of town, they pay the landlord a hundred dollars before they break in?"

"Now that you mention it, sounds like a decent idea."

The marine turned and watched the young man stalk down the sidewalk. His smirk mutated into a grin of joyous malevolence. He stepped away from Hannah and set his bare feet against the cement walkway, raised his open hands. *Bring it on, asshole.*

The young Latin man spit into the grass and kept on coming.

"I told you, man, what I gonna do, you mess with her again. *Hijo de puta.*"

Hannah stood nearby, waiting till the young man got within ten feet, cocking the bat over his shoulder, the marine's full attention focused on his skinny adversary. She waited another second, the batter coming to a stop now, then inching forward into range, the marine's body nonchalant, but his eyes figuring the angles, zeroing in on the guy, his arms, his shoulders.

Hannah picked her moment, ducked in, snatched the keys from the marine's waistband, and hopped back out of range.

The distraction turned the apartment manager's head just long enough for him to miss the first whistling shot. The meat of the bat cracked against his heavy shoulder and sent him lurching sideways. But he recovered quickly and squared off, and it was instantly clear that the young man with the Louisville slugger had wasted his one good shot.

Hannah didn't stay around for the final chapter.

She turned and bolted for the main building. At the row of aluminum mailboxes, she found the name *M. A. Fielding* next to number 206.

Hannah took the steps two at a time, then had to circle the entire building before she located 206. Outside the door, she drew the .357 from her purse, held it in her hand while she used the other to slip the master key into Misty Fielding's lock. She turned it, felt the mechanism open.

She flattened her back against the wall beside the door, turned the knob slowly. When it was open, Hannah took a long breath, reset her feet, then threw her shoulder against the door and lunged inside.

In a squat she swung her pistol in an arc back and forth across the room. No one there.

The air in the apartment reeked of patchouli oil with a faint undertone of marijuana. Hannah shut the door and patted the wall for the light switch, but could find none. The heavy orange drapes were drawn solidly against the sun—only a fuzzy haze lightened the air around them.

Moving deeper into the room, Hannah bumped the leg of a chair and almost went down but caught herself at the last second on what felt like the back of a couch. Pistol outstretched, she edged toward the window. A few feet away out on the landing a toddler bawled, and another one screamed for its mama, and down on Flagler an unmuffled motorcycle rumbled past.

She made it to the far wall, slid her hands around the curtain edge till she found the draw cord, then yanked open the thick orange drapes.

She whirled around. But the room was empty.

It was an efficiency, slightly larger than a cheap motel room. A sleeper couch was opened in the center of the room. A knotty pine counter sectioned off a third of the room. Two mismatched bamboo stools were tucked under the outer rim of the counter. Behind it an ancient refrigerator chugged and fretted, and next to that was a gas stove covered with unwashed pots and skillets. A philodendron vine sprouted from a mason jar filled with water.

In the living area there was a small red card table with spindly fold-down legs. Centered on it was an older model computer and keyboard. On the walls hung several mangled Barbie dolls, grotesque creations that looked like hobbytime projects from the psycho ward.

Hannah checked the bathroom, threw aside the shower curtain. She poked in both closets, looked under the bed. But the place was empty. She lowered the pistol, but still kept her finger against the trigger.

Retracing her steps, she went slower this time, prowling through drawers. A pine dresser filled with underwear and T-shirts and an assortment of socks and cotton tops. A small wall unit that housed the television and on the dusty shelf above it a collection of desiccated beetles and moths. The trash cans were empty and the kitchen drawers held nothing but standard fare. A set of flimsy silverware, a random collection of plates and saucers and glasses.

Inside a sugar jar she found a Ziploc baggie of marijuana along with a small pipe and a packet of cigarette papers. Except for the Barbies, the room was curiously bland. No mail, no check stubs or receipts, no notes on the refrigerator, no corkboard, no sign in the whole room that the occupant had any but the most tenuous connection with the world outside these cramped walls. A life that could be packed easily into the trunk of a compact car.

Her clothes closet was filled mostly with jeans and T-shirts, a couple of dresses, black and blacker, and on the top shelf there was a collection of baseball caps and a short stack of sweaters.

On the bathroom sink Hannah found a toothbrush, a twisted tube of Crest and a stick of deodorant, and a silver tube of lipstick, Passionate Plum. The narrow room smelled of Lysol and mildew and on the rim of a green plastic water glass there was a two-inch palmetto bug waving its feelers. The shower curtain was glossy black with red tulips printed on it.

She went back into the living room and sat down at the computer and jiggled the mouse. The computer came alive sluggishly, grinding its gears and straining. When the opening screen finally winked into view, Hannah settled back in

the chair and sighed with relief to find that Misty Fielding
used the same operating system she did, thus requiring only
a few familiar clicks of the mouse to locate the girl's personal files.

A simple double-click opened Misty Fielding's daily
journal. Hannah scanned the files quickly and found her di-
ary entries were mostly about the men she'd met at the bar
where she worked, men who called or didn't call, men she
slept with, other men she lusted for. Men who hit her. Men
she hit back.

It was the last folder she came to that made her draw a
slow gasp. A collection of Misty's E-mails for the last several months. All of them addressed to Randall. She read the
first one, dated back in August. Then the second, a few days
later. By the third and fourth, Hannah was getting the picture, that from the very first this girl had been beguiling Randall, taking a big-sister tone, flattering him, asking him
about himself, his likes and dislikes, approving of what he
approved, mocking what he clearly disliked, easing the exchange toward increasingly personal territory. No prying
questions. Just that delicate dance, that swelling coo of intimacy.

Randall's E-mail notes were there too, filled with his day-
dreams, his worries, his feeble jokes, his detailed renderings
of his days at school. After reading a half dozen of their exchanges, Hannah's heart was floundering. It was wrenching
to see how vulnerable her boy was, how lonely. With aching
clarity, Hannah saw his sadness, the torment that still bur-
dened his heart. All through the summer and fall he'd been
tapping out these melancholy confessions to a complete
stranger while rooms away Hannah worked on her latest
novel in ruthless silence.

It galled her. How she'd let this happen. How little she
truly knew her own son. Because the chat that flowed between Misty and Randall was not simply more intimate and
more frank, but she was certain that it far surpassed in volume all the accumulated conversations she and Randall had
managed in the last six months.

Her fault. Totally her fault for letting the artificial world she was incessantly creating so totally distract her, preoccupy her thoughts, control her moods even in the hours she was away from the keyboard. Her fault for not paying more attention to Randall's silences, asking more questions, and the hundred other obvious acts that would have kept their bond strong enough to deflect the seductive charms of an angry lunatic like Misty Fielding.

Hannah clicked through a few more random files, saw nothing that might direct her next move, then decided she'd stayed long enough and began exiting. She was almost done, guiding the pointer to its last click, when she heard the scuff of feet behind her and before she could turn, a cylinder of warm steel jammed against the base of her neck.

Her right hand froze on the mouse. In the reflection off the computer screen she made out the ghostly outline of a woman standing behind her. A thin face, straight hair.

"Hello, Misty."

"Look, bitch, you just sit very still now. I don't want to see you so much as take a deep breath. There's two people in body bags because of you already."

Ever so slightly Hannah tipped her head to the right for a view of Misty in the framed poster that hung on the wall just to the right of the screen. In the glass she appeared taller than Hannah, maybe five-ten, with a sharp nose and pencil-thin eyebrows, darkened lips and a ghastly pale complexion, the slutty chic of her generation. She had a long, thin neck and blunt-cut hair that she wore to her shoulders. Wearing what looked like denim overalls over a sleeveless T-shirt.

"You killed Gisela, didn't you?"

"Shut up, bitch."

"You murdered her. You couldn't have gotten Randall away from her without killing her."

"I'm warning you. Just shut the hell up, let me think."

Hannah planted her feet flat beneath the table. Picturing the sweep of her hands as she turned and pushed the gun aside. Getting that image clear in her head, trimming away

the rough edges, stifling the uncertainty. She'd choreo-
graphed dozens of scenes like this, laid them out neatly, each
time Erin Barkley used her wits and her quickness and her
martial arts skills to slither out of danger. But none of that
was any help. Hannah could fabricate fictional worlds till the
end of time and it wouldn't make her any better at controlling the flow of real events. And what cop skills she'd once
had, those fierce, unblinking reflexes, were long gone. Ancient muscle memories, unexercised except in imagination.

"Where's Randall, Misty? What've you done with him?"

The pistol twitched.

"I'm not telling you a goddamn thing, bitch. I should
shoot you right now."

Hannah was looking in the shiny glass of the poster, seeing a man's body fill the illuminated doorway. Something in
his hand, holding it by his right leg.

"Listen to me," Hannah said. "The police are on the way
here. There isn't much time left, Misty, if you want to make
a deal."

She felt the pressure of the pistol barrel slacken against
her neck. The man in the picture frame was holding a baseball bat. He was raising it slowly above his shoulders, coming closer.

"That's all you people ever think of when you're in trouble, making deals. Well, let me tell you, bitch, you're not ne-
gotiating your way out of this."

She could feel the barrel of the gun drift across her skin,
lose its hold. And in the picture frame, Hannah saw Misty's
eyes meet her own, then shift their focus slightly to the right
so she too was looking at the man approaching from behind,
the Marine Corps flattop, the thick neck, the white undershirt.

"Hey!" the man shouted. "What the fuck's going on in
here?"

There was no hesitation in Misty's movements, sponta-
neous and precise. A short chop with the pistol against Hannah's skull which flashed a strobe of yellow light through

the room and made the chair sink beneath her as if she were coming over the top of a Ferris wheel. She felt her chair wobble and the tumble sideways, felt the dull floor rise to meet her, the coarse fabric of the rug burning against her cheek. Eyes open, watching, but dazed, she lay still, her body gone. Watching the legs of the two antagonists. The stumpy marine dancing to the side, twisting as he took a swing. Misty's baggy jeans fluttering in the opposite direction. Hannah felt her stomach swim. Her body anchored to the floor, a useless sack of flesh. Her meat and muscles heavy beyond the pull of gravity, eyes watching from deep inside her skull through a narrow peephole. The two fighters, from their knees down to the floor. She could hear their grunts and pants and curses. Hear the man's warning, the girl's shrill reply. And then the shot of a pistol, then two seconds later, a second shot. Not loud, not deafening, more like the pop of a balloon. A large red balloon at a birthday party for Randall with all the neighborhood kids over at the house. Randall glum but trying hard to join in. Trying for his mother's sake, when a boy Randall's age grabbed a balloon and screamed and ran toward Randall and squeezed the balloon and it exploded right behind him, and her son who'd just turned eight years old, cringed at the noise, a wince so awful to see, she almost wept. And then Randall, her young son, blond and freckled and perfectly made, turned away from his birthday party and marched into the house, straight into Hannah's bedroom and into her closet and tunneled into the pile of laundry, her clothes, her scent, and stayed there, ignoring her pleas, ignoring everything until all the parents came, two hours early, and carted their baffled children home.

Hannah lay on the carpet, sleeping and awake. Watching as the stumpy legs of the marine sagged, and the man tottered briefly and dropped like a thick tree in the open forest, slamming into the rug, rolling a half turn till he came face-to-face with Hannah. Neither of them able to move. Neither able to speak. A half foot from her face, the marine's eyes were open but they were losing hold. Losing the light, the gloss.

Hannah lay there and watched the meanness leak from his eyes until they were calm, then more than calm—utterly, completely neutral.

THIRTY-TWO

"Christ, Hal, the woman was in my apartment. She knows who I am, where I live, everything."

They were parked in front of a pawnshop, a block down on Flagler from the Desert Rose apartments. Misty was still out of breath from jogging all the way from her apartment. Hal stared out the windshield at the traffic.

"None of that matters, Misty."

"Sure it fucking matters. She knows my name, she knows your name. We're fucked. We're totally fucked."

"She's the one that's fucked, Misty."

"Jesus, Hal. I shot Claude McElroy, I shot the fucking apartment manager in the chest. I'm sure he's dead."

"That bothers you?"

"Bothers me? Christ, I killed three people today. Three people, Hal."

"Yeah, three is a lot for one day. Most I've ever done is two."

Hal steered the Taurus into a parking lot a block down Flagler. Found a parking space facing the street so he could see Hannah when she drove past.

"Christ, my picture's going to be on the evening news. The police are going to be looking for me. I'm going to jail, Hal."

"They've been chasing me for ten years. Police, FBI, DEA, Interpol. It doesn't matter, Misty. We'll have the money in our hands soon and we'll disappear. We're not going to be caught."

"We gotta get the hell out of here right now. Forget the money, just make a run for it."

Randall was sitting in the backseat beside Misty. He was staring ahead, not moving, not speaking. Just an eye blink now and then.

"It's all right," Hal said. "We're almost done. We'll get the money, then we'll go somewhere, a vacation. Just you and me. We'll stay in a motel, watch all the pay-per-view movies we want, order room service. It'll be good."

Misty leaned forward over the seat.

"Steal the money? Is that what you're saying? Just take it and run off?"

Hal looked out at the busy street, at all the Cuban stores, some with little windows opening onto the sidewalk where people bought coffee in tiny paper cups, then stood around drinking them.

"It's your old man's money," Hal said. "It's only fair you should get it, like an inheritance or something. That money is more yours than anybody else's. All you've been through."

Misty stared out her window for a moment. Billboards in Spanish. Street signs with the names of Cuban generals she'd never heard of. Her home had been hijacked by foreigners. She didn't have a job, didn't speak the local language. Nothing keeping her in Miami. She drew some air into her lungs. Feeling giddy. Feeling like one of those bugs, a cicada, it steps out of its skin, leaves it behind on the branch, a little transparent crust, its old self.

"That's good, Hal," she said. "An inheritance. That's a good way of looking at it."

"I'm ready to retire," Hal said. "I believe I'm ready to have some fun."

"Are you sure? Steal the money?"

"You think you could show me how to do that, Misty? Have some fun?"

She rested a hand on his shoulder. Felt the electric buzz of his flesh.

"Sure, Hal," she said, a smile cracking through. "It's not like I'm an expert on the subject, but I'd be willing to give it my best shot."

Hannah stumbled back to the Porsche. Her ears were ringing, her bowels had turned to jelly, and everywhere she turned she saw triple images haloed in green fire.

She took the surface streets south. Hitting the beginning of rush hour, a slow, torturous journey. At a red light in South Miami she fumbled in her purse and took out her cell phone, but then sat with it in her lap unable to think of anyone to call for help. Not Sheffield, not Dan Romano, not Gisela.

She snapped the phone shut and laid it on the passenger seat. She steered the car with the excruciating focus of the deeply inebriated. A sticky sheen of blood covered her neck. Blood matted her hair and more blood was spattered on the front of her blouse. But by the time she'd pulled into her driveway, the ache behind her eyes had subsided to merely a thunderous roar and now she was only seeing double. She would live.

In her study, she took out a legal pad and a pen and began to scribble the words she'd been composing in her head. The way she wanted this to end.

She read the words over, crossed out a few, inserted others. Writing not for payment, or self-fulfillment, or some idiotic literary ambition, but for a purpose beyond any she'd ever imagined. To save the only life that mattered.

Every skill she'd learned these last five years, the smoke-and-mirror tricks of language, creating the seductive semblance of truth, mattered not at all. This one had to be absolutely real. This one had to work. First time, only time.

Hannah mumbled the speech to herself and corrected a word or two. When it sounded right, she dialed Stevie Brockman's number and the boy answered on the first ring.

"Funny you should call," he said. "I just finished rereading *First Light*. I thought I should give it another look after meeting you. And I'm glad I did. It's better than I remembered. Much better."

She thanked him, then asked if he still thought he could break into J. J. Fielding's site.

"No problemo."

"Good," she said, then told him what she wanted him to do. She read from her legal pad, dictated it carefully, then had Stevie read it back to her, word for word.

"Okay," he said. "Should I start right now?"

"Right now," she said. "This is life or death, Stevie. This has to work."

"It's all life or death with me, everything I do. That's how I look at it."

She was quiet, nothing left to say.

"Don't worry," he said. "Shouldn't take but half an hour at the most. After you left I penetrated the site, installed a trapdoor. I can return any time, do whatever I want. I was just waiting for your call. I wanted to talk to you again. I enjoyed our conversation."

She thanked him again, then both of them fell silent. She listened to the rustling static.

"Are you all right, Hannah? You don't sound good."

"I'm going to be fine, Stevie. If this works, I'll be just fine."

After she hung up, Hannah sat for a while trying to breathe. Every inhalation drove a spike through the lid of her skull, every exhalation wrenched the spike out. She blinked and blinked again, but her study wall wouldn't stop quivering.

She got up, stripped off her bloody clothes and left them in a heap in the bathroom. She showered in arduous slow motion, changed into shorts and a white T-shirt. She went into the kitchen and loaded a sandwich bag with ice cubes and held it to the knot on her head. The throb had faded but her vision was still blurry.

She opened her purse and took out Ed Keller's .357 Smith & Wesson and carried it into Randall's bedroom and set it beside the keyboard.

She sat for a few moments, inhaling her son's musky, talcum odor. The scent ached in the back of her throat. She wiped the blur from her eyes, set the bag of ice aside, and moved her hand to Randall's mouse.

A moment later she was looking at J. J. Fielding in his hospital bed. He was cranked up to a sitting position and was staring sightlessly into the camera. His lips were barely moving. She rolled the volume knob higher and settled back in the chair.

"I made mistakes," he murmured. "I injured the people I loved. I've been selfish and stupid and I acted out of cowardice when I abandoned my family. I am not worthy of forgiveness, but I still plead that you will find it in your heart to forgive me."

He paused for breath and reached over for his water glass. He puckered his lips around the straw and sucked some fluid into his mouth. It seemed to require a monumental effort. He sputtered, coughed, wiped his lips with his hand, then set the glass back on the table. His voice was feeble, his face more shrunken than it had been only a few hours earlier. The hard shape of his skull was rising to the surface.

Hannah checked the time. It was half past six, over forty-five minutes since she'd called Stevie. Something was wrong. J. J. Fielding was still rambling. Still mumbling his melancholy, useless confession.

The old man picked up a washcloth from the side table and mopped his face, then let it drop to the sheets. Every motion seemed to punish him further. He was panting. His face was twisted. It appeared that at any moment J. J. Fielding might sink into unconsciousness, start his inevitable slide toward oblivion. And the moment that happened, her plan would be worthless. He had to be talking. He had to be moving his lips.

"What's he saying now?"

"Just more blather," said Misty.

They were parked in a vacant lot one street over from Hannah Keller's house. Tucked in among the pine trees, fac-

ing the street so they could see her if she drove past, on her
way to meet J. J. Fielding. In the backseat, Misty had the
portable computer on her lap.

"Still babbling about how fucking sorry he is," she said.
"Whoop-de-doo. Like anybody cares."

Randall was staring at the back of Hal's head. Not a word
since she'd spoken to him on the dock at the marina that
morning.

Looking off into never-never land. Sailing away into
some dead, airless space where nothing moved. Misty knew
about that place. She'd been there plenty of times herself.
Back when her father left. Back when he disappeared without a kiss good-bye, a note, a letter. She knew that look of
Randall's. She knew it from the inside out.

"Tell us an animal story, Hal."

He turned in the seat and looked at Misty. His dark eyes
were smiling.

"An animal story?"

"Yeah, you know, something to perk the kid up. One of
those things about bees or whatever."

"Okay," he said. "I know one about a spider."

"You hear that, Randall? A story about a spider."

"It's called the *Lasiodora*," Hal said, "and it comes from
Brazil."

Misty looked at Randall. It was hard to tell for sure, but
the boy seemed to be listening.

"Go on, Hal. What about the spider?"

"Well, its venom is so powerful the *Lasiodora* will even
attack poisonous snakes. The spider climbs onto a python's
head or a rattlesnake and bites it, then it hangs on through all
the whipping and shaking, till the poison kills the snake. After the snake's dead, the spider pumps more chemicals into
it, stuff so strong it dissolves the snake from head to tail,
turning its insides to Jell-O. Then the spider wriggles into
the snake's mouth and sucks the dead body dry."

"Wow," Misty said. "Now there's a cheery one."

"It's a David and Goliath story."

"What?"

"Doesn't matter how little you are, or how weak," Hal said. "If your juice is strong enough, you'll win."

Hal turned in his seat and looked at Misty. Then he turned further and examined Randall. The boy's eyes were open but that was the only way you'd know he was still alive.

"We need to get rid of the kid," Hal said.

"Get rid of him?"

"Somebody drives by, a neighbor or something, they might recognize him. He's trouble. He could get us caught, Misty. We need to get rid of him."

"Are you saying what I think you're saying?"

Hal met her eyes and nodded.

"Hey, he's just a kid."

"A kid who could get us in trouble. Spoil everything."

"Jesus, Hal. Doing away with a kid, that could be very bad karma. You and me, we're at the beginning of a relationship. It could be like a dark stain on things. We'd be haunted by it."

"It's got to be done."

Hal opened the door and got out. He waited till a car had passed by on the street, then tugged open Randall's door and hauled the boy into the vacant lot and dragged him over into the tall grass behind the car.

Misty jumped out and hustled back there. Hal was hidden behind the trunk of one of the oaks. He had his hands around Randall's throat and was beginning to squeeze. The kid wasn't resisting.

"Wait a minute, Hal. Wait a goddamn minute."

She slapped him on the shoulder and his hands relaxed on Randall's throat.

"Look, we might need him," she said. "We might want to show him to his mother once, let her know for sure we have him. He didn't say a word to her on the phone, she might not even believe it's true he's been kidnapped."

Randall's eyes were closed. His face was red, and there was the bluish-yellow beginning of a bruise at his throat.

Hal looked at Misty, then looked back at the boy. Hal's face was bland. He wasn't mad or worried or anything. Like some kind of Zen master, peaceful and far away.

"Okay," he said. "But he has to lie down on the floor in the back. And if he makes a noise, he's finished. You got that, kid? One noise, you're gone."

Randall just kept looking off at the horizon. Dusk was settling in, lights coming on in the houses nearby. A mosquito whined at her ear.

They walked back to the car and Randall got into the back and lay facedown on the floor.

Misty got in front with Hal and set the computer in her lap.

"What's your father doing now?"

She watched the screen for a few seconds.

"Still yammering," she said. "Jesus Christ, that's got to be the sorriest man who was ever born."

Hal smiled.

"Not half as sorry as he's going to be."

With Fielding's site running in the background, Hannah navigated through Randall's computer and located again those protected E-mail files from **Dad**.

She double-clicked the first one and the gray password protection box appeared. She typed in the word *Pardner* but didn't hit the enter button. She sat there and looked at the seven letters filling the box.

She made a silent pact with God. If he granted her this one, she vowed to radically change her life. She would shut off her computer, exit her fabricated world, and force Randall to do the same. All he'd been doing was copying her. Losing himself in his own electronic universe, cutting himself off from the complications of the real one. Just as she had done, Randall had tried to flee the troubling emotions, entering a place he could control and define. It was a sickness. It was a paltry, synthetic substitute. By God, she would do better, if he would only grant her this one prayer.

She took a careful breath and let it go. Nearby on the desk, Spunky rustled the shredded paper.

Hannah tapped the enter key.

And the E-mail file opened. Thank God, thank God.

Dearest Randall, my son:

I found your Web site today and was so excited I had to E-mail you. I know it has been a long time since I wrote you or spoke to you, but I'm sure you understand how hard it is to speak freely with you since your mother hates me so. I was hoping we might correspond in this manner. If this interests you, please let me know. Of course, please don't mention this to your mother.

Your loving father.

Hannah sat staring at the screen. Her vision was clear, her breath was coming clean and painlessly. After a moment she closed the file and used the same password to open the next one.

Dearest Randall:

It was so wonderful to hear from you by E-mail. Yes, I have been living in Oslo these last few years. I am working at a university teaching mathematics. I miss you very much and think of you every day. And yes, I have a picture of you, but not a recent one. Maybe you can E-mail me something that was taken lately. I'm sure you're a big strong, handsome boy by now.

Your loving father.

She read a half dozen more, the same short, businesslike notes. But with a new subject emerging. Norway. What a beautiful country it was. How clean and orderly it was. And how much Pieter loved his son, how he yearned to have him by his side. And as always a reminder to Randall to destroy these E-mail notes so his mother would never learn of the bond growing between father and son.

Randall quickly tired of the exchange. In one of his recent notes, he wrote:

I'm sorry, Dad, but please stop writing me. I love you but I don't want to do this anymore.

And Pieter's reply was bitterly direct. The loathsome man she'd married.

Dear Son:
I was shocked and sorrowed to receive your E-mail. I can only think that your mother's destructive influence holds you in its power. This is too bad. This worries me greatly. I wonder if I can trust you still with the secret we share. Please write me immediately and assure me that I have nothing to fear. For if I thought my own son would turn against me and tell terrible stories to the authorities, I do not know what actions I might be forced to take.
Your father.

Hannah sat back in her chair. She was shivering and the breath wouldn't fill her lungs.

She managed to lift her hands to the keyboard and opened Randall's final reply, a desperate plea.

Dear Dad:
I promised, didn't I? I haven't told anybody what you did to Granddaddy and Nana, but if you don't stop bothering me, I'm going to tell Mother. I will. I'll tell her everything. So just leave me alone.

And in an instant the story she'd been telling herself for these last five years dissolved. And the new scene played before her, complete and vivid, as if she were witnessing it firsthand.

Five years ago, Pieter Thomasson, her ex-husband, must have been hovering on the edge of their lives, watching, waiting. The coward didn't have the nerve to try his stunt with her around. Then early one morning after Hannah left for work, he showed up at the Kellers' door. Entering through the kitchen, confronting Martha Keller first. Making demands. He was going to take his son away with him to Oslo. He was the boy's rightful father. This was all Ed Keller's fault anyway, for taunting Pieter in the courtroom that morning, provoking him to such rage before the judge that it wrecked his chances for shared custody.

Pieter was carrying a pistol. He expected Ed and Martha to simply cave in. Wave the pistol in their faces and watch them cringe. But Martha didn't react as he expected. She would have none of it, this craven man trying to abduct her grandson. She would have told Pieter exactly what she thought of him. He was sick and deranged. A man who preyed on young girls. A pedophile, as far as Martha was concerned. And in a sudden rage, Pieter must have fired. Ed heard the shots and came running half-dressed from the back of the house.

But the shock of seeing his former son-in-law standing in his living room, made Ed Keller falter for a second, just long enough for Pieter to unload his weapon.

And where was Randall and what did he see? Hannah knew now that he was not on the seawall as he'd claimed. That was a lie, part of the story he concocted to protect his father. So he must have been inside the house. Perhaps eating his cereal in the kitchen, and eyewitness to his father's savagery. And when the last of the shots were fired, what happened between father and son?

Maybe Randall managed to hide. And his father must have searched, frantic, calling out for him. Two bodies on the floor and the killer, the boy's own father, was stalking through the house speaking to his son, trying to cajole him out into the open. Maybe that, or maybe Randall stood face-to-face with the man and refused to leave with him. Refused to be dragged outside and taken away. And his father, shaken by what he'd done and by his own son's repudiation, finally took flight.

No wonder Randall could not speak for weeks. Terrified, full of guilt. Afraid to incriminate his father, afraid for his own life and that of his mother. Locked in a horrible standoff with his own emotions.

Then with every passing year, Pieter's worry grew. His son could incriminate him, send him to prison, the gallows. Even though Randall's cover story held up, Pieter must have been haunted with dread. Three men in a white van, dressed as house painters. An invention of Randall's. A story that had deceived everyone. But Pieter's anxiety grew. When his son reached maturity, would his silence be broken? Would Randall's sense of right and wrong finally outweigh his loyalty to his father?

It must have been that worry that drove Pieter to contact the boy, engage him in these secret exchanges. Test his devotion. And when Randall could take his disturbing presence no more and raised the possibility of revealing the truth to Hannah, Pieter had no choice but to act.

Pieter Thomasson was the tourist from Norway who'd reported his rental car stolen. Pieter Thomasson was the shooter outside Garcia's Café. That was, after all, the simplest solution to his dilemma. With Hannah dead, no further legal action would be necessary. Randall would be terrified, totally alone. And Pieter would simply step forward and repossess his son and spirit him away. Murderer and eyewitness living unhappily ever after.

Hannah stared at Randall's words on the screen.

"I promised, didn't I? I haven't told anybody, but if you don't stop bothering me, I'm going to tell Mother. I will. So just leave me alone."

But he hadn't confided in her. Randall continued to harbor his secret. Corrosive, vile, poisonous, it had burned holes in the boy's soul. The guilt of what he knew but could not tell was more than he could stand. The shame, the terror, the agonizing bewilderment he lived with every day. No wonder he had retreated into his room, and into the safe, electronic universe.

This was the true story. She was almost certain of it.

But it was entirely possible Hannah would never be absolutely sure. This might well be the only version she would ever know. For even if she managed to get Randall home safely, the task of extracting the truth from him about the events of that July morning might prove so damaging, so hurtful that it would be impossible to carry out. She might never know. She might only have this imagined account.

Hannah sat staring blankly at the screen, eyes stinging with tears. She dropped her head into her hands, but just as she began to weep, J. J. Fielding's voice filled the room.

She wiped her eyes quickly.

She took a long breath, then put her hand on the mouse and killed the E-mail screen, moving back to Fielding's hospital room. The old man was talking. He was not apologizing anymore. His lips were moving and he was speaking in the same frail voice, but with fresh words now. Words that, by God, had to work.

"Hey, listen to this," Misty said. She tapped the volume button.

Hal was filing his thumbnail. The point was dagger-sharp. He set the file down and tested the nail against the palm of his left hand. A dot of blood jumped to the surface of his skin. He wiped the blood on the steering wheel.

"Listen to this, Hal. Listen. This is it."

THIRTY-THREE

Frank Sheffield was at his desk at the north Miami field office, cleaning out his drawers, doing it now when the building was nearly empty and when he was fueled by righteous anger and three margaritas from Paco's on the beach. He had his computer switched on, set to *Deathwatch.com*. J. J. Fielding's final minutes on earth.

Frank had bummed an empty Jack Daniel's box from the bartender at Paco's and he'd decided when he filled that one box to the brim with his desk stuff, he was going to declare himself done. Whatever bullshit was left he'd donate to the Bureau's national museum. They could display the stuff in the Hall of Shame wing. Along with the wax statues of all the other idiot agents who'd administered unsanctioned uppercuts to the bellies of U.S. senators.

Frank was sitting in his familiar green leather swivel chair with the nasty squeak in the hinges. Over the years Sheffield must've unloaded three cans of WD-40 on that chair, but the squeak was still there, louder than ever. Now the Bureau could fucking well find the squeak themselves. Pass Frank's chair on to some junior agent, an industrious kid fresh out of Quantico, a squeak specialist.

Frank dumped a handful of yellow pencils into the box, then he opened the flap on a paper envelope full of snapshots, a couple of rolls he'd taken last summer of a few of his three-week romances. Mostly middle-distance shots at the tiki bar, the ladies sloshed, sitting there in the sun, in their bikinis, giving Frank a variety of sloppy grins.

Sheffield dropped the envelope in the trash can, which

was already overflowing with a lot of other sentimental crap. All that was left in the middle drawer was a sheaf of departmental stationery. He was pulling that out to toss it too when an old glossy of Hannah Keller fluttered out. One of her publicity shots from way back when. A leftover from the murder investigation of her parents. He must've stashed it and forgotten.

Frank rocked back in his chair, put his feet up on the desk, and gave the photo a careful appraisal. Didn't take him more than a second to see she'd gotten better-looking over time. Lost the baby fat in her cheeks, the softness around the eyes, the mechanical smile. Five years later and the lady had a hard-edged elegance about her, a no-nonsense stare, eyes that could nail you to the fucking wall and keep you there. She had a better haircut now, did her makeup better, the whole look these days was more natural, more real. As luminescent as Ingrid Bergman but still with a street-tough edge. Somebody you could take home and show your mother and dad, if you had a mother and dad.

A burst of static on his computer speakers woke him from the daydream.

Fielding was talking again. Frank straightened. He could tell immediately that something about Fielding's voice was different. Sheffield leaned forward, rolled up the volume knob.

"I wanted so very much to talk to you in person, Hannah. I was hoping you would come to my bedside so I could take your hand in mine, ask for your forgiveness. But it's clear now that my little plan has failed, and you're not going to make it here in time. I'm dying, Hannah. They tell me I only have a few hours left."

Frank peered at the screen. This wasn't Helen Shane's script. Fielding's mouth was moving, a little out of synch with his words as always. Although the voice sounded somewhat like his, the words were totally different from what Frank heard when he'd reviewed the tape last weekend.

"So what I've done, Hannah," Fielding said, "I've taken

the liberty of making certain financial arrangements on your behalf. I've spoken to my lawyer just now, and he's drawn up the appropriate documents naming you as the sole proprietor of my estate. The money will be yours, Hannah. Yours and your son's to do with what you will. I have instructed officials at the Grand Cayman National Bank to put the account in your name. The full amount is being transferred as I speak. To ensure safety, since I'm communicating with you in this public way, I've sent the account number and identification procedures to your son's E-mail address. These numbers are encrypted, though it is my understanding that Randall, your boy, has the sufficient computer skills to access these files.

"I want you to know, Hannah, that I'm not trying to buy your forgiveness. You may do whatever you want with the money. Whatever your conscience dictates. I simply wanted you and your son to have some small offering, a compensation for the great harm I've done to you and those you loved."

"Hey, Frank."

Sheffield's chair squeaked harshly as he rocked back. Marta Veetro was in the door to his office, giving him one of her big southern smiles. Recently transferred from Atlanta, a thirty-something special agent who'd somehow managed to resist Frank's charms for the last few months.

"I heard your operation shut down."

"Ssshhhh."

He held up his hand and turned back to the monitor. But Fielding was finished now. He was drinking water, mopping his face with his washcloth. Every movement was a struggle. His head dropped back against his pillow and he closed his eyes. In a few hours he would breathe his last.

Frank was on his feet.

"Jesus Christ, she doctored the video. She set a goddamn trap."

"What?"

Marta stepped back out of Frank's way.

"Hey, Sheffield, wait!"

He was sprinting down the corridor toward the alley exit. She yelled after him.

"Somebody called you, Frank. Something urgent from Miami PD."

Frank slid to a stop at the exit door. Marta hurried after him.

"Lieutenant Romano," she called. "Homicide."

Frank waited for her.

"Something about a kidnapping. A kid named Randall."

"Now aren't you glad we didn't kill the kid?"

"It's a trap," Hal said. "I can feel my needle quivering."

They were parked on the shoulder of the road a half a block from Hannah Keller's house. It was dark. No moon. A strong breeze full of moist, yeasty scents, blowing from the west, like maybe there was a storm in the Everglades heading this way.

"What needle?" Misty said.

"The needle in my chest. When it quivers, something's wrong. And it's quivering now. Quivering a lot."

"Fuck," she said. "So what do we do?"

"We just drive away."

"Leave the money?"

"The needle's quivering. This isn't right."

"Hey, this is my goddamn inheritance we're talking about. You're just going to let him hand it over to that bitch?"

Hal looked out into the darkness.

"Let me think," he said. "Give me a second of quiet."

"Jesus, Mother of Mary," she said. "You're just like every other guy I've ever known. Everything's peachy nice until push comes to shove. Then when it really matters, you're going to make the decision all on your own, not even listen to me. Like I don't count. But that's my money in there, Hal. That's my birthright. You don't get to decide what happens with that. I don't care how much your fucking needle is quivering. You hear me? You hear me, Hal?"

"I hear you."

"What're you, stupid? We're this close. All we have to do is walk across the street, have the kid get the numbers off the computer, we're home free."

"I'm not stupid," he said. "I'm not mentally retarded."

"Well, then stop fucking acting like it. This is my money. Stop acting like some gutless moron and let's go get what belongs to us."

He looked across at her. His face was different. Bland like it had been a couple of nights ago when he showed up at her bedside, pinched her nipple. A burst of icy air washed across her neck.

"Sorry for the inconvenience," he said.

"Inconvenience? What the fuck are you talking about now?"

But as Misty asked the question, she saw his hand come through the dark. The right hand, the one with the barb on the thumb. She saw it snake toward her and felt his fingers seize her throat. For a second Misty thought it was a joke, a little playful tussling. The roughhousing some guys resorted to when Misty stung them with her acid tongue. But that impression only lasted a second, then she felt the power in his grip, the cold iron fingers, his hand as sleek as marble clamping off her air.

"I'm not stupid," he said quietly as if he were speaking to someone else, someone far away in his memory. "I'm not retarded or slow."

Little starbursts twinkled inside Misty's eyes. A spray of red and green dots. Brain cells winking out. The handheld computer tumbled from her lap. Her father lay on the floor mat at her feet, sad old man gasping for air. Just as she was gasping.

"I knew it was a lie," he said. "Love and God and fun. A bunch of lies."

She could feel her eyes rolling up, she could hear the snaps and splinters of tissues and tendons in her neck. But through the haze, a thought was forming in her head. No, not a thought, more like a word. A single word. She felt her eyes close, felt her body slump against the car door. Her hand fumbling at her pocket. The word was clear now. A single word. An old friend.

Derringer.

Hannah heard a sharp pop, like a thick branch snapping in the rising wind.

She sat at Randall's desk. His place of power, the one spot on earth where he felt truly safe.

She listened to the wind strain against the house. Listened to the quiet cracklings of the old wood structure as it stood its ground. That wood was heart of pine. Ancient, dense, and heavy. Carpenters dreaded it. Their drills burned out trying to penetrate its grain, their best nails bent double against its iron surface. It was the only organic thing Hannah knew that grew stronger over time. It was tougher on this particular night than it had ever been in its history.

She listened to the old timbers creak and pop.

She had told her story now. Beginning to end. Her words displacing Helen Shane's. And if she was going to see her son alive again, it was because her story had won out. Because it seemed sufficiently real. That was the only trick she knew. Words, words, words. Her story against theirs.

She heard the planks creak, a harsh chirp in the floorboard. She heard the rustle of the avocado leaves, the dry, papery rattle of palms. She smelled the freshening air, a sugary current passing through the house, leaving a ripple across the flesh of her neck. She felt the quietest of shifts in the barometric pressure and knew they were here. They were inside the house.

She kept her eyes on J. J. Fielding. Once more she watched the old man die. The tension in his face relaxing, the slow unraveling of his breath.

They were coming down the hallway. Their quiet passage, their faint disturbance of the atmosphere. She willed herself to relax, to keep her eyes on the screen. She felt the flutter in her gut, the warm, rising pressure in her blood.

They were at the doorway behind her, poised.

She took an even breath and swiveled her chair around. Aimed the .357 at the doorway.

"Well, look what we have," the girl said. "A standoff."

She had a small silver pistol pressed to the side of Randall's head.

"Hold on, Randall, it's going to be all right," said Hannah. "Trust me. Everything's going to be just fine."

The boy opened his mouth to reply but no sound escaped him and he shut it again. He was swaying as if to music only he could hear.

"Put your piece down now," Misty said. "Or I'll drop the boy."

Randall's gaze drifted left and right as though the music he was hearing was sending him into a swoon.

Hannah turned and set the pistol beside the keyboard.

"Did my old man send you the money or didn't he?"

Hannah said nothing. She was watching Randall, watching his loose-jointed waver, his limber dance.

"He didn't, did he? It was all a lie."

"Yes, he did," said Hannah. "It's somewhere in Randall's computer. But I don't know how to get it out."

Misty had her pistol jammed against Randall's temple. Gripping his shoulder with her other hand. The boy looked like he might collapse any second. Like the blood in his veins had vaporized, turned to useless foam.

She studied Hannah for a long moment, then prodded Randall forward.

"Now you get up on your feet, bitch, and stand over there. Better yet, sit down on the edge of the kid's bed. Way back against the wall so you can't come bolting at me. Do it. Do it now."

Hannah sat down on the edge of the bed, then slid backward until her shoulders were propped against the wall.

Misty steered Randall to his chair and eased him down.

"Now, honey, you're going to find the E-mail my daddy sent. Find me that, decode it, and I'll just be on my way."

Randall sat at his desk. His hand reached for the mouse. He stirred it around on its pad. Misty shot Hannah a triumphant smile, then turned back to the computer.

"He listens to me," Misty said. "Hell, he's more my kid than yours."

Randall moved the mouse and Hannah could see the screens changing. He was working his way through the directory, searching for an E-mail file that didn't exist.

"Here it is," he said softly. "I found it."

Hannah leaned forward on the bed.

Misty stooped down and angled close to the screen. Rising from his chair, Randall stepped to the side to give her room.

"I don't see anything," she said. "Just a lot of computer gibberish."

Randall's hand was a blur as he scooped up his grandfather's pistol, and spun, lobbing the weapon ten feet through the air to Hannah. Without a flicker of hesitation, she caught the pistol, found the grip, raised it, aimed, and fired a single shot into the meat of Misty's buttocks.

Yowling, the girl spun sideways. Her own pistol fired, exploding the monitor in a blast of sparks. She tumbled to the floor, sobbing. She ground her face into the wood planks, clutching at her wounded butt.

Hannah tossed the pistol onto Randall's bed and she and Randall stood together looking down at Misty Fielding as she squirmed and writhed like some electrocuted eel.

Hannah lifted Randall into her arms and hugged him, cradling his head against her breasts. He whimpered softly, taking quick, erratic breaths.

"You're all right now. You're safe. Everything's going to be just fine."

But as she spoke the words, she glimpsed through the haze of her tears a wide-shouldered shape filling the doorway to the room.

THIRTY-FOUR

Grunting, the man staggered forward. There was a ragged patch torn through the shoulder of his shirt and the spreading stain of blood.

Hannah lowered Randall to the floor and angled in front of him. Beside the bed, Misty groaned and hammered the floor with her fist.

Hannah watched the man inch closer, a grim smile playing on his face. His eyes were dark and they seemed dazed as if he had been staring too long into a bonfire.

"This is a nice place you have, Hannah. Big yard, lots of trees. Very private."

"I'm so pleased you like it, Hal."

"The kid's lucky, growing up like this. Plus, he doesn't have a father, which might be a good thing too."

Randall took hold of her hand and moved to her side, facing the man.

"So what do you want to do," Hannah said, "sit down and trade recipes?"

The man looked perplexed. His face was running with sweat. He stood between her and the bed where the pistol was propped against the pillow.

"A happy childhood is important," he said. "Not everyone is so lucky. Some kids grow up around dead people. They see naked bodies every day lying on metal tables. Naked women and children and they have to wash and disinfect their dead skin. That's not a good childhood. Not like this place, with the trees and the grass and the birds."

Hannah watched him glance around Randall's room, taking it all in, the desk, the smashed monitor, Spunky in his cage. His smile tinged by a hazy sadness as if perhaps this room was what he'd been yearning for all these years.

"That's your story, is it?"

"My story?"

"What you tell yourself to justify what you do, all the killing."

"It's not a story. It's the truth."

"Oh, yeah, I'm sure, it is. You were traumatized, unloved, molested, whatever it was, it rewired your brain. So none of it's your fault. You're just another victim. The great moral escape clause."

He stared at her, face sheened with sweat. His eyes were vague, drifting in and out of focus.

"I had to wash the dead bodies."

"Big deal," Hannah said. "I'm not impressed."

"He cut off their nipples, saved their pubic hair. Made me smell it. Made me do things to their bodies."

"Lots of kids had it worse," she said. "And they turned out fine."

Hal stared blankly at her for several moments, then shook his head as if to clear it.

"I know a boy," she said, "who saw his own father shoot down his grandparents." Hannah kept her eyes on Hal, but she could feel Randall stiffen at her side. "Six years old and he witnessed his father murder two people that he loved dearly."

She looked down. Randall was staring up at her. His face was crimped with grief but Hannah couldn't stop. Drawing out the last trickle of poison.

"And this boy kept the secret to himself because he didn't want his father to go to prison. He kept silent even though it hurt him terribly to do it. And even after all that suffering and pain, the boy turned out fine. He's a wonderful child, a good son, an honest, brave boy."

Randall held her gaze, something loosening in his eyes, a softening of the tension in his brow. Relief, gratitude, the faint beginnings of a new resolve. And any lingering doubt

Hannah had about what happened that morning five years ago vanished as she looked into her son's sharp green eyes.

"I didn't know what to do," Randall said.

She patted him on the back.

"You did fine, Randall. Just fine."

"Hey," Hal said. "Cut it out, you two."

Hannah turned back to Hal and watched his eyes roam the air around him as though he were tracking a swarm of invisible bees. Then he raised his hand and wiped the sweat from his eyes, gave her another wounded and befuddled look, then trudged across the room to stand over Misty.

The wounded girl peered up at him, groaning.

"An ambulance, Hal. I'm hurt bad. I'm bleeding to death. Please, Hal. Help me."

"Give me the eye," he said. "Give it back."

"Christ, Hal. Help me."

Hal squatted down beside her. He wedged a hand into the pocket of her overalls and came out with a glass marble. He looked at it briefly, then put it in his own pants pocket.

He rose and turned to Hannah.

"Now where's the money?"

"There isn't any," she said. "It's all been a hoax."

"A hoax? What's that?"

"A trick," she said. "A sting. None of it was real. Fielding is dead. He died last August. The money's gone. It was all an FBI operation."

Misty moaned.

"Then where are they? Why aren't they here, the G-men?"

He took a step toward her, his right hand rising.

"You're lying," he said. "You're making up a story."

"It's the truth," Hannah said. "I'm telling you the truth."

Hannah was watching his right hand, hovering like a sightless snake sensing the air. She nudged Randall away from her, separating. Taking a half step to the right toward the open floor. Hal outweighed her by at least fifty pounds. He had the wide-shouldered rawboned look of a farm boy who dug postholes all day. Work muscles. She needed a serious weapon for any kind of chance, but the pistol was across the room. Maybe Erin Barkley could fight her way past Hal to get to it, but Hannah couldn't.

She took another half step to the right.

"I'm going to crush your heart," Hal said. "You first, then the kid, then the girl on the floor."

Hal held his right hand before him like a blind man feeling his way.

"Leave her alone!"

Before Hannah could react, Randall charged the man, fists tight, arms windmilling.

Hal took two steps forward and snatched Randall by the collar, lifted him off the floor, and shook him hard while Randall pummeled Hal's arm.

Hannah spun around to Randall's desk, searching frantically for a weapon. Her gaze lit on the largest, heaviest object she saw, the metal birdcage, Spunky's home, and she gripped it by the sides, and spun back around, and while Hal was distracted by Randall's feeble blows, she lifted the cage above her head, took two quick steps, and slammed it against Hal's skull.

He went rigid, dropped his grip on Randall's collar, and the boy lost his balance and tumbled backward to the floor.

Again, Hannah hammered the bottom of the cage against the crown of his head. The floor of the cage was nothing but a plywood insert, a circle of thin wood. Not enough weight to knock him unconscious, but when she slammed Hal a third time the plywood shattered and the cage snugged down neatly over his head.

Hal threw up his hands and tried to wrench the birdcage off. But his head was trapped inside the helmet of bars, shredded strips of newspaper fluttering in his face as Spunky scrambled for cover. Hal strained against the edges of the cage, pushing upward to lift it off, but he couldn't budge it. The splintered wood was caught against his throat, gouging his flesh with each tug.

Lying on his back, Randall began to kick at Hal's legs. Fierce swipes with his heels at Hal's shinbones and knees.

As Hal took a step toward Hannah, one of Randall's kicks caught Hal's right kneecap and it crumpled him.

Hal staggered to his right, then caught himself, and swung around, lashed out and seized the boy's left ankle. Then he reeled back to Hannah. Dragging Randall with him, he took a lumbering step toward her. His right hand outstretched, coming at her like a man in a deep-sea diving bell moving dreamily across the ocean floor.

The rat was climbing Hal's right cheek, seeking higher ground. Hal shook his head but Spunky held on, tightening his grip on Hal's flesh.

Hannah dodged to her right and Hal stumbled, trying to follow her movements through the confusion of narrow gold bars and shredded paper, and Spunky's panicked scrabbling. With each step, Hal towed Randall behind him, the boy clawing at the floor, trying to pull himself free.

There was no calculation in Hannah's lunge. Simple instinct, blind and furious. She growled and threw herself at him, going for his wounded shoulder, the bloody tear in his shirt. Clubbing it with her fist, then clubbing it again.

Deadly silent, Hal floundered backward. Somehow he managed to keep his grip on Randall's ankle, bumping the boy's head across the hardwood floor.

Hannah went for the wound again. Gouging it now with both hands, digging her thumbs into the damp opening, levering them deep into tissue and gristle. Hal was utterly silent, his face vacant, not even a grunt as he tried to brush her away. But she held on, prying the wound wider, tearing open the flesh.

Then his hand was at her throat. The piercing slash of his thumbnail against her flesh. She tried to wrench away, but Hal held on, stumbling forward, dragging Randall with him. She dug her own thumbs deeper into Hal's bullet wound, deeper through the sinews and sticky webbing of his musculature.

But it was no good. The pain didn't faze him, while Hannah felt herself beginning to drift, felt the numbness seeping into her throat as if she'd gargled Novocain. The blade of his thumbnail had broken her skin, and Hannah could no longer breathe, she felt very very tired. Old and used and worn out. A thick mist rose inside her, spreading through her limbs. She let go of his shoulder and felt herself sinking.

"Mother! Mother!"

At Randall's voice, her eyes drew open. But Hal's thumb dug deeper into her throat, and yellow light flared inside her skull.

Hal brought his face close, peering through the thin gold bars. He gave her a narrow smile, then abruptly he recoiled, his face twisting. He let go of her and began to slap madly at the cage.

Gasping, rubbing her throat, Hannah stepped back and stared through the gold bars. Spunky had sunk his claws into Hal's nose and from that perch the big black lab rat was munching on Hal's right eyelid.

Hal roared and danced backward, shaking his head and clawing at the bars of his helmet.

Then a blast shook the room and Hal Bonner's chest bucked forward as if he'd been slammed by a baseball bat between the shoulder blades, and he stumbled to the right, let go of a long moan, and toppled facedown onto Randall's narrow bed.

Frank Sheffield was crouched in the doorway. He panned his pistol back and forth, then slowly lowered it.

"Are you okay, Hannah? You all right?"

She nodded, then bent down and swept Randall up into her arms, lifting him into an embrace. Her vision was going muddy. With his arms slung around her neck, Randall held on tight as she turned to Frank.

"Good lord, Hannah, why didn't you call me? What the hell were you thinking, staging something like this? You both could've been killed."

She pressed her lips into Randall's damp tangle of hair. She kissed him and kissed him again, then lifted her eyes to Frank Sheffield. She was still flushed with rage. But even then, even with that jittery heart, she could feel a faint smile rising to her lips as she looked at Sheffield. This FBI guy who so obviously should've chosen some other career path. This guy holding his gun with both hands, the pistol lowered, pointing at the floor, but his arms still tensed.

"Is this the guy you've been looking for, Frank?" Getting some quiet irony in her voice, starting to come down a little from the wired pulse, the ragged breathing.

He walked across the room toward her, giving Hal a quick look.

"Yeah, I feel fairly certain that's our boy. But who's that? Who's the girl?"

"That's Fielding's daughter," Hannah said. "She and Hal had struck up some kind of friendship."

Hannah watched as Spunky squirmed his body between two bent bars of his cage, then scooted across the floor to the corner of the room. There he stood for a moment, surveying the scene, then he lifted a paw to his mouth, licked it, and began to clean his soiled cheeks.

Randall clung to her, melting against her body. Frank reached out and touched the back of his fingers lightly against Hannah's cheek. He shook his head solemnly.

"Christ, you're not Erin Barkley," he said. "This could've gone the other way. Gotten real messy."

"But it didn't, Frank. It went this way."

"Man, you're something else. You're really something else."

She blinked her eyes clear. Smiling at him, feeling a tingle on her cheek where he'd grazed it with his fingers. Something inside her relaxing for the first time in years.

"Yeah, you're something else too, Frank. I'm just not sure yet what that something is."

THIRTY-FIVE

Randall sat in an orange chair along D concourse at Miami International. He was dressed in khaki pants and a white button-down sports shirt. One of the new outfits he'd bought this week. Though now he wasn't so sure he liked these clothes. Not as comfortable as his baggy jeans and T-shirts.

A green duffel rested at his feet. His blue passport stuck out of his shirt pocket. The overhead television was tuned to a twenty-four-hour news channel. In the forty-five minutes he'd been sitting there, he'd watched the lead story twice. Senator Abraham Ackerman and Director Kelly of the FBI were standing together on the steps of the Capitol building giving a news conference. Each of the men praised the other for their fine work in bringing to justice one of the most heinous professional killers in American history. Senator Ackerman was holding back tears at he put his arm on the FBI director's shoulder and thanked him again for finding the killer of his daughter.

"Your people took incredible personal risks," the senator said. "I'm proud of every single one of them and I think our entire nation owes them all a great deal of gratitude. My only regret is that your fine agents were unable to capture this madman alive. Because I would have liked to have been able to look him in the eye and let him feel the full weight of my fury."

Randall watched the people pass up and down the concourse. Rolling their suitcases behind them, or tugging them on straps. Across the aisle from him was a group of college girls in skimpy tops and torn jeans. A couple of them were looking at Randall, giggling.

Announcements came over the loudspeaker in Spanish and English. The same male voice repeated a reminder that Miami International Airport was a smoke-free environment. Randall watched two men in cowboy boots across the concourse. They were standing at the window that looked out on the runway. They were smoking cigarettes and glancing around nervously.

It was two in the afternoon on Saturday. The airport was packed. On one side of Randall the seat was vacant. A large woman in a black dress sat in the seat on the other side. She had a gold bug pinned to the breast of her dress. The woman had no luggage, but there was a large black garbage bag stuffed with something lying on the floor in front of her.

Randall sat and stared at the cowboys smoking their cigarettes. Once more he reached up and touched the edge of his passport.

He didn't watch the people walking down the concourse. That could make you dizzy, all those strangers passing by so quickly. It was easier to follow just one person. Watch them approach, watch them pass by, watch them disappear. One after another after another, heading off somewhere. Everyone with an important look on their face. Going on a journey. Going to meet somebody they loved, or somebody who loved them.

A man sat down beside Randall. He was tall and he was blond and he wore dark sunglasses. He had on a pair of navy blue slacks and a white golf shirt and a gray blazer. His loafers had tassels. There was a large gold watch on his right wrist and a gold bracelet on the left.

He sat for a minute and caught his breath. He was carrying a garment bag folded in half and he laid it on his lap.

The man's blond hair was shaggy around the sides, but on top it had thinned and pink scalp was beginning to show.

He had not aged well. His flesh was sagging. There were pouches under his eyes and his ears seemed to have doubled in size. He had stubble on his cheeks and he licked his lips repeatedly.

The man looked over at the college girls and smiled. The girls ignored him.

The man spoke to Randall.

He told him hello. He asked him how he was.

Randall replied that he was fine.

The man asked him if he was going on a trip.

Yes, Randall told the man. I'm meeting my father and I'm going away with him. I'm going to live in Norway.

Norway is a beautiful land, the man said. That's what I've heard.

Randall said nothing. He watched the cowboys drop their cigarettes to the carpet and grind the smoldering butts beneath their boots.

Are you ready to go right now? the man asked Randall. Are you ready for this long adventure to begin?

Randall turned his head and looked into the man's eyes.

"Are you my dad?" he said.

"Yes."

"You're late."

"I'm sorry," he said. "It was unavoidable."

"I wasn't sure if you would come."

"I got your E-mail, son. I was very pleased at your change of heart."

"Mother thinks I'm at a friend's house."

"We don't need to talk about your mother. Your mother is no longer a concern."

Randall was quiet for a moment, looking at the people pass by in front of him. Then he turned his head and fixed his eyes on his father's eyes.

"Why'd you do it?" he said. "Why'd you murder them?"

The man looked over his shoulder. He leaned forward and stared at the large woman in the black dress. No one was paying any attention to them.

"We can talk about this later, Randall."

"I want to know now before I go with you. I want to know why you did that. Why you killed Granddaddy and Nana."

His father took a deep breath and blew it out. When he spoke, his voice was quiet.

"You didn't know them, Randall, not like I did. They were cruel people. Your grandparents were vindictive and spiteful. They tried to destroy my life. They hated me."

"I loved them," Randall said. He looked off at the stream of people. "I loved them very much."

"You didn't know them," the man said. "You only saw one side of them."

"All right," Randall said. "That's all I can do."

"What?"

"You can come out now," Randall said. "That's all I can do. I don't want to do this anymore. You can come out now."

The blond man stood up.

"What is this, son? What are you saying?"

The blond man looked down the concourse and saw the men in blue suits jogging in his direction. He looked the other way and saw more men hurrying through the crowd.

From across the concourse, Hannah Keller stood up from the orange seat where she'd been sitting. The two cowboys tipped their hats at her as she walked briskly toward her son and the tall blond man he so closely resembled.

Who he resembled not at all.

"He's a natural," Frank said.

They were sitting at the Silver Sands tiki bar watching Randall try to paddle the one-man kayak beyond the first line of surf. The waves kept crashing into him, pushing him back, spinning him around. But the boy wasn't giving up. He'd regain his balance, paddle backward for a while, get settled in the calm water, and then try again to crash through that first barrier of surf.

"He's holding his own," Hannah said.

"You seem surprised."

Hannah had a small sip of the Chardonnay. It was Saturday afternoon, a couple of weeks till Thanksgiving. Tourist season about to crank up again. Warm and clear, but not muggy anymore.

"Did you decide what to do, Frank?"

"You mean about Ackerman's offer, the big promotion?"

"That's right. Are you going back? Let bygones be bygones?"

"What do you think, Hannah?"

"I think you probably told him to go take a flying leap."

"My words exactly."

They watched Randall paddling the kayak, angling around for the right slant into the waves.

Frank said, "Boys are pretty tenacious creatures. Something about hormones, I think. Give 'em the right task, the right motivation, they'll keep working at it till their muscles give out."

She eyed him skeptically. He was shirtless. Just a pair of burgundy running shorts. He looked like he hadn't combed his hair in weeks.

"Looks to me like he's just trying to survive," Hannah said. "Trying not to drown."

"Well, I'd call that pretty good motivation, wouldn't you?"

Randall was hunkered low in the yellow kayak. He watched the waves coming, timing his start, then he lifted his paddle and worked it furiously through the water, driving the point of the kayak into the line of surf.

The wave that crested before him was the largest one Hannah had seen all afternoon. For a moment it appeared to be some kind of goddamn monster tsunami, a rogue wave rolling in out of the deep blue.

Hannah jumped down from her stool and sprinted out to the beach. But by the time she got to the water's edge, Randall had broken through the foaming line of turbulence and was floating out on a calm patch of sea. He set his paddle on the hull of the kayak and waved his hand above his head.

"I did it!" he yelled. "I made it."

Hannah waved back.

Frank was beside her in the sand. He handed her the glass of wine.

"See," he said. "Nothing to worry about."

"Yeah, he made it, but can he make it back?"

"Making it back is the easy part."

Frank sat down on a hump of sand and leaned back.

"Sit down, Hannah. Relax for a while. The kid's having fun."

"Fun? You call this fun? He's risking his life out there."

"Yeah," Frank said. "Ain't it great?"